The Dark War CHRONICLES

THE BRIGHT DAWN OF DARKNESS

KURT KRAMER

Library of Congress Control Number: 2025913746

ISBN
979-8-89641-082-9 (Paperback)
979-8-89641-083-6 (eBook)
979-8-89641-081-2 (Hardcover)

PROLOGUE

I will buy up armies and navies,
men and women will devote their lives to me.
And I will rule with an iron hand.

Freedom shall be lost then found
under my loving guidance.
None shall go astray.

All shall worship me and my glory,
the greatest above and the lesser beneath.
All shall proclaim my majesty.

As I pass, men shall hide their honor
and women their chastity.
Children shall weep and wail in fear.

All will know the taste of my everlasting wrath
while the heavens tremble at my power.
None shall dare oppose nor resist my commandments.

The very sun shall hide her face in darkest shame, spewing out
blackest light in reverence to my grandeur.
Her light shall be mine.

All shall be as one beneath me.

-Prophecies of the Dark Lord

CHAPTER 1

He was born to fight. He was strong and agile, quick and vicious; never showing any mercy. No one had ever defeated him; no one could defeat him. He knew this as did everyone else, not just those who had come against him.

Because of his strength and brutality no one dared try anymore. Their fear of him testified of this knowledge, as did the stench of their dread whenever he was around. It kept him alone but he didn't care. He didn't hunt with them, he didn't share their joy in the birth of a young one, and he didn't help them when they needed it. Not that anyone would ever ask.

He let his mind wander to a time when he had attacked a settlement and left rivers of blood running through it. They were fearful of him and all he represented. They called him Red. This wasn't his real name of course, just a name to provide verbal dominance against an unappeasable force. Those who knew him knew they could not defeat him in a fight so they did the next best thing-they mocked him by giving him a hateful name in their language. But instead of loathing his nickname he adopted it.

He now wore that name as a badge of courage and strength; a way of mocking the mockers. It was a name he accepted despite it not being in his native tongue. He would, from this time forth, always be known as Red.

But Red was still alone, ostracized in his own community tight-knit though it was. He would never have the pleasure and companionship of a female. Never know the camaraderie of close friends. Never know the joy and happiness of children. Red was a fighter, the best, and for that he was and always would be alone.

The only company he would ever keep, his only companion and true friend, was his rage. It kept him warm on cold nights, kept him going when he was weak and hungry and allowed him his indignation at the world. It was his passion and only lover; and it was always with him.

A memory abruptly came to him unbidden and flooded his mind. It was a memory of his crowning victory and his greatest shame. Their leader, his leader, roared out his call for a challenger to his leadership, if there was any, as was their custom to do every full moon. He was large, much larger than anyone else in the community and larger by far than Red.

No one had challenged him in many years and no one dared challenge him now; no one except Red. Red, in the heat and passion of youth and with the undauntable ego that comes with never having lost a fight, accepted and their fight quickly began.

It started as an honorable fight, the kind that was expected by everyone. But it quickly deteriorated into a scratching, biting, animalistic conflict with both of them rolling around on the ground like lizaerds. *Rolling around on the ground!* The thought of it still sent shudders through Red. It was not a fight a leader and his challenger should have participated in. Nevertheless, it happened, and Red won.

I won. Those words rolled over and over in his head. That was the point when he became truly alone. He had won, but he could never lead; not after a fight like that.

As always, the anger took over, attacking his nerves and mind like a living thing. Or perhaps it was alive, existing as part of a dark, symbiotic relationship; helping him to continue his existence so it could continue living as well.

Waves and waves of darkness and rage coursed through his body like the cold, agitated ocean pounding against the rocks of the coastline during a thunderous storm. Anger so passionate and overpowering it caused his whole frame to shudder, but whether with moral conviction or emotional pain he still couldn't tell.

He had won; but in winning he had lost everything which was dear to him. His anger knew no bounds and his pride knew no innocent except himself. Everyone and everything was to blame for his situation. As always happened when he thought about the unjustness of his existence, his rage started roiling inside of him like a living thing struggling to get out. He always had his anger; it was his only companion now and he had learned to love it as much as any mate.

Red let his mind wander, more to get away from his previous memory than the blinding intensity of his rage or any personal pleasure. Another memory gently settled on his mind like a dragonfly on the bright Red Serpent Blossom. This one was a time long ago, when he was young, and his mother and father were teaching him how to hunt and fight.

He remembered his mother's advice. *Don't ever challenge our leader or others in our community. If you challenge our leader and win you will become leader and everyone will look to you for guidance. And if you ever make a mistake you will have to take full responsibility for it. If you defeat another in the community you will have their kindred always looking for ways to get vengeance on you. And if you lose you will die.*

Her words at the time seemed to bind him, to tie him up and keep him from doing what he knew he could and should do. He was and always would be a fighter; that's who he was, that's what he excelled at. His vengeful fury swelled in his bosom, sending billows of heat down through his torso and down into his legs, acknowledging its agreement.

He let his mind wander again, remembering a female he had liked very much. She was the one; the one he knew he would love until his dying day. He remembered how beautiful, strong and graceful she was. She too was a fighter, and a good one at that. Not as strong as he, of course, but strong nonetheless. His passion flared at the memory of her. He remembered her eyes, which seemed to become like fire when she was angry or excited.

He knew they would be together one day; at least until he had fought their leader. *Their leader. Why couldn't he say his name instead of only referring to him as "their leader"?* That wasn't important, he realized. What was important was that he would never, could never, see her again. The thought made him sick with sadness and longing, the only other emotions he ever seemed to feel. Surprisingly, those were the only emotions which seemed capable of cooling the hot temper which raged in his soul, if only temporarily.

Then, far off in the distance, he saw something. He squinted, trying to make it out. Would it end up being a meal or just sport? Red hoped for both. He was itching to take out his aggression on something and he also knew he would work up an appetite in doing so. His anger tingled with anticipation; it always loved a good fight.

The day was dying in all its blood-red glory and the sun was low in the sky. Red advanced, keeping the sun directly behind him and staying near to the ground so he would be hard to see. He knew the setting sun, with all of its glorious reds, bright pink and orange hues, coupled with the glare off of the glassy sand, would make it difficult for the other to see him. He moved quickly and smoothly through the cool, still, dusk air.

As he got closer, he realized it was the lone figure of a single man. *A man? This far out in the desert? He didn't belong out here.* Red thought to himself. *Well, it would be his loss.* He chuckled to himself. *His loss of life.* At that last thought his fury roared its approval of his plan to attack. It always agreed with him and, as always, his rage made for an excellent hunting companion.

As Red went in for the kill his blood heated up in anticipation. He allowed his hatred of all things to feed his rage and cause it to boil up inside. Starting deep in his gut and brimming up his throat and into his head, it left a bile-like bitter aftertaste in his mouth as it always did. It was a taste he had grown to enjoy and even desire.

As he closed in he suddenly noticed the man was carrying a staff with a curiously worked carving on it. Red squinted again, trying to make it out, suddenly feeling as if that carving was more important than he could possibly realize. It was a carving of a…

Suddenly realizing what it was, Red wheeled around, beating his wings to gain both altitude and distance as quickly as he could. But he knew it was already too late. As he struggled to get out of range of the Dragonstaff, Red could already feel the tendrils of its magic, like the runners of a vine, taking hold of both his mind and his will. Red had never seen a Dragonstaff before; he didn't know any dragon that had. But once in range a dragon could start to sense its power; its vile, brain-numbing influence. A power which could take away a dragon's spirit and give it to someone or something else entirely.

Too late! The last remnants of his own will now completely evaporated, like the low fog which attacked the early morning desert but which dissipated by full sunrise. He was forced to turn around and head back to the man. This man, this demonic mage, now controlled the strongest dragon in all Dragonmount.

CHAPTER 2

As Red grounded, the man approached him slowly, cautiously; his fear was as palpable to Red as the sand they stood upon. *He is afraid!* Red thought elatedly. But it wasn't just the man's fear of him, there was something else as well. Then he understood.

He is afraid the magic of the Dragonstaff won't work, or at least not enough to control me. But he had to know it was working. As surely as I can feel his mind, his presence, his very being in my head this man must feel my thoughts and presence too. He also has to realize I'm here now only because of the staff.

Suddenly one thought came through: Kam. *So, this vile man's name is Kam. What minion of the Dark Lord would imprison a dragon? What evil must inhabit the heart of one so as to force his will on another more glorious, certainly more intelligent, being? The souls of men are as caliginous as the darkest, moonless night and as far below dragons as lizaerds. And this one was certainly one of the vilest of all.*

Red's anger grew with each passing thought and he strained to move his body and crush this impudent insect. Straining with all he had Red fought the power of the Dragonstaff and tried to inch closer to the man. One swipe of his claw could toss him fifty yards or more. But Red's muscles were locked, frozen like the ancient ice in the Deadlands of the Dark Lord's icy kingdom. He wasn't a dragon anymore but rather a sculpture; the image of a once proud dragon, cut from the strongest rock and shaped by this man's twisted thoughts.

Another thought came to him; fire. If he could blow even tiny spittle of flame this man would be consumed like so much dry kindling. But try as he might it was to no avail. Red could sense that, while the Dragonstaff kept them connected, he could not harm this man purposely in any way. He even tried to swing his tail in the man's direction, trying to swat him like a pesky insect, but couldn't.

Red stared at the Dragonstaff closely, trying to find a weakness within the wooden splinter itself. The staff was about two-thirds of the man's height, or almost the length of dragon's fang, with a dragon's head capping the top of the staff. The dragon's body twisted sinuously around the full length of the staff and appeared to be writhing in agony. The head held a glowing yellow orb in its mouth. There was nothing about the appearance of the Dragonstaff which Red could see to help him overcome its enchantment.

Red growled deep in his throat while his normally scarlet scales, now nearly a deep crimson in color, bristled with rage. Red tried to burn this man's visage into his memory for later reprisal, but found nothing extraordinary about him to single him out. This man was simply an ordinary pestilence like all of his kind.

As Red's thoughts started to entwine more fully with his captor's, he realized this depraved sorcerer considered himself a warrior. Red paused, and for a second the animosity he always held in his heart briefly receded into the recesses of his mind. The word, and more importantly its emotional connotation to the man, came through again-*Warrior.* As Red strained to search his, no, the man's, thoughts as best he could, its meaning became clear-*fighter.*

Red liked that word, warrior, and for a very brief moment Red could almost respect the man. Red also noticed a darkness, alive within this man and similar to his own, yet without the strong emotional memories which gave Red his strength.

It was almost as if the man were pushing his own darkness down, keeping it subdued. It was like a mother dragon using its wings to cover and protect its babies from a rainstorm. He couldn't figure out why anyone or anything would want to keep the power of their rage contained. It was the rage which granted power and inner strength; it made no sense to keep oneself weak when the potential for greatness lay so close.

Kam gagged. The darkness in the dragon was palpable. It was a cold, dark and bitter fury; rage at life itself. It wasn't the type of darkness Kam could see; rather what was in the dragon was a darkness he could feel. It was a putrid, piercingly cold and yet, Kam realized, searing hot at the same time. It was alive and breathing; seemingly conscious, with a heart, mind, and will of its own.

Kam knew that the darkness was, at its core, animosity the dragon felt. There was anger and a bitter disappointment at itself, a cold, vicious resentment at other dragons, and a burning rage at the world. It ate the dragon up inside and Kam wasn't sure he would be able to control it, let alone the dragon. The dragon, with its symbiotic companion, seemed to exist just to spite life itself.

What if I'm not strong enough? He wondered

Abruptly Kam felt a wave of claustrophobia, like being thrown into the deepest depths of the ocean, with water pressing in from all sides. He was being buried alive, swallowed up whole by the earth and ingested inside a rocky stomach. Kam wasn't sure if the feeling of confinement was being caused by just the connection to the dragon or by the living darkness which resided in it. It did, however, force Kam to his knees as alternating waves of blackness and dizzying vertigo overwhelmed him.

The claustrophobia turned into a fierce bleakness, drowning him in its reticent anger. No other emotion would, or could, ever coexist within it. The desolation of its isolation, not from the lack of companionship of fellow beings but from any other emotion, caused a sharp pain in his chest. It was as if his heart was being ripped out, pulled from the protective cage of his ribs, to be laid at his feet. He was being abandoned by every emotion which brought life and the joy of existence except rage.

Every other feeling was drowned out, conquered by a wrath which shouldn't even exist in its present form. But anger without forgiveness, without that absolution which love and friendship brought, turned meaningful life into an empty endurance. Kam turned his head and vomited fiercely, unable to contain it any longer.

Red smelled the pungent odor expelled by this man and looked at the fluid now being absorbed quickly into the dry, arid sand. Did humans have the ability to shoot out acid as a defense mechanism the way he could emit fire? He hadn't ever heard of that before. Maybe it was some kind of magic. If so it wasn't a very effective one. The man's acid traveled in a nearly straight line and came nowhere near him. A man would have to be almost directly over his target to be able to use it effectively, and by that time he would probably be dead.

Red snorted, both at the idiocy of a man's attacking with acid he couldn't spit far and with trying to clear his nose and throat of the rancid scent of this man's caustic fluid. He didn't think the acid was very strong as the sand it landed on remained nearly unaffected by it except for an unusual color change. Maybe that was what it was supposed to do, change the color of the man's attacker and frighten it away. Obviously, men like this one didn't fight dragons very often.

Red snorted again but this time out of a cold, dark humor than for the odor, which was now nearly gone, having dissipated quickly in the hot, dry wind of the desert. Red eyed the man, who still knelt before him as if in worship, and wondered how this man could think himself a warrior. Red was a warrior; this man was nothing more than a soulless necromancer who only happened to have a powerful splinter of wood to gain any dominance over him.

The dragon's thoughts were based on emotion to a much greater degree than Kam thought they could be. Kam came prepared to control a dragon; or so he had thought. The idea of controlling an animal, even one like a dragon, seemed like such as easy task-like teaching a dog a trick. He assumed it would be simple and uncomplicated and with a benign aspect to it. But this wasn't what he expected. He felt as if he was trying to ride a raging bullhorse bareback.

He looked closely at the dragon and for the first time and noticed the deep crimson color of its scales were reflected as deeply in its eyes. He wasn't naïve; even without the connection he knew it wanted to kill him. But the one-track, paranoid view it had of thinking everything in the world was against it was incomprehensible to Kam.

The pure, unadulterated rage it had focused on everything, even its own kind, took Kam's breath away. Of course, he got angry and there were situations where the anger gave him strength to fight and even kill when he had to. But this was different. This felt like the Dark Lord's own sinister emotion seeping through every pore of this creature.

The darkness that raged in the dragon felt like a living, breathing entity. Alive and intelligent, it was constantly looking for targets for its fury. There was an emptiness there as well, a bleakness, like standing on the top of a mountain with a view for miles around and knowing you were the only one left in the world. Kam had felt that aspect of extreme rage before as he also felt it within himself. His anger, which seemed to have directed his life for so long, revolved around his father and the animosity he felt for him and what he had done.

Kam vomited again, tasting the sour, bitter bile in his throat as well as in his mind through the bond with the dragon. The dragon's rage was overpowering and he became light headed. He wasn't sure he could control this dragon. It was almost as if he were controlling two creatures at the same time: the dragon and some other creature of pure rage-filled hatred. Emotion so strong and encompassing it could only be compared to wrestling a hairless and greased Liger. He didn't think it could be done, yet he had to do it. Too much was at stake for him to give up now. He only hoped he had the strength of will to see this through to the end.

Red could sense the darkness-yet-not-darkness in the man's head; it felt more like personal torment, a type of emotional self-flagellation. Sometimes when Dragons hurt another by accident, they would use their own tails to whip themselves to beg for exoneration. He could feel this man's sadness but his darkness wasn't the same. What this man harbored wasn't alive like Red's was. It was driven by this man's past but he kept it down, kept it from acquiring life. He buried it deep inside in a cage of his making where he could manipulate and control it.

Red could also sense this man had killed before and felt he would have the necessity to kill again. But what he had done before he felt had to be done out of some need. Curiously the people he had killed before stayed in his memories in a way which haunted him. This was unlike Red who remembered his victories with pride; most of them anyway. For a dragon victory was everything. Losing a battle could mean death as well.

He'll never reach his full potential worrying about those he killed. You kill, you glory in the victory and you move on.

Suddenly and without much effort, Red caught feelings of what a striking and terrifying Dragon Kam thought he was. *Of course, all lesser creatures revere and esteem Dragons. It is only right. This man is obviously highly intelligent.*

With a start Red realized his own feelings of admiration for this man must be flowing through the mystical tendrils of his bondage to Kam's mind as well and he suddenly felt some of the man's uneasiness slip away.

I will find a way to get past the Dragonstaff and kill you! Red thought, using his anger to amplify it. He was rewarded with both a mental and physical yelp of fear from the man accompanied by a terrified stumble backwards, causing the man to fall clumsily to the earth. Red roared with laughter as only a dragon can; a horrific sound which most who have the hapless chance to hear assume it is either a cry of pain or a challenge to fight. Then Red growled again, making sure the man got a good look at his sharp teeth.

With much effort the man reassumed a standing posture with as much dignity as he could muster. He then started to pace back and forth in front of Red, his confusion evident. He abruptly stopped, turned, and looked expectantly at Red as he started to focus his mind into images and feelings of what he wanted to communicate.

The intrusion of the man's thoughts into his head, not in the meandering, tedious way they had up to now but with a conscious effort behind them, was a bit much for Red to handle. The slow pounding of the forced thoughts caused Red to see stars and made him feel dirty.

The process was made worse as the man slowed his thoughts to an agonizing crawl thinking this would help Red understand him. Red, although finding the idea of communicating with this man extremely repugnant, finally roared mentally *Stop it! Stop forcing your thoughts on me!* This caused the man to again stumble and fall to the ground, something which both Red and his rage could appreciate. He wondered if he would ever be rid of this man and his abhorrent bondage stick.

There is a great… Kam began, struggling to find the right words and rising yet again to his feet…*dark evil which is taking over the lands of man. This evil is enslaving everyone. Many have died protecting their homes and freedom, but we need help. The leader of this evil is a powerful wizard who knows puissant magic and has many dark and vicious creatures helping him, although there are many who believe he is being controlled by the Dark Lord himself. The armies of man are trying to stop him, but it is only a matter of time before we fall, and after us the rest of the known world. That's why we need a dragon to...*

The known world? Red interrupted, only now noticing how exhausted the man appeared. *Who's known world? Certainly not the dragons!* And with that, all of Kam's desires briefly came into focus for Red. The man was hoping the introduction of a dragon on the side of men would create enough of a motive for the elves and other creatures to also join in the fight.

He was hoping for Red's promise to help, even though he knew Red wouldn't last against the myriad of dark creatures at the beck and call of the evil one. He hoped that Red's death, martyr-like, might spur other dragons to join as well, hopefully tipping the scales on the side of man.

My promise to help. Red thought angrily, accepting without understanding how this man seemed to know so much about Dragons. *You want my sacred oath, my Dragonword.* Red understood that Kam knew it was a promise so binding that no Dragon could ever break it. This man seemed to know a lot about Dragons. Red wondered if the man knew that a Dragon had broken his Dragonword once, a long time ago during the Dragonwars. Well, that was one thing Red wouldn't and couldn't give. Not to this man. Not to anyone or anything except another Dragon.

Kam, sensing this, thought back, *If you don't give me your word I will have to keep you bound by the Dragonstaff.* Red simply growled in return. He would not be intimidated by him or any other man. Kam heaved a heavy sigh and turned, walking slowly around in circles, trying to collect his thoughts. It was at this point Red noticed a saddle some yards behind him.

A Dragonsaddle! Dragonsaddles had not been used since the Dragonwars, and they were, physically and mentally, an ugly, binding anachronism from an era long gone. An instrument nearly as depraved as the splinter the man held in his hand. At this point Red redoubled his efforts to break free from the magic of the Dragonstaff, but to no avail. Its magic was more powerful than Red would have thought possible in such a small artifact. Kam sensed all of this and his mind filled with questions.

Why don't you like saddles? He asked, as if any explanation were needed.

Dragonsaddles are a humiliation to dragons. A dragon who agreed to have a man fly on his back was responsible for that man's life and would not allow him to fall or be injured in any way. Dragonsaddles were used by those who did not completely trust dragons, but rather used magic like the Dragonstaff to control them. This was the only reply Red could choke out. He would not wear a Dragonsaddle!

Will you give me your oath you will keep me safe?

Red paused at the question. He wasn't sure what he should do. A Dragonsaddle was considered a humiliation to dragons everywhere since they first were used, an insult to both their honor and integrity. He would not bring anymore dishonor to Dragonkind, he had done enough of that to last a lifetime. *I will,* Red replied. *I give my Dragonword I will let no harm befall you while you ride me. But note this: whenever you are off my back and on the ground, there is no promise. You must provide for your own safety.*

Kam paused, sensing the gravity and limitations of what the dragon was saying. He knew there was little more he could either request or expect at this point. For all intents and purposes, the dragon was a prisoner. And not even just that; he was being asked to sacrifice himself for man in a battle which as yet didn't even involve dragons. With a heavy heart he agreed to ride him without the Dragonsaddle, although they both knew he really had no choice in the matter.

At this point Kam remembered how he had arrived here in the first place. He looked to his right and saw the desert horse he had bought just for this journey about thirty yards away still tied to a wizened old Joshua tree. He decided the best course of action was to just take the horse's saddle off and set it free.

He walked over and unbuckled its saddle, letting it fall to the ground. He then untied the horse and hit its rear to send it running. Abruptly Kam sensed a thought from the dragon, but before he could say anything a shadow passed over him as it half-leapt, half-flew over him to land on the horse and rip it apart in a feeding frenzy. Kam quickly turned away, fighting the urge to lose what little contents he had left in his stomach.

After Red finished, and with the stench of raw meat and blood still in the air, Kam approached him warily, his whole body filled with trepidation. In his mind he wanted to believe the dragon would keep his word. He still didn't completely trust the Dragonstaff, or magic, for that matter. A good solid sword was all he needed to feel safe; although he had to admit a sword wouldn't be much good against a dragon.

Red however was elated knowing that, despite possessing the Dragonstaff, the man was still extremely apprehensive about being around him. However, Dragonword was Dragonword, and so Red lay down he stretched out his leg so as to provide an easy slope for the man to walk up onto his back without any mishap. Not an easy chore given the nervousness and frailty of him and the way he gingerly climbed up on Red so as not to cause Red any pain. With that Red snorted with laughter. *Hurt me?! This man is like the bloodfleas which infest a Lizaerd!*

As Kam reached Red's back questions flooded into Red's mind. *Where do I sit? How do I sit? How do I sit and stay on? How do I keep from falling off when you're flying? How do I stay on when you fly upside down?* And on and on the questions came.

Well, if nothing else, Red thought, *I will get a good laugh from having this man around.*

Kam noticed how, at the base of the dragon's neck where it attached to the body, there was an indention between the shoulder blades and wings. As he sat down, he realized he could probably lay back and even sleep with some comfort. *That's odd*, he reflected to himself, already forgetting how well the dragon could perceive his thoughts. *It's almost as though the indentation exists for the purpose of allowing someone to sit here.*

At that the dragon hurled itself into the air and started beating its massive wings Kam felt his stomach leave his body and he wanted to retch again. A light-headed dizziness invaded his mind.

After about 30 minutes, Kam realized he could get used to the thought of being up in the sky on a dragon's back by pretending he was someplace else. He found that if he stared at the now rapidly darkening night sky, and focused his mind on the many forms of crossing blades, he could trick himself into believing he was still on the ground rocking gently in a hammock. Unfortunately, it seemed just as he was able to convince himself of that, Red's mind would intrude with harsh thoughts about how high they were and what would happen if his wings suddenly broke off from his body. The thought of plummeting to his death jarred Kam back into reality.

Eventually however the slight up-and-down rocking motion of the dragon's body, as well as the soft pounding from the beating wings drumming the air like a tomknocker, put Kam into a surprisingly relaxed state. In fact, the toll of the long journey up to this point was not lost on Kam's body. Inside the dragon's head however, he felt an enveloping and suffocating darkness so overpowering he felt he was physically unable to breathe at times, causing him to become dizzy and lightheaded again.

Are you tired? Do you need to sleep? Kam asked.

Not just yet. Was the reply. *But soon I will.*

Do you know where we need to go? Kam felt it was an effort to put thoughts together as he had not slept in over a day and a half, but the dragon's affirmation eased some of his fears. He did however have a splitting headache which he hoped would not hamper his ability to get some sleep.

Red noticed the man's thoughts get much weaker and even more erratic than before, flitting from here to there quickly and making no sense to him. His rage noted that the man must be sleeping, and Red agreed. Yet even with the man sleeping, or more likely passed out from exhaustion from trying to communicate with a much more intelligent creature like a dragon, Red knew he still couldn't hurt him.

Aside from his promise Red could still sense the magic of the Dragonstaff, still so powerful that even the strength and depth of his wrath couldn't dislodge it. He decided to let the man sleep so he could at least have some time to figure a way out of this. And how would the little parasite know if he was flying slower than he was able?

Red's dark indignation sent shards of heat through to the tips of his wings in impatience, waiting for the time he would be able to tear the man apart and free himself from his witchcraft. Red chuckled mirthlessly; he would be patient, for now.

Chapter 3

Kam awoke with a start from a night terror of falling off the dragon and plummeting viciously to the earth. The dragon seemed to snort and shake roughly in amusement for a moment and Kam wondered if it was his dream of falling which gave pleasure to the dragon. Although he felt rested Kam knew he had slept only intermittently through the night.

He remembered the dragon finally stopping for the night and having trouble falling back to sleep as visions of the dragons's last meal kept intruding into his thoughts. He knew it was being done purposefully as the bloody death of his horse was seen from the perspective of the dragon. He vomited twice more before being able to control his stomach and drift back into a fitful slumber.

As he looked around, he could tell the sun was fairly high in the sky, yet he felt no heat from it. He finally caught on that the dragon's wings were not moving, but instead were folded up, partially obscuring the sun and providing him with shade to sleep in. The continued motion of riding was created by the rising and falling of the dragon's slow, heavy breathing of sleep. He wondered if Red's wings were always set at that angle when he slept or if Red had done it out of consideration for him. Kam chuckled mirthlessly to himself; he already knew the answer to that question.

As Kam's now alert mind slowly reached out to the dragon's sleeping one, he again felt the raging darkness which seemed to permeate the dragon's thoughts continually. There it was-boiling, seething, writhing; like a living creature. It was a giant serpent of molten metal and black ice. Never sleeping, continually writhing and twisting as though in search of food. Alive yet consisting only of the dark emotions of anger, bitterness, and, to a greater extent, hatred.

He now understood that the darkness he felt when he first utilized the Dragonstaff was in fact not a side effect of its magic as he had first thought. Rather it was something which resided in the dragon continually and seemed to represent a loathing of something, but he couldn't tell what. Even so, the darkness wasn't quite as intense or as stifling as it was when Red was awake.

Apparently sleep helps ease the connection a little. Kam thought.

He also felt the bleakness again. As he focused on it, its desolation seemed to create a giant hole in the center of his chest and left him gasping. A realization hit him; the bleakness was actually an extreme sense of loneliness and it wasn't caused by, or part of, the darkness. Rather it seemed to exist on its own and gave him the distinct feeling it was what helped feed the rage which infiltrated the dragon's soul.

Kam shook his head trying to clear it and wondered if there was a way to temporarily block the bond he shared with the dragon. He looked around, trying to figure out where they were. Not knowing exactly how far the dragon had flown while he slept, he could only guess they were in a part of the Northern Desert called the Sand of Fire. It was so named due to its reflection of the sun off of crystallized sand, creating a sense of a blinding firestorm. It was said this was where the final battle of the Dragon Wars was fought and the intensity of that battle melted the sand into bits of glass.

In any case Kam found this bond which now existed between him and Red causing the intersecting of thoughts could be confusing at best and created searing headaches at worst. He hoped both conditions would eventually subside and allow him to focus more on his self-appointed task.

Red roused only a few minutes after Kam, making Kam wonder how much their connection truly affected each other and if his waking up caused the dragon to arise as well. It was something to consider anyway.

After a couple of minutes both were wide awake and they took to the skies again. For Kam to be flying high in the sky on the back of what he felt was a very large, hairless rat was bad enough, even an abomination against nature to say the least. But the fact this rat was hoping to serve him up as a meal and was held in check by only a small staff of magical driftwood didn't help matters any.

He could still sense the dragon's presence constantly in his mind; a dark, anger-filled essence which filled his whole soul with anguish. Fortunately, without full effort and focus, their communications seemed more abstract and ineffective. Less informative and more emotional. It was also less exhausting, Kam found to his immense relief.

After they had been flying for some time, Kam couldn't ignore the rumblings in his stomach anymore. Between trying to keep the dragon's emotional influence in check and controlling his paranoia about flying he had worked up quite an appetite.

He concentrated on figuring out if it was his stomach he heard growling or the dragon's appetite coming through. He came to the conclusion that the dragon was still full from his horse. *His horse!* No one he knew had ever eaten horse meat before and the thought nauseated him.

As he pulled some dried and salted beef out of his small knapsack, he remembered he was nearly out of water. In fact, if he hadn't found the dragon when he had, he probably would have died of dehydration within a day or two. As he focused his thoughts on getting water Red replied, *We will arrive at Dragonlake before the sun has left the sky.*

Kam received an impression of the lake and its location from the dragon. Interestingly it was an aerial view, with a large desert on one side and dense tree cover on the other. As they flew over the southern tip of the desert, which bordered Dragoncountry on its southern side, Kam allowed his mind to wander as the barren desert flew by below him in a crazy quilt of tans, browns, umbers, and the occasional gray of an exposed rock.

Thoughts of friends, some of whom he hadn't seen in a long time and others who were not around anymore, filled his mind. It was one of his friends who had jokingly suggested getting dragons to help during the siege of the Great Wall in the borderlands. That idea is what had inspired Kam to begin his quest to enlist the aid of a dragon.

Not enlist, imprison. Came Red's abrupt interjection.

Kam ignored the interruption, allowing his thoughts to continue. So many had already died, many he knew and loved, in the defense of their families and homes. This war, what so many now called the Dark War due to the perceived influence of the Dark Lord, had taken its toll. Creatures of unthinkable descriptions were found roaming the land, indiscriminately slaughtering people. The sage who started it all, Gogam, lusted after power. Fortunately, there were many who aligned themselves with those who were fighting to preserve their homes and families just as he had.

Gogam sounds like a typical man-wanting power and control and forcing others to do his bidding. Red injected again, with more than a little sarcasm.

This time Kam focused on the dragon's comment. *Do you think I like being here? Do you think I like having to force you, a creature many don't even believe still exists, to fight for us? Gogam will not stop until he controls everything. And when he does, he will rule as though he is the Dark Lord himself, brutally taking what he wants and killing those who will not obey him.*

Red seemed undisturbed by Kam's outburst and left Kam with the impression Gogam would not be able to take Dragonspire by any means. *What is Dragonspire?* Kam asked.

Dragonspire is the highest mountain in Dragoncountry and where most of the dragons live.

Kam sighed. He appreciated the fact dragons were powerful, intimidating creatures physically and probably magically as well. He just wished he could get it to understand just what was out there. The desert surrounding Dragonmount was difficult to get through, but not impossible. Dragons were just so enamored of themselves and oblivious to the outside world they couldn't understand what was at their own front door.

Enamored of ourselves? Dragons are the greatest creations in the world! We are the pinnacle of all that exist! Nothing is greater than a Dragon!

And yet I control you with just a piece of wood. Kam responded.

The silence in Kam's head vibrated with loathing and hatred and caused Kam to feel he was bathing in a pool of rancid tar. Kam immediately regretted taunting the dragon and having to force it to help him in what was still just a war of men. Yet Kam knew Gogam wouldn't stop until he enslaved the world.

After that Kam kept his thoughts to himself by not having any at all. He whistled tunelessly, sang old children's songs, thought about what he had for dinner every night for the past two months and on and on. He found it took a lot of energy to literally think of nothing. It was like being in a house completely engulfed in flames and being in the center of the conflagration while trying to ignore the heat. As far as the dragon went all he felt were intense stabs of emotion so strong it caused his head to ache.

They finally came to a large pond, which Kam seemed to instinctively know was not Dragonlake. The dragon grounded saying he needed a drink and Kam gratefully got down, accepting the solid feel of the ground beneath his boots with renewed appreciation.

Kam kept his thoughts under control as best he could and didn't look back as he walked to the edge of the water. He wanted the dragon to think he wasn't afraid to turn his back on him, but the intense tightening of his stomach screamed otherwise. When he reached the edge of the pond he looked down at his clothes and for the first time saw a number of dead bugs covering his shirt.

They both bent down and drank water that tasted both cool and sweet. It erased much of the grime Kam felt in his throat and allowed him a chance to clear his mind for the moment. He glanced over at Red but found the dragon ignoring him by watching some birds fly around the water.

He also realized, and this was reconfirmed by his newfound personal experience, dragons were highly intelligent. He wasn't sure if all dragons were as dominated by their emotions as this one was, but based on their limited communications he could honestly say this dragon was brighter than many people he knew. And with that thought Kam was certain he felt a lessoning of the sharp mental jabs and rage-filled headaches which allowed him to relax a little bit.

Unfortunately, Kam was forced to climb back onto Red andexperience the wonder of flying again. The simmering rage which the dragon harbored seemed content with giving Kam a small but annoying throb in the back of his head which the pulsating vibrations of the ride exacerbated. Kam wondered how insects managed to compensate for the flying they did on a daily basis. In either case he was grateful when the dragon suggested they ground for the night about an hour later.

Although it was an area ripe with low laying hills and shadows grappling to rule the landscape, Kam still felt the dragon purposely landed hard so as to shake him up. The dragon couldn't allow him to fall off, of course, as it was large and causing him to fall off could injure him severely, breaking its Dragonword. Still, it wasn't a pleasant grounding, as the dragon called it, and Kam slid slowly off and stood unsteadily on his feet.

Kam took some shaky steps forward, allowing a cool breeze to waft across his face. The lake, which seemed to suddenly appear out of thin air about ten feet in front of him, shimmered magically in the soft, silvery moonlight. It was a beautiful sight and for a moment Kam was homesick for the house he grew up in, itself not far from a lake. However, as Kam strained his eyes to gauge the size of the lake, he realized he couldn't see the far shore. He wondered just how deep the lake might be.

As the pangs of hunger started to assail his stomach again, Kam was surprised when the dragon said it would already be able to see the closest permanent settlement of man to Dragonspire. They just needed to fly high enough. He didn't know what the dragon meant by permanent and hadn't seen anything himself but assumed the dragon's eyesight was probably much sharper than his. More to his surprise however was when the dragon mentioned that there was an area near there where dragons willingly met with people.

Dragons meet with people? Kam asked incredulously, forgetting for the moment the queasiness that had entered his head.

Red peered at him with eyes now glowing gold and orange, reflecting the colors of the sunset and heralding the day's demise.

Dragons have a fondness for cow meat, but sometimes in the desert around Dragonmount, lizaerds steal some of our breeding cows. When that happens, we need to trade for more cows with people.

Kam did nothing to hide his surprise. *Most people think dragons are not real and never were. Only a few people still believe dragons even existed at all. Only one person I ever met knew of you and your kind and where to find you.*

Red, who had started drinking water by the gallons, stopped and again looked at Kam with the fiery colors of sunset mirrored within its eyes. *Is this the one who gave you the Dragonstaff?*

When Kam responded affirmatively Red continued. *I want to meet this person.*

Although the dragon responded neutrally Kam could feel the swirling tide of emotion surround him, barely contained like an overflowing lake threatening to overwhelm a dam. He started to feel claustrophobic, as if he were in a tiny closet with the sides pressing in on him. He held no reservations about what the dragon intended to do; the person who provided the information and staff was as good as dead in the eyes of the dragon.

With an abrupt loss of appetite Kam spread his sleeping roll on the ground, laid down and turned away from the dragon and the now bloody sky behind it. He only hoped the color didn't portend the danger he felt it might.

CHAPTER 4

The next morning Red awoke bright and early from a very lucid dream of taking a bath. It literally felt the water washing over him while using a brush to scrub the dirt off. When he found that the man was already up and wading around in the lake he briefly wondered if that had any connection to his dream. Then without a further thought Red launched himself up and over the man and into the deep part of the shimmering blue lake.

For a brief second he elatedly caught the man's surprise, visually and mentally, as Kam looked up and uncomprehendingly and saw a large object pass above him. Red hit the water with a massive splash and the ensuing wave caught the man and carried him to the shore where it spewed him unceremoniously onto the grainy sand.

Coughing and sputtering Kam gave Red a look as vile as the thoughts he sent over, causing Red to laugh hysterically. The terrifying uproar scattered birds from some nearby trees, which apparently hadn't been told there was a dragon nearby splashing in the lake. Red eyed the birds hungrily, vainly wishing they were much larger than they were. It was then he realized just how hungry he had become.

Red looked around, trying to find something to eat. With water here there should be animals as well; but he got no sense of anything even remotely close. He was surprised as there were supposed to be many lizaerds out around the lake which the Dragons who came to trade with man would eat. Then it hit him, a smell he knew very well. His eyes narrowed as he looked over at the tree line and saw the tail of a lizaerd wrapped partially around a tree. He slowly crept over to the trees, sloshing through the water as quietly as he could.

Wait! The man thought nervously. *Where are you going?*

I am bound to you, Kam. I cannot leave you. The influence of the Dragonstaff keeps me enslaved to you. Even you must feel that.

Kam paused, another question forming in his mind. *What is a lizaerd?*

Something Dragons eat. It is a creature, larger than one of your horses, which lives in the desert. You had to have seen them. They wouldn't be afraid of a small thing like you.

The man paused, his dislike for Red's sarcasm was obvious. Red simply snorted and tried to focus on his prey again. Suddenly Red's only friend, the omnipresent darkness, screamed in his mind, blocking out any possible conversation with the man. It sent shards of searing heat to the tips of his wings and left his face feeling hot and flushed. It was an abrupt realization, not unlike the slap to the face baby Dragons received from their parents' tails when they did something wrong, and caused Red to stop mid-step.

He had referred to the man by his name. His NAME! Red turned to look at Kam…the man…and saw incomprehension in his face. He didn't understand, or somehow couldn't hear, the thoughts going through Red's mind. Red intended to keep it that way and his constant companion grimly agreed.

He turned back and continued on with the hunt, trying to get to shallower water where he could effectively leap on his prey. When the water reached only to the tops of his claws he crouched, readying himself for the pounce. Then, with a giant leap he covered the distance and flattened a few small trees as he snatched up his large, juicy meal.

Kam watched as a dark, indiscriminate color splattered against nearby trees and oozed down the dragon's face. At first, he assumed it was a very dark red. However, when he looked closer, he would swear the color was more of a deep, almost black color with a hint of green in it. But the murky darkness of it, even in direct sunlight, made it impossible to truly hazard a guess. But what was clear was the dragon's joy at both the hunt and the meal.

Ominously, just a few minutes previous, Kam seemed to be cut off from the huge animal. It was like someone next to you trying to tell you something over a tremendous din of a hundred people shouting. You could catch the sound of their voice but couldn't make out any words.

For a moment he worried the dragon staff might be losing its power, but that idea just didn't feel right. It was more like someone or something was trying to block their conversation. At any rate Kam didn't really have a choice in the matter. He would continue on with his plan and hope for the best.

Kam looked away as Red finished his meal and cleaned himself up. Even so, he expected to feel sick; but when he didn't, he began to wonder if he should be relieved or worried. The dragon drank many more gallons of water before proclaiming himself ready for flight. Kam obligingly climbed back up and made sure his knapsack and newly filled water bottle were secure.

With a tremendous leap into the air, and with nearly the loss of the contents of his stomach again, Red took off. Once in the air however Kam noticed a marked increase in his ability to accept being on the dragon's back and appreciate the view which went on for miles. The patchwork of different hues of colors, now being more along the lines of browns and various shades of green from the myriad plant life, gave the landscape the look of a giant's massive comforter. The extraordinary view took his breath away.

Red is lucky to be able to enjoy this kind of view all the time. Kam thought to himself.

We now live in a mountain surrounded by desert because we were driven there by people. Red responded

Kam felt guilty for that. He knew he had nothing to do with whatever happened centuries ago. He didn't know or even begin to understand how or why that would happen. That is unless all dragons were all as ornery and belligerent as Red.

You used my name. Red stated.

Does that bother you? Kam cautiously questioned, afraid of agitating the dragon further. The resulting silence, and lack of even a spiteful response, was even more curious to him. But he let the matter go and focused instead on trying to understand the layout of the land as seen from the dragon's perspective.

Being able to see the movement of troops, signs of weakness in the enemy's lines and knowing where their leaders were situated were all valuable pieces of information which could easily turn the tide of any battle. And to think it could all be discerned by one man on the back of one dragon.

They flew on in silence with Kam preoccupied with the strategic impact of dragons. He played and replayed in his head various scenarios of different battles, both historical and fictitious, and worked out different outcomes based on the influence of one dragon. When Red announced they were close to the settlement he had seen Kam was surprised. Not only had he not gotten sick but he had completely lost track of time. He wondered what Red must be thinking of his view of the tactical advantage of a dragon. Strangely, this time only a sense of puzzled anger reached him.

As Red swooped in low to find a place to ground, Kam looked out over the broken landscape with huge swaths of charred land broken up with sections of shattered and twisted trees. It looked as though a tremendous battle had taken place here only a short time ago. Then the scene quickly changed to become even more bizarre.

Huge structures of some sort appeared, but Kam had no idea who or what had built them. The structures seemed to comprise a massive city, much larger than any he knew of currently, and looked like children's blocks stacked atop one another. Some of the buildings he saw he assumed were for people to live in but were much taller than he had ever seen before. There were even some with multiple sections sticking out from a central axis. All of them looked to have been knocked over due to an ill-tempered giant.

Many of the structures seemed to be broken somewhere above what would have been a sixth, seventh or even eighth floor. Yet the remains of others were much higher. *Buildings higher than four floors!* Kam thought excitedly to himself. It seemed incomprehensible; but then it was obvious they weren't made of wood or even brick.

The building material looked more like huge, solid pieces of light-colored stone, worked to a smooth finish and without the seams or coarseness found in typical buildings made of rock or brick. He could also see metal bars intermixed in the stone as if they had just grown there naturally.

Trees and other plants were growing here and there between large slabs of the smooth rock, including flowers he had never seen before in his life. The colors and looks of these plants alone would have left him speechless even if they weren't part of some ancient civilization full of wondrous sights and mammoth stone structures. Yet despite the breathtaking aerial view he could see no people.

Near the outskirts of the giant structures Red found a group of smaller buildings which at one time was probably surrounded by a beautiful garden but which now consisted only of an area overgrown with tall grass. Red grounded there and gave Kam an intense look. Kam realized that this is what people were to Red, creatures of damage and destruction.

I don't know this area Kam thought, *but I believe it's called the City of Stone.*

A better name would be the City of Broken Stone.

Kam gave Red a withering look and a few choice words, but the dragon seemed not to notice. However, as the sun was starting to get low in the sky Kam suggested spending the night there. The sun, which was behind the remains of a few of the taller structures, gave the area a bright halo. The wondrous colors of the beginning sunset made it seem as if the area was on fire, and he had to wonder if that was the scene when this incredible place was destroyed so long ago.

Kam had terrible nightmares that night. First there were dragons carrying large rocks which they hurled at buildings higher than the eye could see, and when the rocks hit the buildings, they burst open with a tremendous force, causing the structures to collapse. Then there were men marching to battle, leading hordes of deformed and twisted creatures to fight other creatures like themselves. The creatures had armor of bone and muscle, weapons which sprouted directly from their bodies as well as heads of various animals, including dragons.

The scene shifted again to that of people trapped in caves and underground lairs, people who looked normal except for having an extra arm or two, multiple legs or a face full of eyes. These people were attacked by others who were more animal than man; tiger people walking upright on claws dripping with blood or some type of creature with a head that was split nearly in half by a mouth filled with rows of triangular shaped teeth.

The scene shifted yet again and Kam saw rows of people adulating others who had large heads with long finger-like noses and many arms. Then there were others who looked strangely plant-like who seemed to be teaching their followers. He also saw many who allowed themselves to be killed in the name of peace, their corpses being trodden over by the armies of other, more brutal people.

Then there came the largest battle Kam could comprehend or envision. It seemed as though all of the people Kam had seen before were a part of it as well as other creatures like dragons. He saw powerful magic being used and people who appeared to be indestructible. He knew, somehow, he was witnessing the final battle of the Dragonwars. The carnage and destruction were horrendous and he knew that this war would change everything that was to come.

Kam awoke with a start. The view of the broken city looked so much like a graveyard full of broken and tilted headstones that Kam quickly became depressed. How could people, in an era so obviously full of wonder, magic and potential, have fallen so far? He shook his head as he wondered how he and one lowly dragon could influence the convergence of so much evil and darkness.

He looked over at Red and saw him sleeping peacefully. At least he seemed to be sleeping peacefully; Kam really had no idea what a dragon was supposed to look like when it was sleeping, peacefully or otherwise. Kam sighed and got up out of his sleeping roll.

The closest building near them looked like a huge house except for the fact it had a massive hole in the wall allowing Kam to see inside. He entered but only saw stacks of old, yellowed paper with a lot of writing printed in neat rows on them. He tried to pick up one of the papers to look at it more closely but it crumbled to dust in his hands.

He continued to look around and to one side of the large room he had entered he saw many tables. Most of them were overturned and broken as if a large fight had broken out. But on the one table which seemed to have been spared the wrath of whatever had done this was a stack of blank paper which had a bright, white sheen to it.

As he picked up the top sheet words magically appeared and glowed with an inner power. However, something seemed wrong. The words which appeared were incomplete, with some of the letters not appearing. Kam touched the paper but it didn't feel right; it was too smooth and slick, almost like glass, but flexible. Even more disturbing was when Kam lightly ran his finger over the surface the words changed, almost like turning the pages of a book.

Kam's attention was diverted from the object he held in his hands as a rumbling, which seemed to be quickly getting louder, reached his ears. It was a stampede of whatever animals were in the area and Kam needed to get to Red before either of them got hurt. He gently stuffed the mystical tome into his knapsack and hurried back outside where the rumbling had now grown quite loud.

He looked around trying to get a bead on where the noise was coming from; unfortunately, Red's body was between him and the sound. Kam paused as he watched the rise and fall of the dragon's chest as it continued with the slow, heavy breathing of sleep. With an exasperated grunt of understanding he went over to the dragon and kicked him as hard as he could in the leg.

The ensuing pain shot up his leg and caused him to yelp loudly in agony. It did get the snoring to stop though as Red woke up and moved his hind leg gingerly.

My leg hurts. Red said.

Kam hobbled over to a large rock to sit down. *Your leg hurts because my leg hurts.*

Red's head swung around from the far side of his body to get a close look at Kam. *What did you do, fall down again?*

I was trying to get you to stop snoring.

Dragons don't snore. Red's mind seemed to move around inside of Kam's head for a second before belligerently saying, *you kicked me.*

It feels more like you kicked me. Kam shot back.

Red moved slowly, purposely taking his time with getting up. The dragon slowly rose to his claws. He stretched each leg individually, although more gingerly for the leg he complained was sore, while balancing on the other three. He then stretched his neck out its full length and rotated his head, first to the right and then to the left. Finally, he extended his tail its full length and whipped it around back and forth a few times as if to make sure it was fully attached.

Despite having been just immobilized with the pain in his leg, Kam had to laugh at the maneuvers. It seemed an awful lot of work to go through just to get up.

At Kam's laughter Red swung his head around so that he faced Kam squarely from only a few feet away. As soon as Kam stopped laughing and looked up, he gave a yelp of surprise and fell over backwards, this time allowing Red to laugh heartily and causing the dragon's whole body to shake. For that brief moment while the dragon was laughing, Kam noticed the darkness in the dragon's head receded a bit.

CHAPTER 5

She knew she was good. She could fight better than most men, and as good as most of the others. But he was different; quick and strong, with a far better mastery of the blade than anyone she had seen before. And his weapon! A spear made of what looked like some type of dark stone. He used it with a skill and accuracy to rival any sword, or any other weapon for that matter.

His lean frame was taller than average and had the strength of someone far larger. Disconcertingly his dark hair and eyes matched the color of his spear, and like the spear they had a sharp, almost flint-like edginess to them. His gray skin had the look of granite and gave him a decidedly deathly pallor.

As she paused to catch her breath, sweat running down into her eyes, she tried to remember how he had lured her into this room. She had received a note asking for a rendezvous and telling her where to go. She didn't know who had sent it since there was no signature or seal, but assumed it was her employer. However, she had enough faith in her abilities that the lack of accountability for the note had seemed only mildly bothersome at worst.

She entered the room and found it empty, or so she had thought. She looked around the room before facing the far wall where she saw a colorful, if violent, fresco painting. She became mesmerized by the scene and the myriad color variations.

The artist had used brighter colors to represent the strong and violent action with ocher blood spilling across the lower part of the wall and spreading onto the floor. The darker overtones showed the tryst between the Dark Lord and his minions as well as the concourses of the Heavens with their Golden Ones, painted with what appeared to be real gold.

She blinked in surprise as the characters appeared to move. The timeless battle of good and evil was being played out right before her eyes. Men and demons were locked in combat with weapons swinging and man and beast dying.

She could swear it wasn't a painting but rather a window in the wall looking out over an actual battlefield. In the end it was his throaty chuckle, an evil sound mimicking someone choking to death, which caused the enchanting spell of the fresco to finally dissipate.

They engaged again, breaking her out of the spell of her own thoughts. The whole time they kept exchanging one thrust and parry with another he kept leering at her. He made a dramatic point of staring at her full bosom, and displaying a condescendingly smug smile, trying to intimidate her.

As they fought, she realized that she would need to find a way to escape. She wouldn't be able to defeat him, he was too good. It was not an easy conclusion to reach, but she didn't want to die. Not now, not ever if she could help it.

So she fought on, pressing her attack before taking a step back to glance around the room. She did this over and over; engage, pivot, step back and glance at the wall which had just been to her side.

She lost count how many times she performed the maneuver, unable to believe there was only one door and no windows in the room. And the door wasn't just closed but he had managed to place a bar across it as well! She was sure the room was empty when she had entered.

He stared at her again, licking his lips as he stared at the sweat-soaked garment which now clung enticingly against her body. His chuckling, his leering, all designed to intimidate her. Unfortunately, it was working. He was getting inside her head, and worst of all he knew it.

She didn't know his name, but knew him only by his look and reputation. She knew he wouldn't kill her. He would do things much, much worse. Things she couldn't think about right now, things she couldn't allow to distract her from being focused on fighting him. But she couldn't help herself. She didn't know what kind of man he was, if he was even a man at all. But she couldn't bear the thought of his touching her.

Exhaustion was starting to set in. She could hear her own breathing now and it sounded ragged. How long had they been fighting? It seemed like hours with no hope of his letting up. And the worst part-he still hadn't broken a sweat.

She came to the realization he wasn't a man; no man could fight as he did, look as he did. He was a monster in a man's skin. He was a rabid dog with a heart as black as night itself. Perhaps even the Dark Lord himself.

Again, he attacked, pressing her up against the wall. Their weapons crossed and his face came close; not more than a foot away. Abruptly he leaned forward and she turned her face quickly as he ran his long, black tongue from her chin up to her forehead. It's slick, smooth surface was as cold as a river stone. She shuddered in disgust and pushed him away.

She was gasping for breath now. She estimated that they had been fighting for at least two hours. She also understood why he picked this room. He didn't come here to give her instructions involving her employ, they were here simply for his pleasure. She belatedly realized he must have had this planned for some time.

She watched him closely-his breathing hadn't changed. His rough, cool skin felt like sandpaper and his dark, ink-stained teeth now made him look as though he had just risen out of a grave. She had tried to kick him a few times, but each attempt was met with the stoic density of a boulder.

She attacked him again quickly, violently, for a few seconds then she stepped back. He of course advanced and she would defend briefly, then attack viciously again. He would never allow her to leave; at least not without getting what he wanted. She knew that. But this game he was playing with her did allow her a chance to try and think of a plan of her own.

She pivoted around him again so that her back was to the door. She devised a plan, a risky plan, but it was the only one she could think of. It had to work.

She took a few steps back and tried to catch her breath again while inching towards the door. When she felt the door was right behind her, she attacked. He retreated a little, and parried her attacks with ease. Following that she quickly stepped back and hurled her sword at him, point first. It was a gambit she never in her life thought she would be forced to do, but desperate times called for desperate measures.

She turned to face the door as the sounds of him parrying her thrown sword, the clanging of metal on metal, and her sword hitting the ground signaled that she only had a few seconds left. She struggled to lift the crossbar and found she couldn't.

She looked at it closely. Somehow, he had put retaining bars across it to hold it in place. She was sure there hadn't been any retaining bars there before! She would need to unlatch the two vertical bars as well as the horizontal one before she could take out the wooden crossbar.

He started to laugh that evil, deep chuckle of his that now sounded like rocks grinding against each other. It was a sound that would send chills down anyone's back. She swallowed hard and turned around.

She still had the dagger strapped to her thigh. She didn't think he knew about that. But that could only be used as a last resort, after he was-she shuddered at the thought- already on top of her. She didn't think she could stand the thought of him being on her, grabbing at her, ripping off her clothes. She wanted to throw up, but she knew she didn't have the luxury of that right now.

He advanced slowly with his spear outstretched towards her. She was patient. She knew she had to be to get out of this. He approached her slowly and came to a stop with the spear-point just barely touching the soft, indented pocket at the base of her throat.

She felt it lightly touch her, almost as if he was trying to caress her with his spear. He laughed again but this time it sounded more like a giggle. The maniacal laugh had now transformed into a demonic chortle.

He looked her over from her head to her feet and giggled again, sadistically. Oh, she wished she could beat him in a fair fight, or even an unfair one for that matter. The world would be much better off without him in it.

Barely moving his wrist and hand, he flicked his spear to the right and left side very quickly. The tip easily cut threw her blouse and underclothes, leaving them barely hanging on. He backed up a step and flung his spear across the room. She frowned. What was he trying to do? Suddenly he came forward, put his left hand around her throat and clutched tightly. As quick as that she couldn't breathe.

She reached up and tried to pry his hand away with both of hers. He was too strong, unnaturally strong. He did that insane laugh again. She wanted to kill him. She wanted to kill him so bad she could taste it. Her whole body ached with the desire to end his life. But now was not the time. She had to be patient.

He grabbed her blouse with his right hand and ripped it completely off. She was left to stand there in her shredded camisole and skirt. In one quick movement he threw her on the ground and pounced on top of her. He grabbed her wrists and pinned them above her head with his left arm, and with his right hand followed the curves and contours of her body from her shoulder down to her left thigh. It took all of her self control to keep from screaming.

As she watched, spittle slowly seeped out of the corner of his lips. It gradually eased away from his mouth and gravity brought it towards her until it paused about four inches down. As he breathed it swung, pendulum-like, back and forth before it continued to ooze towards her face again. She forced herself to keep her eyes open, to be patient and think.

As he tried to pull her skirt and petticoat down, they caught on her right thigh where the knife was strapped on. He tried using his feet to try to force them off, pushing so hard some of the stitches in her clothing gave way and the straps for the knife sheath bit into her leg causing blood to drip around her thigh. Surprisingly both the cloth and the straps held.

She knew she had to do something, and quickly, before he looked down and saw the knife. "You don't need to be quite so rough," she said in as sweet a voice as she could manage under the circumstances.

He paused, his spittle still hanging in midair, now about two inches from her face.

"I'll be happy to help you. You've already ruined my top; you don't need to ruin my skirt as well."

He stared at her, uncomprehending. And finally threw back his head and burst out laughing. The spittle swung up and over onto his cheek and landed there, but he didn't seem to notice.

When he looked down again there was a line of moisture glistening on his cheek in a line reaching from his mouth to his eye. Ironically it gave the illusion of his shedding a tear for her situation. Again, she wanted to throw up and again she forced herself not to.

His arm which had pinned hers above her head eased up. She slowly reached down with her right hand, smiling the whole time. In the back of her mouth she was biting her tongue to keep herself focused, to keep herself from allowing the fear to overwhelm her. She forced herself to look him in the eyes and not turn away. She bit her tongue so hard it bled, her mouth filling with a metallic taste, but she kept the smile on her face.

She felt the knife and pulled her garments over it while she slowly eased it out of the sheath. Thoughts swirled around in her head as to where she should stab him. She wasn't sure she could kill him, or even if he could be killed; but she had to try. She at least needed to cause a great deal of pain. She needed to slow him down enough to give herself a chance to escape.

That most tender spot men have was already in close proximity to the blade. Right now, it was where she dearly wanted to stab him. But she felt there was a good chance it wouldn't hurt him enough. Not to mention with him already on top of her she might not be able to get away. She slid the knife slowly, seductively, up her body; holding it with the blade against the inside of her wrist. She decided the best place to stab him would be the throat.

To keep him from suspecting anything she took her left hand and caressed the right side of his face, avoiding the wet spot that still lined his cheek. She lightly touched his lips. She finally ended up with her left hand lightly caressing the side of his throat, so as the right hand came up to the other side, he wouldn't suspect anything.

She steeled herself to move quickly and brutally. As she drove her knee violently into his groin, his face instantly contorted into one of rage and pain. She quickly brought her right hand up and out and tried to bury the knife in his throat with all of her strength. In that instant he suspected what she was doing and his left arm came up and blocked her attack. She put so much force behind the motion however, that as her arm slammed into his, the force caused her arm to slide down his and the knife bit deeply into his left shoulder.

He rolled over and off of her, keeping his injured side up and reaching for the blade. As soon as he was off of her, she rolled away and jumped to her feet. She nearly stumbled and fell forgetting that he had pulled her skirt and petticoat part way down.

She quickly pulled them back up around her waist and grabbed her shredded blouse to cover her camisole. She got to the door and realized she needed both of her hands and let her blouse fall and started dismantling the metal bracing keeping the heavy wooden bar in place.

She dared not turn around. She wanted to stay focused on opening the door. She knew that if she turned around that she would slow down, and if he caught up to her, she'd never have another chance. He was yelling something in a language she had never heard before. But even though she didn't understand him, she could imagine what he was saying. As she lifted the heavy metal bracing off, she finally turned; he'd gotten up and was just a few steps away from her with her dagger in his hand.

She got a firm grip and swung the brace with all of her might. He brought up his right arm to block it, but she swung so hard it hit his arm and pushed it back. It then struck his shoulder and glanced off and up and hit him in the head. He went down to his knees with an angry snarl.

She set her feet and swung the brace again, utilizing it as she did a wooden bat she used when she played batball as a little girl. This time she struck the front of his head and knocked him down to the floor. She stood there in shock, looking down at his faceless head while it oozed what looked like black mud.

His face abruptly disappeared into the floor while a new one slowly seemed to get rebuilt where it belonged. She then lifted the brace and brought it down on his head as hard as she could.

His body collapsed on the floor, his mouth still working furiously with mud and foreign words spewing from it. She went back to the door and hoisted the wooden bar and hurled that at him for good measure. It struck him full in the chest, although she never saw it connect. By the time it hit him she had already opened the door and fled. She knew she'd need another chance to get him. Another chance to finish the job she couldn't do now.

Rage filled him, and it was made all the stronger by the burning desire he had for her. He had toyed with her too long; he could see that now. It allowed her to think up a plan to escape, and she did.

He couldn't remember the last time he was with a woman, or even wanted to be with one. But this one, Sakura, she was everything he could want.

She was breathtakingly beautiful, to the point he ached for her. Then there was her ability with the blade. She was impressive by anyone's standards. And she kept up with *him*, a man who couldn't even remember how old he was because he had lived so long.

He thought about that for a moment. Perhaps calling himself a man was a stretch, but still he had been a man at one point. An unimpressive geek of a man which everyone he had known made fun of. But now he was like a god compared to others, one who deserved respect and whatever he wanted.

But what he wanted was her.

He sighed, a low rumbling sound which coming from an ordinary man would make people think his lungs were about to give out. But for him the sound was not unusual, especially given his unique genetic makeup. Now he was just one of a handful of others, some of the most powerful beings on the planet.

He got up, his anger now simmering just below the surface but at a controllable point. He would get her eventually; that he knew. Her escape now just meant he could fantasize about her that much longer.

He walked over to the door and picked up her blouse. Holding it to his nose he inhaled deeply. Her scent was as intoxicating as her physicality had been just moments before.

He felt himself grow hot again. His longing for her was growing. He didn't understand completely why he wanted her-does any man really know what attracts him to a specific woman? But he knew his desire was stronger than anything he had felt in centuries. And it made him feel alive.

The sound of loud footsteps coming up the stairs echoed down the hallway. He knew he could take out the City Guard without any problems, but that was not his task. He had already strayed too far from his mission by going after a personal prize, and his Lord wouldn't like that.

Holding on to her blouse like a well-deserved trophy, he grabbed his spear and disappeared before the guards arrived.

CHAPTER 6

Wyk made his way quickly towards the royal hall. It didn't look good for one of the King's Guard to dally after receiving a summons to see the king. He was returning from the barracks where he had just inspected the men when he had received the summons.

His men, he reminded himself. He was no longer doing this for king and kingdom alone but now had his own heart invested with his detachment. Not that he had ever looked at himself as not being a part of the group; but it was different now. He was in charge and the blame for any failure or poor behavior would fall directly on his shoulders.

He entered the cavernous hall where some of the kingdom's most noted rulers had dreamed dreams of conquest and war and had been a part of arbitration and peace accords. This place had hosted courts and weddings and balls. He always stood in awe of this place whenever he was here.

Unfortunately, he was here less and less these days. There always seemed to be some place he was needed more than here, despite being part of the King's Guard.

"Captain Wyk!"

He turned at the call of his name. It was Jesse, his second in command. When he had been given this command his first act was to bring Jesse with him. A good friend, Jesse always amazed him with his feats of strength. He was compactly built yet his lean body displayed a regimented discipline of exercise which allowed nearly every muscle which existed in the human frame to be seen.

Jesse was always in uniform. Often, he was in his formal colors, but more frequently than not he was in his "casuals" as they were known, as he was now. Wyk felt the blue shirt with gold epaulets and braided gold ropes and red pants with vertical gold pin stripes were too garish for fighting men to wear, but he had to admit Jesse looked good in them. And apparently everyone else felt the same way.

Jesse reveled in standing out and attracting the gaze of men and women alike. However, even now with his casuals being worn a size too small, he was a constant reminder of the professionalism which Wyk expected of his men at all times. Wyk loved him like a brother.

"Captain Wyk," Jesse continued, "There's been a crime. A woman was brutally attacked and had her, um, clothes ripped off."

Wyk frowned. Any crime committed was bad news of course, but he especially loathed hearing about attacks on women and children. When he was young his own mother was viciously attacked and killed. After that he promised himself he would never let that happen to anyone else.

When he found out the creed of the King's Guard taught respect for all, but especially women, children and the helpless, he knew he had found his life's calling. He felt himself honor bound to join. Anything less would have been sacrilege and an affront to his own personal beliefs.

"I appreciate your concern for the welfare of the King's subjects, but we are not the City Guard. This crime should be left to them." Wyk said.

"But the victim was the king's special guest. The one who was to accompany us on our…" Jesse paused, searching for the word he needed. "…quest." He finally finished sheepishly.

Wyk paused; a quest? This was the first he had heard of it. If the king wanted someone to go on a fool's errand he should lay that task to the regular soldiers. The King's Guard was not created to be the servant for the king's every whim. They were the best blademasters in the kingdom and specifically charged with protecting the king and his family. Going out on trips to do special requests for the king and his friends was not part of their calling.

"The king asked me to fetch him something," Jesse continued. "But he wanted you to go up to his chambers."

Wyk sighed. Going up to the king's personal chambers was not something he looked forward to. The king was almost always more offensive there.

Giving Jesse a curt nod he continued up into the heart of palace. He walked past the stunning artwork and tapestries which adorned the hallways. He thought about how the current king had gone out of his way to waste his people's money on irrelevant opulence. The sight of it all sickened him.

He neared the door of the royal chambers and some of the chambermaids talking very excitedly in overly loud whispers passed by him. Their gossip was about the assault on the woman. He couldn't believe the maids were so brazen as to talk about the incident right in front of the king's chamber door.

Wyk entered the chambers. The first section was an ante-room off of the main royal chambers which allowed some privacy for the royal couple and gave more area for guards to be posted there if the need arose.

Wyk knew the guards at the door he just entered were some of the best, but there were only two of them. In the event a large group managed to enter the palace, a larger contingent of guards should be waiting inside this room to protect the royal family.

Wyk passed by the two guards who gave him slight nods of recognition. Jasom Smythe, Captain of the City Guard, was inside with the king and looking none too pleased. He was dressed in his dress uniform, the one reserved for special events or visitations from other dignitaries. He seemed to take no notice of Wyk's entrance but continued talking as if no one had entered.

"...and I personally investigated the area where the crime was committed thoroughly. In the room I discovered her sword and some dirt, but nothing else. No one saw or heard anything."

The King turned slightly to look at Wyk with a look of contempt. Wyk didn't take it personally; he knew the King felt that way about all of his subjects. His weasely face and narrow, dark eyes only heightened his look of his disdain. He was disliked by Wyk and everyone Wyk knew. Yet he was still the king and Wyk would follow his orders to the letter.

Now, as always, the king was adorned with the most costly clothing and jewels Wyk had ever seen. This time his pants, vest and coat were woven with what appeared to be gold thread, giving him the appearance of a god who condescended enough to descend out of the sun itself to be with his subjects. Wyk was sure there had to be some thick, soft cotton undergarments worn below it, but was also sure the suit still had to be extremely uncomfortable to wear.

The shimmering gold thread reflected the sunlight streaming in from the window, left open on purpose no doubt, creating a blindingly golden sunrise within the room. Wyk felt tears well up in his eyes but refused to look away from the king's radiant amber visage as the others in the room had done.

"Wyk, I want you and your men to look into this attack. We can't have friends of the royal family being attacked in the castle as if they were common peasants on the street," the King said darkly.

Wyk frowned. He didn't like where this was going at all. If he accepted the King's pronouncement there would be contentious feelings between the City Guard, who rightly should be investigating the crime, and the King's Guard. He couldn't have that; the Guards worked in close proximity to one another. An issue like this could cause conflict between them, and that could jeopardize the effectiveness of both groups.

He bowed on one knee and said, "With your King's permission, I would humbly suggest that the City Guard continue looking into this. Our commission is for the protection of the king and his royal family and whatever royal…quest the King sees fit to send us on." He even managed to choke out the word *quest* without much of a pause.

Now it was the King's turn to frown, not a pleasant look even for a person whose countenance was already far from fair.

"I believe this crime is intricately woven into the reason for the quest. I will say this one time only-you and your men will look into this crime until you leave for your journey. You have that much time to help the City Guard discover who did this. Are we clear?" The king said, and in a manner so as to let Wyk know he had better understand.

"Yes, your Majesty." Wyk grunted.

With that Wyk turned and tried not to storm out of the chambers. As he passed by Jasom, he was treated to a look nearly as vile as any he had seen the king dole out. He couldn't blame him; he would be upset too if he were in his shoes.

Outside the palace Wyk found Jesse surrounded by four beautiful women who were giggling like young farm maids. He wasn't surprised; Jesse always seemed to be around women during his off hours. He seemed to attract them like flies to honey. Unfortunately, this could also cause some trouble as well.

Nearby he saw a group of six men glaring at Jesse with a mixture of jealousy and anger. A common problem whenever Jesse started to socialize. Wyk would often see trouble of this sort brewing around him, but knew it often would come to nothing as most men would think twice before starting trouble with the King's Guard.

As Wyk approached he realized Jesse had already noticed the men. Most wouldn't catch it in Jesse's outwardly relaxed appearance-his casual stance and frivolity with the girls gave him an unassuming air and seemingly ill-prepared for an attack. But Wyk knew how to read men. Under the façade Jesse was tense, looking much like a lion ready to pounce on prey. He decided to stand back and see what would develop.

The men seemed to gather in among themselves a little bit tighter, talking in whispers so faint Wyk couldn't discern what they were saying. As they started to scatter to go their apparently individual ways, Wyk could tell that the randomness in their movements was actually an orderly and systematic series of paths designed to spread out around Jesse. He tensed, but still kept to his commitment not to interfere.

The group's casual scattering slowly developed into their ploy to surround Jesse. Wyk found himself grudgingly admiring the men for their ability to appear as though they were heading in different directions and keep their true motives hidden. They had received some military training at least. That much he knew.

He also knew Jesse had noticed them as well as he turned his body in such a way as to corral the women into a smaller, tighter group in order to keep them safe. But the placement of his feet, along with his slight pivots hidden in bursts of laughter, showed he was keeping an eye on the men as they approached him.

The six men finally had Jesse surrounded in the classic six-pointed star configuration. They were set up in such a precise manner that there was no opening for Jesse to escape through. They too were trying to look as unassuming as possible as they tried to figure out how to get Jesse away from the women while keeping him from getting away. Not that Jesse would need to escape; Wyk knew he would use their formation against them.

As the men slowly advanced on him, Jesse made an excuse to the women about having to leave for a minute to go to the privy. And he said it loud enough for the men to hear. Saying you were going to the privy was the most unassuming reason one could give for leaving a group.

Wyk watched as Jesse's first few steps were taken quickly. Wyk knew he did this to put distance between him and the women as well as the four men who were behind them and to his side. That meant that only the two men in front of him would need to confront him first.

When Jesse was just a step away, they both turned towards him to attack him simultaneously. But the two men made three mistaken assumptions: they didn't expect Jesse to have noticed what they were doing, they didn't expect him to move as quickly as he did, and they certainly didn't expect him to strike first.

Jesse quickly took a small step sideways so he now had one of the men directly in front of him and the other a little to his right. As the man directly in front of Jesse pulled his arm back to land the first blow, Jesse moved a little farther to his left and under his attacker's arm. As the man's swing went harmlessly over Jesse's head he slammed his elbow into the man's face so hard Wyk heard his jaw break.

The man would have dropped straight to the ground if Jesse hadn't caught him and pushed him in front of the second man who had started to advance on Jesse.

One down. Wyk thought to himself.

The other man who had been in front caught his companion and paused, a look of amazement at what Jesse had done crossed his face. Jesse took the opportunity to step forward and hit that man in the stomach, just below his sternum, punching in and up. This caused him to drop his companion. Meanwhile his breath come out with such an audible *OOMPH* that Wyk was sure people down the street could hear it.

Two down. Wyk thought as a smile started creeping up his face.

The women still hadn't fully registered what was happening, but the other four men had. The two men who had been on either side of Jesse were now just one step away. However, Jesse was facing the man to the right he continued in that direction, slamming the palm of his hand into the man's face, breaking his nose and knocking him unconscious. But before that man could hit the ground Jesse grabbed his arm and, twisting violently, threw that man into the other assailant who was now coming in from behind.

The unconscious man's head smacked into the other man's face with a sickening crack and both men slumped to the ground.

Four down. Wyk's smile had deepened considerably.

The last two men finally got around the women and moved quickly towards Jesse. Jesse repeated what he had done initially; moving forward and to his left so he could attack one of the men and use his body as a shield to keep the other from attacking at the same time. This time however Jesse used a strong side kick into the man's groin to stop him. That man went straight down in front of the other, slowing him down.

Five down. Wyk had to shake his head in amazement at his friend's prowess.

As the last man standing stepped across his friend's prostrate body, Jesse did a roundhouse kick with his left leg. This time the last attacker learned from his friend's mistakes and ducked below it. Unfortunately for him the kick was only the first of a combination Jesse let loose with. Right after his kick Jesse spun with a wicked backhand to the man's head and he collapsed like a sack of potatoes.

Wyk ready to count all six of the men down when he saw that the fourth man, the one who attacked from the side and had his partner thrown on him, had gotten up from under the unconscious body.

His face was a bloody mess, looking worse with the sheer look of contempt he was throwing at Jesse. But before he did anything he suddenly noticed all of his companions lying on the ground unconscious.

He then took one more look at Jesse and decided retreat was the better part of valor and took off running.

The four women finally seemed to realize what had happened. Three of the women had shocked expressions and stood speechless. The fourth woman however eyed Jesse up and down with an admiring look on her face. They all, however, joined in clapping along with some bystanders after the impressive display of the King's Guard in action.

Jesse definitely had a way with women. Also, with fighting; which made Wyk very happy Jesse was on his side.

"Jesse!" Wyk called out, "Come here for a minute."

He knew Jesse wouldn't enjoy having to leave his newfound harem without having spent some "quality" time with each of them. Wyk smiled to himself. Jesse had more virility than any other man he knew. Even more than a lot of men put together. No, Jesse would not be happy at all.

When Jesse came over his first words were, "They attacked first."

Wyk started to chuckle in spite of himself; then quickly forced himself to stop. He couldn't let his men see that he found humor in a situation like that.

"We have work to do," was all he needed to say. Jesse was, above all else, a true Guardsman for the crown. He took great pride in that and it was the only thing which could take him away from the arms of a pretty women. After a brief goodbye to his new friends, and some promises for the next time they met, they headed straight for the scene of the crime.

CHAPTER 7

On their way to where the attack took place, a small room in one of the more ornate towers ironically called the Pious Room, they passed several of the City Guard moving through the hallways. What bothered Wyk the most wasn't the sullen silence of the City Guards as they passed, he expected that. Rather it was how quickly all of them seemed to have found out about the king's pronouncement. It was like women gathering in the marketplace with nothing else to do but gossip.

"This is not the way to run an investigation," Wyk said. "Pitting the King's Guard against the City Guard by having us do their investigative work doesn't help the situation at all."

"I think the king did that on purpose." Jesse said bluntly.

Wyk flashed a quick look over at Jesse. He could tell by his friend's expression he was deadly serious, as well he should be. Mocking the king or insinuating incompetence was not something the King's Guard should be doing lightly; or at all. Wyk wondered if he should say something to him, but thought better of it. Jesse knew how serious his comment was.

They finally reached the Pious Room, a chamber neither of them had visited or heard of before, after ascending many steps along a spiral staircase. At the top of the staircase was a short hallway which led straight to an open door.

They entered the small, empty room apprehensively. There was some dirt on the floor about eight feet in and the wooden bar from the door was inside on the floor close to the dirt. There were a few splatters which looked to have been made by someone throwing mud into the room.

Something Wyk noticed quickly was that near the wooden brace was the metal cross brace which kept the bar secure. The cross brace really served no useful purpose. It didn't strengthen the wooden bar so it really did nothing other than to give whomever was inside a stronger sense of security.

Wyk looked around the room and saw it was not very large, about twenty feet by twenty feet. But somehow the art on the far wall gave it a feeling of being much smaller; perhaps enhanced by the scenes painted on the wall of crowds of people in violent conflict with each other.

There was no other opening, which only added to the claustrophobic sense a person would have. As Wyk looked more closely at the war-like images painted on the wall he got the unnerving feeling that the people were moving.

Wyk blinked a few times to clear his vision and looked again at the brutal images. They were indeed moving; attacking each other in slow motion but with such a brutality and bloodthirsty zeal as to be repulsive.

The scene, painted on the far wall facing the door, seemed to represent the Dragon Wars. However, he wasn't sure how he knew that as there were no dragons depicted anywhere in the scene.

Wyk continued to watch the battle rage. It gave him the unnerving feeling of falling through a hole in the sky while watching the battle taking place on the ground below. He thought he was going to lose his breakfast until he averted his eyes quickly and stared at the ground.

To his surprise he noticed a reddish flickering as if a fire was burning somewhere in the room. He again checked the wall before looking quickly away and saw some of the painted figures carried torches while others were busy igniting whole villages and razing them to the ground.

So, this wall supplies ambient light. That's why it isn't dark in here despite the complete lack of windows. He mused to himself.

But the red flickering he had noticed was faint, and a much stronger golden light, like that of sunlight at dusk, permeated the room. He glanced up again and this time noticed that the blood in the painting was ocher instead of red.

The blood must somehow be providing the rest of the light. There must be some sort of magic in the paint used.

Too late he realized he had stared too long at the painting again. However, even with that knowledge he seemed unable to pull his eyes away from the macabre scene depicted on the wall. Suddenly Wyk remembered he was not alone, a thought which seemed difficult to formulate given the hold the room had on him.

Using strength of will he didn't know he had, he managed to glance over at Jesse and saw him as spellbound by the wall as he had been. The look on Jesse's face however seemed serene, almost beatific. Wyk watched as Jesse's eyes seemed to be following something moving along the wall, traveling from one side to the other.

"Jesse, what do you see?" Wyk asked.

"Horses, many of them, and they are running across the plains with a beautiful golden sunset behind them."

Wyk paused at his friend's statement. The magic must work differently for each person. But why paint a room using magic? And why have everyone see something different?

"You've never been here before, have you?"

The question startled Wyk as much as a glass shattering next to him while he slept would have. He turned and saw that Jasom had followed him in. The Captain stared straight and hard into Wyk's eyes, carefully avoiding letting his eyes wander and subtly letting Wyk know how to avoid getting lost in the painting again.

"No, I haven't. And quite frankly I don't understand the use for this room." Wyk said, returning Jasom's gaze with equal vigor.

"This room is used to question suspects in crimes they are alleged to have perpetrated. The painting can different for each person, although most people see some sort of battle taking place. The movements and colors keep a person's mind so focused they cannot lie. Just look at your friend."

Wyk glanced over at Jesse again and was surprised at his posture, something he failed to notice the first time he looked. He was standing with his shoulders slumped forward and his head hanging loosely to one side. His arms looked as if they were fake, the wooden arms of a puppet hanging loosely by its side until its master took them up by their strings.

Jesse's legs, barely supporting the weight of his body, appeared ready to give way at any moment. Jesse looked to be asleep despite standing up; the only differences being his eyes were still half open. A thin stream of spittle was slowly oozing out of his mouth and on to his tunic.

"Jesse!" Wyk called out loudly.

With a start Jesse turned toward him, eyes quickly opening wide as if he had just been awakened from a deep sleep. Jesse looked at him uncomprehendingly at first, taking a few seconds before he seemed in control of his faculties again.

"We need to leave, now!" Wyk said.

Jesse just nodded his head in agreement.

As they walked out the doors Wyk thought he heard Jasom chuckling to himself.

He knew it, blast him! He knew what would happen when we came into the room.

The thought just made Wyk all the angrier at having been made a fool of. At any rate he knew what he would tell the king and hoped that would be the end of this charade.

Wyk checked around the base of the tower despite the lack of any windows whatsoever. There soil had not been disturbed and there were none of the mud splatters that they had seen in the room. This crime was definitely a mystery; one which he felt could not be solved before he left on the king's errand… except for the guards at the foot of the stairway leading up to the room. The only sign of anything untoward having happened appears to be a vicious attack on a potted plant." Wyk said.

Wyk hated being so crass to the king, even if the king didn't deserve respect. He half expected the guards next to the king to draw their weapons in defense of the king's honor, or at least in defense of the king's station. Surprisingly, or maybe tellingly, they didn't.

The king eyed him suspiciously. It was almost as if he thought Wyk was lying to him or creating some fabrication in order not to have to continue with the investigation.

It's the girl that's lying. Wyk thought to himself.

He turned slightly to focus on her standing to the left of the king. She was breath-takingly beautiful and was eyeing him with large, blue doe-like eyes which seemed to be condemning him for not believing her. Wyk frowned, wondering why this whole charade was still going on.

"I feel that the City Guard is more than capable of solving this mystery and catching the attacker. They have proven themselves in times past and have shown a tremendous ability to both retain the peace and keep crime in check in the city." Wyk said.

The king gave Wyk a belittling look from his raised throne. It gave Wyk the impression the king was looking down at him from a high mountain, keeping him from being next to him both physically and, more importantly, as his peer. Wyk figured all royalty had the hubris to feel superior over their subjects to some degree. It was the main reason Wyk neither liked nor trusted anyone of royal heritage. But this king seemed to view himself as being perfectly flawless, forced to condescend himself to reign over the incompetent people surrounding him.

"Very well," the king finally proclaimed, "if you and your men are incapable of catching even the basest, most corrupt and largely unintelligent denizens of the lowest reaches of the kingdom, then you may as well leave and start on your quest now and be constructive in some aspect of your life."

Wyk just stood there, unsure of how to react or respond. If it had been anyone but the king himself who had said such vile things about him and the King's Guard, he would have drawn his sword and requested a fight for his honor right then and there. This king wasn't just crass, he was malicious and vengeful.

"My guest Sakura has requested to escort you on your quest. She feels uncomfortable and doesn't believe herself to be safe here in the kingdom." The king continued.

Wyk groaned inside. Now he was a baby-sitter for a girl who made up stories just so she could have the attention of the king! Although he was sure the City Guard would take her slight about not feeling safe in the city badly, they must also be relieved at being rid of her. As he looked at the Guards standing next to the king, he could see the pity in their eyes for him having to cart her all over creation.

"As your liege desires." Wyk said, trying not to sound as pompous or patronizing as the king did. But thinking he failed miserably.

Once outside Wyk turned to Jesse to gauge his reaction to what had just transpired. Based on Jesse's dark look he figured Jesse was angry with him. It wouldn't surprise him; after all, even he felt he was out of place with the king. But the Dark Lord take him, the king was out of place first!

After a pause, and Jesse's continued withering look, Wyk had to admit that the king had the right to be rude, but he did not. It was not the King's Guard's place to rule over the king. He mentally kicked himself for allowing the king to get under his skin the way he did. It was immature and unprofessional.

Wyk sighed and glanced up at the sky. To fully prepare for whatever the king wanted them to do would take some time. Maybe even as long as a week or two, depending on where the king was sending them.

If they were crossing other kingdoms then they would need to send out a King's Request for Passage of Foreign Troops through the land. If it was a place unknown to them then there was the necessity of maps or information about those areas.

Wyk sighed again. He would love to get away from here as soon as possible, but it looked like they would be spending more time in the kingdom than he would have liked. Especially with the king on a potential warpath for Wyk's hide for being insolent to him.

A dark mood settled over Wyk. He glanced at Jesse and knew his friend was thinking the same thing he was. The only bright spot in an otherwise dismal future was his friend Jesse. He could always count on him.

CHAPTER 8

Abruptly a shaft of pain struck Kam in his stomach so hard it drove him to his knees. The only comparison he had was of a blade being driven deep into his body and then being violently twisted. The pain was as excruciating as it was debilitating and he doubled over and fell to the ground.

The pain struck again, harder this time, and caused him to writhe in the dirt. While his body was wracked in the throes of agony his mind reached out in the only way it could, to the only being around who could possibly help him.

Red! His mind pleaded. *Red, I need help!*

Just at that moment the realization of what was happening came to Kam in the form of Red's loud retching.

Red, Kam thought, *are you sick?*

Nothing came through their bond except a burning which extended from his gut to his mouth.

Red, what's wrong?

I ate a bad lizaerd. I will need food again shortly.

How often does this happen to dragons?

Not often. Dragons' stomachs are very strong and usually don't spit up food. There was something bad about that lizaerd, something different. It tasted like it had been dead many days even though it was alive. That has never happened to me before you cursed my life with your presence.

Finally, after a few long minutes the pain subsided and Kam was able to get up again. He felt he needed to help; not out of any sense of guilt but simply because he felt one person should help another. He knew Red would probably hesitate to eat another lizaerd from this area so he went back into the house to see if there was any food for the dragon.

As he wandered around inside, he saw a table which had been flipped over but which wasn't lying completely flat. As he bent over, he noticed some cloth protruding from just under the lip of the tabletop. He lifted the table and was rewarded to see a shriveled, bony hand grasping what looked to be a piece of metal fashioned into a makeshift knife.

He let the table fall with a surprisingly loud crash and kept looking. Although he really had no idea what dragons ate besides fresh meat, it would be a simple matter to ask it and see if it found anything palatable. Unfortunately, the building he was in was cleaned out of anything even remotely edible from what Kam could see.

Suddenly he felt Red's consciousness flood into his mind with the force and shock of a freezing cold waterfall. Without thinking he turned towards Red, who had swiveled his long neck to look around and behind the outside of the building Kam was in. In the recesses of Red's mind Kam sensed pensiveness, an anxiety which was unclear and confused. It was almost as if Red was feeling an emotion for a situation described to him but which he had never experienced before. The darkness, which Kam sensed was hoping for a violent confrontation, was also there.

Kam himself began to fret, wondering if the danger was real or just Red being paranoid. He wasn't sure if it was even possible for a dragon to be paranoid. He looked outside but with the exception of some odd plants and flowers which, although extremely beautiful with their bright colors and exotically shaped flowers, he saw nothing.

Let's go. Kam thought anxiously as he ran towards Red's clawed foot and climbed up as quickly as he could. Suddenly he noticed a hesitation in Red's mind, a questioning of what was bothering him. Red himself couldn't place his concern and he was curious as to what was making him feel so apprehensive. The dragon turned around and started to walk down the road, swinging his head this way and that looking for possible causes for the disquiet he felt.

Red walked quickly down the road which led from house-like structures to the larger, broken buildings. The road had a hard, lightly colored surface which was unnaturally free of dirt and overgrowth. However, there were large deposits of earth along each side of the road with weeds and flowers growing along the mounds, framing the road with color. The mounds also made Kam think of how easy it would be for archers to hide and shower them with arrows.

Even before they reached the first of the large buildings, massive chunks of stone appeared on the road like so many wildflowers in a grassy field. Although the road was wide, with the structures set back from it a short distance, Kam guessed it was still not wide enough for Red to open his wings fully to allow for him to become airborne.

The ground feels funny. Red thought. *It tingles the bottom of my feet like I'm walking on small, sharp rocks.*

Kam noticed his own feet were tingling too. He knew he was feeling what Red felt through the bond and he had to admit it was an odd sensation. It made him think of the times when he had kneeled too long and felt what seemed like the jabs of many tiny needles against the soles of his feet. He didn't remember noticing it the previous day, but when Red grounded, they were already exhausted and had fallen asleep quickly.

Why is he wandering around the ruins? Kam thought to himself. *I can sense his hunger; he should be looking for food, but he's not. All I can sense is his apprehension.*

As Red roamed around the ruins trying to understand his own uneasiness, Kam sensed a feral quality to this broken city. Patches of wild plants and twisted trees sprouted up between slabs of pale rock with chunks of debris thrown about here and there forcing Red to maneuver uncomfortably as he walked around them. Piles of small bones littered the street with sections of the road showing the blackened scars of past fires. A few pieces of road were torn out like a giant dog had dug holes to bury their bones.

The valleys created by the hilly uprisings of the once proud structures in this former Mecca of humanity kept them out of the direct light of the morning sun as a chill breeze blew across them. Red continued to weave his way through the roads innately, following something which only he seemed able to sense. Kam couldn't sense what Red was conscious of even through the bond.

As they went along, intermittent noises started to come at them from every direction. There were soft, insect-like clicking from the brush, loud airborne shrieks, and heavy grunts which emanated from the shattered remains of the tall metal and stone buildings. Kam started to wonder what was causing the noises but soon stifled his imagination as the creatures his mind conjured up grew more hideous with each passing moment.

He caught a quick glimpse of what appeared to be a large lizard, about the size of a house cat, like the ones he had seen a few people own as pets. But as it took to the air in startled flight he gasped in surprise. It was a small dragon! It screeched menacingly at them as it flew through a broken window into a building and out of sight.

What was that? Kam asked Red. *It looked like a baby dragon.*

A feeling of resentment came through the bond strongly, surprising Kam with its intensity. *I felt no connection to that creature.* Red snorted. *It wasn't a dragon; it's something else.*

More thoughts, quick and fleeting, came through to Kam. He couldn't pick up on them but did sense that Red knew more about the dragon-like creature than he was letting on.

As they passed one especially unique-looking building, which surprisingly seemed unaffected by the chaotic devastation which had occurred all around it, Kam sensed an ancient spirituality. There were many small spires along the top of the main structure giving it a slightly foreboding look. But the most prominent aspect was two immense towers at opposite ends of the building, each topped with long, spear-like spikes reaching skyward. They were at least double the height of the main building and higher than many of the broken structures in the city.

Yet the building, which must have been dwarfed by the other structures which now lay shattered at its feet, must have seemed insignificant at the time and Kam briefly wondered what it must have been used for.

Maybe it was a place to torture Dragons. Red muttered mentally while still keeping his mind focused on his ethereal feeling of apprehension. The darkness in the dragon roiled at this feeling, deeming it a matter of personal safety and seeking to extinguish whatever was causing it. Red's anxiety caused the darkness to send out daggers of searing heat and tendrils of freezing cold into Kam's mind.

Kam thought about all he had learned about dragons and what he had gained from being with Red. He had heard nothing about the raging darkness which seemed to exist within it like a feral animal. As the darkness thrived on Red's intense emotions, Kam noticed his own agitation grow as well. It was becoming more and more difficult to keep his own emotions in check and he was afraid his own feelings might be giving power to the boiling, roiling hatred within the dragon.

This place reeks of man. Man long dead, as all man should be. Red thought, interrupting Kam's own thinking.

Kam gave a mental shudder, though in response to Red's feelings towards humanity or the general unease Red was still feeling he wasn't sure. He began to wonder if dragons could lose their minds the way some people did. If Red was losing his mind, would it affect his own as well? He had too many unanswered and unanswerable questions.

He must feel small and insignificant here among these false mountains. Red mused. He wondered why man would build such ugly facades of nature when there was so much natural beauty in the world. And the stench! The stink of man was everywhere despite there not having been anyone around here in, well, a very long time.

Red sighed. He would rather have been flying over this city of broken stones. However, he would have lost the…scent was the only word which seemed close to what he was feeling. Only it wasn't a smell exactly; it was more like a sensation in his mind.

Red couldn't understand why he felt uneasy here. Well, beside the fact it was the home of many of Kam's kind at one time. He was sensing something else, some magic, and a lot of it. A dark, evil magic which sent chills of joy radiating through his darkly angry friend who resided within him.

Why do you like dark magic? Red asked his long-time companion.

The darkness within him remained silent, but Red could feel its joy in the discovery of the magic which resided here. Red had never before contemplated the differences between good and evil magic. To him there was just one magic, the first magic-Dragonmagic, which was always good. Any other magic which existed was a corrupted version of Dragonmagic. At least that's what he had always thought. For the first time in his life, he wondered if that were true.

Maybe we can join with this power. Red's bitter confidant said gleefully to him. *Maybe there is enough power here to destroy this man and the staff he wields against us.*

Red grew increasingly troubled at the path the conversation was taking. His anger, his very hatred of life, he considered his one great inspiration. It's what motivated him and helped him survive. He accepted this. But he was not wormcrazy; at least not to the point where he couldn't differentiate between his innermost feelings and another entity talking with him.

Who are you? He thought to himself.

You know the answer to that, old friend. Came the reply.

Red paused. He wasn't sure what to do. He reached out with his mind to that of his flesh and blood captor, trying to touch his mind as before. He could, but the connection was weak. And while under any other circumstance Red would be ecstatic about *that* happening, there was definitely something unnatural about what was going on. Red walked through the streets, searching for a hint as to what was happening to him. His only clue was the clear, strong sense of magic that existed here. What he couldn't understand was why he didn't notice it the night before.

Red came to another intersection of four paths. There seemed to be many intersections of paths in this man-created forest of stone. He tried to focus on the direction he sensed the magic, but it was difficult. It was almost as if the city was reeking of magic the same way the stink of man permeated everything in this place.

Suddenly Kam's thoughts came shooting through the connection. They were surprisingly clear since his…since his feelings acquired a life of their own.

Why are we stopping? What are you sensing?

Before Red could answer, his newly sentient anger said *Turn heartside and head straight down the road.*

Red turned left and slowly made his way between the large chunks of debris. Kam's questions again started coming through but he ignored them. As they passed an exceptionally rocky area pockmarked with huge craters in the road and extremely large chunks of rubble Red caught Kam's thought *I wonder if all this damage was caused by dragons during the Dragon Wars?*

Red snorted. *It figures you blame others for everything bad that happens. It's obvious this city of man was destroyed by some dark magic your kind created.*

Kam was curiously quiet after Red's retort and they continued on in relative silence. Even the darkness within Red remained strangely silent. However, as Red moved closer to where he felt the essence of the magic, he got the unnerving impression the darkness within him was chortling gleefully.

Red moved beyond the section of road which had been disastrously torn up and onto smoother ground. They were still in the City of Stone, but this area looked as if it had sustained much less damage. There were faded yet colorful mini-structures along this path, large enough to hold a few people. Red guessed them to be small, separate living areas for people, but Kam's thoughts broke through to disagree.

I believe they are wagons. He thought. *You would hitch up a horse and it would pull it.*

Red snorted. *Here was another reason that shows how Dragons are better than man; man doesn't have wings!*

The ground became smoother still with much less debris on it. There seemed to have been no buildings built on the area they were approaching. It had a natural, if wild, beauty in the growth of trees and plants; nothing twisted or distorted. Red heaved a sigh of relief with the impression they were at the outskirts of this massive man-made alter to their ability to stack stones on one another.

Suddenly out of nowhere a group of bizarre creatures surrounded them. They appeared to be part man and part other creatures. Red had never seen anything like them before. Suddenly Kam's worried thoughts burst into his head, overwhelming his own.

Those are Halfers!

Quickly the idea of creatures which are half-man and half-animal entered Red's mind; twisted creatures which Kam considered to be servants of the Dark Lord. Within seconds Red and Kam were completely surrounded by the strange creatures. Their animal-like features of tusks and fangs and snouts all seemed to be oozing with saliva as if they were about to feast. As Red prepared to let loose a ball of fire at a group of three of them standing close together, he suddenly realized Kam had slid down his leg and drawn his sword to fight.

The man thinks he needs to protect me! What arrogance!

For a moment Red considered allowing Kam to fight all of them himself, knowing he would fail. But the writhing darkness inside wanted this confrontation. It was a chance to kill, no slaughter, these creatures and allow Red the opportunity to take out his rage at being impotently enslaved because of some man-made dark magic. It wanted Red to let loose with everything he had and destroy these creatures; no, to completely erase them form the face of the earth.

The desire of the darkness became Red's own. The urge to fight, to destroy, became his reality as bursts of liquid energy pulsed through Red's whole body. He felt a tingling all the way down to the tip of his tail and he prepared to decimate these insignificant man-like darklings.

CHAPTER 9

Kam knew Halfers ate those they killed, and any fight with a Halfer was a fight to the death. As he turned to face them and keep the dragon's hindquarters behind him and protected, he got his first good look at them. They looked to have been designed by a child playing with potato men and a cornucopia of wooden toy animal parts.

Some had the long, muscular limbs of a cat while others had the strong, coltish looks of a horse while still others had the thick, brutish look of what appeared to be the limbs and body of a bull. Their heads were uniformly twisted and deformed, half animal and half human. However, all of their features displayed a definite feral quality.

One of them seemed to come out of nowhere and attack. Kam was so taken aback by its appearance and speed that it nearly took the sword out of his hand. The lower half of the creature was so twisted and entwined within itself that it appeared to be a blur. Yet somehow it was able to move with amazing speed. Its arms, if that's what they could be called, were bizarrely deformed serpents with hissing, snapping heads in lieu of hands. Its head was also reptilian, although also so twisted and deformed as to be barely recognizable as such.

One of its arms/snakes shot out towards him, aiming for what he thought was his throat. He quickly parried it and cut off its head. The creature roared in anger and pain while blood spurted out leaving Kam drenched in red.

As Kam advanced on it, he watched the other arm/snake of the creature warily. Too late he realized he made a grave error in thinking the headless limb was now useless. The creature feinted with its good "hand" while it whipped the headless stump around one of Kam's legs. As the Halfer pulled its limb violently Kam fell hard to the ground, his sword knocked out of his hand.

The other limb with the serpent head still attached shot out, trying to bite Kam in the throat. He barely managed to catch the snake limb just below its head and hold on to it. It squirmed violently in his grasp, threatening to break free at any moment.

As Kam wrestled with the good limb, trying to keep it from biting him, the Halfer now used its headless limb to beat Kam whip-like across his body. Kam lay gasping as the beating knocked the wind out of him. Thinking frantically, he let go of the serpent's head with one hand and grabbed the whip-like tendril. Using the creature as leverage he was able to pull himself up to a kneeling position.

The creature appeared stunned for a second by Kam's ability to get back up, if even only to a kneeling position, and Kam used that moment to grab his sword. He swung and cut the still snapping serpent arm off close to the shoulder.

While the Halfer screamed in rage, he slashed across the creature's chest, cutting through skin, bone and organs. The Halfer stood there for a moment looking stunned; then with its chest bursting open and its organs spilling out onto the ground it fell over, dead.

Kam got up and quickly scanned the area. He noticed several of the creatures up against one of the buildings in various forms of being crushed. Some had bones protruding out of their chests, others had their arms and legs, or at least what would pass for those limbs, completely flattened like a picture in a book and still others had their heads crushed in.

Red must have used his tail. Kam thought.

He also realized the connection appeared to have weakened, or at least become less discernable, during his fight. Abruptly a feeling flooded through his mind that Red was in trouble. As he turned to see what was going on, he saw the creatures had used ropes to pull Red's tail and head down to the ground as well as having pulled two of his legs out from under him so he was lying on his belly. There was even one looped around his snout preventing the dragon from opening his mouth. But these weren't regular ropes; they looked as if they were made of metal! Many more creatures had appeared as if out of thin air to grab onto the ropes so that Red was unable to move.

Kam had an idea which seemed to come into his mind as if from Red but the sensation was different. There was none of the usual tangible, caliginous anger which seemed to permeate Red's thoughts. Instead, this was more like pure evil, almost as if it was from someone or something which was separate and distinct from Red yet emanating from the dragon nonetheless.

It caught him by surprise but hit so strongly that without thinking otherwise, he ran forward and swung his sword at the metal ropes. The sword cut through the metal as if it were just old twine, releasing Red's head that quickly.

In that instant Red flashed out with fire, burning many the creatures and sending an oily-looking thick smoke and acrid smell into the air just behind the screams of pain. Most of their attackers were able to quickly retreat for the moment, their initial advantage eliminated. Kam nearly threw up again as the scene now surrounding them included some of the still living Halfers having the metal rope melted across their bodies.

At nearly the same time Kam felt a burning himself in his left leg and he collapsed to the ground in agony. He looked down to see an arrow had entered in from the back of his thigh and was protruding a full third out of the front. Kam had been shot with arrows before but this one seemed to have hit every conceivable nerve in his body, causing the pain to radiate outward to his foot and up into his chest.

Through the haze of pain, he remembered hearing Red roar in agony as well at the same time he was hit by the arrow. Kam looked behind him and saw Red favoring one of his hind legs. He felt Red's pain in his leg as if he too had been shot. He didn't know if what he felt from Red was the dragon's feeling of pain caused by Kam's getting shot, forming a vicious circle of shared pain empathy, or some kind of mental echo reverberating between himself and Red. There was of course the possibility that Red had been injured in the same place at the same time but that seemed unlikely.

Kam scoured the scene behind where he was standing. He was rewarded with seeing the top of a bow protruding up over a large boulder from which he assumed was the Halfer who shot him. This time the Halfer stuck its head over the top of the rock and lifted his bow to aim for a shot at Red. Kam recognized the bow as a Halfers' broadbow, a large wooden bow which was rumored to be able to shoot up to five stretches. However, at the range from which he was shot, the arrow should have gone right through his leg and through whoever was standing behind him as well.

Unless... He thought for a moment. *Unless the archer wasn't an archer at all.* What if this creature had found the bow, or killed its owner. He, she, *it* may not know how to use a bow. As he watched the creature let loose another arrow, this one at Red. The arrow clearly did not have the full string of the bow behind it and it was handled awkwardly, missing Red by a good two feet. Kam had to wonder how he was lucky enough to have had an arrow strike his leg at all.

He looked back at the protruding arrow. He knew enough not to try to take the arrow out; if he did, he could lose too much blood and black out or even die. But the pain! Instead, he focused on finding a way out of the Halfer infested area.

Abruptly Kam sensed something; two things actually. The first was a sense of movement coming towards him very quickly. The second was a voice in his head saying, *Get up you clumsy lizaerd. If these creatures don't kill you, I'll step on you myself! I'm not here to protect you!*

Kam rose wobbly to his feet. He scanned the direction from which he sensed the movement. The distorted figure of a man was coming at him very fast. Kam dove and rolled clumsily to his right, swinging his injured leg up and over his body carefully so as not to jar the arrow. In the same movement he held up his sword to block the downward swing the approaching figure was using to try and finish him off.

Just in time he caught the creature's blow and blocked it, leaving an odd, dull thumping sound against his sword. He frowned in surprise as he focused on the creature's weapon. It was a sword made of what appeared to be bone. As his eyes wandered up the form of the figure he gasped. He was now fighting a Darkblood. What was a Darkblood doing here with these creatures?

As Kam studied the Darkblood more intently he saw it had a sword-like extension made of what had to be extremely hard bone growing right from its arm midway between its elbow and wrist. The blade was its widest where the creature's hand would have been and extended out about three feet from that point. Extending behind the elbow was another, smaller blade about a foot long. That blade was narrower and looked more like a long dagger.

The bone was yellowed and chipped from many fights, but obviously very hard. And it had the same bony growth covering its head similar to a helmet and practically no hair. There were also bony plate growths on its back and chest, providing protection in much the same way as armor.

Its other arm, instead of being another sword or a shield, was a long neck and head similar to Red's, covered in dirty, brownish scales. Unlike the first creature Kam fought, the head on the end of the arm/neck looked fully developed and even able to think on its own. It would growl and snap at Kam one second then pivot around to look behind the creature as if expecting others to come to its aid.

Kam struggled to regain his footing, but was unable to. He had to continue to block the creature's powerful blows raining down on him while on his knees. The dark, boney extension seemed well able to take any punishment his sword could give, with only minor chips and scratches marring its already resolutely gritty finish.

When the dragon headed arm finally seemed to understand there was no one else coming, it turned and slowly advanced at Kam. The head of the arm wove its way carefully below the dancing blades, seeming to take pleasure in knowing Kam had to keep both hands on his sword hilt to match the Darkblood's strength and to keep from getting skewered.

Suddenly out of the bottom of Kam's sword hilt a blade extended itself, shooting out directly into the head of the creature. It screamed in pain once and then dropped to the ground as the blade retracted on its own back into the hilt where it came from.

The Darkblood turned and with its own cry of fevered hysteria fled from Kam, the dragon-headed appendage with its long, forked tongue dragging lifelessly along behind it. Then before Kam even has a chance to try to understand what had just happened Red's thoughts again entered his mind.

They have me tied down with metal ropes again! I need your help!

Kam saw that Red was again incapacitated with the strong metal ropes. Many of the bindings were looped around large pieces of rubble. So fixated were the creatures on Red that no one paid any attention to him.

They thought dragon-hand would have finished me off. Kam surmised. *Now it's my chance to help.*

He struggled to his feet, arrow still protruding from his leg, and hobbled over to Red. Bracing himself for what he knew would be excruciating agony, he half-ran, half-limped alongside the dragon, slicing the metal ropes all the way down the length of his body. None of the creatures seemed to focus on him until he was nearly done, and by then it was too late.

Red broke free from the few metal ropes still holding him down and let loose a volley of fire which Kam noticed had a decidedly green hue to it. Most of the creatures were instantly incinerated, as was any vegetation in the area. Even many of the large pieces of broken rock seemed to shrivel up like a raisin. The remaining creatures ran, galloped, and slithered away quickly, disappearing into the very ground around them.

Are there any others left? Kam felt the question in his head rather than heard it.

I don't see any. That time your fire looked green. Why was it green?

I used my Dragonmagic, came Red's reply. *And I still feel drawn someplace down this path.*

Kam still sensed the molten rage of darkness in Red's soul; but also something else, something new. It was almost as if Red had another dragon living in his head. Red existed with his seemingly endless hatred, but also another raging element coexisted within him. Perhaps the other something even fed off of Red's own anger. It was disconcerting, especially since he still hadn't gotten completely used to having Red's own emotions inside of his head.

Kam clambered onto the back of Red, asking if they shouldn't turn around. But Red ignored him and they continued on down the path. Kam broke the arrow at both ends but left the shaft in his leg. The pain seemed to have numbed a bit around the area where the arrow penetrated, but the rest of his body throbbed with every heartbeat. He wondered if the arrow had been poisoned. He looked carefully at the arrowhead but saw only his blood dripping from it.

Not far from their recent battle Kam noticed a structure about half a mile up on the right which sent shivers down his spine. It was approximately five stories high and didn't seem to have been damaged as the other structures had. It had layered sections of the smooth, light-colored rock most of the structures had at approximately ten foot intervals. Between those layers there appeared to have been open sections which had been filled in with layers of jagged, loose rock to cover the gaps. Even from this distance Kam could see were many narrow openings through which arrows could be loosed at unwanted visitors. Kam sensed that was Red's destination.

As they approached the unusual building Red slowed down. Kam realized there were no structures of any sort in the immediate vicinity of this building. He wasn't sure if whoever was currently inside had done this so as to keep any approaching enemies in the open or if it had originally been built like this, having an open area around it for a purpose long since forgotten.

As Kam looked along the top of the building, he could see many guards peering down at them. Surprisingly the guards didn't seem to have their bows notched yet. Near the base of it were two large doors which, if opened, would have easily allowed Red to enter. At this point one of the doors was partially open and there was a large group of men in armor with weapons drawn standing and waiting.

Red approached them warily and stopped just short of being able to stretch out his neck and snap at them with his jaws. Kam could see them much more clearly now, and this new view only increased his nervousness. A few of the men he had seen standing there were in fact Darkbloods, weapons and armor of bone growing from their bodies.

Some of the others were Halfers with snouts and jaws and tusks and fangs. Some of them had skin bristling with hair while others had hides looking every bit as tough as any leather he had ever seen. These Halfers had various features derived from animals, but all had the same ferocious look in their eyes.

The rest of them were creatures of the type he had seen before, the ones with snakes for limbs or heads at the end of arms or some other hideous mixture. Some even had multiple arms with tentacled protrusions in their palms and heads growing out of their stomachs. But the one person who drew his attention the most was a single individual; ironically the one most like an ordinary man. His only oddity was his shiny, black, obsidian-like skin with hair and eyes to match.

Kam shuddered; this man looked like rock, and it was obvious he was the one to be feared over all the others. It was also apparent by the way the others looked at him that he was the one in charge. What Kam couldn't understand was how these groups could be together. Everyone knew Darkbloods, and their distant cousins, Halfers, were sworn enemies. It was even heard that Darkbloods ate not only any creatures they caught and killed, but even their own kind; something Halfers never did.

The obsidian man raised a staff which unnervingly appeared to be of the same material as his body with a black diamond-like jewel on top. Kam squinted at it. It seemed to have a dragon carved on it as well, similar to the Dragonstaff he possessed.

He noticed three distinct differences however. It was about three times the length on Kam's staff and the dragon wrapped around the top of the staff seemed to be bowing its head before the black jewel. The other difference was that this staff had other animals and creatures carved on it as well. All seemed to have bowed heads or were looking down away from the jewel.

Red shuddered and Kam sensed a desire in him to leave, but felt Red was powerless to do so. Kam could sense that the darkness in Red's head, the one which now seemed to have a mind of its own, was keeping him here. The evil which was in him was replacing Red's own will.

Whoever or whatever else was in his head had control of Red's body. Kam stiffened as he realized the implications of what he was thinking. This man had a staff which could control Red, and perhaps other dragons, and could have them attack whomever and wherever he wanted. With a start Kam realized he had done precisely the same thing.

But my reasoning was to help humanity, not hurt others. He said to himself. *My cause justifies my actions.*

Does it? Red's faint retort sent chills through Kam's whole body.

That talk can wait, Kam thought to Red, gratefully hoping to put off having to judge his own actions for a time. The obsidian man smiled; a cold, emotionless act which showed perfectly set teeth as smooth and sparkling as polished gems. Yet instead of being the pure black Kam was expecting they were a deep crimson color, as if the man had just feasted on bloody meat.

Red, we need to leave! Kam was shouting in his head, but he sensed his thoughts were getting swallowed up inside a starless, moonless midnight sky. It was like his feelings were getting blocked by something large and evil. He focused on the Dragonstaff, willing it to overcome whatever vileness was in Red's head.

Red, we need to leave. We need to leave now! He repeated, using such force he was rewarded with a mental jerk within Red's head.

Red seemed to shake himself all over, reminding Kam of the dragon's morning ritual for getting up. Kam was rewarded with more clarity of thought from Red, and as Red ran the few feet he needed before lifting off the ground caught the look of surprise on the obsidian man's face.

As they left the broken city behind, Kam sensed something, like an egg being laid gently in a nest, deposited in Red's mind. He wasn't sure what it was, but knew he would have to ask Red about it later.

CHAPTER 10

They had been flying for some time, although Kam didn't know exactly how long. His mind continually wandered, briefly touching on all of the things he had seen thus far since his time with the dragon. It was almost as if the dragon was like a magnet, pulling in trouble like metal shavings.

What if it isn't the dragon causing this? Kam wondered. *What if it's me?*

What if I'm the cause of all this evil following us around? What if I'm the cause of the darkness festering inside of him?

Kam sighed and looked ahead at the dragon's head, bobbing slightly in time with his great wings beating the air. Just then he noticed the dragon seemed to take in an extra-large breath of air before releasing it loudly.

Did Red just sigh too? Was it possible for him to feel the same sense of futility and weariness a person can?

Of course we sigh. When the Great Dragon created Dragons, He also created people and everything else which is alive. He did it so we could see how much greater we are than His other creations so we know what to be thankful for.

Kam was dumbfounded. So much so he didn't notice he had referred to Red as a *him* instead of an *it*. And the connection which had been losing its strength in the City of Stone was back to where it was before. He could even sense the arrogance of Red again.

Why would you consider yourselves better than all other creatures? Kam asked. *And why do you believe you were created?*

Only a wondrous being like the Great Dragon could conceive of creatures so glorious as dragons. Can man fly? Can man heal others with his mouth? Does man have the ability to communicate without sound, unless he uses dark magic to capture a dragon as you did?

Kam thought about all Red said for a moment. It was true that, after initially leaving the city and flying for a brief time, Red set down and touched Kam's injured leg with the tip of his tongue. He allowed some of his saliva to ooze around the arrow and hole. It not only caused it to go numb and but also allowed Kam to pull the rest of the arrow out relatively pain free.

Red then had his tongue tip, one of them anyway, briefly flicker into the open wound. By doing that he had been able to inform Kam that there had indeed been poison on the arrowhead. Red then let Kam know his saliva could nullify the poison and help heal the wound.

It seems your Great Dragon gave you at least one gift for the benefit of people. Doesn't that make man the higher creation? If man was below dragons as you say, why did he provide you with the means to help them?

Insolent man! Don't you think we help ourselves the same way we can help you? All this proves is that everything was created by that same Great Dragon and that everything, even people, has some of the Great Dragon's power in them.

Kam didn't agree with that, but he didn't want to make the dragon angry by disagreeing. There was a certain twisted logic to it, albeit with much moralistic relativity, something he would expect from a politician. He did find it interesting that dragons believed in a Great Dragon. Although he wasn't sure what he believed, he knew there were some people who believed in a higher being of some sort.

But how, he wondered, *could anyone believe in a great and loving being when there was so much darkness in the world, and with the Dark Lord himself seemingly ready to wipe out all of humanity at any moment?*

Maybe the Dark Lord will rid the world of the pestilence that is humanity, and allow dragons and other creatures to live in peace.

Kam snapped out of his reverie with a jolt. He kept forgetting how clear and lucid the thoughts between him and the dragon were at times.

If he wipes out people, don't you think he will also go after dragons? Kam asked. *Dragons are too intelligent and powerful to leave behind untouched.*

This time it was Red's turn to be startled. *You believe dragons to be intelligent and powerful?* He asked Kam.

I do.

Red realized he may have been too harsh to Kam. If a man can call a dragon intelligent and powerful, maybe there's hope for him yet.

Kam pondered much of what had gone in the past day of being with Red. He opened up his mind to allow his thoughts to flow freely, even though he knew his thoughts would get through anyway.

As he remembered what had gone on, Red remained strangely quiet. There were no criticisms of him or of people in general. There was no burst of angry outrage, just the darkness which Kam always sensed; sitting, waiting, like a vulture on a tree branch by an animal it was waiting for to die. Watching and waiting.

Yet being in Red's mind was almost as if he was in a cave with two animals; he could sense they were there in the darkness but couldn't tell one from the other. They had different smells and made different noises, but he knew there were two of them.

He knew one represented Red's hatred at being held by the Dragonstaff and, to a greater degree, Red's loathing of life. Kam could tell something had happened to the dragon which had pushed him over the edge emotionally. However, Kam had no clue as to what that was. That was the one thing, the only thing, which the dragon was able to keep from him.

The other was a more sinister presence which hadn't been there before their arrival at the city. Someone or something had gotten into Red's mind and had now made a home there. Kam figured it was the obsidian man with the staff of animals. That man, that...*thing*, had reeked of evil and somehow had gotten into the mind of his dragon...

YOUR Dragon? Red snorted, a sound which Kam was beginning to understand dragons made frequently to represent a variety of emotions. *How am I your Dragon?*

Kam paused, not sure what to say but knowing he didn't want to upset Red anymore.

You have... Kam paused, unsure of what to say or even how to express it. *Something inside you, using you, filling you with hatred.*

Red snorted again. *The only thing inside of my head filling me with hatred is you!*

But Red knew the man was right. His emotions had come alive; they now had a mind of their own and were communicating with Red as one dragon to another. He wasn't sure how that was happening, but he knew he didn't like it.

After flying for a few more hours Kam noticed that the tree coverage had gotten noticeably thicker. He looked in both directions but only saw more forest as far as he could see in either direction. He also saw a type of tree he had never seen before-tall and broad, these trees looked to be a cross between always greens and great woods. Abruptly Red landed at the edge of the forest at the last open area before the canopy removed any sign of the ground.

Are you tired? Kam asked.

That is not why I'm stopping. Red responded. *From here I have to walk, I can't fly.*

Kam sensed there's more to it than that, but he couldn't figure out what it was.

Dragons have an old agreement, since the Dragonwars, not to fly over this area unless they are carrying food. Red continued, as if reading Kam's thoughts, which he was. *This is the quickest way across for long flights in either direction.*

Kam, still on Red's back, waited for him to continue but Red didn't seem to feel the need for any more information to be dispensed. Finally, Kam, irritation clearly in his thoughts, asked, *an agreement with whom?*

Red's long neck swiveled around so his luminescent eyes were turned on Kam, giving Kam the unnerving feeling of how a bug might be looked at by a boy who was about to squash it.

I don't know what you call them, but Dragons don't get along with them.

As Red thought this, an impression came to his mind of a giant bird-like creature with the body of a big cat but with great wings and a beaked head.

A gryffyn. The creature you are talking about is a gryffyn. But no one has seen one for hundreds of years; there aren't any more.

You are wrong. Red replied. *They live in this forest.*

As Red wandered through the woods, Kam noticed there were areas of large spaces between tree trunks; large enough for Red to go through without too many problems. He looked up and saw the canopy reaching high and stretching hundreds of feet across for each tree. Even so Kam felt an oppressive weight pressing down on him, as if the trees were closing in around him. He half expected the huge branches to reach down and snatch him right up off the ground.

Kam also felt the heavy presence of Red's darkness settling on his consciousness like a heavy blanket. It was very unsettling and seemed to have a physical weight, causing his head to bow and his shoulders slump. He knew that at this moment the presence he felt within Red was also bothered by their traveling through this forest. That somehow it too was unsettled and sensed this was a dangerous place.

He didn't know exactly what was causing the emotional burden on Red, but he could feel that he was part of it. However, he could now also somehow understand it existed before they ever met; although being held captive by somebody would invariably cause anger in anyone. But this was something much more profound. It was the one area of Red's mind Kam couldn't get to or understand.

Red didn't seem to notice, but continued walking through the woods as though he had no problems. Or maybe it was just that Kam didn't know how to read a dragon like he did a person.

How do you feel right now Red? Kam asked.

Red seemed either not to notice the question or else was simply ignoring him. Kam sighed. Trying to talk with a dragon was about as hard as… as talking to a girl. You never knew what they were thinking, you never knew what they were feeling, you never knew what…

You are comparing me to a human female? Red's question cut through Kam's reverie like a hot knife through tallow.

*I…well I… I was just, uh, trying to understand…no, I was just noticing how it's difficult to understand you and how it's difficult to understand girls…*Kam's thoughts trailed off at the end, his train of thought lost, afraid he had hurt the feelings of his traveling companion.

Red swung his long neck around so he could see eye to eye with the vermin on his back and snorted.

Saying I am one of your women is like saying a dragon is a lizaerd. They are different.

No! Kam's thoughts struggled to come through and be understood. *Not that you are a woman but that you are like a woman…*

What are you trying to say? I am not a woman but I am like a woman, which then makes me a woman. So, you are saying I am a woman. Red responded.

Kam's thoughts seemed to become even more jumbled, causing Red to sigh. Apparently, humans can say something is like something, but not something even though they just said it was something. He wished this man could control his thoughts and not let them escape his head, even if they were connected by the Dark Lord's own magic to torture dragons.

The Dark Lord is a wise one. Red heard the thought clearly. *He created a means to keep the dragons at bay by allowing man to torment them.*

Red blinked in surprise. The thought seemed to come at him from the man, yet not. And the words didn't seem the type of words a person, or at least this man, would say.

They walked on with relatively little going on in their heads, until the darkness in Red's head spoke up. *Just leave the man in the woods. There are many hungry animals which can do the job you can't. Let them eliminate him, after which you can dispose of that stick of his.*

Red wondered whether Kam could hear his other companion talking as well. He never said anything about it and he seemed to have a gift for talking incessantly about nothing, or at least about nothing that concerned them. Red shook his head to try and clear his thoughts, causing his whole body to shake at the motion.

What's going on? Kam's question came quickly, anxiously. *What's happening? Are you okay?*

Red just sighed. He must be going crazy. Unless…*Wait!* Thought Red with venom. *What if it was the man's magic causing him to go out of his mind? Only powerful magic, evil magic, would allow a man the ability to control a dragon in the first place.*

Again, Red's thoughts turned towards how to stop this man from controlling him. *Maybe if we got the man to eat something poisonous, we could be rid of him.*

Again, Red was startled by the other voice inside his head. All he knew for sure was it wasn't the man's thoughts. The voice was… different. It also wasn't the thoughts of another Dragon as he discerned other Dragon's thoughts differently than this one. He didn't understand what was going on but knew he had to try to focus, if only to find a way to get this bloodtick of a man out of his mind and out of his life permanently.

The next few days went by painfully slow. Kam sensed Red's desire not to communicate and let it go at that. They traveled in silence, eating and drinking whatever they could find in the woods. Kam was amazed how Red could go for long periods without needing water. But when they did find water, as they did their third day in when they came across a large, shallow watering hole, Red drank for a full two minutes.

I wonder if he can smell where water is. Kam pondered. *How else would he know where it is?*

On the fifth day since entering the woods they finally left the trees behind. Kam sensed Red was happy to leave it behind, and not just because he could now fly again. Red had kept his thoughts down to a minimum, but Kam still felt as though there was something about the woods which bothered his large companion. Something else made him uncomfortable. But for all of his searching Kam didn't see anything looking even remotely like a gryffyn.

Just past where the trees stopped a large field started which went on as far as Kam could see. It looked to be farmland; half seemed to be in fallow and the other half produced tall stalks of something which looked vaguely familiar. However, Kam also noticed many trees separating large sections of the field which appeared to bear fruit. He squinted at some.

Those are starfruit trees! He thought excitedly. *I haven't had starfruit in a long time.*

There was no response from Red and, as Kam had felt for the past few days, all of his thoughts seemed to be muted. It was as if someone inside his head had built a stone wall between them that only allowed the more focused thoughts to come through.

Let's go over to those trees, Kam said excitedly. *I'll get you some starfruit as well. They always bear so much fruit that even you should be able to get a couple of mouthfuls from one tree.*

As they approached one of the starfruit trees Kam's eyes widened; the tree seemed as though it should be bowed over from the weight of the fruit it was bearing. And the starfruit! They were larger and plumper than any he had ever seen. Some of the fruit was so large that it lost its eponymous appearance, looking more cylindrical than star shaped.

Kam quickly ran over and plucked one. As he bit into it juice came streaming out of his mouth leaving a sweet, succulent trail of sticky moisture down his chin.

As he chewed, he glanced over at Red who now had a long strand of saliva streaming down out of his mouth, his jaws performing a faint chewing motion despite having nothing in his mouth. Kam looked away sheepishly for a moment then quickly gathered a large armful of the sweet fruit, noticing for the first time every fruit looked to be perfectly ripe.

As he dumped one armful unceremoniously into Red's massive jowls, he realized he would need to put in at least two more armfuls just to have enough for Red to be able to chew. As he went to collect more, he noticed something unusual; there were no fallen fruit lying around the base of the trunk.

After his third armful into Red's gaping maw the dragon started to chew the fruit; unfortunately for Kam he soon found out that dragon's lips not only don't close when they eat, but rather pull away from their teeth. This caused a flow of starfruit juice to come squirting out at Kam, nearly knocking him off of his feet.

As Kam stood there, drenched in starfruit juice from head to toe, Red began laughing. It started in his belly and worked its way up, sounding like an unimpeded sneeze erupting from his large frame.

In that instant Kam felt the darkness within the dragon recede as darkness does when a candle is suddenly brought into a pitch-black room. So great was the difference in Kam's mind that for a minute it was as if the darkness no longer existed in either the dragon or himself.

In that moment he abruptly saw with startling clarity the dragon's life and true, underlying emotions.

Clear as Crystal Lake where he used to play in as a boy, with the bottom looking so vivid as to not have water covering it at all, he saw much of the dragon's young life. This window into Red's life came with all of the pain and pride it harbored. Then, like a curtain being draped over a window the darkness returned, bringing forth its familiar feelings of anger and resentment. The abrupt reappearance of whatever was inside Red was stark and painful, like a sharp knife being drawn across Kam's hand.

Red looked at Kam and then back at the tree. Kam sensed his hunger and desire for more of the fruit, but as Kam suddenly registered what Red was thinking of doing, he tried to jump back but it was too late. The dragon swung his great tail and hit the tree with a resounding *whack,* causing almost every last one of the starfruit to fall out of the tree at the same time. As Kam stared in wonder the dragon's wondrous tongue started to whip in and out of Red's mouth quickly, snake-like, taking in large handfuls of the fruit which stuck to it like feathers sticking to tar.

Kam looked over to see the neighboring tree, one he didn't recognize, move and shimmer in the sun, its spectacular red, orange and yellow leaves moving and fluttering like flames from the force of the concussion of Red's tail. Although not far away, Kam squinted his eyes as he watched the sparkling and flickering of the fire-colored leaves become more pronounced and definitely untree-like.

It stated to look as though the tree had sprouted thousands of small wings and was preparing to fly out of the ground when Kam realized the brilliantly colored leaves had now become an actual mass of fluttering wings. The insects became airborne, leaving behind a tree with its now bare branches like skeletal arms reaching heavenward, imploring for a prayer to be answered. The image filled him with cold despite the warm sun.

The butterflies now swarmed towards him en masse, as if his scent were attracting them. Kam seemed to wake with a start as the butterflies, beautiful and mesmerizing to watch with the sun glinting off of their ginger and gold wings, started to flutter very decidedly towards him. He reached for the hilt of his sword even as he felt silly thinking of drawing it against the radiant kaleidoscope of their tiny, beating appendages.

As they drew closer, he became aware the butterflies were flying very close together, with his eyes being unable to discern the individual insects even at this close range. As they stated to swirl around him, he realized he was tense, with his hand still gripping the hilt of his sword.

The butterflies flew around and past him, their wings beating against his body like the faint heartbeat of a much larger creature. As a stinging pain registered in his mind, he quickly unsheathed his sword and started swinging through the air with broad strokes, trying to stop as many of them as possible from coming close enough to him to… well he wasn't sure what they were doing. But he had never heard of butterflies attacking anyone before.

A large gust of wind seemed to come out of nowhere which blew the butterflies not only off and away from him but scattered them, causing the group to disperse. Kam looked in the direction from which the wind had come, knowing full well it had been Red's doing, who was also suffering the aftereffects of the painful stings of the insects. Kam took the moment to inspect what the butterflies did to him.

Surprisingly he felt a combination of relief and adulation emanating from Red before he realized it was his own feelings being mirrored back to him through the bond. As he looked on the ground he could see many of the butterflies lying there, some cut into shreds and others having had their wings blown off, and he realized they weren't alive; at least not in how most animals were.

There was no blood or bodily juices flowing from them and no guts oozing out of their damaged bodies. Rather there were tiny strands of hair protruding from the crushed and cut bodies, hair which didn't seem to contain any blood or anything else which would usually be found in living things. He picked up one which he had apparently "killed" as it was cut clean in half vertically, separating it into front and back halves.

The first thing Kam noticed were the wings, which were nothing like anything he had ever felt, seemed to be of some type of material he had never seen before. It was smooth and glossy and similar to silk, yet it felt much more durable than any cloth he knew of. This fabric was stretched tightly over and around a light metallic-looking frame which constituted the wings and body. It appeared to be a type of extremely light-weight metal unlike anything Kam knew.

The body seemed to be made of the same material as the wings but was of a different shade than the wing structure, looking more like burnished steel in color. Kam didn't know what kind of magic could have created such creatures, but he knew the pain he felt had come from the edges of the wings as they had fluttered around him, and he could see he was bleeding from innumerable cuts on his arms and legs. He felt many cuts on his face as well. His clothing had fared a little better, with little nicks and cuts but for the most part having protected his body.

He glanced over at Red and asked, *what magic is this?*

It is not magic. It is something else.

Kam paused. Not magic? How was that possible? It clearly wasn't a living creature but some sort of magically created one. Yet he knew Red could sense magic; that had already been shown to him in the city.

Thank you for helping me. If you hadn't blown them away, I don't know what I would have done.

Then in that instant it became clear-Red hadn't done it to help Kam but rather had done it because of their bond. He too had been feeling the pain from the cuts the butterflies' wings had inflicted.

They both stood watching the last of the strangely ominous, yet bizarrely beautiful, butterflies which flew erratically away. The image left Kam feeling he was watching men stager out of a tavern when they've had too much lingonberry wine. Kam turned to look at Red to see if there was any sign that the dragon knew what the butterfly-like creatures were. At that moment he sensed from Red a feeling of confusion; not just because the dragon didn't know what the flying flame-colored, butterfly-like creatures were, but also because of something else.

Kam frowned in concentration trying to read the feelings which were pouring over him from Red. Then as quickly as that everything became clear; Red couldn't sense any life in the flying creations. Kam didn't realize dragons could sense the presence of other animals. That new revelation made him understand just how little he actually knew about Red.

That's how dragons hunt, Kam mused to himself. *They sense other animals, then they can pursue them.*

Kam realized the tall plants were in fact corn stalks growing on the field they landed on and started heading for the stalks. The ears of corn shone brilliant gold in the light like the noon-day sun casting its reflection on a placid lake.

As he reached for one it came to him that he had never before seen corn growing without a husk the way this one was. He paused in mid reach; he could see the full ear of corn and that it was without blemish. But was it edible? Still, it looked good and he was still hungry.

As he bit down into the corn it was sweet and crunchy, yet without the hardness of uncooked corn. Its color was a beautiful, even, golden yellow. To Kam's complete surprise there were no indications of any insects having gotten to it despite the corn not having its protective sheath. And all the corn as far as Kam could see was the same; completely ripe and without any husk.

As he looked around, he picked up on Red's growing unease, due in part to his own feeling of something not being quite right. He tried to gauge if Red could sense any other animals around but Red didn't, leaving the big dragon as perplexed as he was. There were no draft animals to help with the farm and no other sign of life. Kam felt an uneasiness enter the pit of his stomach. He turned to Red to suggest they leave when the ground started to shake.

Kam reached out with his mind to Red to see what the dragon thought. He realized that where the dragon came from landquakes happened quite frequently. However, Kam was decidedly not used to the ground beneath his feet shifting and moving and quickly made his way towards the dragon. Red's feelings about Kam were quite clear; he hoped the landquake would swallow him up and allow Red to return to his previous solitary life.

CHAPTER 11

Abruptly Red lifted his head and seemed to look past Kam. Even before Kam was swallowed up in Red's surprise and shock, he saw it on the dragon's face-a widening of the eyes, a slight crouching of the legs to prepare for anything. His mouth pulled back to show long, razor-sharp teeth and a hissing sound not unlike that which snakes make when they are about to strike filled the air.

In an instant the ground Kam was standing on seemed to come alive, lifting Kam high into the air and throwing him a good twenty feet like so much chaff in the wind. As he came down, he kept his senses enough to roll with the fall; but as luck would have it his scabbard turned perpendicular to his leg and across the front of his body. When Kam landed and rolled, his still injured leg landed full on the scabbard sending branches of pain shooting out in all directions.

As Kam finished his roll an incredible roaring filled his ears, deafening him. It took him a minute to regain his feet, the pain from the newly acquired bruise sharpening on his thigh.

As he looked back towards Red, he saw a tremendous battle was taking place, a battle between Red and a creature Kam had never seen before. It looked like a giant worm of some sort, with the part of its body protruding from the ground already longer than Red's full length. Its body was segmented in a way which made Kam think of an earthworm, but each individual section was large, at least six feet in length. Its circumference however was much narrower than Red.

Protruding from its body all around its circumference were short, stubby legs and round disk-like appendages. The legs and disks were alternating along the length of its body that Kam could see. The worm had partially wrapped its body around Red and the disks seemed to be able to cut through the dragon's scales. Thin streaks of blood, somehow contrasting with the angry crimson of his scales, were now noticeable all over Red's body. At that same instant Kam noticed the pain form what seemed like a thousand cuts simultaneously hit him all across his body.

The two titanic creatures turned and twisted around each other, like two dancers doing a slow ballet, trying to get a hold or position which would enable them to get the advantage over the other. As Kam watched wondering how he could help his companion his eyes were momentarily blinded by a bright flash of light coming from the creature's body.

His heart seemed to skip a beat as he realized some of the creature's skin had been torn away and a metallic sheen shone through. The sun reflecting off of it was sending blinding daggers of light flashing all around and temporarily blinding Kam with its brightness. Kam stood speechless as understanding slowly took hold of his mind.

A metal creature? What sort of magic is this?

Kam strained to understand what was going on through Red's mind, but only bits and pieces came through. He knew the dragon wanted to get airborne so it could have the advantage. He knew Red wanted to use fire against this thing but because of the angle of the worm's body pushing up against Red's neck, Red's head was wedged up between two of the creature's legs which kept him from being able to use his fiery breath.

Red was clawing at the creature with his full strength but his claws didn't seem to be able to penetrate the worm's metallic hide. And drowning everything else out was pain, overwhelming pain in one of Red's wings from where the creature's disks had cut far through the shoulder and into the bone. The injury was deep and caused the dragon's blood to fountain out in that spot, covering the worm in a gruesome red overcoat which soaked into the outer hide of the worm to create a macabre sight.

Kam knew he needed to do something quickly to help Red or he might lose his only chance to have a dragon help him. Pulling out his sword he ran forward and stabbed the worm as deep as his sword could penetrate, almost to the hilt. But before he could pull his sword free to attack the worm again it twisted its body and raised itself higher, lifting him up off the ground as he continued to grasp his sword. He ended up on top of the section he impaled, his sword still buried deep in the worm's body.

He braced himself and pulled his sword out; but before he could attack again the worm's body undulated, raising the section Kam was on higher and putting him directly across from the section which was holding Red's head. It was as if the worm's body was forming the letter U with Kam on one side and Red's head on the other.

Kam gauged the distance between his section and the other and leaped across the chasm over the lower part of the worm's body. As he leapt, he brought his sword high over his head.

He fell short of reaching the top of the other side but before he could fall off, he plunged the sword deep into the worm's body again, this time reaching the hilt with his blow. Although the impalement was nothing more than a pinprick to the monstrous creature, it did allow Kam to pull himself part way up where he could again gain some measure of support by allowing him to grasp the base of one of the legs. He was now close to the creature's legs which were holding Red's head against its body.

Suddenly the worm's head, if it could be called that, rose into view in front of Kam. The front of it had no discernible eyes or nose, or any other facial feature for that matter. All that existed was a mouth, the opening of which, although slightly smaller than the diameter of the worm, was filled with metal disks for teeth, angled this way and that, making Kam think he must have fallen into some bizarre nightmare.

All of the disks were spinning and showering dirt and Red's bloody gore everywhere. Yet despite that horrendous scene, a scene which would have made even the most hardened warrior flee the battle, Kam knew what he had to do.

As he balanced himself as best he could atop the worm's gyrating body, he pulled his sword out and swung it, trying to cut off the one of the legs holding Red's head against its body. Unfortunately, he lost his footing in mid-swing and started to fall; but instead of holding back and trying to regain his footing, he continued his swing, severing one of the legs completely off. As he fell backwards towards the field below, he saw Red wrench his head out of the grasp of the other leg.

He hit the ground with a thud, his breath getting brutally knocked out of him. The only thing which saved his ribs from being broken was the soft, freshly tilled earth on which he landed. He struggled to inhale, forcing his lungs to expand despite having them feel as though they had just been flattened by a stampede of horoxes.

With his eyes watering he painfully sat up and watched as Red launched a stream of fire directly at the worm's head. The orange-red flames completely enveloped the front of the worm. Almost immediately the fire went out and Kam gasped at what appeared. The entire front end of the worm's skin had been burned off and the creature's head now looked like blackened steel. It was now unmistakably obvious that this was no living creature but some sort of man-made atrocity likely devised with the help of some ancient and arcane magic.

In freeing his head and letting loose with a volley of fire Red had managed to escape the worm's grip. Red was now also on the ground, but Kam knew, both visually and from the jagged pain which seared his shoulder, that Red was unable to fly. It would be a battle fought only on the ground.

The blackened head of the worm advanced slowly towards Red. At that moment with its darkened face and spinning disk-like teeth it appeared more as a servant of the Dark Lord himself than of anything devised by man or magic. Red's fire seemed to have done no permanent damage to the thing other than superficially.

As slowly as the worm advanced Red retreated. During the heat of battle Kam hadn't realized just how much pain Red was in; but even with his own injuries Kam could feel through the bond just how much agony the dragon was in. Kam felt every injury from the deep cuts to the shredded shoulder still supporting the weight of the wing. Kam had to keep himself from frantically searching over his body for blood and wounds which were not his; yet he felt the pain of those injuries to the point of almost believing they were.

Abruptly Kam felt lightheaded and for a moment felt he might faint. He knew what was about to happen, but even knowing he was still surprised. He knew in that moment that for Red to use his magic while he was as severely injured as he was could prove fatal. He knew, without knowing how he knew, that when a dragon used its magic, it takes away from the dragon's energy, and when a dragon was as seriously injured as Red was, it could easily cause the dragon to black out or die.

As Red belched out his Dragonfire, the bright, beautiful green flames shot out towards the worm's head. The worm, almost in anticipation of the attack, moved with an unbelievable amount of dexterity to the point of appearing almost graceful in lifting its head clear of the flames.

The flames surrounded a point on the worm four to five segments behind the head, causing it to glow briefly before melting at the onslaught of Red's magic. The rapidity of the melting of that segment of the metal body made Kam think of a red-hot knife cutting through a ball of butter, with the butter pulling back from around the edge of the knife due to the heat.

Its head hung there for a moment, almost as if it was taunting Red, letting him know that even in pieces it would continue to live, much like its actual earthworm counterpart. But finally, slowly at first but with increasing speed, the head fell with a loud crash on the ground about twenty feet in front of Red. The crashing of its body, although less climatic, signaled the end of its life.

As Kam ran forward to see how Red was, he noticed the pain eased a bit. It didn't take him long to understand why. Red was stretched out on the ground unconscious, with only the slow rise and fall of his great chest showing he was still alive.

Kam quickly ran back to the edge of the field where the butterfly tree was. He had noticed earlier that there were other trees and foliage around it away from the field where they now were. As he raced over, he silently hoped he could find both a rubbergum tree and a fleshbush. Although both were fairly common, he was in an area he didn't know and seeing things he couldn't even have imagined before. He also wasn't sure if either would even work on a dragon.

He spied a large rubbergum tree and ran over to it. Besides being able to utilize the sap, rubbergum trees also grew gourds, fairly large, woody pods which were for the most part hollow except for some water they contained.

He quickly cut down some of the lower hanging gourds and dumped out the water they had in them. After cutting deep gouges in the tree, he set the gourds propped up against the trunk to collect the sap and then went in search of the fleshbush. He found a few fairly close, and with a relieved sigh started to cut up many of the large fronds.

With several of the leaves under his arm he went back and picked up the now full gourds and carried everything back to the dragon. He had been gone for about 30 minutes and was concerned the dragon's condition had worsened to the point where he might have died. The bond seemed almost nonexistent now, and Kam chalked that up to Red's severely weakened condition. Fortunately, he found the dragon still breathing, although not conscious yet, which he reasoned was probably for the best although he couldn't tell how near death the dragon was.

He quickly circled the dragon trying to find the worst injuries to look at first. Red had many deep cuts, but none looked life-threatening except for the shoulder injury. Somehow those disks had cut through the tissue surrounding the shoulder, leaving part of the white bone exposed.

Kam quickly shredded the leaves and laid them carefully into the gash. It required him to push the shredded fronds as far into the wound as possible to help the tissue repair faster and to stem the bleeding, and Kam knew from experience how painful that could be. He didn't know if he could save the wing but he had to try.

Red didn't move at all as Kam carefully but firmly pushed the shredded fronds deep into the wound, but he did hear a high-pitched sound which he assumed came from Red. He also felt his shoulder ache even more as he tried to tend to the wing.

Before he could apply the rubbergum he had to raise the wing so as to close the gash, and then find a way to support it while the sap solidified. Surprisingly he found that it didn't take much effort to slide the wing, which was much lighter than Kam would have thought, against Red's body into its natural resting position. Fortunately, that position plus a few branches he cut off from the nearby trees to use as crutches to support the wing, were enough to keep the wound closed.

He climbed onto Red's back to apply the rubbergum sap. He unceremoniously dumped the rubbergum sap onto the shoulder, knowing that in this case more was probably better. As he covered the entire shoulder with the gooey, sticky mess, he suddenly felt exhausted. He knew he hadn't slept well and with the intense pain he had felt earlier he quickly fell into a deep, dreamless sleep.

CHAPTER 12

Wyk had been practicing hard. Sweat rolled off his body like giant waves rolling into shore during a storm. His clothes were matted to his body, outlining his lean, muscular frame. His hair was slicked down and looked as though he had poured syrup all over it.

He had practiced against three of his men simultaneously. It was a practice he tried to do at least once a week. He felt you could never be too ready to fight multiple assailants, especially on a battlefield.

Jesse, who had been conspicuously absent all morning, had probably been with a woman; or perhaps more than one knowing him. But Wyk couldn't complain; Jesse kept himself in better shape than anyone he knew. He deserved to have some time off now and again.

Just then he spied Jesse coming straight towards him with a determined gait. As soon as he arrived, he glanced around at the men who were standing nearby talking and joking. Wyk gave a slight nod to one side and Jesse followed the movement, moving away from the other men.

"What did you find out?" Wyk asked, now realizing Jesse had done at least some of his duty that morning.

"I don't know where we're going, but I know it's somewhere far. Probably near some swamps." Jesse said.

Wyk pondered what he just heard. Going far was a surprise in itself. He figured the king's errand would be somewhere in the area, somewhere they could get to and back in a few days at most. Now it seemed he had it all wrong.

For a moment Wyk briefly considered asking Jesse how he came about the information, meager as it was. But since Jesse hadn't offered an explanation, he felt it better not to bring it up. He didn't want to put his friend on the spot of having to choose between being loyal to him or to whomever he had gotten the information from.

Wyk started to walk back to his living quarters with Jesse following him dutifully. As he left the practice area, he caught sight of the woman who said she had been attacked. She looked at him coldly before continuing on in the direction of the training area.

Wyk nearly stopped to go and watch what she could do. She had a loose robe on, presumably to cover herself after practicing and keep herself warm, but Wyk doubted that. He was sure she was trolling for men, hoping to find someone to support her and her expensive lifestyle.

She had a beautiful face Wyk had to concede. But even though he had never talked to her he was sure he knew her type. She lied about getting attacked to draw the attention of men who would "comfort" her and, naturally, buy her whatever she wanted.

He had no time for women like that. In fact, he had no time for women at all. As far as he was concerned, they were just a waste of time and money; even the nice ones. They would suck up a man's money and free time leaving him beached like a large fish; unable to breathe, unable to swim, unable to do anything.

He was nearly to his chambers now. Although officers were allowed to live in a place of their own, he chose to live and sleep in the guards' quarters. They were supplied by the king and paid for by the people. He always felt guilty thinking about living outside when money from the people, collected as taxes, provided a descent living area.

"Jesse," he began. "Find out as much as you can about our…quest." He finished, choking out the word.

Jesse nodded solemnly and Wyk wondered how he felt about the whole situation. Not that it mattered, if the king said go, you went.

After cleaning up Wyk went to inspect the men. He loved to catch them off guard, going in at different times on different days. He felt the men should always be prepared for anything.

As he walked through the bunkhouse he stopped in front of Glenne. He was a good man, if not the sharpest or cleanest. Or the best at anything for that matter. But he was true to the Guards.

This time however Glenne's shirt had more than a few wrinkles in it and wasn't even tucked in all the way. He couldn't let him slide-the others would see that and feel they could be as lax as him.

He stopped directly in front of Glenne and eyed his shirt while raising one eyebrow. It was a look he had perfected and one which always succeeded. This time was no different. Glenne's eyes dropped and his face went beet red. The others could see that, but still more was required.

"You will do one hundred rounds around the practice area and bunkhouse." Wyk said sternly, realizing even as he spoke it was far too strict a punishment for the infraction. But then Glenne always played it close to the edge and maybe this would teach him a lesson.

It was a very strenuous workout for Sakura that day. She practiced alone, as she almost always did everyday outside of her town. She practiced forms with and without her sword. She practiced hand-to-hand combat, knife throwing, nearly everything someone could think of as a way of fighting.

But although she practiced alone, in her mind she was fighting him-that creature which had gotten the best of her. Every time she closed her eyes, she saw him leering at her. Every time she took a breath, she saw him reaching for her chest.

Without realizing it she had stopped practicing and was standing, her body shaking as if it was the middle of winter. She hated what that monster had done to her, what he had nearly done to her. She was terrified and she couldn't deny it.

She focused herself and started practicing again, harder this time. She would defeat him the next time he tried anything with her.

She took a moment to catch her breath after an exceptionally long workout and noticed a couple of men quietly standing nearby staring at her. They looked like novices by the way they held their swords. However, she couldn't be sure if they were staring at her because of her skill or her looks. Knowing men, it was probably a little of both.

Wanting to get the image of the demon thing out of her head she challenged both of them. They looked at each other with surprised faces before smiling greedily and accepting. That told her all she needed to know-they were staring at her before because of her looks.

As she entered the ring the slow-looking one asked, "What do we get if we win."

Before she could stop herself, she said, "What do you want?"

Now they glanced at each other excitedly, mouths fairly watering at the thought of what they could get.

"I think we should each get an hour with you to…have fun with." The dimwitted one answered.

She gave a tight smile. This would be enjoyable.

"If you win, you each get me for one hour to do with as you wish. But if I win, I get your clothes, your money, everything you have on you now."

They chuckled darkly, as if she were a man who had just told them the dirtiest joke they had ever heard.

"That sounds good," the slow-looking one said. "That sounds fair."

With that they both attacked her simultaneously, surprising her with their speed. Their swordplay, however, was far worse than she thought it would be. She had to allow them to put her in awkward positions, having them nearly win time after time to make it even a modicum of a challenge for her.

After about 20 minutes the two men finally figured out that they wouldn't be able to beat her. The dimwitted one, showing far more intelligence than she first gave him credit for, said, "On second thought maybe we should just let her go. It wouldn't be fair for us to take advantage of a woman like that."

She smiled another tight smile, but her eyes showed her true emotions. "If you leave now, you can drop your clothes off at the side of the ring. And don't forget your swords."

The two men again glanced at each other and then rushed at her one last time. This was even better than she had hoped. Deftly dodging their frantic attacks, she resoundingly slapped them on their bottoms with the flat of her sword. She hit them so hard they fell to the ground, unable to stand.

"If I were you, I would take off your clothes now or I'll be forced to take them off the only way I know how-without your arms and legs attached."

The two men again looked at each other and quickly shed their clothes before they took off running. Sakura chuckled briefly to herself as she watched their white rears flash in the sun. Their skin was so pale she almost needed to turn away.

She quickly sobered up however as thoughts of the taunting, leering man came back. She knew she would have to do better than beating two simpletons of the likes she had just thrashed to beat him.

She sighed lightly and bent over to get the swords and moneybelts the men left behind. Maybe she could give the items to an orphanage or some needy person. She knew she didn't need it.

She walked back to the castle slowly. She didn't like staying there, but it kept her off the streets. It also kept her away from men who could draw attention to her as they tried to outdo each other for a chance to be with her. At times she felt men were nothing more than rutting pigs or dogs in heat.

Sometimes men behaved as if they had no brains at all. Or maybe they behaved that way all the time. Maybe that's what she needed to accept-that men were nothing more than the basest of animals, incapable of aspiring to true greatness.

Deep down she knew that wasn't true, there were some great men out there. She remembered reading about one great general among her people-Tsuyoshi Kiyamoto. He led the armies during the Dragon Wars and was able to unite different factions of humans, elves and dwarves against an army of dark spawn and dragons.

She shook her head slowly. She was always amazed when she thought of those groups, even united, defeating a horde of dragons. Granted, there were some dragons on the side of General Kiyamoto. But the number of dragons that fought against them far outnumbered their own.

Deep in her heart she felt as though she had been born in the wrong era. She should have been part of that war to preserve humanity, not fighting for the Dark Lord's lackeys as she was now.

A terrible image fought its way to the surface of her memories. She tried desperately to push it down, to keep it out of her conscious thoughts, but it was in vain. Forming clearly in her mind was the nightmarish image of the man who had tried to...

She sighed heavily. The memory of the attack weighed far more heavily on her than she would have liked, or would like liked to admit. That creature was evil and had a black heart beating in a dark soul.

The thought of him sent shivers down her body. She knew for him to touch her again would drive her insane. She truly believed she would have to kill herself if that thing succeeded. It was a vile, degenerate conception, even for the Dark Lord.

She entered the castle and headed straight to the king's quarters. He was always there, using his servants as toys for his twisted fantasies. He was nearly as bad as the creature that attacked her. But she had to see him to get information.

She walked up to his door which was flanked by two guards. They started to draw their swords when they saw she had no intention of slowing down, but the look she gave them had them quickly step aside.

The guards here are good men. She thought. *But it's obvious they have no respect for the king.*

She entered without knocking and found the king cornering a small, petite serving girl against the wall. With her entrance the king stopped and threw her a withering look. Sakura quickly waved the serving girl over and was surprised to see that instead of a small, young woman she realized the serving girl was barely more than 11 years old.

Quickly shooing the girl out she glared at the king, who suddenly seemed in a more amicable mood when he recognized her.

"Oh, my radiant Sakura. Yes, how are you today? You look like you've been working out. Please lay down on my bed for a minute and rest. Let me massage your tired muscles."

Sakura glared at him menacingly. "If you touch me, I will cut off your hands."

The king backed away so quickly he stumbled over himself and fell down on his ample rear. Sakura had to fight to keep from smiling.

"Look, we need to work together. There no need for hostility."

She paused a moment, pondering what he said. Her people, above all else, valued the business relationships which gave them their notoriety and money. They were true to any and all contracts they made, down to the letter.

"I'm sorry." She said begrudgingly. "I've had a rough past few days."

"Ah, yes." The king said. "I know you have. He told me what happened…"

"What!?" She exclaimed. "He told you what he did? He met with you?"

Now it was the king's turn to pause, obviously unsure of what, or how much, to say.

"Let's not talk about that. Whatever happened between you two should stay between you two." He stated politically.

Sakura's eyes narrowed and she clenched her jaw. But she knew now was not the time to go over that. She needed information.

"What exactly are we looking for?" She asked.

A malevolent gleam appeared in the king's eyes as a wicked smile touched his lips. He licked his lips nervously, or was it greedily she wondered, before continuing.

"It's a sphere the size of a child's ball. Your people call it the sacred orb I believe. I found out its rough location, plus a few other clues as to its whereabouts. I want it. No, I need it, desperately. I can give it to you for your people when I'm done with it. But until then I need to use it."

Sakura's heart nearly stopped at the words 'Sacred Orb'. If what he was saying was true, then she needed to find it. Her people would worship the ground she walked on if she could bring it home. No one would look at her different ever again. She would finally be accepted as one of them.

However, she had no reservations about what the king wanted it for. Nor did she think the king would ever turn it over willingly. He was a greedy, self-centered narcissist who only wanted power for himself. But if she played her cards right, once the orb was retrieved, she could get close to the king and slit his throat.

The thought sent shudders through her, both physically and mentally. Not for slitting his throat-that part would be easy. But allowing him to get close to her? He was barely above the level of the beast that attacked her. No, she would have to play it coy. She would pretend as though the king might get something from her but she would string him along until the right moment…

"I'll help find the Sacred Orb if you promise to give it to me when you are done." She said, trying to sound enthusiastic.

The king smiled a dark, malevolent smile full of treacherous thoughts. "Then maybe we should consummate our new agreement? The royal bed is extremely comfortable."

"I can't stay any longer," Sakura lied. "I promised some of the guards I would spar with them. It would look bad if they found out I missed our agreement because I was in the king's chambers."

The king seemed to ponder this for a minute before reluctantly nodding his head. "You are right, of course. Perhaps another time."

"Perhaps," said Sakura as she turned so the king wouldn't see her holding back her vomit.

Chapter 13

"I haven't been able to get any more information about what we're supposed to do. What about you?" Jesse asked.

"Neither have I." Wyk replied.

Jesse sat next to Wyk on the ground below the snapapple tree. The sun was low in the sky and the brightly colored clouds hovering in the distance in various shades of red made them look angry. Jesse knew Wyk would let him know what was happening as soon as he did, but he still felt anxious about not knowing.

Just then a quartet of cheerful salutations made both of them look at the four women walking by. They were returning to the city with basketfuls of snapapples balanced carefully on their heads. They playfully watched the two men before they started to giggle uncontrollably. Jesse smiled and waved, causing the giggles to be magnified. Wyk on the other hand simply looked down, admiring the grass growing around him.

"You really need to find yourself a nice young woman," Jesse said. "Someone to wash and mend your clothes, cook meals for you, and especially keep you warm at night."

"What if it's already a warm evening?" Wyk asked innocently.

"Then with any luck you'll have a very warm evening." Jesse said with a mischievously knowing smile.

Wyk chuckled at his friend's sense of humor. It tended to be a bit lopsided with his focus being on women so much, but Wyk could understand where Jesse was coming from. It wasn't that he disliked women, he just found his pursuit of perfection in his service to the king more fulfilling.

"You know," Jesse began, his voice taking on a much more serious tone. "I've heard there are some people looking to force the king to consider stepping down."

Wyk eyed him warily. Force the king to step down? Was that supposed to be a nice way of saying they wanted to overthrow the king? That would make them traitors and for that they would be hung.

"It seems there are many people who find the king to be a bit…overbearing."

Wyk began to wonder where this conversation was going. Did Jesse know the people he was speaking of? Was he saying he supported their beliefs? Jesse was a good man and Wyk couldn't see him bending the rules for anyone. Not even his mother.

Their conversation was interrupted as Glenne walked over to them.

"The king will see you tonight at 6:00, Wyk." Glenne said. "He said he will give you all the information you need to begin your journey."

"Did the king actually say journey?" Jesse asked.

Glenne shook his head and looked sheepish as he said, "no, actually he said quest."

Jesse and Wyk gave each other knowing looks. They didn't know what they were looking for or where it was, but chances were it wouldn't be good.

Sakura came back from the royal guests' shower room. Opulent by nearly anyone's standards, she was embarrassed to shower there and get anything dirty. But the nice thing was that as she was the only guest currently staying in the palace, she had the shower room, and the entire wing, to herself.

She entered her bedroom and took off the towel she had wrapped around herself. She stood in front of the highly polished brass reflection stand and looked over her lean, taut body. She was always surprised that men and women viewed her so differently.

When men saw her, they invariably thought of only one thing. With women though, it was different. Some women thought she was a woman of the night, trying to earn coin by pleasing men. Others thought she was the wife of some high ranking official, and others thought her a foreign dignitary. She could play any of those parts, and more. She could be anyone in order to accomplish her mission, whatever it may be.Now she needed to be a thief. She needed to break into the room of the man she knew would lead the group in search of the orb.

She had to know how much he knew and where his allegiance lay. Any information she could get on him would help her to understand the situation better.

First, she did some stretches to help her focus. hen she slipped into a well-fitted dark suit known as a *shinobi shozoku*. It would help her to avoid detection while moving around outside in the dark. It also covered most of her face and made it difficult to see her eyes. Then she left her room and slipped stealthily into the night.

Wyk was nothing if not punctual. He felt the hallmark of a good soldier was perfection in the small things. Unfortunately, the king was probably busy with kingly matters involving a serving maid or two and it took about an hour to see him.

When he was finally allowed to see the king, he was even more surprised to find he was being taken to the pious room. Fortunately, he now knew what to expect and steeled himself for it.

The guard escorting him stopped outside the doorway to the room and gestured that Wyk should go inside. Wyk noticed the guard looked nervous and figured he had been in the room before. Upon entering Wyk quickly noticed the king was seated facing him, with his back to the cursed wall.

The chair the king was seated in had not been in the room when Wyk had visited previously. That meant the king had his servants lug the large, padded chair up the stairs to place it there. This king's self-centeredness knew no bounds.

Wyk focused on the king's eyes. He noted that, even with his gaze strongly held, he could through his peripheral vision see colors swirling around behind the king. They fairly screamed to be looked at.

"Well, Wyk," the king began, "I see you're punctual as well."

Wyk felt his face grow hot. The king knew he had been on time yet still had him wait for an hour before seeing him. He knew it was a power move, an attempt to intimidate someone through the manipulation of their time. It bothered Wyk that a king would see fit to try and intimidate a man whose very life was devoted to serving him. He knew he couldn't let it get to him.

Wyk stared at the king, who seemed content to wait until Wyk's eyes started roving, but they didn't. Wyk's eyes were glued to the king with such intensity the king began to squirm uncomfortably in his padded chair. Finally, with a disgusted grunt of dissatisfaction the king began again.

"You will find me the sphere," the king said, then paused expectantly as if wanting Wyk to finish his thought. Wyk, however, had no clue as to what the king was referring to.

"A sphere?" Wyk asked, more to break the silence than for anything else.

"Yes. It's like a child's ball."

"A child's ball?" Wyk repeated questioningly.

"No, no. It's not a child's ball. It's like a child's ball. Hard, like one of those balls made of dried reeds they kick around."

"It's a sphere of dried reeds." Wyk said, playing dumb so as to garner as much information as possible.

"No!" The king said emphatically. "It's definitely not made of dried reeds. It's a, ah…" Here the king stopped with a surprised look on his face. After a moment a slow smile squirmed up his cheeks and Wyk knew the king was on to him.

"Let's just say it looks like it's made of stone, only it's lighter. You must be very careful with it and not entrust it to anyone else. You must be the one to hold on to it get it out. Do you understand?"

Wyk eyed the king suspiciously. There was obviously more going on here than the king was letting on, but at this point Wyk couldn't figure out what.

"Here is all the information you need." The king said, handing Wyk a scroll. Wyk took the scroll, noting how heavy it felt. He subtly ran his fingers along the paper and noted it was unusually smooth and had a very dense feel to it. He briefly wondered if he was strong enough to even tear it.

"Listen to me." The king said sternly. "You must commit this to memory and then burn it. Do you understand?"

Wyk nodded, realizing his face held a confused look but unable to change it. Besides, he knew the king wouldn't offer up any further information.

"Now go."

Wyk turned quickly, still being careful not to look at the wall. As he exited the doorway, he noted with interest that there were now no guards outside. Apparently, the information he got was of such a sensitive nature the king wanted to take no chances on anyone else finding out about the child's ball made of stone. The whole thing reeked and made Wyk feel as though the king was simply trying to get rid of him for a while.

Wyk tucked the scroll inside his tunic and headed straight for the informal practice area some of his men used during their off hours. Jesse was meeting him there to do some light sparing which Jesse had suggested to reduce the stress he knew would come from Wyk meeting with the king.

They had a light workout without weapons. Wyk noted with appreciation that this time Jesse wasn't questioning him about his meeting or their task. He was grateful that Jesse picked up on his lack of desire to talk about it.

Before heading off to dinner Wyk decided to head back to his room and change. He really didn't feel the need to after the workout, it was because he felt dirty from meeting with the king. It was not an experience he had ever had before.

As soon as he entered his room, he knew something was wrong. As a soldier he had built up a sixth sense, the ability to feel when something wasn't right. And right now, he felt as though someone was in his room.

Without sunlight coming in through the window and without having any lit candle the room was effectively pitch black. But even in the darkness he had a sense of movement coming from his right.

Instinctively he ducked and swung out with his leg to trip whoever was there. The intruder jumped and Wyk's leg brushed just under his feet. Then from his crouched position Wyk kicked out and was rewarded with a connection to the stomach, sending his assailant flying into his wall and letting out a surprisingly high-pitched grunt.

Standing up quickly Wyk moved in to punch the intruder, but received two hits to his head for his overconfidence. Shocked, he fell back a few steps. He wasn't just surprised that the man was able to get to his feet after the kick he had administered to his gut, but also that he moved in as quickly as he did without making a sound.

Suddenly sensing movement coming in at him Wyk threw up his arms and blocked a one-two punch combination aimed for his head again. He expected, but was too slow, to stop a sharp kick to his own stomach. Fortunately, he had time to tighten his stomach before contact was made. The kick ended up having only a minimal effect. Stepping in he swung his elbow and partially connected with his attacker's head, powering his swing through a block. He then stepped forward again and brought his knee up forcefully but caught the back of the intruder's thigh as he had turned and kicked out at him again.

This time the kick was not as powerful as before, partially due to his knee connecting a second ahead. But it was enough to send the assailant falling backwards off balance. He reached out to grab the other man's arm to keep himself up when he felt the arm twist violently away from his grasp. Instead, he grabbed at the man's shirt.

With a surprised gasp Wyk immediately let go and continued falling backwards. Meanwhile he heard the assailant scramble through the window as he landed on the ground with a loud thud, getting the wind knocked out of him.

He knew the intruder was long gone and he sat up ruefully wondering how much he should tell Jesse.

Chapter 14

"Let me get this straight," Jesse said. "You were falling backwards because you lost your balance. You reached out to grab this guy's arm to keep from falling. You missed his arm and instead grabbed at his chest. Only it wasn't a his chest it was a her chest?"

Jesse looked at Wyk skeptically. It was obvious he had been attacked-he had the bruises to prove it. But there were very few men who could take Wyk in a fight. Sometimes Jesse wondered if even he could. But a woman? It didn't seem possible.

"So, how was this chest you grabbed? Because if it was soggy and flabby, it was probably an old woman I know who sells fish in the marketplace. She's mean and could probably take you in a fight. Just her language would be enough to take most men down."

Wyk stared hard at Jesse. He could see his friend was having a hard time trying not to laugh. But by the light the woman could fight. She could handle herself like any man he knew, especially in dark quarters. He hadn't even practiced blind sparring since he was a recruit.

"I also found this." Wyk said, trying to avoid Jesse's overt expressions at trying to hide his amusement.

Jesse took the object from Wyk's hand.

"It's a candle. It's small, easy to hide and probably just bright enough to see by without attracting attention through an open window. Anyone could have bought this in any city anywhere."

"I know. It isn't much help, but it lets me know I wasn't crazy." Wyk said.

"I think your bruises were enough to tell you that." Jesse smirked.

"Well, here's something that will really put a smile on your face. We are going to start incorporating blind sparring into our training regime beginning immediately. It's amazing what you notice when you're forced to rely on your other senses. I think it will do the men some good."

Jesse was caught off guard by the pronouncement. He hadn't done blind sparring since he had first joined the King's Guards. Well, if it made him a better fighter, so be it.

It felt like the silence in her room was berating her in a way she never could do herself. How could she be so stupid as to allow the Captain of the Guard to catch her in his room! What was his name again, Wyk? Granted, he was a well-trained officer in the Guard, but that was no excuse. Not only that but he fought well; too well.

The Assassins' Guild members trained hard; harder than anyone else she knew of. She should have been able to take him out easily. His ability at blind fighting nearly rivaled her own, and she had been training for years and was one of the best.

She inspected herself carefully in the reflection stand. She had bruises on her arms and face, but makeup could conceal those. What surprised her was the massive bruise marring one side of her perfect bosom. A bruise in the rough shape of a large hand print, which looked almost claw-like, marred her left breast.

She chuckled softly to herself remembering his reaction in realizing she was a woman. Suddenly it dawned on her-this was not a good thing. Most men, and nearly all women, discounted her abilities. If anything, untoward happened, it was almost always thought to be the work of a man. Sometimes a deranged man, but always a man.

She looked at herself again. Being a woman was her best, greatest disguise. With that gone she could be considered as a suspect in nearly any crime. Especially as he now knew how well the woman in his room could fight. Now she needed to play the weak woman extremely well to throw suspicion off of herself.

She sighed. It was a ragged, tired sigh. There were times she wished she could just leave the Guild; leave it and never look back. But the Guild was not so accommodating. Those who were a part of the Guild were a part of it for life. She herself had assassinated some who chose to leave. It simply wasn't allowed.

At least she was good at it. Better by far than most of the women and better than nearly all of the men. She had the skills and the natural ability to exceed in nearly every aspect.

She looked at her reflection once more. She wondered what a man like the Captain of the Guard might say about her if she weren't an assassin. Would he say she was pretty? That she was worth fighting for? Maybe even dying for?

She shook her head. Thoughts like that could get her in trouble. She knew he would be the one to watch out for. If anyone could figure out her secret it would be him. She would need to stay close to him, but not too close. Fortunately, she was trained in that as well.

"What do you intend to do?"

The man asking the question was bland. He was neither good-looking nor ugly. His hair was of a color that seemed to be any color except that which would be noticeable. He was of average build and average height. If he were to stand next to someone else no one would even notice him.

The king noticed him however. He knew what he represented; or rather who he represented. He knew the power which stood behind him. This bland man was not to be trifled with.

The king was impressed the man got this far. Obviously, he had no small amount of ability, but you could never guess that by looking at him. The king knew enough to tread carefully around this one.

"Well, what do you intend to do?"

It was an open-ended question-one which eliminated simple, one-word answers and required an explanation. That way the person giving the answer could be held accountable.

"I have set everything in motion." The king said slowly. "Everything that was required of me I am doing."

"It doesn't look that way to us." The bland man intoned slowly.

The king frowned. There was something strange going on here, but he couldn't quite put his finger on it. It was almost as if a stray thought regurgitated from some long-distant memory stood up and asked politely to be remembered.

"We don't see you performing your duties as requested. We have an agreement-you do what we ask and you can rule this kingdom anyway you want. But you are not fulfilling your end of the deal."

The stray thought was screaming now. It was jumping up and down and waving its arms frantically. He knew it was important. Although why it was important now with this extremely vapid man in front of him, he couldn't say.

"What do you have to say for yourself?"

The king paused in thought. He needed to stall, to buy himself some time. At least until he got the orb.

"I am putting everything into place as you asked. It's just taking a little longer than we had planned for."

The dull man stood in silence, unmoving. It made him seem as though he was contemplating the fate of the world, which he might very well have been. Then it dawned on the king why this man was so important.

"You have 10 weeks to complete our instructions or get taken down. There are many others who could sit where you're sitting."

The king swallowed hard. He remembered that the benign-looking man and those like him were a means of communication with others far away. They could see through his eyes and hear through his ears. When they spoke, the words issued from his mouth.

He knew what was coming next but he also knew he had to take it or they would come after him with things far worse. He tried to take in as much air as he could to hold his breath, but he knew deep inside that it wouldn't help.

Suddenly the bland man burst into flames. They were a bright, unearthly color which consumed his body quickly. Yet despite the pain he must have felt no sound escaped his lips.

The smoke which quickly filled the room looked as though it dissipated quickly, but the king knew better. Soon his skin started to blister and his lungs burned as if they were on fire and a massive headache nearly blacked him out. This would last a few hours, but it was designed to keep those working from forgetting who their employer actually was

It worked.

He studied the candle carefully. What he first thought was nothing but an ordinary candle turned out to be something more. Out of curiosity he had lit it the night before and watched it burn. It had an extremely small flame and gave off very little heat and barely lost any wax during the fifteen minutes or so he kept it lit.

However, the most unusual thing about it was the light it gave off. Looking at it from the top Wyk found it to be exceedingly bright, yet when looked at from the side its luminosity was much less. He also found that he could point it and the flame would burn sideways instead of continually pointing upright. This gave it the ability to send a spot of light wherever he pointed it instead of casting a warm glow around the whole room.

He didn't know how the candle was able to do that. If he didn't know better, he'd say it was magical. But for some reason he had a feeling magic had nothing to do with it. He felt it had more to do with its actual construction.

He frowned in concentration, trying to think of a time when he had heard of something like it before. However, no thoughts came to him. He finally had to admit it was something truly unique.

He began to wonder if the candle had anything to do with the journey the king was sending them on. He didn't see how that could be, but if the king said anything to his lady-friend then she might be inclined to gossip, especially for a bit of coin.

Wyk's thoughts suddenly veered to thinking about the woman. She was, he had to admit, the prettiest woman he had ever seen who was in that line of work. If fact, she was undeniably the prettiest woman he had ever seen, and that was saying a lot.

But a woman like that would be helpless in a situation where there was danger. She would probably cower behind a horse at the first hoot of a nightowl on a moonless night. Or worse yet she might throw her hands up in the air and run around in circles, screaming.

Wyk started to chuckle at the thought of her doing just that, then he paused. Somehow that just didn't seem to fit her. He wasn't sure what she would do in a dangerous situation, but he had a feeling he might be surprised.

He forced his thoughts back to the candle and tried to figure out what it meant. It was a specially made candle using s process which he believed most candle makers wouldn't know. It was perfect for a thief to use though.

With nothing left to show for what had happened to him the night before he left to see how preparations were going for their trip. He also had to make time to visit Nix, an old friend of his. Nix said he had something special to give him and to bring some of his Guard friends with him. Knowing Nix, that could be interesting.

CHAPTER 15

When Kam finally awoke, he looked at the position of the sun and realized he must have slept for over twelve hours. It was the morning of the day after the attack of the metal worm. He was still on Red and turned his full attention to the dragon.

Red seemed to be breathing a little easier and Kam noticed the sharp pain he had felt in his shoulder the previous day had eased to a dull, albeit extremely painful, ache. He slowly crawled across Red's back to look at the injured shoulder.

As he thought he couldn't see much. Although the rubbergum sap seemed to have held the wing joint in place despite the fact Red must have moved his injured wing at some point while Kam slept, there was no way Kam could see the injury beneath the solidified amber glob.

He took a moment to grow introspective, a luxury he hadn't had much of since the bonding. He wondered at how powerful his new sword was. It sliced through metal without any problem. He remembered his friend giving him the sword for this very trip. He hadn't expected the sword to be as powerful as it was, but he wasn't complaining. The only regret he felt was in leaving his father's sword behind while he wielded this one.

Fortunately, the shroud of darkness which seemed to surround Red's mind constantly seemed to have dissipated for the time being. Kam wasn't sure why, but was grateful nevertheless. He slowly slid off of the dragon's broad back and set out to find food and water nearby for the two of them.

As he walked, he again looked closely at his sword; it wasn't even scratched. Its brilliant shine gave the impression of having just been polished; but Kam knew that wasn't true. He hefted it, trying to remember how it felt when he had first pulled it out of its sheath. He was positive it had felt a little heavy at the time, but now it seemed the perfect weight for him.

Kam walked around slowly, trying not to awaken any other metal creatures which might be in the area. Due both to the severity of their injuries and sheer exhaustion, they hadn't traveled from where Red had collapsed after his fight with the worm. Despite its mutilation and seeming "death" he was hesitant to pass by the magical worm-like creature again. He walked away from it, towards some trees off to the far side of the field.

On the other side of the trees he found a small river, one which ran perfectly straight and seemed to be in a man-made canal of some sort. He pulled out the two small water skins which he always carried on trips and filled them with water, knowing he would need to make numerous trips just to supply the dragon with one small mouthful.

As he finished filling up the skins he suddenly stiffened, the hairs on the back of his neck stood up and he felt dizzy. Turning quickly, he found Red behind him, head hanging low and his large body swaying from side to side. The dragon crouched low and dipped his head for a drink. It was nearly nearly a minute before Red lifted his head and starting to turn as though to head back to where he had initially collapsed.

Abruptly another wave of dizziness hit Kam accompanied by nausea. Kam fell to his knees while Red fell onto his stomach and blacked out. Then, as suddenly as it had hit him, the dizziness and nausea left, but not before Kam blacked out too.

When he came to this time Kam figured it was early morning, just before dawn. He thought he must have been out another sixteen hours. He knew it must be due to the connection he had with the dragon and not with any injuries he sustained, but that provided little comfort. Sure, he probably he wouldn't starve or die of thirst, but he still wasn't comfortable having to suffer with the dragon. He started to wonder what women would say if they had the chance to have their husbands suffer with them while they were pregnant, but quickly shook his head to clear it of that unbidden and unwelcome thought.

He finally decided to stretch his legs a bit and see if there were any other potential dangers in the area. Although he didn't want to, he knew the first thing he should do was to go back and check on the worm creature. He walked over and approached it slowly, sword drawn. There was no movement coming from the head. The rest of the body also seemed still and no sound emanated from either section. As he walked around it the size truly staggered him; it made Red look small!

He went to where the dragon breathed green fire onto it and froze, gaping in amazement. True to its appearance the skin did indeed seem to be of some metal, which had melted. However, whether that was due to the extreme heat of the dragon's breath, the acidic nature of it or some magical quality he didn't fully understand he didn't know.

Kam lightly rapped on the outer part of the worm with the hilt of his sword. Except for emanating an unusually high pitch, the sound was definitely metallic. He then took another step around to peer into its insides, and was again shocked at what he saw. There was no blood at all, just some fluid which had a whitish color to it forming a puddle on the ground. The fluid continued to drip from the severed and melted ends of countless small tubes which seemed to make up the bulk of its insides.

As Kam looked closer however, he noticed that there were two layers of skin. The outer layer, which consisted of a metal skin covered by what vaguely felt like cloth, was some inches apart from the second layer of metal. The gap between the two layers was filled with dirt which Kam assumed came from the field.

So, either this creature was in the process of shedding one layer of skin and having a new one develop, or it always has the two layers and somehow pushes dirt between the two in order to travel though the earth. Kam mused to himself.

Shaking off a cold chill which seemed to come out of nowhere and run down his spine, Kam continued to wander around the area. Bordering the field were trees of various types. He recognized many such as the rubbergum, mountain apple, star fruit and pine. There were at least as many trees he didn't recognize. He also noticed an absence of sound, which was unusual given the fact he was essentially on a farm, and farms were always noisy.

He gathered as much corn as he could carry from the edge of the field to take back to Red. As he walked back, he pondered why a farm would have a large creature like the one they had just fought on it. And why were there no people or insects or structures or anything else? As he passed the great worm's head he glanced once more into the gaping jaw with its slanted discs, giving it the impression of a pumpkin jack head. Then a glint in the corner of the mouth caught his eye.

He bent slowly over and peered into the hole. Wedged between one of the rollers and the side of the mouth was a glint of green light. It seemed to be imbedded in a clod of earth, so Kam took out his dagger and tried to pry it out. It took a few minutes but he finally managed to free it.

As he studied what appeared to be a piece of metal, some loose dirt fell away and he realized with a start he was holding a finger. With a startled gasp he dropped it. Chiding himself for behaving like a schoolboy he picked up the finger, which was still plump and fleshy and not more than a few days old. He saw that the green glint came from a ring which was still around the finger. He slipped the ring off and threw the finger to one side.

He had no idea what the ring was, but the color it gave off reminded him of Red's magical fire. He slipped it into his pocket and again headed back towards the dragon when he noticed one of the creature's disks on the ground. It was only about three-quarters complete and the section which was missing appeared to have been dissolved by Red's fire.

He hefted it; it had a good weight to it and felt surprising well balanced in his hand, as if he could use it to throw. He touched the edge and found it to be extremely sharp, despite what he assumed was constant use underground. He decided to keep that as well and slipped it into his pack.

As he approached the dragon he was relieved to see him drinking more water while tentatively moving his wing slightly.

How is it? Kam asked, hoping the dragon could fly again, yet knowing that would be impossible for the foreseeable future.

Red stopped drinking and turned his long neck to look right at him. At the same time a jumble of thoughts, feelings and even physical distress came through the bond very strongly. All of which made Kam wonder why he didn't get all of that before the dragon turned to him. Kam wondered if either he or the dragon were able to control the intensity of the bond now that they've had it for a while.

You helped me. Was all Red said; yet Kam sensed the deep gratitude the dragon felt for saving his life. He also sensed the animosity Red felt because a person had helped him. Truly dragons were as bad as women when it came to emotions.

My wing. You helped my wing. It is healing well but I won't be able to fly for a long time. Then almost as an afterthought Red added, *you will need to find yourself another dragon to help you.*

Kam wasn't sure if Red was touched by his helping him in the fight and was sincerely letting him know he would need another, healthier dragon to help or if he was looking for a way out, which wouldn't be surprising after all. But the latter wasn't the impression Kam got. It was more of a concern Red wouldn't be able to help coupled with a feeling of obligation towards him, although those feelings were muddied and hard to read.

Kam tried to guess where they were and figured they could probably walk to the nearest town in three days; then to the city in another seven days, putting him behind his schedule by a considerable amount of time. He sighed again.

Are you able walk without much difficulty? Kam asked.

Red snorted but Kam couldn't sense if it was due entirely to the pain. The pain was making the bond between them hazy and Kam still felt the throbbing ache in his shoulder too. But there was something else...the pain was somehow keeping the dragon from dwelling too much on the darkness within it. It was as if the pain was disturbing the heavy canvas curtain which had kept the light out and allowed the thick, pervasive darkness to fester in the dragon like an infected wound.

With the darkness at bay, at least for the moment, light was allowed to return. Ironically, despite his injuries, the life-threatening battle seemed to be lifting the spirits of the dragon more than anything else.

Almost as if he lives for the fight. Kam mused to himself. *Maybe that's all he has left to live for.*

Kam could understand that feeling; needing to do something and not allowing friends or family to break your focus of what must be done. He also figured the animosity the dragon felt towards life, including his own existence, was probably the result of a conflict within his community of dragons.

Abruptly a thought entered into Kam's mind like a tidal wave, nearly overwhelming him to the point of his falling down. It was backed by an enormous surge of pain which ebbed back to where it had been as soon as the thought crystallized: *You think you understand about Dragonnation?*

Kam paused, as much to recover from the abrupt onslaught of pain as to gather his wits. He had been looking in the direction they had to travel but now turned to face Red. To his surprise Red's head was not two feet from him; so close he could feel his hot breath coming out like a blast furnace with the stench of burnt blood and old, rotted meat. It was a smell Kam did not think he would ever forget.

As Kam eyed the dragon with his huge, luminescent eyes looking as large as the moon and his lower canine-like fangs, each as long as his forearm, he suddenly felt sorry for Red. He had obviously suffered great anguish among his own kind, but what that was Kam couldn't fathom.

He had already caught through their bond that something happened of such a great magnitude it had forced the dragon out of his community. Then to heap more indignity upon him, Kam had emotionally and mentally castrated him by taking away his free will. Ironically it was humanity's freedom Kam was trying to fight for and the hypocrisy of it was not lost on him.

I don't know your people, your kind, but I know something great and terrible happened to you. Kam said, choosing his words carefully. *Something which you believe was so heinous that you buried it deep in your soul under layers of anger and regret. I understand that much, as that happens among people as well.*

As Kam stared at the dragon, he came to understand that he and Red had more in common than he first thought, or ever would have thought for that matter.

You now feel I have a soul. Do you truly believe that?

The question startled Kam, and for a moment he didn't know how to answer. But he knew the best way to handle this would be to be open and honest with the Red. Not just because his mouth full of razor-sharp teeth was a mere two feet from him, but because he also felt a kind of kinship with him. A kinship he hadn't felt with anyone in a long time.

I believe everything has a soul, from the smallest insect to the largest dragon. Kam replied. *And you and your kind seem to be as intelligent as any person I've ever known. I can't see why The Light wouldn't have provided you with a soul as well.*

Red seemed to be mulling over what Kam had just said. Then he responded, *I'll take that as a compliment.*

Kam was again startled, but for a different reason this time. He could have sworn the dragon was laughing at him.

They had been traveling for the better part of the day and Kam was beginning to worry about Red. Although it was the dragon's idea to have Kam ride on him as he could walk faster than a 'mere person' as he had put it. He knew that Red must be exhausted. His body was still trying to overcome the battle and severe injury he had taken to his shoulder. Their direction had been paralleling the river/canal so thirst wouldn't be a worry, at least not yet. But Red needed to eat as well; if for nothing else than just to help him get strength back so he could heal quickly.

Kam had been surprised at one thing though. The dragon's scales seemed to be able to heal quickly, much quicker than any person could. The dragon had sustained many smaller injuries than the shoulder wound such as scratches and deep cuts from the worm creature. But where scales had been cut open a sticky liquid had oozed out with the blood and solidified, in essence becoming part of the scale and sealing the cut.

Kam had discretely tried to poke at the new, hardened area with his dagger while riding the dragon and found the newly solidified parts seemed as hard as the original scales. He noticed the ooze also had a reddish color to it so when it hardened it seemed to match perfectly with the rest of the scale, thus making it difficult, if not impossible, to discern that there had been any desecration in the first place.

Evening was fast approaching and Kam knew they would have to stop for the day. Red said, *we should sleep here for the night. It will allow me time to heal. Dragons heal better when they aren't moving.*

Red stopped by a wild mountain apple tree, then lay down and curled around it with his injured wing on the inside by the tree. Kam slid off after grabbing some apples while standing on top of Red's back where he could easily reach them. As he was about to take a bite he had an idea.

Would you be able to use your, uh, non-magical fire without tiring yourself out too much? Kam asked timidly.

Red stared at him blandly. *It takes very little energy for me to use fire without magic. Do you want me to cook your food so you can get rid of the taste and be able to stomach it?*

Now it was Kam's turn to stare. *Actually I, ah just wanted to roast these apples before I ate them. It makes them taste sweeter.*

What do you mean by 'sweeter'?

Kam thought a moment before finally answering, which he did while forming a small pyramid with the fruit in front of Red. *I'll tell you what, if you roast these apples for me, I'll give you one and you can see for yourself.*

Red barely seemed to exhale when a little burst of fire came out and torched the apples and the grass around it for about five feet in every direction. Kam took one of the hot, shriveled apples from the stack and tossed it from hand to hand to cool it.

Wait until it cools down and I'll toss it in your mouth.

Red peered at Kam and with sarcasm careening through the bond and said, *I just spit fire from my mouth. That apple is not too hot for me.*

Kam gave a sheepish grin and tossed it into Red's open jaws. As he watched he got the feeling Red was playing with it, using his tongue to roll the apple around in his mouth. He then understood the dragon was trying to get as much of the flavor as it could in its mouth.

A sense of surprise and even a little delight struck Kam, and the unexpected reaction brought a smile to his lips. Then, without warning, Red rose and bringing his body a little ways away from the tree so his injured wing wouldn't be affected, blew a torrent of fire onto the apple tree. Instantly it burst into flames, throwing light and heat in all directions. As a dumbfounded Kam looked around to make sure no unwanted creatures might see the flames and come visiting, he asked, *Why did you do that?*

I wanted more. Red said.

But even as Kam was about to respond and say that the fire would completely consume all of the apples and the tree, Red put his mouth right to the flames and seemed to inhale them, causing the inferno to be extinguished.

How did you do that? Kam asked.

Without looking at him Red said, *I am a fire dragon. I can do more than just throw fire; I also have control over flames. At least over fires as small as this one was.*

The tree, now looking for all intents and purposes as one which had been dead for some time, had all of its leaves completely burned off. Yet surprisingly most of the apples were still hanging on, looking like the dark, shrunken heads of those which are said to adorn the Dark Lord's throne. The steam and smoke swirling around the tree only added to the ambiance of the gruesome image.

Kam gave a shiver and watched as Red thrust his head into the middle of the tree and inhaled loudly. The apples hung on for one brief moment before they all seemed to agree their fate was inevitable and let go, creating more of a vile vision by making it appear the dragon was now devouring the shrunken heads. Red drew his head back and started chewing, spewing what little hot and steaming juice they had left on Kam.

As the heat registered in his mind Kam inhaled to let out a cry when, just as unexpectedly, he felt something slimy wrap around him and everything seemed to cool off. It took him a moment to realize the dragon had encased him in its tongue. But that was not all; somehow it had taken the heat off of him so that now he felt normal again.

As he looked over at Red, he tried to express gratitude for the help in not getting burned. He understood it was more the dragon's ability to somehow absorb the heat rather than the actual physical contact of his tongue made. Interestingly enough all he felt from the dragon through the bond was what seemed to be indulgence.

As Kam started to eat one of his own roasted apples, he now sensed a smug happiness within Red. He wasn't sure what that meant, but he did know one thing; the viscous, omnipresent darkness had receded. It was as though those life-sapping curtains had been drawn back, allowing life-giving light back into a room which had not seen it in far too long. Kam smiled to himself; Red seemed much more human now.

I heard that, and you don't need to ridicule me.

At that point Kam did something he hadn't done in a long time, he laughed.

CHAPTER 16

They continued on their journey towards Kam's home, the kingdom of Austine. Red knew the man was figuring out how long it would take them to get there; and using his walking speed instead of flying the man had figured about 10 days.

But with him riding on my back he now figures about 7 days. Red thought to himself. *He looks to get us there in three days if he can. But there's no way we can without my being able to fly. Walking is for man, not dragons. Dragons were meant to fly high in the sky, soaring over the land and the lesser creatures on it.*

A thought suddenly flashed into Red's mind courtesy of Kam, and Red understood there was a way, a shortcut, which would cut out about four days of walking.

If we can finish what we have to do quicker, then let's do it. Red said, interrupting Kam's thoughts.

There is an element of danger… The man started. *There is the Sea of Sand we would need to cross and…*

A sea of sand? No dragon has ever spoken of such a thing. Do you mean an area of great sand such as surrounds Dragonmount?

A desert? It's like a desert only the sand is so fine it behaves like water. It can swallow a man whole. Was the only way Kam could think of describing it.

Red pondered this new information for a moment. *You believe I am tall enough walking that I can walk through it?*

The man's silence gave him the only answer he needed to hear. The man was going to sacrifice them uselessly and foolishly so he might die with the knowledge he *tried* to accomplish what he set out to do. Truly this man had no brains.

No, Kam continued. *There are stories of boats which cross it; ferries which will take you across if the price is right.*

Red thought about what the man said. Apparently, people couldn't fly so to try and make up for their inadequacies they go across sand in boats. People truly are useless and a scourge wherever they live.

The continued walking in silence until dusk, then they made camp and settled down for the evening. Red could still remember savoring the apples the man had gotten. He had never tasted anything so delicious in his life. They were sweeter than a young lizaerd's flesh, and very nearly as satisfying.

At the thought of the apples Red's mouth started to water and he hoped the man might find him some more to eat. Just then he caught something coming through the binding with the man; he was apparently *laughing* at him! As if this insect had any right to find any reason to laugh derisively at him. He was in no position to...

You're right.

The words, although softer now as though the words were coming from far away, were nevertheless clear. His old friend, the darkness, which had just recently found renewed strength in its own life, was talking to him again.

What do you want? Red asked.

I want to help you to rid yourself of this man, this bloodtick, which infests you. You can't kill him while he has you binded, but I can. You know I can.

Was the answer truly from his non-corporeal companion, or was he going wormcrazy? At this point Red felt as though his mind was being overcome by something far darker than anything he ever harbored in his soul. And it could talk with him! Despite the abuse the binding generated from the man, and his inability to tear the man to shreds to free himself, he felt he should fly lightly where this matter was concerned.

As Red walked the way the man told him, it dawned on him no dragon had ever been this far away from Dragonnation since the end of the Dragonwar, except for those few Dragons which went out on trade runs for the Dragonclans. Red sighed. He never wanted to be one of those Dragons who went and traded for cows; he was always happy staying within Dragonnation.

But now that you are outside of your beloved domain maybe there is more you can do.

What are you talking about? Red asked. *What would I want to do away from Dragonnation?*

You can't fool me, the voice, or was it his madness, continued. *You could wreak havoc among the nation of men. They have not had contact with Dragons in many years. You could finish them off before they could bring any weapons or magic against you.*

Red paused at the last statement. All dragons knew people had powerful magic at their disposal and that it would be death for dragons, especially a single dragon, to take them on. This voice had to be madness to have him fight a useless fight to his own death.

And yet, to die fighting would be a noble way for a dragon to die. Not like the Dragons now whom sit around Dragonmount simply passing on knowledge which was passed on to them over countless years. They never taste of battle or the glory of victory. You know I am right. Attack man and die like a Dragon.

If the voice was really part of him speaking out, why would it want him to die? The end of Red meant the end of it as well. Red was puzzled.

Why do you want me to die? Red asked himself. But for a reply there was only silence. *Why do you feel the need to have me die? Is it because a person controls me?*

Red wasn't sure why he asked himself that, but he knew it must have come from somewhere. After a moment of silence, he thought he would try a different tact.

Why do you want me to fight people alone?

I don't want you to fight. Came the reply, and for a second Red didn't realize it was the man talking to him and not the other voice. *I want you to fight the darkness, and I will fight by your side.*

Red peered at Kam solemnly. He didn't understand anything that was going on. He did notice one difference; his bitterness, his resentment, his only true companion, was not as close to him as it once was. Despite the newly acquired ability to converse with him as a dragon would, he felt as if a huge rock which he had been carrying on his back suddenly broke in half, leaving much less weight pressing on him.

He knew it had, in part, to do with the man traveling with him. Despite the binding and control the man was exercising over him, he had to admit the man showed courage in the battle with the wingless Dragon in the field. He also showed concern for Red's welfare above and beyond the fact he wanted and needed him to fly. Red sensed a genuine concern, and unbelievably even affection, from the man. He couldn't explain it but it was there.

Red sighed again. This trip was going to be a long one.

Later that day they finally arrived at the Sea of Sand. Red noticed a strange smell in the air which had grown progressively stronger as they got closer. It was reminiscent of a place he knew long, long ago when he was but a youngling. He watched as the man, after having carefully slid off of his back, gingerly approached the edge of where the sea started. It was easy to see as the ground changed from a tan, roughly textured sand to nearly blindingly white sand which moved in the wind the way water did.

As Kam cupped a handful of the grains and let them slowly pour out, Red got the impression that he too sensed something odd. Kam also noticed the odor, a faint aroma but one nonetheless, but which didn't seem out of place to him. Red focused on his memories, trying to recollect what the smell reminded him of.

Then, like a physical blow, the memory hit him. At that same moment the voice, that awful voice that wanted him to kill and die for no reason, struck up a cacophony of sound that reverberated through his body and rattled his teeth.

YOU MUST ATTACK THIS MAN! YOU MUST ATTACK EVERY MAN YOU SEE! YOU MUST END THE INDIGNATION OF BEING BINDED TO THIS ONE! YOU MUST KILL! KILL! KILL!

As Red watched, the man threw his hands up and forcefully covered his ears. He bent over and waves of nausea hit Red, although he knew the feelings were coming from the man. After the commands the voice gave it stopped, and the silence seemed overwhelming. It was hard for Red to believe how a voice in your head can make you notice the silence in your ears.

The man looked up at Red with true concern in his eyes, but before he could communicate anything Red said. *It's not sand, it's salt.*

The man paused and looked back at the expanse of whiteness. Then he cupped a small amount of the substance and put it to his lips. Suddenly he was violently spiting it out of his mouth. He had apparently tasted it and through the binding Red could tell it tasted like salt, but the taste was so strong, so abnormally potent, he was forced to spit it out quickly. Through their connection Red understood how Kam was confused about how the smell could be so faint for a salt so puissant in flavor. Dragons obviously had a more effective sense of smell. No surprise there.

It should be called the Sea of Salt, not the Sea of Sand. Red thought to Kam.

Wha…what was that yelling? That came from something inside of you, something dwelling in the darkness within you. The man said.

Red wasn't sure how to reply. Should he tell the man he's crazy? He didn't think it would matter to him in terms of keeping him binded. And what was the man saying about something being inside of him in the darkness?

Red suddenly noticed Kam had approached him and was now standing almost directly below his head. Red tilted his head down so he could look full at the man.

There is…something…inside of you. Kam began. *I think it's magical in nature. I didn't notice it there until after our confrontation in the City of Stone where we fought the Halfers and Darkbloods. I think we should have a wizard use magic on you.*

Red snorted. Have another person use magic on him? He was already binded by magic. An evil, dark enchantment no Dragon would ever use on another Dragon.

With another loud snort Red turned away and tried to figure out how this man would have them get across. The Sea of Sand appeared to be as large as the area around Dragonmount, and probably more dangerous. Red eyed the salt suspiciously; after their confrontation with the worm, he didn't know what to expect. He wondered if a creature such as that one could live in a salt sea.

Over there. It's by the mountain.

Red glanced back at Kam, who was now shading his eyes with one hand and pointing with the other. As Red followed his gaze he saw that far over to heartside was a small hill which the man was referring to as a mountain.

A mountain? It was more like a large rock than even a hill. It was nowhere near the size of Dragonmount, or the mountains which radiated out from it.

Red was anxious to for them get on their way. He hadn't heard from the other voice, the one in his head, since its outburst. He hoped he wouldn't have to hear it again. Every time he heard it, he felt sure he was going wormcrazy. Maybe the madness was what he needed to break the binding spell on him. Then again, maybe it was the binding spell which was bringing on the madness.

With a start he realized Kam was staring up at him again, concern plainly written on his face. Red growled; a deep, bone-vibrating noise from deep in his gut and was rewarded to see the man step back a few paces. Yet Red obligingly stretched out his leg and caused his scales to bristle slightly, allowing the man a relatively easy climb up.

Ready? Red asked as sarcastically as he could.

Yes. Was the only answer Kam gave, and Red could tell the man still wasn't entirely used to the idea of being on him; but he also sensed he was a little relived that they weren't flying even though he seemed to be getting used to it. But there was something else. He could sense it; it created a tingling throughout his body and left a metallic taste in his mouth.

There is something different, something magical about you now. Red said.

He could sense Kam's confusion and wariness about the statement. Apprehension as if what the man felt was happening to him was somehow contagious, like a loathsome disease, which he had caught. He knew that the man was worried about the darkness he said he could sense. It frightened him.

How do you know? The man's question broke through his thoughts, bringing him out of his reverie.

I can taste it. Red responded.

Red could sense many half-formed questions rising to the surface of the man's thoughts, yet none formed into coherent communication for him to understand.

As if anyone can understand a man's thinking. The voice inside Red's head said in a much more subdued and quiet manner than before.

Although Red was still uncomfortable with the voice communicating with him, he had to agree that this was one time the voice was right. There was no understanding people. They had no honor in their lives or in their fighting.

However, this man did show courage in battle with the magical worm. Red told the voice. *And he risks his life for many he does not even know. He is an unusual man and I am starting to believe he may have a Dragonsoul in him.*

Red knew what he just said could be, no probably would be, taken as blasphemy in Dragonnation. But it was true dragons could sometimes be reborn in other bodies for either very great deeds or very bad ones.

But why would a Dragonsoul enter a man's body? No Dragon would choose to be a weak, pathetic man! The voice asked, starting to sound very unsteady.

Red couldn't answer that one; perhaps it was because the Dragonsoul was supposed to be a light for people; to help them to become better than they were and to be an example for them. For whatever reason, all Red could think about was whether or not the voice in his head was his own. If it was his own then he would have to say he was Dragonwylde. If it was someone or something else then perhaps Kam was right and there was a sentient darkness, a living entity of evil, inside of him. He wasn't sure which circumstance worried him more.

CHAPTER 17

As they rounded the hill Kam had pointed out, Red could see a ship about the length of his body sans his neck and head. But it was elegant and exquisite with its long, narrow lines and sharply pointed edges. The head of the boat had a dragon's head carved into it, making Red snort in contempt.

Above it floated two large cloth pouches side by side, which also had points at both their front and rear ends. And, rising above all else, were two extremely tall wooden spears which had cloth wrapped around them. Red wondered why the boat was so narrow. A wider boat could carry more of whatever they wanted to put in it.

Those spears are the masts and sails and the long, pointed aerostats are balloons to help keep it afloat, Kam answered. *The narrowness of the boat makes it lighter and requires less lift to hold it up. There is also less drag as it moves through the salt.*

Red said nothing. The overall look of the boat even without the masthead was dragon-like in appearance, to the point of making him wonder if a dragon possibly helped these people build the ship. However, he also had to wonder how he would be able to traverse these salt seas in it as it was obvious the ship was too narrow and had no room anywhere for him.

They also do cargo runs I've heard. Kam said. *They tow some kind of raft behind the ship across to the far side of the sea for trade in the various kingdoms.*

Now you're to be treated like so much extra weight, like a dragon carrying a breeding cow. The voice in Red's head said. *Just extra weight.*

Red snorted and turned his head to shoot a glance at the man. Kam didn't seem to notice the other voice in his head this time. With a small sigh of relief Red began to think the voice was indeed magical in nature, and not him going Dragonwylde.

Then tension mounted again as Red realized that this was another type of magic, another act of control by someone else exerting their will over him. The thought brought his companion to the surface once more.

You wish me to leave?

The voice was back, louder and stronger than it had been in a while. It was to the point where Red finally made the connection between his own emotions and the voice. But before he could respond the voice continued. *That will not happen. I am here because you need me. You need my guidance.*

Red closed his eyes and sighed. The passionate fury subsided a bit, and he felt calm again. The darkness, the power of his feelings and the despair of his life, seemed to melt away. At the same time he felt lighter, the feeling of having an immense weight lifted off of his back occurred again.

This time however the fervor and vitality of the voice, which he could now sense as being right at the edge of his consciousness, ebbed a bit. It was as if it acquired part of its strength, of its very existence, from his feelings of madness or rage. Or maybe it was a combination of both. He didn't like thinking he might be Dragonwylde, if even just a little bit.

He was curious as to why the man couldn't hear the voice, though. With their connection he should be hearing it as well, yet he seemed to have heard it just the one time, when it spoke in an exceptionally "loud" voice. This was all too much for him. He just wanted to live his life without anyone controlling him.

At this point they were very close to the town where the boat was docked. As they approached many of the townspeople started scurrying around like lizaerds when a dragon flew by. Some even went and got weapons thinking he was going to attack them.

Great, thought Red. *How am I going to get us out of this one.*

Great, thought Kam. *How am I going to get us out of this one.*

As the men and women ran around grabbing weapons and preparing for what they thought was an attack by a dragon, Kam sighed.

This isn't going to be easy. He thought to himself and Red.

Kam had Red stop and slid off. He then approached the town alone, slowly, so they could see he was looking to talk with someone. One man did come out to meet with him; a tall man with dark green hair and whose arms were bare nearly to his shoulders in the common loose fitting and light-colored shirt the men of the sea normally wore. His skin was nearly as dark as a cocoa bar. His eyes had the squinty look of a man who had been out in the bright sun far too often.

As the man approached him, Kam could see he was keeping a wary eye on Red, not that he blamed him. A dragon, any dragon, would be an impressive sight, especially when up close and walking towards you. The man stopped a few feet in front of Kam, but his full attention remained on Red.

"Is that your dragon?" The man asked cautiously.

Kam instantly felt red-hot indignation flow through the bond and he stifled the urge to laugh. He did notice however the consternation which now came to him didn't have the usual darkness attached to it. It was a bright, like standing in the summer sun at midday, something which Kam found quite preferable to the flaring darkness.

"Yes." Kam replied hesitatingly. "The dragon is…with me. We are looking for passage across the Sea of Sand. Both of us; my, er, the dragon can't…doesn't wish to fly."

The man seemed not to believe him at first, gripping his sword so tightly his hand became white knuckled and he flexed his muscles as if preparing to attack. Finally with a grunt of acceptance, he turned slowly and walked back to the buildings where he let out a series of loud whistles forming a tuneless song Kam didn't recognize.

After seeing the townspeople getting weapons and running to what had to be pre-assigned positions in defense of their town, Kam was relieved to see the towns people relax a little. They still gave Kam, and especially Red, looks of distrust and pure animosity. It was almost as if they felt Kam and Red had reaped destruction on them in a former time.

Kam, with Red trailing behind, approached the town slowly, following the captain. Everyone moved to the far sides of the surprisingly dusty road, giving them plenty of room to walk. Kam didn't need to be able to read their minds to know what they were thinking. He could understand the fear in people at the sight of the dragon, but hatred? One man came forward and spitefully spit on the ground at Kam's feet; but it was the look the man gave Red that made Kam wonder if the action was truly aimed at him. Either way he couldn't put up with it anymore.

"We have done you no harm," Kam said slowly before the man who had spat at their feet could turn and leave. "Why are you treating us this way? We simply want passage across the salt and are willing to pay for it."

The man stopped and, narrowing his eyes even further, looked at Kam suspiciously. Then through lips still damp from spittle said, "We have been attacked by dragons nearly every year. They come and take our livestock and kill many. We don't like dragons here and would kill you and yours now except for our captain forbidding it."

Red, with indignation clearly in his thoughts, said, *No Dragon has attacked any human since Dragonwars. This man is not telling the truth.*

Kam knew Red believed what he said, and he didn't think Red was lying. But there might be something else going on; maybe a small group of renegade dragons or a few ostracized ones living outside the boundaries of the normal dragon habitat. Whatever it was, these people were very apprehensive about allowing a dragon to walk among them within the confines of their town.

Kam looked around and noticed that most of the residents were heeding the words, or rather whistles, of the captain. But he also noticed the furtive glances from behind shuttered windows and arrow points protruding from around corners as they moved slowly down the street.

How could they possibly fight a dragon? Kam asked Red. *Their arrows wouldn't be able to penetrate your scales.*

I can sense their arrows are cursed with powerful magic, allowing them to hurt me. I also smell feebleworm, Red continued. Then as if sensing Kam's next question, continued, *Feebleworm, if given to a Dragon, can very quickly drive it wormcrazy. Some Dragons have even attacked other Dragons when they have the feebleworm in their blood. Eventually a Dragon will go completely Dragonwylde and will even die from it.*

Kam felt sick to his stomach at the thought of a worm inside of a dragon causing it to go crazy. It would be a horrible way to die. He wondered if those worms could affect humans the same way. That made his concern increase all the more.

In the middle of what seemed to be this town's main street there was a large, circular area cordoned off with small, sandstone-like blocks around it. In the center of that circle was an enormous skeleton in the shape of a large creature having an immense mouth full of large, sharp teeth, a huge fish-like tail which was horizontal instead of vertical and four massive legs each with four large toes on them. The skeleton vaguely reminded Kam of a sea creature he had heard of called a whale, but he knew enough to know they didn't have legs on them.

As they approached the edge of town by the sea near the large boat Kam had seen before, the captain turned abruptly and said, "This will cost much. Do ye have enough on you for the passage?" As the captain eyed Red he said, "Four gold pieces…for you and twenty for the dragon."

Kam slowly pulled out his purse and opened it. Although he was hoping to have flown all the way to the kingdom he still came prepared for what he thought was any contingency.

"That's quite a bit of money…" Kam started, knowing that bargaining was part of the fare agreement, but wanting to get it over as soon as possible. "But I think this should cover it." he finished.

With the last words Kam pulled out a green emerald the size and shape of a small egg. The captain's eyes opened wide as he realized what it was, then just as quickly they returned to their normal squinty look.

"How do I know it's real?" He asked, his breathless voice denoting he already suspected it was.

"Have it checked out in your town. There must be someone here who knows gems."

The captain slowly took the emerald from Kam, his hands shaking as he reached for it. Carrying it as gingerly as he would a real egg, he went back down the road and stopped in front of a particularly dilapidated structure. He paused, again looking at the stone in his hand before disappearing into the building.

Kam took the opportunity to get a good look around. He could now see there were many boats of varying sizes and shapes moored to docks, some of which looked makeshift and very rickety in nature. He could also see that the largest boat was the one he had first noticed and it dwarfed most of the other boats.

As he turned to look out over the fine salt which comprised the sea, he noticed many small boats near the shore being paddled by their occupants with very strange looking paddles. These paddles had some type of broad attachment midway up the long handle and seemed to help propel the boats quickly through the salt. Some of the boats had individual occupants while others carried two people, but they all seemed to be fishing; although for what Kam couldn't imagine.

After a moment the captain reappeared with a large smile on his face, a smile Kam wasn't all too fond of.

"When do you want to leave?"

"Now, if we can." Kam replied.

With his smile growing even wider, probably at the thought of getting rid of the dragon all that much sooner Kam mused, the captain let out a series of sharp whistles. Kam was amazed that anyone could whistle that loudly and the sound echoed in his ears for a minute after the captain had stopped.

Men came running at the whistles, most of whom quickly swarmed over the ship, while the rest went to retrieve a large raft of some kind. As Kam watched the raft was affixed by long ropes to the stern of the ship. Kam felt unsettled as he watched, knowing the feeling was emanating from Red. He could sense Red would rather fly than cross the salt on what he considered was a small piece of wood.

"How did you know this area is salt? Most of you awayers think it's sand." The captain's question broke through Kam's viewing of the ship and its preparations. He turned to face the captain.

"My, er, the dragon knew. He is very intelligent and quick to notice things." Kam wasn't sure why he added on the last part, but he sensed confusion and a certain amount of pride coming through the bond with it.

The captain looked over at Red with a certain amount of respect.

"Does your dragon need something soft to make him comfortable?" The captain asked gravely.

Kam glanced over at Red, who was staring at the raft as if it would sink the moment he laid his body on it. Through their bond Kam sensed Red wouldn't need anything, but the dragon was still hesitant about floating across.

"Are you sure it will support his weight? He is, uh, much heavier than he looks." Kam finished sheepishly.

The captain looked at him as if he pronounced the sun would rise at sunrise the next day; then he continued on as if Kam hadn't said anything.

"He should be comfortable enough. There are blankets we can spread to make sure he doesn't get any splinters." The last word was said with a slight cough, which Kam was sure was done to hide a brief laugh.

As Red registered what the captain said from Kam's thoughts, he turned his large red eyes towards Kam and said, *Dragons don't get splinters.*

"We were planning on leaving tomorrow," the captain began, "because we have a schedule to keep. We dock at various towns around the sea on different days for the people to trade. But with your extra cargo…" And with that the captain cast his eyes towards Red. Kam was hoping the voyage would only be a day, as that was what he had heard. But with the captain insinuating on an extra long voyage, Kam began to wonder.

With the boat loaded and the captain content with the preparations that had been made, Kam was allowed to board. Red gingerly boarded the raft. He had to avoid the ropes which were fastened to both sides of the raft and tied to balloons of their own.

The captain gave a penetrating whistle which signaled someone on shore. Kam wasn't sure what the whistle was for until the raft suddenly started to wobble and he knew the support logs beneath it had somehow been removed. As they moved slowly forward the raft rocked back and forth for a minute and for a moment Kam thought it might flip over; but it leveled off and Red settled down as best he could.

They eased away from the dock and traveled slowly at first until the sales high above the balloons were unfurled. Kam was amazed to see that on the deck of the boat there was very little airflow, yet the sail just above the balloons were straining at their lines like a racing horse about to be let loose. The boat, despite the obvious weight it was pulling, moved along at a fairly brisk pace.

As Kam looked around to see what each of the crewmen was doing, he noticed all of them had scarves tied around their heads and mouths to the point of leaving only a slit for the eyes to see through. Covering the slits was a type of goggle Kam had never seen before. He gave the captain a puzzled look.

"Sometimes the wind picks up and you can get salt in your face." The captain said while handing over a pair of old, faded blue and red scarves and a pair of well-used goggles to Kam. "These will help."

Although not wanting to seem unappreciative, Kam nevertheless put them in his pocket for the moment. He really wasn't in the mood for wrapping himself up.

"You might as well settle in." The captain said. "We won't be arriving at your destination until the morn. And have your dragon relax too; we wouldn't want him to upset the raft now, would we."

As Kam looked at the captain, he noticed movement behind him and tried to focus on what it was. It appeared to be a miniature island, only it was moving, and keeping pace with the boat.

"What is that?" Kam asked, pointing to the island.

"It's a whale, and a big one at that." As the captain squinted, he suddenly exclaimed, "That's ol' Berthla. She's the Queen of the sea. She's been around here longer than anyone around. See that white streak down the side? Some friends of ours got it in their heads that if they caught her she would grant them any wish they wanted."

With that last statement the captain roared as if someone had just told him a joke that no one else seemed to get, which in Kam's case was exactly that.

"Why would they think if they hunted her, they would get their wish granted?" Kam asked.

"Well, I suppose someone told them." The captain replied with a malicious gleam in his eye. "Thing is, now we don't have any more competition from them. I guess it was a win-win situation; for us anyway." And with that the captain broke out laughing again.

Kam could sense Red had noticed the whale as well and he felt a combination of interest and what could only be described as bloodlust. He was amazed at the simple brutality of the dragon and how everything revolved around his ability to fight. Yet he knew from the pieces he glimpsed from Red's darkest thoughts that there was more to his life than just fighting. There was some sort of community that existed among his kind and that there were other qualities of life enjoyed by dragons.

Kam paused and tried to sense what he had come to think of as the pit-that pitch black part of Red's emotional state which seemed to lead him around the way a large, strong bulbear can be led around by a ring in its nose. He tried to reach out with his mind and sense it, but it was difficult now as the darkness seemed to have receded farther into Red's innermost consciousness. It also lost strength to the point where it was a mere wisp of its former self.

While they sailed Kam paid a lot of attention to the salt surrounding the boat. It behaved much like any large body of water; it had an ebb and flow and moved as if currents were raging beneath its surface. It reminded him of the way Red's darkness swirled within him.

Large, immovable chunks of an opaque substance were scattered across the sea like so many crumbs. The salt was thrown against these rock-like substances in much the same way water crashed against the seashore. Even so, he noticed areas which seemed perfectly frozen in time, as if a painter had captured that very moment to memorialize for all eternity.

As Kam was staring out across the saline seascape, the captain must have noticed and came alongside him and said, "Those rocks of salt are all over this sea. A good sailor knows where they are."

"How did the salt form into the big chunks?"

"No one knows for sure, but it's hard as rock. It's like the salt just melted together into giant lumps."

As evening descended Kam took one final look at Red before bedding down. Red was asleep and his slow, heavy, rhythmic breathing threatened to lull Kam to sleep as well. Just then the captain came up behind him and asked, "Your dragon asleep?"

"Yes. He'll probably sleep until we arrive."

"'He?' Don't you mean it?" The captain responded with what sounded like incredulity.

Kam paused; he hadn't thought about how he referred to Red. Before being bonded He thought dragons were animals; no, below animals. Creatures of pure destruction giving no other thought to life other than what they knew to do instinctually. But Red had taught him differently.

Dragons were highly intelligent and came from a society similar in many regards to people. They had familial structure which enabled parents to teach their young about the norms of their society. But most of all they made choices about their actions, something which went far beyond mere instinct.

Then there was the bonding. All the animals he knew could be trained to listen to people. But dragons were different. Red wanted his freedom, however unhappy he was with it. He wanted to live his life the way he wanted, not bound to someone else's will. As unhappy as Red was, his freedom made it all worth it. That was something Kam could not only understand, but also appreciate.

As Kam started to reply to the captain he looked around and saw he was alone. The captain had apparently not expected an answer to a question he understood to be a given. Wearily Kam walked slowly to his room, which was little more than a bench in a closet, to sleep. As he crawled atop the hard wooden bench, he fell asleep worrying about Red and his injured wing.

CHAPTER 18

The violent swaying of the ship should have woken Kam, but it didn't. It was the short fall onto the floorboards, causing him to dream of falling off of Red's back midflight. For a moment he was confused as to where he was, and the loud whistling which saturated the air all around him didn't help. He felt as if he were living at the top of a high mountain while a gale swirled around him. The noise was deafening.

Quickly he ran up the stairs and burst out onto the deck into what he assumed would be the bright dawn of morning. Instead, he was surrounded by twilight. As he peered to where the sun should have been he saw…nothing. A large dark cloud comprised of millions of flying insects was blocking it. The swarm looked to be getting closer to the ship, as if heralding a danger which it felt the deafening whistle of wind wasn't communicating strongly enough.

Men on the boat were scurrying around like so many rats, tying down anything which might fly away. The wind was pushing at his eyes so strongly he closed them for a minute and instantly regretted it. He found it nearly impossible to open them again in the face of the savagely strong winds which were applying so much pressure to his eyelids it felt as if they were glued shut.

He finally managed to open his eyes a crack, just enough to witness a crewman shove a folded-up piece of cloth into his hands. It was only then Kam noticed that he, and every other member of the crew, was wearing the cloth and goggles over their faces and looked for all intents and purposes as thieves bent on robbing each other.

The swarm was definitely closer now. But their flight seemed to be erratic, swirling around in circles with no apparent purpose or destination in mind. Kam had seen men so drunk they could barely stand or move in a coherent manner. Then it hit him-they were not insects but rather salt from the sea tossed into the air like so much foam off of the top of a mug of ale. It was a saltstorm.

Just as the churning maelstrom of salt hit the ship, he shut his eyes as tightly as he could. But somehow the salt wormed its way between his eyelids and into his eyes, causing a searing pain like nothing he had ever felt before. He opened his mouth in agony and instantly the salt invaded his body. As if that weren't enough, every inch of his skin caught fire with the stinging pain of a thousand angry fire-ants attacking him as the salt bit deep into his flesh.

However, compared with what he felt next that was nothing. With the salt assaulting his mouth and throat he felt water flow out of him. First his mouth, then his throat and on down instantly dried up and lost all of its moisture. The pain of the salt hitting his eyes and skin couldn't compare to the uncomprehendingly painful effect of having every bit of moisture leave his body. He felt that in another minute he would be nothing but a fleshless, bleached skeleton like those he found in the desert.

A cool darkness abruptly sheathed him in a soothing cocoon of nothingness. Somehow, he was insulated against the saltstorm. Yet even though the salt had stopped pelting him with its insidious desire to rob him of all feeling except pain, the residual burning from his previous flogging still haunted his body. And the wind had died down to a faint wisp of its former self.

When he opened his eyes, he saw that Red had placed himself between him and the stormy upheaval which still tossed the ship like a paper boat on a choppy lake. Red was doing his best to straddle the relatively narrow boat with his front legs while keeping his rear legs firmly on the raft. Kam could feel through the bond his balancing act by continually shifting his weight to avoid helping the tempest to capsize the boat.

Then, as quickly as the riotous onslaught of salt and wind enveloped them, it ended. Kam turned towards the stern and saw the haze of salt move on. This time however the tiny brackish crystals glinted playfully, even joyously, as though pleased they had moved on from the ship infested with men. The sparkling star-like crystals cascaded over each other like a thousand tiny fireflies dancing in the now clear light given off by the great ball of fire in the sky.

Red maneuvered gingerly back to his raft, being careful to neither step on any of the crewmen nor to cause the boat to tilt too far to one side. Kam watched as the crewmen went about and checked the boat for any damage with a well-practiced ease. They scoured the riggings, railings and especially the lines holding the sacks of air for even the slightest wear and tear. To Kam's surprise they looked like they found none.

The storm's passing seemed to have taken the wind with it. The day became calm and peaceful, with the boat not making much headway in the sea. The crewmen cast long looks at Red as though he was somehow responsible for both the previous squall and their current lack of propulsion. He knew through their shared link that Red sensed the rising animosity towards him as well.

The rest of the day was a slow and monotonous. Kam found himself surprisingly exhausted at the end of it and was grateful to lay down for the evening.

The sun hadn't yet lifted past the horizon when Kam awoke to the sounds of heavy footfalls above him. He knew the location of his closet was at the stern of the boat just below the top deck, and he couldn't understand why there was so much going on above him. Kam quickly jumped out of bed grabbed his sword and went topside to see what the commotion was about. He was surprised to find five of the crew along with the captain diligently trying to cut the ropes connecting the raft with Red to the boat.

Kam smoothly pulled out his sword and asked, "What are you doing?"

All six of them turned as one to look at Kam, arms still outstretched and knives still poised above the ropes, some of which had already been partially cut through. The men looked sheepishly at each other then focused their attention on the captain.

The captain simply pulled out a sword of his own from a scabbard which seemed to be hidden in the folds of his baggy pants. The other men followed suit, instantly dropping their knives and pulling out their own swords from the scabbards strapped to their backs. Kam stood facing the armed group, one sword against six.

With a guttural growl Kam leaped forward, his sword creating a swath of blood and limbs as he cut through two of the crew members with one stroke. Three of the other men surrounded Kam as best they could on the small upper deck now slippery with blood. Only the captain continued to hack at the ropes holding the raft to the boat.

Kam took out another of the crew with a vicious slash to the neck after a quick feint to the stomach. The headless body toppled over sideways as if in slow motion while the remaining two crew members positioned themselves between Kam and the captain.

As Kam readied himself to fight the remaining two crewmen, he heard the sharp sound of a rope giving way followed by two more in quick succession. Knowing he didn't have much time, he tried to communicate with Red through the bond, but felt as though the dragon was in an unnaturally deep sleep.. He tried yelling but nothing seemed to be able to wake Red.

Just then arms came out of nowhere from behind him and pinned him to the deck. His sword was ripped out of his hands and tossed to one side. Then as he tried to fight off the crew who were swarming over him like ants, Kam suddenly had his mind opened up, as if a heavy fog had suddenly been blown away by a stiff wind.

Red was now at least partially conscious and very angry. With a deafening roar Kam felt rather than saw the fire which spewed out of Red's mouth and engulf many of the crew around him who were unlucky enough to be standing up and not pinning him down. One in particular had the top half of his body ending up like a mallow which had become blackened and shriveled up from being left over a fire too long.

The others of the crew practically flew off of Kam in a desperate bid at escape; but Red wouldn't have it. Amazed, Kam watched as Red, standing up on all fours, pinpointed little spits of flame and took out the crew one by one. He didn't know Red could be such an accurate shot with his fire.

As Kam grabbed his sword which had been left to one side out of his reach, he glanced around the top deck of the ship. He saw the captain hunched down behind the rear gunwale, afraid to stand for fear of becoming charcoal. But he was still signaling his crewmen with sharp, loud whistles. Most of the crew which came up onto the top deck had bows and arrows to fire at Red. Just as the arrows were loosed Kam mentally yelled to Red to be careful.

Opening his mouth as wide as it would go, Red created a broad barrier of flame which torched the arrows before they could reach him. Even so, Red instinctively slid further back towards the rear of the raft, keeping the arrows as far from him as possible. The dragon's weight forced the back end of the raft deeper into the salt while causing the front end to lift up.

The wooden arrow shafts burned up before getting anywhere near Red, but the metal arrowheads were still propelled forward towards their target. Fortunately, the raft had lifted up enough in the front that the arrowheads all struck the bottom of the raft. Unfortunately, Red lost his footing and slid into the salt.

As Red floundered for footing in the salt sea his tail flailed around and struck the boat mid-deck, smashing a large hole in its side. As Kam watched, the fine salt poured into the boat like water, causing the boat to list dangerously to one side and sink lower into the fine brackish grains. Kam, along with the captain and crew who were topside, started sliding down across the deck towards the smooth granules as well.

Kam wondered what it would be like to drown in salt. Knowing he had a better chance than Red of staying afloat in the salt said, *Red! Try to get to one of the islands of salt. they are stable and hard like rock!*

He wasn't sure if Red cold hear him or not, but he quickly slid down the ship and into the salt. There he floundered around trying to stay afloat. As the boat listed dangerously to starboard, Kam could see it was only the buoyancy created by the balloons which was actually keeping the boat above the surface at all.

Almost as if reading his thoughts, which Kam realized was probably the case, Red shot flame up towards one of the balloons. As the fire hit the outer skin of the balloon nothing seemed to happen. The skin was strong enough to withstand the fire for a few seconds, then abruptly the balloon exploded in a large fireball.

The force of the explosion caused a secondary one as the second balloon also detonated. The force of the near simultaneous explosions toppled the masts as if they were matchsticks and drove the boat down into the salt before it broke in half at the spot where Red's tail had hit it.

As Kam struggled to stay afloat, he was surprised to see Red floating effortlessly on the salt. *How can you do that? How can you maintain enough buoyancy to stay afloat?*

I have raised my scales and spread my wings to help me to stay above the salt. Red replied.

Kam wasn't sure what Red meant by having his scales raised. He remembered seeing Red's scales hackled the same way a dog's fur will raise on the back of its neck when it is angry or ready for a fight. He wondered if dragons could raise all of their scales and put that thought aside for later. He was more concerned about Red's wings being outstretched-especially the injured one.

Red understood Kam's concern and replied that he felt no pain, which meant the rubbergum dressing was holding and not letting any salt into the open wound. Kam was still worried about the pressure being put on the wing joint even as Red also readily admitted his wing was not close to being able to be used for flying.

Kam looked around and saw that some of the crew had found their way into a few of the lifeboats which had been tethered to the side of the boat along both sides. He saw a large section of wood which had somehow survived the destruction of the ship floating nearby. He splashed over and quickly clambered on.

One of the oddly shaped oars had also managed to survive and floated nearby, although its mate was nowhere to be seen. He grabbed it, again noticing it had a flat end like a traditional water-based paddle would and a downward facing shield partway up the shaft. He soon realized the shield was designed to keep the fine salt from flying into the boat and eyes of its user.

How do you feel? Kam asked Red as he neared him.

I am fine but there are many large rocks moving around in the salt sea. He said. *But I am getting a sense of life from some of them…*

Kam paddled over to a large salt rock extending out of the water. It appeared to be the size of a small island with more than enough room for Red. He wasn't sure how the salt formation, large as it was, would take to having Red's weight on it. Would it roll over or sink into the sea? He had no idea.

Come up on this rock, Kam thought to Red. *You can rest up here. Just be careful climbing up.*

Red came over and slowly and started climbing up on the protrusion. Kam, trying to prepare himself for any contingency, grasped his makeshift raft tightly and held his breath. The little island, however, didn't move at all. Puzzled, he began to wonder if some of the salt islands were in fact columns reaching all the way down to the bottom of the salt sea, however deep that was.

As Red climbed up the island, Kam followed as best he could while pulling the little raft behind him. As he breached the top of the small hill next to Red, he let out a gasp. There appeared to be many such islands of salt which they would have sailed past had the boat survived a little longer. Some of the islands were huge, and resting on many of them were large creatures, mostly whales, many of which dwarfed even Red.

The whales were large in the front with a mouth that split their heads. The head became part of the body with no discernible neck delineating the two parts. The body tapered somewhat at the tail which had a flat, horizontal end used for propulsion. Yet the creatures also had squat, thick, powerful looking legs with which they could climb onto the large islands of salt. At this point the creatures seemed to be sunning themselves. At that moment Kam realized he was sensing puzzlement from Red.

What's the matter?

I…I sense dragons. Those…things are giving off a sensation like I would feel if I was near dragons. The sensation is not strong; but still, it is there.

Kam wondered at why the dragon could sense these creatures, which appeared to have no discernible similarity to dragons at all, and not sense the small flying creatures in the city of rock which appeared to simply be baby dragons.

I don't know, Red said, puzzlement still clearly in his mind as if he too had been wondering the same thing.

Kam walked around their small island, which at times seemed hard as granite while at others had sections give way and crumble beneath his feet like sandstone. The latter caused him to slip and gave him small scrapes. The scrapes of their own were of no consequence; however, the exposed under layer of his skin coupled with the salt being rubbed deeply into it caused Kam to yelp with the painful burning and Red to snort with mirth at the same time.

The pinnacle of the island was a tall, narrow peak which looked like a chimney. After Kam scaled it with a surprisingly arduous climb, he stood and took stock of their location. From this island they were not more than what he figured to be a mile from the shore on the other side of the sea.

From that height he could also see other islands, most of which were as barren as the one he was on. There were some islands that were covered in a type of low-growing, pale-colored lichen, which at times seemed to develop the courage to actually sprout small, slim twigs and leaves. The mainland however had trees and grass growing almost to the salt's edge.

Do you think you can swim? Kam asked Red.

Red gazed at Kam, then raising his long neck he looked over to the mainland.

Yes. I can take us there.

Kam slid down from the pinnacle smoothly. He then climbed up Red's back and they set out across the remaining stretch of sea. They had just barely started out when a loud commotion behind them caused them both to turn their heads. One of the large sea creatures seemed to be attacking one of the few dinghies which had survived the sinking of the ship. The men were yelling and gesturing at it wildly, as if the creature would cease to attack the boat by merely knowing of the presence of men on board.

One of the men had an unusual looking spear which he hurled at the creature. The strength with which he hurled it made Kam think it would go right through a person, but it merely bounced off the creature's tough hide and slid into the salt.

Then, with a quickness which belied its great bulk, the creature turned its head, opened it cavernous mouth and took a massive bite out of the little boat, leaving only shattered pieces of wood. Kam could sense Red was impressed with this creature and felt his bloodlust start to boil inside of him.

From being with Red Kam knew dragons loved to hunt and kill; it was their nature. But with the size of these creatures coupled with Red's injury he felt Red would have a hard time taking on one of these behemoths. Fortunately, Red agreed, although more for the reason of his injury than the size of the creatures.

Swimming dog style it didn't take him long to get to the other side. When they arrived at the beach, it was hard for Kam to notice where the salt ended and the sand began, so smooth was the blending of color between the bright salt and the smooth, white sand.

As with one mind, they both start looking around for food and soon found some wild game nearby. After a few hours, and with the smell of both raw and cooked meat hanging heavy in the air. They relaxed for a little while under one of the immense trees that seemed to follow the shoreline.

As they lay there, a poem his father had told him when he was very young came back to him. His father said it was written by an honorable warrior who had lived millennia ago.

We live in deeds, not months and years
We should not count time by heartbeats
He most lives who thinks most,
Feels the noblest and acts the best.
Kam heard a snort and knew Red had been listening.
What do you think? Kam asked Red.
It sounds like the typical tripe a person would make up. He replied.

But…but doesn't it make sense? I mean, think about it for a minute. Which is more important: the length of our life or how we live it, what we accomplish?

Red didn't respond directly, but Kam could hear his thoughts as if they were his own. He felt as if his head was spinning like a tornado. Different thoughts, judgments, feelings, and even biases, were being thrown around. Ideas were being accepted, discarded and then accepted again quickly. Red was thinking faster than Kam had ever assumed he could.

Kam understood what was going on; he had times where thoughts seemed to come and go quickly. His mind could look at many things simultaneously while quickly sifting through a myriad of ideas trying to grasp a situation. He again thought about how similar dragons were to people.

As Kam listened to Red's thoughts, he realized not only did Red now seem to have less of the thick, debilitating darkness in him, but he also found an incredible intelligence emerging. Or was it just that he was only now noticing?

Chapter 19

They decided to walk down the shoreline to try and find a road which would allow Red more room to walk between the barrier of gigantic trees leading inland. As Red's shoulder was still injured, they knew walking was their only recourse. As they walked Kam couldn't help finding the humor in the fact that the salt still washed up on the sandy shore in much the same way water did.

The trees form an effective barrier against the large creatures which inhabit this area. Red commented.

Kam said nothing but he glanced up at the towering vegetation and nearly stumbled. The tree trunks were massive; but more than that they were growing extremely close together. They also paralleled the shoreline to the extent Kam knew they had to have been grown there on purpose.

The limbs of the trees, some nearly as massive as the trunks, were so intertwined that it was impossible for Kam to say where one branch started and another ended. He tried looking between the trees to see how far back they extended and saw more trees close behind those in front, limiting their view. The dark shadows caused by the dense canopy blocking out the sun didn't make things any easier. The proverb about being unable to the forest for the trees came to mind. The tree line formed a tall, thick wall that would be impossible for any creature larger than a person to breach.

Kam frowned, uncertain of what they should do next. He continued to ponder their destination-the kingdom of Austine-and knew they had to get there as quickly as possible. He wasn't sure when the evil of war would invade that area, but he knew they needed to be ready. The prince, who was a good friend of his, understood the severity of the danger as well as Kam and was willing to do something about it.

They had walked for some time and still had not seen an opening. Kam was getting worried wondering just how far the tree line extended.

Is it possible to fly for even just a short distance? Kam asked. *The creatures which live in the sea are large and can't fly, so maybe the trees don't go in far...*

Red stopped walking and swung his long neck around so as to face Kam.

My shoulder is badly injured and I cannot fly. If you are willing to go into the forest and see how far it extends then we would have some idea how far I would need to travel.

Kam could sense Red's idea-to burn a path through the trees. He turned inland and entered the woods. He was instantly shrouded in an oppressive semi-darkness as the huge trees blocked out much of the sun. Given the closeness of the massive pillars of wood, Kam quickly felt claustrophobic. He forced himself to remain focused and scanned his surroundings with the practiced eye of one who had learned a painful lesson from not having done so before. He soon realized that it would be impossible to find anyone hiding in these woods if they didn't want to be found.

Red could even hide behind some of these trees. Kam thought to himself.

He continued to look, scanning up into the higher branches as well, realizing a house could be built high enough in the trees where arrows from a bow wouldn't reach it. With the foliage being as dense as it was it would even be possible for a person to miss the house altogether.

He continued to walk deeper into the woods. Suddenly he was startled by an overwhelming silence which permeated the air. There wasn't even the chirp or wing flap of a bird or the soft buzz of an insect to show there was any other life besides himself. For a brief, frightening moment Kam was overwhelmed by the feeling of being inside a coffin.

That sounds refreshing. Red interrupted, seeming so loud that Kam jumped.

You are just used to being alone, my friend. Kam said, finally grasping exactly what kind of life Red had been leading. He also caught the shock from Red at his use of the term friend.

You understand nothing. Red suddenly interjected. *You cannot understand what has occurred in my life or what has been done to me.*

As quick as that Kam sensed the burning darkness was back, stronger if that were possible. It burst forth, causing a headache so painful that Kam dropped to the ground in agony, feeling as though he had been dipped in boiling ice. The pain was so great it that if it wasn't for the waves of nausea anchoring him to his body, he thought he would have died. Even so, he found he couldn't think or speak. His vision blurred and the pain caused a loud and distinct ringing in his ears which seemed to last forever.

STOP! Was all he could manage to Red.

Through a thick, foggy haze that seemed to envelope him he thought he heard Red say something. It was at that point where the pain abated enough for him to comprehend what Red was thinking.

What's the matter? Red asked. *What do you want me to stop doing?*

That pain, Kam gasped. *Didn't you feel it? Where did it come from?*

Kam sensed a bewilderedness emanating from Red; a confusion which was both sincere and unsettling. As Kam lay on the ground, the pain washing over him gradually drained away. After some time passed, he finally felt he could sit up.

Red mentally regarded him with what he could sense was a mixture of anger, incomprehension and a little...*concern*? The latter surprised Kam so much he questioned himself as to why the dragon would have concern for him.

I don't. Came the response.

Kam sat there, slowly allowing himself to feel normal again. He realized the intense emotion and pain he felt was what Red probably felt all the time. He wasn't sure why the full impact hit him now or why he didn't feel it before. He guessed it had something to do with Red being a dragon in the first place. He got up and walked back in silence to where he had left Red.

Why are you filled with so much hate and anger? Kam asked.

Red just looked at him, giving Kam no sense of his having understood what he had just asked. Kam asked again, trying to enunciate his thoughts more clearly, if that were possible. This time the flood gates opened and a torrent of thoughts, feelings and images crashed into his mind with such emotional force he almost blacked out. He had to force himself to stay conscious and focus on what was in his head.

There were two dragons fighting, with Kam watching from the perspective of one of them-Red. The other was a much larger dragon who was obviously the leader. It was a fierce and lengthy struggle with the two fighting for supremacy. They grappled in the air; wings flapping quickly as much to keep them from being torn to shreds by the other's claws as to keep them skyborne.

But the leader of the dragons made a mistake and his wing was injured by a fierce slash. The wound to the wing Kam/Red saw to be not very serious, although it made it difficult for him to fly. He landed and cried out his challenge for a later time when his wing was healed. Kam knew through their bond that when dragons fight a challenge for leadership, if one is kept from flying the contest is postponed until both dragons may fight in the air again. Kam/Red thought the leader was looking for a way to end the fight, at least for now, as the injury meant his loss/death.

But the leader didn't stop there. Hearing the insults the larger dragon hurled allowed Kam to understand what Red had suffered through his entire life. Being one of the smaller dragons meant Red would always serve the larger dragons in some servile capacity. Kam had never seen a society which social standing was set, at least in part, by a person's size.

But Red's pride would not allow him that; he attacked the larger dragon on the ground. The fight continued with Kam/Red clawing and biting in a frenzy that took Kam's breath away. When they were done there weren't any pieces left of the other dragon larger than the size of a horse.

In that moment Kam understood Red's shame. He saw Red's parents turn away from him, tails between their legs. Other dragons, also shamed by what they saw, turned away with lowered tails between their legs. All of the dragons turned away from Red because of his actions.

Then another dragon, one a beautiful golden color that reminded Kam of the golden sunrises on the coast during the only family trip where his father had been present, continued to look at him. She also turned, more slowly than the other dragons had, but still continued to watch Red. Kam felt hot, seething shame twist in his gut and knew that she had been special to Red.

As the images spun in his head, he felt a volley of emotions hit him with the power of a fighter's punch. He knew Red was ostracized from the dragon community and finally understood how the shame had turned into the fury which now survived like a living thing inside of Red. He knew the greatest pain Red felt was the pain he caused the golden female because he had loved her deeply. And the anger that was caused by both the shame he had brought on her and her refusal to stand by his side throughout his ordeal.

Then it returned with a vengeance; the searing hot anguish as if someone had taken a freshly-made sword, still hot from the furnace, and plunged it straight into Kam's head. This time however the darkness followed into Kam as well; twisting and writhing like a serpent in his skull trying to escape from a trap. The sensation, although within Kam's head, was almost physical in its brutal tactility.

With a low moan Kam felt the scalding, oozing tar-like essence leave his consciousness and flow back into Red. What it left behind was not unlike a burning infection which felt as if it had left puss filled blisters in his brain. It was all he could do to empty his water skin over his head before the cool darkness of oblivion swallowed him.

Now do you understand? Red asked, sounding very drained and tired.

Kam came to with a start, not knowing how long he had lain there. He looked around, still trying to overcome the disorientation from the onslaught of thoughts which had caught him off guard. But since Red had allowed him to see and experience his life, he felt he needed to clarify what had gone on.

You felt it necessary to fight the, uh, head dragon after he landed? Kam asked.

Yes. The life of a small dragon in Dragonnation is not a pleasant one. Also, I let his taunts get me angry and I lost control. But I also wanted to win and both of us knew I would have eventually. He was afraid of me and he wanted to put off fighting me for as long as possible. And I wanted to show I was as good as any other dragon, large or small.

Kam thought about this for a moment. It was a sentiment he could understand, even agree with. Being regulated to menial tasks serving others simply because you were smaller than someone else didn't sit well with him. Then another question started to come to him but he quickly thought about something else, hoping Red hadn't heard what he wanted to ask.

What is it? What is the question you want to ask? Red seemed resigned to get everything out in the open at this point.

*Well I…*Kam paused. Not sure how to proceed. *If I understand your culture correctly, when a dragon turns away from another dragon and puts their tail between their legs it means they are shamed by the action of another dragon, right? And you felt that about your father and mother?*

Yes.

And you felt that way about your ah, girlfriend too, right?

My what?

The female dragon you like. Kam responded, in a way he hoped was understandable.

When Red didn't respond he continued. *But your girl dragon friend, she was upset but she didn't show that you had shamed her, but you felt she did. Why did you feel that way?*

Red stared at him for a long while and Kam felt him puzzling out things in his head. *She had her tail between her legs. She didn't accept me!*

Kam knew Red felt that way and he also knew he felt betrayed. But he thought maybe Red's emotions were getting the better of him and affecting how he saw the facts.

Look into my mind and watch what you showed me. Kam said. *I saw your memories and felt your feelings, and I think one is affecting the other.*

As he felt Red's mind enter his mind in a way he had not felt before, less like an intrusion and more like someone standing next to him trying to see what he was looking at. Kam relaxed and let his memories of what Red had just shown him come through.

He felt the paralyzing shock of Red's emotions when his girlfriend turned away, clearly not happy at what had happened. But he also felt Red mentally jump when he saw that she did not put her tail between her legs. In fact, she held it straight up, making Kam think she was making it easy for others to notice she was not showing the life-shattering condemnation the others had shown Red.

The change in Red's demeanor was instantaneous. The darkness dissipated abruptly at the sheer joy Red now felt. Kam sensed he was bonded to a completely different dragon, one whose outlook had not been marred by a traumatic mistake made in his life. However, the absence of the searing, oppressive weight of the darkness was brief and Kam again felt its presence, watching and waiting for the right moment to manifest itself again.

Not wanting to dwell on the evil he felt not only in Red but which had entered his own head, however briefly, Kam tried to change the subject to one of a more positive note.

Your girl dragon friend, the one you like, her name is Gold?

Yes.

But in your memories of home, I saw other dragons which were the same color. Do you call all dragons by their color?

Dragonmount is not my home anymore! Red responded, anger flowing through the bond easily. Then, softening a bit he continued. *Yes, but Dragons communicate in much the same way you and I do; using thoughts. The images we have when we talk about a certain Dragon lets the others know who we mean. When we do say the name of a Dragon based on their color, we say it a little differently for each Dragon, even though it is the same word for you.*

Although Kam could easily grasp Red's explanation through the bond, he wasn't sure people could understand the same concept explained by him verbally. He could appreciate that vocalized dragon was guttural and to a human ear might sound like just so much growling.

From Red he perceived that dragons could differentiate between hundreds of slight variations in color, creating just as many variations for a single word. Yet each dragon could perceive that word as it was meant, without any misunderstanding.

That meant where several dragons of a specific color, such as red, were together, dragons would be able to differentiate them by the variations in their individual shading of red.

Kam tried to think of as many words for the color red as he could-crimson, scarlet, ruby, burgundy, cherry and blood. Then there were the overtones of other colors which would add to that list such as maroon, pink and orange.

Kam shook his head. Dragons could see and describe the color red with a nearly infinite amount of words based solely on the color. And since no dragon apparently had the exact same shade of color, their shading became their name. It was a lot to take in.

I have one more question, Kam began.

You want to know why I never used my Dragonmagic when we were fighting in the air.

Yes.

Dragons cannot use Dragonmagic against each other when fighting over a challenge for leadership. The only time we would it is against anther dragon we feel is our enemy, and that has only happened one time in the history of Dragons-during the Dragonwar.

Kam sighed. He never realized just how complex the culture of dragons was. More and more he realized dragons were not that dissimilar to people. An observation he would never have made before meeting Red.

When they finally got up Kam noticed how tired and drained he felt, but he knew instinctively it wasn't his own body he was sensing but rather that of Red's. The throb in his shoulder returned with a vengeance and his stomach felt as if it was gnawing on itself from hunger.

As he watched Red advance to the nearest tree and push against it with his tail, he was surprised to see the tree doesn't even shake at all. Red then turned to use his body to push against it. However, the outcome was the same; the thick tree didn't even sway an inch. Even the branches seemed impervious to Red, mocking him by bending back in half instead of breaking.

As Red's emotions advanced from irritation to outright anger at the tree, he used his full weight and strength to alternately push and pull on the tree. In spite of the immense pressure Kam knew was being exerted on it, the tree barely quivered and lost only a few leaves.

Even with a constant stream of flame shooting from Red's mouth, the heat of which Kam could feel despite standing back many yards, seemed to have no effect on the great arboreta. These trees were somehow immune to fire.

After a few moments of effort Red turned with a confused look and an incomprehensible amalgam of emotions. Kam could sense many conflicting feelings but no darkness. It was almost as if the darkness within Red went into hiding, afraid of its inability to help Red in this situation. Yet raw, unblemished rage did come through strongly and he wondered how Red could be angry and not have the darkness follow.

Kam backed away even further as Red took a step back and used his magic. The bright green fire hit the tree and surrounded it with radiant emerald flames, giving the effect of gems shooting out of the tree. The effect was not what either Kam or Red expected. Instead of razing the tree it caused it to wither. The tree slowly parted down the middle with both halves sagging to the ground. Red continued to spray all of the trees in front of them with his beautiful green heat, moving slowly forward as the trees bowed in obeisantly before his blistering onslaught.

After slow, tedious progress past what had been six trees Red stopped, obviously exhausted. He left behind something more akin to an abstract painting of a landscape, with the trees looking like bizarre lumps of clay left half-finished on a potter's wheel.

As Kam walked up to where Red lay panting on the earth, he realized Red had managed to penetrate only about a hundred yards into the forest due to the enormous size of the trees. He turned to survey the stark section Red had just razed, when he realized the trees behind them looked a little less like the melted lumps than they had just minutes before.

As he watched, the trees Red had just burned, or dissolved Kam realized, he saw the trees get noticeable larger and taller. Not only that but small shoots seemed to be pushing through the earth from all around where the trees had just stood.

They're growing back! Kam said, nervousness lacing his thoughts. *And it looks like the roots of the trees are sending up shafts of wood to spear whatever hurt it.*

Red turned his great head slowly. A jumble of thought and feelings poured into Kam's head, many of which sounded like language only a sailor would say during a storm. Suddenly Kam felt a sharp pain in his foot which caused him to jump and turn to see what had bitten him. It took him a second to realize the pain came from Red where a shaft of wood shot up into him.

Confusion reigned in Red's thoughts as he stared dazedly where the wood had gone into his foot, penetrating his scales. Kam didn't need to have the bond to know Red couldn't understand how a wooden shaft managed to penetrate his scales or to know Red was as concerned as he was about getting out of these woods.

Red turned and looked up as if measuring the trees. Kam followed his gaze and realized these trees weren't just immense. They spread wide and their interlocking branches created a dense canopy, which seemed to exist from the tops of the trees all of the way down to nearly the ground. The branches were thick and dense so as to even cause a bird to hesitate to fly in among them. They were also tall, much taller than Red if he stood upon his rear legs.

I have an idea. Red thought. *Get on my back.*

Kam quickly clambered up, feeling relieved to get off the ground and the garden of sprouting spears. If this vegetation could penetrate dragon scales, then nothing was safe here. Images of the City of Stone and the twisted trees and other growth which had pushed their way up through the rock broke into Kam's thoughts.

Climb onto my head. Red said, breaking into Kam's sordid imagery.

Kam had a flash of misgiving as thoughts of getting closer to Red's mouth didn't seem like the best idea. But he obediently climbed up Red's now hackled neck scales, using them as handholds as if he were climbing up a mountain. When he reached Red's head, he tentatively crested it and sat nervously. He wasn't sure what Red had in mind as nothing came through the bond. Not for the first time he wondered if Red could control what thoughts came through; a talent he wished he possessed.

Move forward.

Although those two words were all Kam perceived, he knew instinctively Red meant for him to edge onto his snout, an idea Kam did not relish. However, he continued up past Red's eyes with each of them gauging Kam's movements. This gave the dragon a decidedly creepy, cross-eyed look.

He went halfway out along Red's snout, and to stay on with any ease he had to dangle his legs on either side of the partially open mouth. Even though he knew Red couldn't eat him, his position still seemed precarious. Thoughts of his "accidental" ingestion by Red previewed by a long and slippery slide straight down his throat attacked his thoughts. Suddenly he felt Red shaking all over as if he had just gotten the shivers from a sharp drop in the temperature.

Don't make me laugh! Was all Kam could catch.

Abruptly Red seemed to nod his head, causing Kam to be momentarily suspended in mid-air with nothing below him. He had the horrifying thought of Red allowing him to plummet to his doom. Then he felt a blast of hot, smelly dragon breath. The fervent, furnace-like air lifted him high into the air, even higher even than the tops of the trees. As he went up, he received a single thought/word from Red, which was more of a command, literally forcing him to obey.

Look!

Then, almost as an afterthought, *See how much farther we have to go.*

As Kam looked, he realized they were more than halfway through this section of the jungle until it opened up. Perhaps another fifty yards or so was all they needed to get through. Then, as Kam started to pivot in the air, somersaulting head over heels, he had a view of where they had come from, although from a vantage point of being upside down. He could see how the first two trees had already grown back to nearly their original height and the others were not far behind in their growth.

We need to hurry! Kam yelled with is mind. *The trees are growing back quickly!*

Kam figured those to be his last words as he suddenly realized he was falling very quickly. He looked up, although he realized with a sickening thought it was actually down as he was now falling headfirst. He saw Red watching him and slowly opening his mouth wide. Kam closed his eyes and prayed his demise would be quick.

With a sickening squelch he landed in Red's mouth on a soft and moist mattress. He was instantly covered in a wet, gooey slime from head to toe. As Kam waited for his slide of death, figuring it to be a slippery trip to a pool of whatever flaming stomach fluids dragons used to digest their prey, he again said a quick prayer. This time his prayer was for his mother and sister to be safe.

He hit the ground with a jarring thud. He looked up into the face of what can only be described as Red smiling, teeth bared and tongue partially extended. If he didn't know better, he would have thought the dragon was preparing to eat a delicious snack. He knew Red was smiling by the simple fact he felt no darkness in him; none at all. He was simply taking pleasure in Kam's situation.

As Red continued to burn his way through the last of the quick-growing forest, Kam followed close behind, with thoughts of tree shafts spearing him like so many swords penetrating his thoughts. At that point he could swear Red was laughing at him.

I'm not as large as you, Kam thought disdainfully. *And I can't breathe fire or knock down a house with my tail.*

He was now sure Red was laughing at him. He also noticed the living, pulsing entity which normally seethed inside Red's mind having receded a bit, almost as if it were hiding in the furthest shadows of Red's mind. Or maybe it was just pushed there by the light of Red's recent outbreaks of humor at Kam's expense.

Either way, as soon as Red turned back to the task at hand the darkness returned with a vengeance. It came crashing into Kam's skull like a wave pounding against the cliff-side, causing Kam to fall to his knees and not just in amazement. The return of the darkness felt as if Kam had been struck with a physical blow. He couldn't understand how someone as intelligent and beautiful as Red could have something as evil as... well, as whatever it was that existed inside of him.

It took a moment for Kam to notice Red had stopped burning, or melting, the trees and had turned to face him. Kam felt his face grow hot. He hated being connected to another person where every thought, every feeling sifted through. Then Kam sensed something…a small sense of wonderment. Why would Red be feeling that way?

Then he seized upon it-it was because he had referred to him as a person. There was some confusion also coming through, confusion because Red couldn't understand how Kam could think of him as a person and he wasn't sure if it should be taken as a compliment or not.

They continued on in silence, with the only discernible sound being that of Red's jade firestorm as he exhaled sharply. Kam caught some sense of the intensity of Red's focus through the bond as he used his unique magic to dissolve away the thick forest. It was an intensity Kam had not suspected was required as he had assumed the dragon's magic was simply an extension of himself.

As they walked Kam noticed a thick branch, longer than he was tall and thicker than his calf, which must have fallen as the tree trunk gave way. He quickly grabbed it and examined it closely. He was amazed at the light yet well-balanced heft to the sizable piece of wood. He thought it might make a passable walking staff.

THUMP.

Kam walked straight into one of Red's hind legs without realizing Red had stopped. It was then he realized they were in open land, having finally cleared the forest. Red's exhaustion was evident through their bond and caused Kam to feel as though he had just run a few miles as fast as he could.

Without another word both of them collapsed to rest. He realized only now just how much energy it took for Red, and he assumed all dragons, to use their magic. It was just one more thing he hadn't known about them.

Kam turned to see the path Red had just made and saw that the trees had already started to regenerate themselves. He knew that within about sixty minutes they would have grown back completely to where they had been before Red's fiery devastation.

Absently Kam handled the branch he had found just moments before. It had a different feel to it now-smoother and narrower than it had been. He looked at it and blinked. It had somehow been transformed into a perfectly sized walking staff.

He looked around in confusion, wondering if maybe the branch had been cracked and some of the wood had somehow split off without him realizing it. However, he knew in his heart that was improbable, especially given the smoothness and new, rounded shape. It was a mystery he would need to look into in more detail later.

CHAPTER 20

Red awoke with a start, his senses more alert than he remembered them ever being without any danger present. The sun had not yet risen and the clear, dark night was lit by hundreds of glowing pinpoints of light. He knew he had used a lot of Dragonmagic the day before; more than he had ever used before at one time. It had exhausted him beyond any tiredness he had ever felt.

Now however he also felt alive and refreshed and, more importantly for him, extremely clear headed. It was a feeling he hadn't experienced in a very long time. It vaguely reminded him of when he was a young dragon, full of life, energy and mischief. He chuckled softly to himself; even as a full-grown dragon he was always getting into trouble.

He thought about the trees which couldn't be destroyed and marveled at how he could sense no magic in them. Yet they obviously had magic-even his Dragonmagic couldn't keep them back for long. What kind of powerful magic would allow trees to withstand Dragonmagic and allow the shoots to penetrate his scales? Whatever power it was it was beyond his comprehension, and that worried him.

He slowly rose to his feet and turned to look at the man curled up on the ground next to him. Kam had managed to fall asleep in the nook his hind leg formed at the knee. Red carefully excised himself from Kam so as not to wake him then turned to stretch his limbs. His injured wing, which he flexed and rotated, seemed to have healed even faster than he thought it would be able to. He wondered if using his Dragonmagic had done that.

Ever since he had been a cub, all dragons warned him that using too much Dragonmagic can wear out a Dragon and make them vulnerable to attack. He had been exhausted after the extensive use of his Dragonfire, but he now felt better than he had in many years. He wondered if in the days of the Dragonwar dragons used their power so much that they actually grew stronger, and that maybe, over the years, his kind forgot that.

Red turned his attention ahead. They mountains which he had seen from that small, floating piece of wood he laid on to go across the salt still seemed so far away. Kam knew them by the name Highwall Mountains. It figures people would give natural beauty like that such a silly name.

A mist seemed to cling stubbornly around them, giving the illusion of the mountains burning. He knew he could walk there within a few days, but the man binded to him would need to get on his back again or they would be slowed considerably.

Red shook his head; the dark mist in his mind seemed to have receded. He couldn't even sense it at the moment. Perhaps it was because of that his mind felt clearer than it had in a long time. He felt young and strong and…proud again. Proud to be a dragon, proud to be a Red and proud to be alive. It was an exhilarating feeling and he just wanted to roar out his strength to any and all to fear.

The sound filled his own ears and seemed to echo from all around him. He felt Kam jump to his feet and heard the man's heart pounding as if it would burst from his chest. He felt his mind in his own, trying to understand what was happening.

Red roared again, but this time it wasn't a challenge. It was a laugh erupting from his body with the same force, the same volume, as his challenge. It felt good to laugh like that again and it felt good to feel the man's abject terror at the sound. Life was good.

The next few days were uneventful. Even the dark entity which existed in Red seemed content to pass the time without commotion. Although water was plentiful there was little around besides very small game to help to quench Red's hunger.

The sun was high at midday on their third day of walking. Red, with Kam riding on his back, reached the base of the very tall, very long series of mountains. Red knew through Kam that these mountains marked the edge of the kingdom they were trying to get to. Red could tell Kam was worried about not being able to cross them without Red's ability to fly.

Do not worry, Red said. *My wing has grown much stronger. I think I should be able to fly tomorrow.*

A sense of relief flooded through the binding as the man's effervescent hope again bubbled to the surface, nearly causing Red to throw up. How can a man live like that? How could a dragon live through the hope something could happen?

You train, you grow stronger and you do what you can. To hope you will be able to do something or, worse yet, to hope something will happen which is beyond your control is like hoping you will find a meal the next day. Either you will or you won't.

A stray thought, coated with humor and self-satisfaction and inflated with self-importance, floated into Red's mind from Kam. Apparently, the man thought Red had referred to him as a dragon and he took that as a compliment.

A Dragon fights and, through fighting, either wins or loses. Honor is in winning; but if you do lose, you work harder to win the next time. There is no hope, only strength.

Puzzlement came through the binding. Red could sense confusion at how Red, or any dragon, could go through such a dark life without the light of hope guiding them. Red snorted.

This man was definitely wormcrazy enough to think going through life with the false premise that good things would just happen and that those you would fight would fall dead on the ground in front of you simply out of fear made no sense. Hoping for something which couldn't be, which couldn't possibly happen meant it was a false hope. Worse yet, it was a hope rooted in fantasy.

Red traveled a short distance paralleling the base of the mountain range looking for food. He could smell the gamey, wild scent of some large animals and his stomach growled. The scent was reminiscent of the man's pack animal which he ate when he was first binded. Kam called it a horse and it was very tasty and like nothing Red had ever eaten before.

He continued to follow the scent until he found a small herd of animals about the same size as the horse; but these definitely weren't horses. They had eight legs and a massive head full of sharp teeth. Yet for all their ferocious appearance they ran around in terror when the wind changed direction and they caught a whiff of Red's scent.

They were fast but not as fast as Red. He caught one and bit down heartily. The taste was reminiscent of the horse but different. It was good and he ate two of them to fill up his belly and give him strength for the day.

As he walked back to where Kam was tending a small fire, he noticed he was looking a little pale, even for him. Kam always seemed to get sick whenever Red ate a meal and he found that amusing. After all, he ate meat too, if not raw like Red did.

As he approached him his tongue worked on a piece of meat wedged between two of his teeth. Normally a dragon's teeth work like knives, slicing game into thin shreds of food which are then too small to get lodged between their teeth. But this time a substantial chunk of meat had managed to avoid being sliced and was at just the right angle to bother him.

Can I help?

Kam's query came as Red was getting agitated. He didn't want the man to know he could use his help, yet he needed it now. Kam walked over and drew his dagger.

Hold still, I don't want to cut you.

Red almost responded indignantly that the man couldn't possibly cut him but caught himself. With no scales inside of his mouth he supposed it was possible a sharp knife might be able to do just that.

He waited patiently as the man worked on the piece of meat, using the sharp point to scrape it out. When he finally got it, the pressure Red had been feeling against two of his teeth was gone and Kam was holding a chunk of flesh on his knife and staring at it.

Red could tell the man was hungry and that the dried fruit he had been eating wasn't doing enough for him. He also could tell that the fresh meat was making Kam's stomach growl.

Go ahead and eat it. I'm not sick.

The thought of eating the meat he had just pulled out of Red's mouth was turning the man's stomach and Red gave a low chortle of delight. Before Kam could do anything Red used his tongue to flick the meat off of the knife and into the fire. The fire spit out sparks as if angry something was thrown in.

Now it's cooking. You can eat in a little bit.

Red could sense Kam was torn. The smell of the fresh meat cooking was making his stomach growl so loud Red could hear it. He watched and listened as the man debated with himself whether or not to eat the cooking flesh.

Finally with a sigh of resignation he went over to the fire, stabbed the meat with his dagger and held it up to cook evenly over the flame. Red didn't know why but he had a feeling of winning an important battle. He didn't understand it but he took it with pride. Now if he could just get the man to throw the Dragonstaff into the fire...

A few hours later he tested the strength of his wing. He said he was ready to try to go over the mountains. Surprisingly, he found that his uninjured wing had gotten a little stiff as well due to his lack of use. The man was impatient to go, that much came through the binding loud and clear, yet he still waited patiently for him. Red was surprised how much concern the man seemed to have for him.

Red did some tentative attempts at flying and found that although his wing was much stronger, any attempt to actually fly for any length of time put a painful strain on his shoulder and he had to land. But his continual flying and landing had given him an idea as to how they might cross the mountains. Kam didn't seem to have sensed anything about the idea and was a little surprised, albeit hopeful, when Red proposed it to him.

After having Kam climb onto his shoulders, he started running as fast as he could towards the base of the mountain. The lower half of the mountain had a fairly steep incline, but not so steep that Red couldn't use his momentum to continue moving up it. After about an hour Red had gone approximately halfway up and was starting to breathe hard, something he wasn't used to.

From that point the slope grew increasingly steep, becoming nearly completely vertical. Here he turned to using his claws and wings to half-climb, half-fly up the mountain side. Thrusting his claws into the hard rock and using his wings to provide some leverage was clumsy, tiring work and his weight frequently caused large chunks of rock to break off and fall. The loud noise of the rock cracking apart and hurtle down the side of the mountain made Kam more than a little edgy.

Although Red tried not to use his wings very often, there were many places where the rock was so hard his claws barely penetrated it and he had to flap his large wings to keep from tumbling back down the side of the mountain. He was using his wings far more than he planned to, and the exertion was taking its toll. His injured shoulder had an intense, deep burning while his lungs felt constricted inside of his chest.

Then there was the man's influence. His unease, and at times outright fear, when Red slid backwards seemed magnified inside Red's head. He knew what was causing it; the darkness, which had often been distant and indistinguishable of late, had returned. Its presence was subtle, but noticeable. It wasn't communicating with him as it used to, but it was there.

Once it seemed to understand that Red could again sense its influence, it ceased trying to be coy about its existence. Once again outright hatred of the man and all he stood for cascaded through Red's mind. It even seemed to exacerbate his injury, causing his wing to stiffen up to the point of near uselessness. Fortunately, Red finally found himself just below a ledge which he could climb onto.

Once on the ledge Red collapsed. His wing seemed all but useless and his own heart was pounding so hard he could feel it throbbing through his whole body. The darkness, which at times saturated his whole consciousness, had but one thought-to plummet down the mountainside killing both of them.

It was not the kind of insane thought Red would harbor, but the darkness seemed to feel that if sacrificing itself was the only way to be rid of the man then so be it. And if that meant Red would perish as well then at least he would be free again. But Red didn't agree. Freedom was life, not death.

The anger energized the darkness and filled him. The dark evil seemed to possess him, as if it was the owner of his body and not him. He knew what it was going to do; take the man and throw him off the ledge.

He didn't know if it could do something. Or if the magic of the Dragonstaff didn't affect it the same way it affected him. He did know if he let it take over his body to the point of killing the man then he would never be in control of his own body ever again.

What's the matter?

Kam's question broke through the burning grip of darkness and brought the recognition of pain back into Red's consciousness. It was as if a separate void, or bubble, formed around the darkness and allowed it to exist inside of him. Yet into that void came the pain, flooding every pore of his mind and blotting out the evil essence which had resided there just moments before. Red's pain, echoing in Kam's head, kept the darkness at bay. It was as if the darkness shunned the pain the way some creatures fled the light of day.

Kam seemed oblivious to the darkness which still resided within Red, but not to the pain. Red saw Kam fall to the ground in agony clutching his head. Red saw spots swimming before his eyes as he fought not to lose consciousness.

The darkness existed at the edge of his perception, surrounding the pain but not entering into its field of existence. For that and that alone Red was grateful for the agony he was in. He would nourish it if it would help him to keep the darkness form settling into his mind and taking over.

The pain did finally to start to recede when Red laid still and didn't move. To Red's surprise the darkness didn't invade his mind again. It settled at the perimeter of Red's mind, waiting like the great winged birds which sometimes circled Dragonmount after a large slaughter, hoping for scraps. The image sent shivers through Red's body like the blistering cold wind from the plains of ice.

Red watched Kam get up slowly and stare at him. A jumble of emotions came through the binding, but the most pronounced was that of concern. Red snorted, a soft, halfhearted sound which was more reminiscent of a cub than a full-grown dragon. But Red did notice that the concern, much like the pain, seemed to cause the darkness to wither and shrink back as if it were experiencing a physical attack.

Before Kam could say anything, Red said, *I am weak. The climb took much out of me. I will need to rest until tomorrow before continuing.*

Kam didn't respond for a moment; then he simply nodded. Red sighed, moved in as far away from the edge of the cliff as possible, which wasn't far given the small area of the ledge, and curled up to sleep. He felt Kam lay down in the crook of his leg again.

Red sighed. It seemed he should be upset with the man for using him as a bed. But not only was he not upset but the tactile feel of the man against him gave him a sense of comfort. He could tell the darkness wasn't happy about it though, and that was okay with him.

<h1 style="text-align:center">CHAPTER 21</h1>

The next morning Red arose early. The sun was starting to rise and the sky was turning many shades of his favorite color-red. The mist, which had been holding tight onto the mountains for the past few days like a baby Dragon getting suck, was gone. Red looked up and could clearly see the top of the peaks rise majestically above him. He felt he could surmount the summit by midday if he moved quickly. That is, if the darkness didn't try to have him leap to his death.

Red's injured wing was incredibly stiff and sore and the other one wasn't much better. Yet contrary to what he was expecting the damaged wing also seemed much stronger. He glanced down and saw Kam was just waking up. *Good,* Red thought to himself. *We can get an early start.*

The darkness was nowhere to be sensed when Red and Kam started up the mountainside and he was hoping to keep it that way. Moving swiftly Red traversed the remaining distance to the top without mishap, much to his relief. He sensed relief in the man as well.

Once there both he and Kam scanned their surroundings. The cold air filling Red's lungs and the wide, panoramic view afforded by the summit gave Red the joyous feeling he normally got from flight. The brisk wind only added to the sensation of being skyborn.

Red glanced over at Kam and noticed him pulling his clothing tighter around his body. He sensed the man was cold, something which had never come through the binding before when he was actually flying with him. He wondered briefly if Kam noticed that too. He also sensed extreme elation that they had finally arrived.

Red was puzzled; they were on a mountain top in the middle of nowhere. Why was Kam happy they had arrived here? Red looked around again and this time near the mountains saw an immense castle surrounded by small structures and encompassed by a massive wall. How could he have missed that before?

Red sighed. He must have been caught up in the moment when he had been reflecting on being skyborn again. A sudden, shocking thought attacked his mind-what if he wouldn't be able to fly again? What if his wing had healed as much as it could and he was now forever limited to ineptly flying low to the ground for very short distances at a time? How could a dragon, how could he, live like that?

Red shook his head. That thought had to have come from the darkness in him. It must have. He had to move forward with the hope that his wing would heal and that he would…Red caught himself and a cold chill spread throughout his body. There was that word, *hope*. It wasn't possible. Dragons didn't hope; dragons *did*. That's all there was to it. Hope was an emotional weakness, a false desire to inspire for the impossible.

Red shook his head again, but what of hope for the possible? Was that still foolish? His wing healing was possible, wasn't it? Or was it just so much Dragonwylde thinking? He didn't know and didn't think he could figure it out himself; at least not with that thing inside of his head. At that moment Red could swear he heard laughing close by. He looked down at the man again but only saw him looking up with concern.

Are you okay? Kam asked.

Red swallowed hard. He needed to think straight or they would both be in trouble.

Kam continued, *There is a ravine going down the side of the mountain to our right. If we go down the mountain in it no one will see us from the city and we can keep from frightening everyone.*

Red exhaled loudly. When would this torment end? He had to find a way to destroy the Dragonstaff. Men were always killing each other. Maybe this one would get himself killed by others once he went inside the place of people.

A sharp pang of guilt followed closely by regret for the thought shot through Red's chest like an arrow. Why did he feel bad thinking about this man's death? He was just one more person in a world already covered by the scourge of them.

If he were to die by the hands of someone else, Red could return home to Dragonmount and be free again. Well, not to Dragonmount itself; he had been banished to a place where he could not interact with others in Dragonnation. Still, he would be free.

Red looked at Kam again. This man was not as bad as most, he supposed. Except for the cursed magic he used on him. He briefly wondered if there were any magical items like a manstaff he could use on this man to get him to destroy the Dragonstaff.

Climb up, Red thought. *I will take us down in the broken part of the mountain.*

Kam wasted no time in scampering up to his spot between Red's shoulder bones. He did so quickly and with the evident ease of much practice Red noticed. It was an observation which did not sit well with either Red or his dark companion. It felt as if the darkness wanted to say something but which it kept to itself.

As Red moved gingerly down the ravine, he couldn't help but to cause small landslides of loose rock and dirt down the side of the mountain. There were times when Red slid several feet, his claws unable to find purchase, giving him the feeling of an uncontrolled fall.

It became apparent that the ravine was filled with rock which had been loosened over the years by ice and rain. However, after a number of times of that happening, Red started to enjoy the sliding. He noticed that even the man began to find a certain thrill in it.

It was at that moment Red realized something; he had started to view Kam as a man, an individual and not necessarily representative of his kind. He wasn't sure when that happened, but he did find it odd. He had even attributed some noble characteristics of dragons to him. He wasn't sure why, but he felt the act of taking away the generalization of him was a dangerous thing.

Then there was the darkness. He still wasn't sure what it was or where it came from. It seemed to have taken all of his anger, that which used to motivate him, and turn it into its own private reservoir of emotional energy. Red tried to think back to when he first noticed the darkness as a separate and distinct entity within him. It wasn't long after their fight in the City of Stone when Red saw the other creature which had a staff similar to Kam's.

Abruptly Red felt Kam's presence in his mind. He knew the man hadn't just entered now but had been there for some time. His thinking was a worried jumble of thoughts and images; barely coherent to a dragon but probably normal for his kind. Kam formed a question but left it unasked; Red however could sense it. Kam wanted to know if it was the Dragonstaff causing the darkness to rage within Red.

Suddenly Red lost his footing and the smooth sliding he had been enjoying turned into a rolling tumble down the mountainside. Red instinctively brought his wings in close, sheltering Kam and his injury. He then used his claws as a means of both braking and regaining control of his descent. He came to a slow, rumbling stop and noticed they had been falling quicker than he originally thought and were now more than half way down the mountain.

Red slowly spread his wings and tested them. Fortunately, they had not been injured anymore and Red breathed a sigh of relief. He had been worried they might have been crushed under his own weight as he fell.

Thank you, Kam said simply.

Are you okay?

Red could sense Kam's bemused acknowledgement. He could tell the man felt Red had done what he did in order to shield him.

I protected you with my wings so you would not get hurt as I am forced to by your binding, Red said.

Kam sighed and reiterated his gratitude anyway. Dragons definitely were as stubborn as women; of that much he was sure. After confirming the Dragonstaff was still secured to his side, he looked around for his newly acquired staff, thinking the worst. As he scanned the loose rubble which lay strewn around Red's feet and down the mountain he felt a curious sensation around his arm.

The staff, which he had hoped not to lose during their precarious slide, had somehow gotten much shorter and narrower and had wrapped itself around his arm like a snake around a tree branch. He gently took it in his hand and it became soft, almost like a cooked noodle. He uncoiled it gently and it straightened and became firm again, although much shorter than before.

Kam's surprise at the ease with which the wood became malleable and then firm again was mirrored in his head by Red's own surprise. He knew Red could understand what was going on by his own reactions, but he also knew the dragon felt absolutely no magic emanating from the wood. Yet how could the wood respond as it did without the benefit of magic?

Red continued on down the ravine at a much slower rate, taking great care to watch his footing. Without further mishap they were at the base of the mountain before nightfall. Kam set up a small campfire and relaxed. They were close to the city yet hidden within the ravine on the side of the mountain.

Kam knew it was only a matter of time before they were discovered. He needed to figure out how to hide a large, red dragon so as not to frighten anyone. There was only one person in the kingdom who knew of his journey and would expect to see a dragon, and that was the same one who had given him the dragonstaff.

Kam slid off of Red and unrolled his bedroll. He sighed and slowly drifted off to sleep. He slept fitfully that night, constantly dreaming of soldiers with living halberds attacking Red. The weapons became serpents of wood and entwined Red, tearing up his wings and penetrating his scales. In the end Red became a living piece of wood, a carving which caused death to the soldiers by breathing out salt and burying the King's Guard. Kam awoke to the bright morning sun shining in his eyes and thoughts of suffocating under an avalanche of salt.

After his heart slowed from the nightmare he tried to focus on Red. The dragon was nearby but not in sight. He could gather from Red's thoughts he was flying low and fast over the plains, his wing much stronger and nearly completely healed and providing him with an exuberant sense of freedom. But there was more. Red had sensed other dragons nearby; something which Kam found difficult to believe. Yet he too could sense the other dragons through Red, and it was a unique sensation.

It was almost as if someone were calling him, only he could hear it in his head, not his ears. But the calling was not a conscious effort of someone trying to communicate, but a feeling caused by their simple proximity to his location. It was very difficult to understand and even more difficult to accept.

It wasn't that long ago when he had a difficult time believing dragons still existed, even after his friend assured him they did. Yet not only could he now sense that there were dragons not too distant from the castle itself but that he was even connected to one mentally and emotionally.

In the end he realized he shouldn't be surprised. He found that people, most of them anyway, could have the truth right in front of them but refuse to see it. People would see only what they wanted, real or not, and everything else would just be hearsay and falsehood despite facts.

It was the same attitude he saw whenever he tried to tell people about the war that was coming. They just didn't want to believe it. He hated to admit it but he really was just like everyone else.

You are not like others of your kind.

Red's interjection broke into Kam's thoughts again, startling him. Yet for some reason Kam found Red's comment oddly reassuring.

He really wasn't that far from the city. Red's brief commentary, which seemed to be the only communication Red was willing to participate in, helped Kam make his decision. He decided to set off on foot towards the main road, with his staff now growing long enough for him to actually use it to walk with. Fortunately, he met a farmer with a wagon full of fresh produce headed to markets and he caught a ride. Although it was slow going it still saved him hours of walking.

Once inside the city gates he hoped off the cart and with a quick show of gratitude to the farmer made his way slowly down the main street. He knew which direction to head, but other than that his friend's directions were very vague. 'Look for the nameless shop and you will find me,' was all he had been told.

As Kam walked down the busy road, he noticed the shops on either side were butted up against each other with no space or alley between them, an unusual occurrence for a town as large as this one. He eventually came to an especially weathered shop front which stood out despite the surrounding shops having a similarly derelict look. In dire need of paint and repair, the glass in this particular storefront was surprisingly clean and clear and free of any cracks.

As he looked up, he noticed two broken chains dangling from a crossbeam where the sign of the shop should have hung. However, above the top of the front window across old, warped planks of wood were painted the words 'Weapons and Armor'. He noticed there was no mention of magic as it had been outlawed in the kingdom for some time now.

He entered slowly and noticed just one other person, a woman, in the shop. He glanced quickly around and saw that the shop was bare but for a few books on a small shelf behind a long, low counter. An odd circumstance considering a shop needed to sell merchandise in order to get coin. The woman announced her name as Julianne and stated she was the apprentice.

"Are you looking for someone?" She asked Kam.

"Yes, I'm looking for Nix" Kam said, and as soon as the words came out of his mouth a ruckus seemed to break out just outside the front of the shop.

"So, he thinks a simple repel spell can keep ME out! He will pay for his insolence."

As Kam looked out the window to see who had spoken, his eyes were instantly drawn to a man standing there. He was tall and muscular, with gray-white skin the color of ash and bright orange-red hair which looked a lot like flames.

As Kam watched, the man's hair moved, but not as wind moves hair, tousling it about and getting into a person's face. It was more like an actual fire. It had the unnerving appearance of flames emerging and ascending one minute and then disappearing quickly the next, only to be replaced by another blazing tongue of heat. It was one of the most disconcerting things Kam had ever experienced next to having a dragon inside his head.

At that same moment Kam experienced a chill of icy apprehension. It was similar to the darkness within Red but without the hot, bitter anger stoking it. This apprehension had the distinct presence of evil about it. It was cold, calculating and definitely willing to kill.

The fire-haired man glanced over at Kam through the window but quickly turned away as if he were simply a fly which had suddenly appeared but could be easily squashed without any effort. He instead glared at Julianne who had suddenly and noiselessly appeared next to Kam, briefly startling him.

"Where is your Master?" Flame-hair asked her, his voice dripping with contempt. His eyes, the color of the blackest coal, formed in the most sinister expression Kam had ever seen on a man, and a thin half-smile painfully twisted his lips. It was a smile if cockiness, as if this man knew only corruption and depravity and was proud of it.

"Tell him Ignis has returned…as promised." The implication in those last two words was not lost on Kam. He was here to get something, and someone would pay if he didn't.

"He's in the back helping a customer, but should return momentarily." Julianne replied calmly, as if what was happening was a common occurrence.

Ignis looked up and down the road he was on. He seemed to only notice now that the shops were built wall-to-wall for some distance with no alley to utilize to avoid circumventing a long walk to get to the rear of the shop. Ignis' eyes narrowed to mere slits while his hair blazed even brighter. He then turned abruptly in one direction and started to walk away.

Kam exhaled slowly and belatedly noticed that a group of four men who had apparently accompanied fire-hair now turned to follow him. They were dressed in loose robes, clothing much the same as monks. However instead of the usual drab green-brown robes with white trim monks normally wore these robes were a deep crimson, as if they had been dyed in blood. However, it was the belts that truly stood out, looking as if they were made of fire. Only instead rising skyward these flames burned horizontally around their waists.

All four of the men with the one called Ignis had staffs with them. Two of the men had long, smooth staffs and two of them had rough, thick pieces of wood which appeared to be branches which had just been cut off of trees. The two monks who had the long, smooth staffs had black hoods and the other two wore yellow hoods. Kam knew by reputation that they were warrior monks.

The black-hooded monks were Monks of the Sword and the yellow-hooded monks were Monks of the Empty Hand. The latter monks were so named as a euphemism, due to the fact they used magic without actually admitting to it, as all magic was illegal.

All of the hoods were up showing at this time they had no intention of fighting. However, their faces could still be clearly seen and all of them had tough, hardened faces set like steel. Not the kind of men you'd want to fight against or meet in a dark alley.

"The master is out back, Kam. I can take you out through the back door, but he wanted you to have this first." She said as she walked toward the back wall of the shop. Behind the counter Kam now saw a surprising number of weapons hanging, which he had apparently failed to notice earlier. She grabbed one of the sheathed swords and handed it to him. She then turned quickly and led him to the rear of the shop before Kam could question how a woman he had never met before in a shop he had never visited before could know his name.

As Kam followed Julianne, he pulled the sword part way out of its sheath and inspected it. It had a long, curved blade, thicker than any he had seen before, which was white and very similar in appearance to alabaster or fine bone china it was a beautiful sword and stunning to look at. The dark, polished wooden handle was plain in appearance yet striking in color.

The sword was beautiful in a way one would expect a work of art to be beautiful rather than an instrument of death. It looked like anything but an actual sword used for fighting. The sheath looked and felt like leather of some sort, but not any type of leather he recognized.

When Kam looked up, he belatedly realized he was already standing outside with Julianne, not far behind a man dressed in the bright, comical colors of a shopkeeper. He wore a gold striped tunic with bright blue pants. Around his waist was a large black belt, typically the only piece of clothing worn by a shopkeeper not of a bright color, and black shoes polished to a mirror-like shine. The shopkeeper also lacked the typical bright, conical cap also prevalent among people in his trade.

The shopkeeper turned and Kam gave a start. It was his friend Nix standing there, yet he seemed to be looking at him for the first time. He knew him as a quiet, soft-spoken individual who was neither too old nor very young, neither handsome nor plain and neither tall nor short. In fact, without his shopkeeper clothing on, he might pass by on the street entirely unnoticed and ignored. The exact person one wouldn't expect to be a shopkeeper. Shopkeepers were as vibrant in personality as they were in dress, often bordering on the deafening and rude in order to draw people in and keep their attention.

Besides his clothing the only other exceptions to his appearance which stood out were his intense blue eyes and his snow-white hair and beard. Both of the latter of which were short and well kept, with the beard having a good point on it. His hair and beard gave off a feeling of having passed through a blizzard in the northlands and retaining the worst aspects of the frigid cold and ice.

Nix was watching a large man lightly practicing swordplay. With him were others he obviously knew well as their banter about being too feeble to hold a sword correctly and how one's mother was a far better bladesman betrayed. The large man was obviously the leader and all of them were of the King's Guard based on the insignia on their clothing. When the large man took his sweat-soaked shirt off Kam saw he was muscular with broad shoulders developed from having to do hard work all of his life.

"Wyk," the shopkeeper called, "if you're ready, put the armor on and see what you can do."

The leader of the group gave up his sword to one of the men there and walked over to a small, circular field they had fenced in to form a practice arena. To one side was an open crate. He reached in and pulled out a set of armor like nothing Kam had ever seen before, and he had seen many types in his life.

There was the Western Isles' thick, heavy steel armor (universally considered to be the ugliest yet strongest armor around) to the Arabias' light, shiny aluminium armor, which looked very handsome in midday but stopped nothing short of a child's toy ax Then there was the extravagantly plumed and painted armor of the Fremany.

Kam had seen some magical armor too, or at least that was what he had been told. He'd even seen elfin armor on a few occasions; but that armor was extremely rare and expensive. Elfin armor was more often gotten as a gift for helping out the elfin people. It was then usually passed down from father to son as a source of pride within a family.

As Wyk started put the armor on Kam couldn't help but notice its bright bronze color, which shone like the sun, and looking as if it had just been polished. As the leader and his men emptied the crate, Kam saw it consisted of many more pieces than any other armor he had ever seen.

The helm was three full pieces; a back side, which had two extensions protruding up like small ears, a head section which went up and around the sides and the conical visor, which was placed in the head section and stuck out not unlike a bird's beak. The helm reminded Kam of the older style bascinet helmets which also had a distinctly bird-like appearance.

Each arm consisted of five pieces. There were two pieces each for the upper and lower arm plus strange looking gauntlets which had sharp extensions on the fingers. The gauntlets looked as if holding a sword would be next to impossible.

The body consisted of the traditional two-piece front-and-back plating with a small, nub-like extension protruding out of the lower back. The leg armor was similar to the arm pieces, including foot coverings which also had sharp extensions extending from them. Kam realized then that the armor appeared much too small for Wyk's body; yet as it was being put on it seemed to expand to fit Wyk as each piece was put in place.

It must be some type of one-size-fits-all magic armor Kam surmised, chuckling softly to himself at his comparison to some of the more modern garments sold to those with coin enough to spare.

When he had the armor completely on Wyk entered the arena and shouted, "Okay. Go ahead and attack me."

With that command the other men grabbed staffs and clubs which were lying around the practice ring. The men then formed a loose circle around their leader. But their hesitant steps and cautious looks to each other spoke volumes to Kam. They obviously weren't prepared to attack someone who could send them to the dungeons for a very long time, even though their wooden implements would probably cause little discernible damage to the armor.

Kam watched as Wyk looked around and gauged the veracity of the men under him. Kam knew he was wondering what kind of inspiration he could give his men to have them attack him. Finally, Wyk yelled, "Remember, this is your chance to hit me freely with no repercussions. None at all."

Apparently Wyk said just the right thing as the men gave each other confident smiles and moved in quickly. However, right before the first blow was struck the armor seemed to change slightly, to blur a little, as if seen through watery eyes. All of the separate pieces seemed to merge together and became a single piece of armor without seams, instead of the many pieces that had been put together just a few minutes before. The newly altered armor had a distinctly animalistic look to it and one that was vaguely familiar to Kam.

The attackers must have noticed it too because they paused for a second, a couple of them in mid-swing. Then without further hesitation they attacked. Gently at first, then with more and more ferocity they bludgeoned their leader. For his part Wyk, who was just standing there like a statue, kept egging them on by yelling, "More. Do more. Hit harder. I can't feel a thing. Are you even trying?"

The clubs seemed to have no effect on the armor with the exception of a dull ringing sound. *But a good sword hitting armor can do more damage that a stick,* Kam chuckled.

"They are just making sure it is what I promised, Kam." Nix said. The shopkeeper appeared as abruptly at his side as his apprentice had done not long before, and seemingly able to read his thoughts.

"It is known as Dragon Armor and it was created during the Dragon Wars many years ago." The shopkeeper continued.

"Dragon Armor? The Dragon Wars? I've heard stories, of course, but I never realized..." Kam began, now thoroughly interested in what he might be seeing.

At that moment Kam felt a slight pressure in his head, like a small mouse was shifting its position in order to get more comfortable. He knew it was Red and that he was listening to every word. Kam had to wonder if he knew about the Dragon Armor. He made a mental note to bring it up later as Red was not saying anything now.

"That the armor was still around? Of course it is. The magic used to create it and the other two was the most powerful ever used. And they were successful in their attempts to create something so powerful it could challenge the dragons themselves."

The shopkeeper paused as if contemplating what to say next, then he continued, "There were three sets of armor which were created, called in the old tongue Aurum, Argentum and Pyropus in reference to their appearances of gold, silver and bronze respectively. Of course they weren't actually created using those metals, but that is the appearance they were given so as to be differentiated. You see, each armor had different abilities, different strengths. They were created with one purpose in mind…"

"…to slay dragons." Kam finished for him. Everyone knew the old tales, but Kam never figured on actually seeing something from those times, mush less something which was so vital in turning the tide of what was certain defeat into victory over the dragons.

"You realize, of course, that the armor didn't bring about a victory." Nix said as if he were still reading Kam's thoughts. "But rather brought about a stalemate between the forces of good and evil. The evil forces, including those dragons which chose to fight on the side of darkness, realized the toll a protracted conflict would cause. The evil leading them, as is in its nature, chose to fight again another day when it felt the possibility of losing was minimized."

"Dragons that *chose* to fight on the side of evil?" Kam asked incredulously, "I thought all dragons were…"

"Were what? Born evil? Born hating people and all that represents good?" The shopkeeper gave a loud snort. "Surely you don't think all people are good, do you? Or all dragons evil? I would have thought that by this time with your new friend you would know better." Without waiting for a response he continued, "Many dragons were blinded into joining the side of evil by some of their own. There were some dragons, a small few, who stayed with the side of good."

Suddenly there was a loud crack as one of the men with Wyk had seemingly gotten overly excited in the testing of the armor and hit it so hard that his staff, a good four inches thick Kam noticed, broke at the end as he struck the armor. Wyk inside could be heard laughing as he exclaimed, "I didn't feel a thing! What do you think about that?"

There was some mild cheering as everyone let out a sigh of relief, especially the man who had broken the staff. Wyk took off the helm, which apparently allowed him to as none of the previous seams were showing. He then approached the shopkeeper.

"So far so good, right Nix? Shall we try swords now?"

Kam hadn't realized it before but now some long-forgotten memories, lessons taught by his father when he was young, bobbed to the surface in his mind like ice floating down a freezing river. The name 'Nix' meant snowstorm or hailstorm in the old tongue. Unusual to be sure but befitting a man whose very presence brought chills to Kam. But before Nix could answer Wyk, someone came up behind them and said in a frosty tone, "I believe you have something of mine."

As they all turned in unison, Kam recognized the flame-haired man, the one named Ignis, and his friends dressed in their red robes with the hoods still up standing there. Ignis, with that same cocky half-smile frozen on his lips, a smile which never seemed to reach his wintry eyes, said in an even colder voice, "I would like my armor back."

CHAPTER 22

Suddenly, it hit Kam why Ignis's name kept bothering him, almost as if he had heard it before. In one sense, he realized, he had. Ignis meant firestorm in the old tongue. Another unusual name and for some reason it irked Kam, until he realized why. You almost never heard the old tongue spoken anymore. Kam was amazed he even remembered the meaning.

While pointing to Wyk Nix said, "It's not mine anymore. It now belongs to him."

Ignis looked at Wyk coolly, with dark, slitted eyes, before saying quietly, "I want my armor back."

"I don't believe this is your armor anymore; if it ever was." Wyk responded, with far more courage than Kam was feeling at the moment.

Ignis looked at his men briefly before stepping back and yelling, "Take it." As if waiting for just such a command, the Monks of the Empty Hand raised their arms and lowered their hoods. They meant to fight for the armor!

At this point Kam noticed his knees starting to shake in fear. *In fear!* Kam had been in many fights in his day, but he couldn't fathom why this time in particular he felt so frightened. It was as if they were attacking him simply because his life was worthless and should be ended. Or as if his death would make the world a better place.

Coupled with the fear Kam also felt anger emanating from the monks and their leader. Pure unadulterated rage. The same fury he felt coursing through Red from the moment he used the Dragonstaff to bond the dragon to him. But this time, instead of anger directed at everything and everyone, he felt it directed solely at himself.

Kam abruptly felt something cold and hard pressed into his hand. It was some sort of amulet which Nix was prodding him to take. As his hand closed around it the fear and trepidation he had felt melted away and the hot, boiling anger aimed at him subsided, leaving him calm and ready to do anything necessary to protect himself. As he glanced down at the amulet, he saw that it appeared to be gold except for the fact that it was mostly covered with rust.

When Kam looked up again, he saw that Wyk had backed up away from everyone else. The monks however hadn't remained as passive. They started to throw apple-sized orange-red fireballs at the armor. The fireballs seemed to disperse as soon as they touched the armor with no perceptible damage. Wyk made sounds within the armor which made Kam think he was laughing.

However, Nix's apprentice Julianne didn't take the attack as lightly. She quickly raised her hands and let loose streaks of fire at the monks in Wyk's defense. Without any hesitation both monks ceased throwing fireballs at Wyk and turned towards Julianne while at the same time their tree branches glowed with an eerie dark green light. Her fire seemed to hit some sort of protective shield which caused the flames to encircle the monks but not to burn them.

In the instant before the monks could respond to Julianne's attack, Nix knocked her arms down and stepped in front of her. Then with a look that matched his own stony words he said, "Leave this one alone."

The monks turned as one to look at Ignis, almost as if they were imploring him to allow them to attack Nix and Julianne. With a slight shake of his head, Ignis answered their unvoiced question and then uttered one word, "Again."

This time as Kam's eyes followed the fireballs, which looked larger than before, he noticed something unusual. Right before they struck the armor they started to dissipate slightly. It was almost as if there was a type of shield around the armor as well, nullifying some of the magic. When the weakened fireballs did strike the armor, they seemed to break up quickly, dissolving into wisps of magical vapors which disappeared rapidly. When the monks saw that nothing could be accomplished, they stopped and turned to Ignis again.

"Stronger." Ignis said, again uttering just one word to the monks.

The monks turned back to the armor and heaved fireballs again. Only this time the fireballs were twice as large, bluish in color and fairly crackled with magic. Kam felt the hairs on the back of his neck rise whenever one of the monks sent a ball flying towards the armor.

The outcome however was no different. Finally, the monks stopped their attacks and again looked over to Ignis who, without making a sound, nodded just once.

This time the monks used fireballs which were less like fire and more like a child's drawing of a ball made of lightening. And the color! Kam couldn't believe his eyes, with what he could see of them anyway. They were white like the hottest metal heated at a blacksmith's shop and as bright as the noon day sun, with streaks of green and blue in them. They were also louder, with much more of a piercing, almost thunderous, crackling to them. With the use of this magic Kam saw their bodies deflate a little, as if they were exerting a tremendous amount of physical strength in creating them.

As these balls of lightening struck the armor, a physical blow appeared to have been struck. With each ball Wyk seemed to stumble back about half a step. But because of the brightness of the balls, Kam couldn't be sure if these magical balls of lightening also lost some of their energy right before they struck the armor. The armor itself, however, still showed no signs that the balls were damaging it in any way.

After a few seconds of this intense bombardment, Ignis stopped his men and all quickly went quiet. After a moment Wyk and said, "If that's the best you've got, you'd better leave now."

Kam glanced back at Ignis and noticed his cocky half-smile was still there. In fact, it seemed as though nothing had changed about it at all, as though it was etched on his face as a sculpture might be carved in granite.

Kam realized it would take a lot of hubris for someone to have things not go their way and yet still feel confident. *Unless*, Kam thought, *he was hoping this was how things would turn out.*

Ignis glanced over at the other two men and quietly, almost imperceptibly, said in that same hard, cold voice, "Your turn."

At that the two other warrior monks approached Wyk. Wyk moved around slowly and gracefully, with much more agility than what Kam thought possible wearing the heavy, full-body armor.

As the monks attacked with their staffs, Wyk, who had since picked up and drawn his sword from where he had put it earlier, clumsily blocked their blows. For the life of him Kam couldn't figure out why Wyk bothered to defend himself as he seriously doubted those long, slender staffs could do any damage to the armor where powerful magic and thick clubs couldn't before.

Then the tactics of the two monks changed. Instead of randomly attacking with their staffs they started to alternate, with one hitting high and the other low. The one swinging low tried to trip Wyk up by thrusting his staff between Wyk's legs and twisting it violently to one side.

Wyk however avoided every attempt at trying to trip him by either maneuvering with the twist of the staff so as not to fall down or by jumping completely over the staff. Kam didn't see how it was possible for someone in armor of any sort to be able to jump, and Wyk was managing to leap two or three feet straight up into the air.

"Switch!"

The command from Ignis was in a voice which sounded like a waterfall plunging down on top of Kam and which would crush him violently. While managing to somehow keep his composure, Kam noticed the monks now pulled their staffs apart and exposed long, narrow, jet-black swords which looked to be made out of some sort of stone. They continued to hold the sheath part of the staff as well.

The monks continued to fight, and the speed of the blows they rained down on Wyk grew faster and faster. Kam, although just short of being a master bladesman himself, had to admire the speed and dexterity these monks exhibited. Their tactics were impeccable.

While using the sheath end of the staff to hammer blows upon Wyk's head, they were simultaneously using them to partially obscure his vision. This allowed them to strike repeated blows upon his arms and body with the swords. This caused considerable nicks, cuts and dents to the armor.

Then it finally happened. While trying to block a strong swing from one of the monks Wyk's sword was knocked from his grasp. Kam watched as Wyk was now reduced to using only his arms to block their blows. After about thirty seconds of vicious attacks Ignis let out a sharp whistle and the monks stopped.

To Kam's amazement the monks were barely breathing hard after their punishing work out. However, it was the armor everyone stared at. Despite the severe dents and scratches in it, the armor was still in one piece.

Wyk's arms were not lying on the ground as Kam feared might happen, especially considering the unique, and probably magical, black swords the monks had used. Kam was sure parts of the armor would need to be remade from scratch. Glancing over at Ignis Kam realized it was the first time he noticed the smile he so despised actually slip slightly.

"It's not what you're looking for so you may as well return home, old friend." The last two words of Nix's statement shook Kam initially. Then he realized the intent behind it was to say that although they might have been friends once, that time was now long past. Ignis noticed it too and he gave Nix a look as if fire would shoot out of his eyes at any moment and consume Nix completely. Suddenly, Ignis' face took on a new look, almost contemplative, which sent shudders down Kam's back.

"My turn." Ignis breathed, as he advanced on Wyk. "You'll do well just to survive me, human. Understand, you must allow yourself to merge with the suit, to become as one with it, for its full magic to work."

With those words Ignis held both of his arms outstretched, palms vertical. From his right palm what looked to be two steams of water gushed upward, twining around each other in a surprisingly beautiful ballet. After extending up about three feet the two geysers merged and solidified into a sword of water which, as Kam watched, stiffened and hardened into ice. But it was ice like he had never seen before. It was clear blue and looked extremely cold, although Kam couldn't understand how he knew that. It also caused the air around it to pop slightly and a slight mist to form around it.

Out of his other hand two tongues of red-orange flames shot upwards. The flames danced and twined around each other until they also extended about three feet. At that point the flames merged and solidified, forming a white-hot sword of fire radiating heat that Kam could feel from where he was standing.

Holding the two swords expertly Ignis attacked Wyk. Wyk however had not wasted any time in going over and grabbing his own sword again. It was apparent Wyk thought his sword would be of some benefit, but Kam highly doubted that.

Ignis and Wyk started to fight. Although Wyk was a part of the Kings Guard and probably also a master bladesman, it was painfully obvious to Kam that Ignis was at least as good a bladesman as Wyk and as good as any man he had ever seen. Ignis attacked again and again with both swords equally well and having only about a quarter of his blows blocked. Even worse, as they fought the awkwardness of Wyk's armor seemed to grow worse with each passing second.

Ignis's fire sword struck the armor again and again, causing red hot sparks to fly out and rain down on the ground. Kam wasn't surprised by that, but what did surprise him was what happened when the ice sword struck the armor. Blue sparks, with cold so intense Kam could only imagine that they could burn you just as badly.

Ignis moved like a dancer, smoothly moving around Wyk using many martial forms to attack. Some Kam had never seen before, but others so difficult in maneuver he couldn't believe they were even humanly possible. Nothing seemed too difficult for him.

At one point, Ignis attacked with both swords before spinning to his left to strike first with his fire sword, which Wyk managed to block, and then with his ice sword striking Wyk solidly across his torso. The sword struck with such strength Kam could believe Wyk would have been cut in two were it not for the armor.

They continued to fight, the armor still taking much of the hits until finally Nix yelled, "Throw your sword down and just use the armor, Wyk."

The timing of his statement was ironic considering right as he was saying it Ignis struck Wyk's sword solidly with both of his. Both swords cut through Wyk's blade, leaving 2 pieces of the sword on the ground and Wyk holding his hilt with only a dagger-length of metal left on it.

Fortunately, Wyk seemed to have heard Nix and dropped his sword and took up a defensive stance bare handed.

Now, instead of a single sword, Wyk was able to use both of his arms to block the attacks. Even so, his movements looked awkward, trained as he was to use a sword and not his arms to parry a blade. Many of Ignis's blows were blocked, but more often than not his lightening fast strikes continued to pummel Wyk on his by head and torso.

Finally, as if on cue, both Wyk and Ignis stopped and stepped back. Wyk's posture, hunched over with his hands on his knees, gave away his exhaustion. Amazingly Ignis appeared only mildly winded.

Kam noticed Ignis held that same cocky half-smile on his face, albeit if it were possible with even more malice to it. And he appeared to be studying the armor. Kam turned and focused on the armor as well, striving to study it carefully. Although there were dozens of dents and scratches in it from all of the fighting, what caught his attention and made him gasp in astonishment was a large gash across the chest.

Kam couldn't believe a sword, any sword, could do that much damage to that armor. Yet even as he watched, the armor seemed to blur again, the way it did when Wyk first put it on. The ugly gash now seemed smaller and less jagged and some of the dents which he had seen just moments before were now gone. But that wasn't possible. It was almost as if the armor was healing itself.

While Kam puzzled over what he had just witnessed, the two men started fighting again. As if from a distance Kam heard Nix yell, "Allow the armor to fight Wyk, don't force it. Allow it to become part of you."

Unbelievably Ignis increased the ferocity of his attack. *There's no way Wyk could have heard what Nix yelled.* Kam thought. Yet Wyk's whole demeanor slowly changed. He became lighter on his feet and his movements were quicker, as if he wasn't wearing any armor at all. And he was able to block more and more of the fiery haired man's attacks with his arms.

At one point, Wyk brought one hand down to strike, but Ignis in his pride didn't even bother to block it. He simply leaned back about six inches knowing Wyk would miss him cleanly. But as Wyk's gauntleted hand came down, Kam saw the talon-like extensions on the gauntlet grow. Long, razor-sharp blades extended out, and their new length was more than long enough to reach Ignis and scratch him deeply across his chest.

With a savage yet inhuman cry of pain that surprised Kam, Ignis leapt back a good five feet and looked down. His shirt was shredded and darkened. Kam looked but he could see no blood flowing out.

He should be losing a lot of blood, he thought.

Wyk appeared to gain confidence at this turn of events, attacking Ignis quickly and viscously. He brought the claws to bear so swiftly his hands became a blur. He slashed, cut and blocked as if he had been born to fight in the armor and had spent years training with it.

He was almost as fast as Ignis now, almost but not quite. However, as the fight wore on, it became apparent Wyk was adapting more and more to the armor and its abilities. Part of this was noticeable as the armor's healing ability grew quicker and quicker until it got to the point where it seemed nearly instantaneous.

Finally, as if trying to end the fight for good, Ignis slashed his sword of fire so as to cut off Wyk's head. Wyk blocked it with his forearm and then grabbed it so as to keep Ignis from swinging it again. Too late Kam realized that was just a feint. Just as quick Ignis tried to bring his ice sword down onto the helm of the armor; but Wyk's speed had improved immeasurably. He reached up with his free hand and actually caught the ice sword and held on. Ignis glared at Wyk as he struggled to pull his swords free but couldn't.

As Kam watched he slowly exhaled, not realizing he had been holding his breath. There they stood as if frozen in time. They were marble statues glaring at each other for all eternity; immobile and unmoving. Two titans struggling to finish what they had started.

As the two of them remained locked in their silent struggle, Kam got a cold, dark feeling in the very center of his being. Without understanding why, he sensed this is what Ignis had hoped for all along. With a blaze of light and heat, heat which even Kam felt, the sword of fire blazed bright and caused Wyk's gauntleted hand holding the sword to start to glow. The sword of ice also seemed to blaze, but with a cold so powerful that it too reached Kam.

Not understanding how any of this was possible, Kam realized the gauntlet holding the sword of fire had now turned white hot while the other gauntlet had turned a deep blue and had ice forming on it. Kam couldn't understand how Wyk could continue holding the swords with the temperatures he was experiencing or how he could ignore the extreme pain he had to be in.

The strain finally seemed to affect Wyk and he fell to one knee. Suddenly Kam caught a slight movement out of the corner of his eye. The nub, which extended from the rear of the armor just above the lower back, was longer. Even as Kam watched the golden lance thickened and elongated; even developing a nasty looking pointed end. Then as the long, metallic whip swung around Kam was astonished at its full length. In fact, it resembled nothing short of a tail.

How did that happen? Kam wondered as he stood transfixed at this new development. Showing flexibility beyond what Kam would have thought possible the tail edged its way between Wyk's legs. After a brief moment it shot out at Ignis, penetrating about half a foot into Ignis' stomach and causing a look of astonishment to cross the flame-haired man's face.

As the tail slowly withdrew the swords Ignis carried dulled, as if the magical energy they had been receiving had been turned off. Out of the newly created hole in his abdomen where his lifeblood should have poured out, something which looked like muddy sand darkened the ground around him instead.

Ignis's swords retracted into his hands so quickly it seemed as though they just disappeared, and the absence of any opposing force caused Wyk to take a stutter step forward to catch his balance. Ignis grabbed his stomach and fell back a couple of steps, oozing more black sand on the ground.

He turned and walked slowly over to where Kam and Nix stood, still holding his stomach. But as he walked, he seemed to gain strength and Kam wondered if he was really healing that quickly. But he never lost the cocky half-smile that he seemed to hold onto perpetually.

"So, *old friend*, it looks like my visit wasn't in vain after all." Ignis sneered at Nix.

It's then Ignis seemed to finally notice Kam, looking directly in his eyes as if he could communicate with him mind to mind.

"I want the sword you have," He sneered in a gravelly voice. "Its magic is far beyond your comprehension."

Abruptly Kam felt an essence enter his mind with a sensation not unlike when Red communicated with him. However, this one was much more menacing, more vile, than even the darkness inhabiting Red. Then, like an old memory surfacing and overwhelming all other thoughts, his reflection of Red brought the dragon's mind full into the forefront of his own.

The dragon's presence seemed to collide with Ignis's, and the effect was two-fold. Kam immediately got a painful headache and a second after that Ignis's influence fled his mind. So quickly did the arrogant man's presence in Kam's mind cease, that it caused a physical reaction, sending Kam back a couple of steps to catch his balance. It was the only time since their initial meeting that Kam saw a completely different look come upon the fiery-haired man's face; a mixture of surprise, confusion and total hatred.

Ignis swiftly regained his composure, and his infamous smile, putting it on as quickly as if it were a glove.

"There appears to be more to you than meets the eye, boy." Ignis uttered with pure contempt. "One day we'll meet and you and your pet will need to stand on your own."

The latter was said as if he were granting Kam a special gift; that of another day of life which could be taken away at any moment. It was a gift which he had the right to do with as he pleased and which he had total power and control over…

Without realizing it Kam had put his hand in his pocket. He had released the gold medallion Nix had given him, but now he grasped it again. As before he felt it go cold in his hand. He rubbed the medallion with his thumb and to his surprise he felt it go rough under his touch. He wasn't sure why but grasping the medallion somehow helped him stand against the waves of fear and discouragement which came crashing into him like a bolt of lightening striking him.

With the anxiety and fear in him diminishing, Kam looked Ignis straight in the eyes. He wasn't about to let this man get the better of him today. With his cocky smile firmly back in place Ignis turned and strode quickly away with the monks following close behind. Kam had a bad feeling he would be seeing him again.

CHAPTER 23

Wyk came walking slowly over to where Kam and Nix stood. Kam was surprised at how quickly he had removed his armor.

"This is amazing armor Nix. What do I owe you for it?" Wyk asked.

The shopkeeper just laughed and said, "Nothing. Just keep fighting the good fight, old friend. Put the armor in a safe place and tell no one about it. Have the men with you now sworn to secrecy. You won't need it for some time."

Kam glanced over at Wyk, who just looked at the shopkeeper with something akin to a mixture of love and respect, before he turned and went back to the crate to put the armor in. Nix watched him, the same look in his eyes, with a little concern mixed in. It was the same look Kam's mother had given him when he told them he was leaving to find his own way in the world. It was an innocent time for him, a time before he knew what the world was like and before he knew what the future held for humanity.

Abruptly images of his sister filled his mind. He had not seen his sister since he returned home more than a year after his mother's death. Being away meant he found out about her death months after the fact, and he had always felt guilty about his sister having to deal with it alone.

As he thought of her now, he realized she would be nearly 18 years old and still living at the same boarding school. His mind clouded with thoughts of her school. Everyone knew The School, as it was referred to instead of its actual name, was simply a prison for those who showed any aptitude or ability to use magic to any degree. He felt bad for her despite her strong ability in defensive magics, gotten from their mother's side of the family.

Nix and his apprentice headed back inside the shop and Kam followed. He put all thoughts of his sister aside while a thousand questions started swirling around in his head. So many in fact he didn't know where to begin. He had seen some bizarre things in his life, but what he had just seen he couldn't begin to understand. That meant magic was involved.

Nix turned to look at him patiently, silencing his thoughts with a knowing look. He turned to his apprentice and excused her, then waited until she left. He then began by asking, "What do you know about the Elementals?"

Kam just stood there, stunned for a moment.

"The elements? Like water and earth and things like that?"

Nix looked thoughtful for a moment and then smiled. "Many years ago, even before the Dragon Wars, the Elementals lived. No one knows where they originally came from, only that they are eternal. They are comprised of, and strong in the use of, elemental magic. Each of them is strongest in his or her base element. They can also look human, although they are not. Today you met Ignis. Do you know what Ignis means in the old tongue?"

Kam's father had taught him a little of the old tongue, although he wasn't sure why. He didn't know anyone who understood it anymore, although he knew a few words. But Ignis was one word he did know.

"It means a large fire." He responded.

"That's right. That's who you met today, Firestorm. He is the leader and one of the most vicious of the Elementals."

"But I don't understand," Kam began, "he seemed to possess powerful magic, he's still just a man. Not some mystical, eternal creature made of fire."

Nix sighed, as if this explanation had been given a thousand times before and always with the same response. He paused for a second, as if trying to figure out a new way to explain it, then his face lit up as though a brilliant thought had just occurred to him.

"I have an idea. Just ask the dragon what he knows about Elementals. I'm sure he can give you an earful, I mean mindful. Just remember, you must get him to rid himself of the darkness he carries inside. All creatures, man included, has some darkness within them. It is different for everyone. For the dragon, it's his rage at life. But you must be careful not to allow his emotions to cloud and overshadow yours."

Kam's jaw dropped in surprise and anger at what Nix said. *How can he know what's been going on with me?* Kam thought.

He knew Nix was a sorcerer of some power, but it was almost as if he could read his mind. An uncomfortable fear settled on Kam and his hand edged closer to his sword. He felt he needed to defend himself against whatever evil influence Nix was exerting over him.

Nix eyed him warily, seeming to know what thoughts were flowing through Kam's head. Without any conscious effort Kam's other hand reached into his pocket and touched the medallion. The bitter cold and harsh roughness of its surface pushed away the clouds of self-doubt and fear like a sun breaking through a dark and deeply overcast sky.

Kam came to his senses with a start, as if out of a deep sleep. "Wha…What just happened?"

Nix smiled; a sad, cold smile lacking even the smallest amount of warmth.

"Elementals have an ability to turn men's emotions against them. The medallion I gave you helps to keep that particular skill of theirs in check."

Kam wondered if the medallion would also help him with the overpowering darkness he felt within Red. The intensity of Red's anger coupled with the raging darkness could fall like a thick fog on his mind, keeping him from thinking clearly. He knew from experience how much effort it required to keep his own sanity from being completely engulfed.

"Tell me more," Kam said. "I want to learn."

"You wish to understand everything; yet there are things which are worse than nightmares. Those things, once known, cannot be unknown. Are you sure you want to travel down that path?"

Kam wondered what could be more terrifying than many of the things he already knew and had seen in his life. Heinous acts committed by men in war were bad enough, but his newfound knowledge of the existence of Halfers and other dark things seemed like nightmares sprung to life. He didn't think anything could be worse.

"Yes, tell me everything." Kam said.

"Elementals have the ability to instill fear, anxiety, depression and even loathing against those around them. They draw their strength, in part, from the weakness created by this ability. The weaker a person's mental and emotional fortitude the greater an Elemental's ability to use their magic.

"That medallion I gave you helps to hinder an Elemental's poisonous influence. When you hold the medallion near an Elemental it will go cold and corrode. This shows it's keeping the Elemental's negative energy from affecting you. When they aren't around the medallion regains its full luster."

Here Nix paused. He looked straight at Kam as if he could see into the depths of his very being. It was a look Kam found unnerving.

"What you need to understand is that the ability to truly overcome the effects of an Elemental comes from the soul," Nix continued. "You must develop your own inner strength to truly overcome the dark magic they exude."

Kam was silent for a moment, trying to take it all in. He thought about the fire-haired man and the battle he had with Wyk.

"Wyk wasn't affected because he was wearing the Bronze Dragon Armor when Ignis came. That armor protects the wearer from much of the Dark Master's influence." Nix said.

Abruptly Kam felt new and stronger waves of rage flow over him through the bond. The unexpected intensity caught him by surprise and he had to fight to keep from blacking out. Nix noticed him sag and quickly held out his hands for support.

"Are you okay?" Nix asked quickly. "Do you need help?"

Kam looked at him blankly for a second before responding. "I'm okay," he said. "But do you have anything to lesson the connection between me and the dragon?"

"I wish I did," Nix responded. "But now I don't think even destroying the dragonstaff will help."

After that statement Nix paused, studying Kam intently. Then he continued, "But let me tell you something, as I mentioned before you ever got the Dragonstaff, the best way to get a dragon's help is with their dragonword, their sincerest promise. A dragon willingly submitting and choosing to help is the best way to go. How long have you had this dragon bonded to you now?"

Kam sighed. "A while." he said, trying to sound as if he had everything under control. "But you were the one who gave me the dragonstaff to use in the first place."

"Yes, but my intention was not to have you two bonded for any great length of time. I had hoped that whichever dragon you were able to bond, would see your thoughts and understand the severity of the situation and agree to help quickly. I never imagined you would find a dragon with the kind of poison in its soul that this one has."

Kam nodded his agreement. He knew only too well how the darkness was affecting both of them.

Nix's face grew more somber as he continued. "The longer the dragon stays bonded to you, the more you two will come to know each other's thoughts and feelings. The sensation of being one in thought will actualize to the point where your thoughts will become one. There will come a time when, even if you try to break the bond by destroying the dragonstaff, the bond will remain until one of you dies. You should know a person who has bonded with a dragon usually ends up killing themself."

Kam pondered this new information pensively. He always thought he would die fighting. He never figured his death to be of his own choosing. It reminded him of what Nix said earlier about Elementals and how they can cause self-loathing. He could understand how that might lead someone to want to die so much they choose some form of self-destruction over life.

"I have already sent an emissary of mine to the king to request a search for a special artifact. I think you and your friend should be in the group to look for it. It could very well hold the only hope for the coming battle against the Dark Lord."

Kam looked at Nix soberly. "Would you be going as well, Nix?"

"Unfortunately, I have many other obligations I must fulfill. But know this, at the last day I will myself fight for the cause of light and, if necessary, give my life for it. But for now I must go, and you must return to the dragon."

As Kam turns to leave, Nix asked, "How do you recognize evil?"

Kam turned back. Not sure how to reply he asked, "What?"

"How do you recognize evil?"

"Well, evil is full of darkness, evil always lies…"

"Wait." Nix interrupted, "do you think evil always lies?"

"Well, yes." Kam answered hesitantly. "Evil lies all the time, doesn't it?"

"Even evil knows the truth and even evil can speak the truth for its own ends. When evil wants someone to do something they wouldn't normally do, it will say nine truths before getting to the one lie in order to get what it wants." Nix said.

As Kam pondered this he again turned to leave and head for the door before he remembered the sword he had received. He turned quickly to ask about it and realized he was standing alone. Suddenly Julianne came in through the back door and asked, "Was there something else?"

Kam replied, "I haven't paid for the sword."

"Don't worry," she responded, "It was meant as a gift. I was also asked to give this to you. It was meant as a means of understanding that which you will one day treasure more than your own life."

With an ease and lightness decrying the solemnity of what she had just said, Julianne handed him a neatly folded piece of parchment. Then she turned and without another word disappeared through the back door. Kam left and headed up the road. The streets seemed unusually quiet and empty given that it was about midday. He took that time to open the parchment and read it.

One evening an old man told his grandson about the battle which goes on inside all people.

He said, "My son, the battle is between two wolves inside us all. One is evil-it is anger, envy, jealousy, sorrow, regret, greed, arrogance, self-pity, guilt, resentment, inferiority, lies, false pride, superiority, and ego.

The other is good-it is joy, peace, love, hope, serenity, humility, kindness, benevolence, empathy, generosity, truth, compassion and faith."

The grandson thought about it for a minute and then asked his grandfather, "Which wolf wins?"

The old man then smiled and replied, "The one you feed."

Kam thought a moment about what message Nix was trying to tell him. He was sure it had something to do with Red, but what? He decided instead to focus on the artifact Nix told him he needed to get. He would have to find a way to get himself to become part of the group going out to look for it.

CHAPTER 24

R ed headed for the dragons. He knew there were two of them and he sensed they were not too far away. But it was still a slow process due to his walking.

Dragons couldn't usually know which dragons they were sensing unless they knew them well. And Red hadn't been close to any dragons for many cycles. In spite of that Red knew instantly he had known these two before.

One brought a sharp, clear image of the beautiful and graceful Gold he had once loved. She often had fire in her eyes, as he knew she would this day when she saw him. The other...the other was more difficult to bring to mind. An old friend, certainly, from before his shameful fight.

He continued on foot. He had thought about flying but decided against it due to his proximity to the city and his not wanting to appear clumsy in trying to use his injured wing. As with the City of Broken Stone this area reeked of people, but not just their stench. There was the smell of cooked meat, an abomination to any dragon. Plus, there was the smell of other things in the air, things being cooked but not meat; things he had no name for. But the biggest difference was that this place smelled alive.

He continued on foot, avoiding any possibility of having people see him by taking a long route around this City of Man stench. The place where he felt the dragons were was on the far side from where he and Kam had parted at the foot of the mountain.

As he walked, he allowed certain memories to come crashing in on his conscience. His beautiful Gold, his banded and the one he would have been sealed to, would not be happy to see him. His shame had brought her shame as well since everyone knew she was to be his. Thinking of the shame she shared with him caused him to feel heat in his face as though the sun itself came down and touched him.

His heart beat for her again now that he knew she was close; close enough to touch and twine tails with. She always had a calming effect on him, and it was especially apparent now. All of the old animosity he held for his kind was gone. Even the darkness seemed to shrivel up in her presence. She was the light of the day to him, and always would be.

He walked for some time and knew he was getting close. He swiveled his long neck back and forth as he tried to get a bead on where they were but found he couldn't. His binding to the man was hindering his ability to track other dragons. And he still couldn't see them despite the fact he was in a large, fairly open area now with no cover to speak of except a dense growth of trees nearby.

He walked towards the grove of trees and discovered that it was just a few large trees surrounding a single, massive tree. The immense size of the largest tree surprised Red as it was easily larger around than his full length and had a multitude of vines and woody protrusions extending from its heavy branches to the ground. The vines appeared to have grown and thickened and formed into support trusses for the larger branches.

Red slowly went around the trees and found another open area. This one caused him to stop short and stare at what he found. His throat constricted and he felt lightheaded.

Four men with some cattle were standing in front of two dragons, a blue and a gold. The dragons seemed to be communicating with the one of the men. Much to Red's surprise the cattle, which were not in any kind of enclosure, seemed complacent to just eat grass. They paid no attention to the dragons.

Red had a memory of his mother flash into his head. She told him how, when she was young, she had been chosen to go and trade with the men for their cows. Those breeders had been new and had not known to put up a temporary enclosure for the cows. Nearly all of the cows had stampeded madly at the first sight of the dragons, killing two of their breeders.

However, two of the cows had stayed behind, not showing any fear at the dragons' presence at all. His mother told the man who was brought to communicate with them to use the two cows still there and breed herds with them so as to raise cows which wouldn't bolt at the sight of dragons. She knew the dragons needed the cows but, she still felt it was better to have the men breed more of the ones they would prefer.

His mother was reprimanded severely for not having brought any cows back. But within three years nearly every cow brought had been from the stock of those first two cows and from that point on the breeders never again needed to build enclosures.

The cows now were easier for the dragons to keep in Dragoncountry as well, although this didn't sit well with all Dragons. There were those who gloried in the chase of their meal, however brief that chase might be. After all, cows were not known for their speed or agility in avoiding capture by a hungry dragon.

As the memory left his mind, the void was again filled with the all-consuming darkness and its intense hatred. It filled his mind with its disturbingly vile presence. Red wondered if other Dragons would be able to hear the darkness in him. However, as Gold and the blue dragon seemed completely oblivious to Red's existence he doubted if they could even sense him at all.

Red knew the Dragons had been communicating with the breeders by simply pushing forward amounts of human treasure, usually gold, which they had brought with them. They would continue pushing the valuables forward until an amount could be agreed upon with the breeders.

Both sides knew the amount would total all of what the dragons had brought with them. It was a silly game, with both sides knowing that the Dragons would not return home with any of the gold they had brought. The traders would then give the Dragons all eight of the strong, healthy breeding cows they had with them.

Red was watching the meeting intently when suddenly both Dragons started looking around them, as if searching for something. He suddenly realized they were sensing him and they should be able to pinpoint his exact location quickly, especially with him being so close. But they kept looking to their side, away from Red.

They must be as confused as me at sensing another Dragon here. Red thought. *Still, it doesn't make any sense that they can't find me when*

I'm this close. Then it hit him! *Of course, my connection through the Dragonstaff must be confusing them. They're sensing the man's location instead of mine.*

Then at the same moment both dragons looked directly at him. Red's prideful loathing made him stand straighter and stride all the more confidently towards them. The men who were there also turned to see what the Dragons were looking at. When they saw Red, their jaws almost fell to the ground. Never had more than two dragons come to trade with the breeders at one time.

The men looked unsteadily at each other, grabbed some of the boxes of gold which were already in front of them and left running. Red found it interesting that they only took about half of what had been brought.

They probably thought this was a trick of some sort and that they were going to be eaten. Red snorted to himself.

As Red looked back at the two dragons, his mind seemed to clear of all intrusive thoughts. He now recognized Blue; he was a dragon he had been very close with and had been like siblings when they were younger. That is, before Red was forced to leave.

The other dragon was Gold, his Gold. The dragon he had been banded with. Both dragons were staring at him with a mixture of loathing, detachment, animosity and fondness.

Fondness? Why would they be feeling fondness for me? With a start Red realized the feelings of fondness were not coming from his old friend as he had started to suspect, but rather from Gold.

Why does she have feelings of fondness for me? Red pondered, *especially with all that's happened.*

As both dragons started communicating with Red simultaneously, he realized that none of the animosity he felt was actually coming from Gold. All of the condemnation was coming from the one friend he had thought would be able to forgive him in time.

However, he could also sense both dragons discomfort. He knew they could also sense his shame at their being able to feel his anger so clearly. And then he realized they should be the ones feeling shame, not him. It was their fault he was feeling this way in the first place, not his.

As the intensity of his anger grew, the other dragons grew noticeably more uneasy. Gold finally broke the silence and asked, *what are you doing here?*

It was at that moment Red had his first epiphany, his first true Dragonchange. So long had he been away from Dragonkind. So long had he held his anger inside. so long had he taken upon himself the human name of Red that he understood his Dragonname not as it truly was, but as the name he gave himself out of rage. And it struck him now that his anger, his hatred, was not just at everything else, but also at himself. And for the first time in his life he felt true shame.

I'm here with a man to help. Red replied.

Blue and Gold looked at each other pensively, confusion coming through very clear.

What are you talking about? Blue asked, his eyes narrowing and the scales on the back of his neck bristling so loud Red could hear it.

There is a darkness coming, Red began, trying to remember the exact words Kam had used, *and it will wipe out all life, including all Dragonlife, if it is not stopped.*

He felt Gold's emotions of pity and empathy strongly. He knew she wouldn't believe him; no dragon would. Their Dragonworld was one of strength and no group of creatures could ever defeat them. But Blue's feelings were different. Red couldn't make them out clearly.

So, you think to show yourself to be great in the eyes of Dragonworld so you can return and resume your place there? You are as wormcrazy as you ever were. Blue said, finally allowing Red to understand his emotions.

With Blue's pronouncement, Red felt Gold's pity grow into sorrow for him. She was genuinely grieved for all that had happened to him, and all that had become of his life. Red finally understood the depths of her emotion for him, and his emotion for her. At that moment Red grasped that he would do anything, absolutely anything, to win her back. He didn't care about Dragonworld, or any part of the rest of the world either, for that matter.

It is too bad Gold is banded to me now. Blue then announced triumphantly.

Red felt as if he had been hit in the head with a landslide. He *must* have misunderstood. He looked imploringly at Gold, his eyes begging for some hint that what Blue had said was false. Gold's feelings were a mixture of so many emotions he got dizzy just sensing them. Then a touch of relief when Gold said, *Not banded, not yet. We're just promised.*

As Kam walked down the narrow roads through the older area of the town where the magic shop was located, he noticed how deserted the other shops looked. In a town this size you would expect to see shops bustling with activity; *some* activity at least.

Even the smaller, more esoteric shops like herb and remedy, magic crystals and the like. They should all be getting some coin. But today most of the doors and windows lay shuttered, almost as if they were expecting the darkness to roll down the road now and attack their daily life.

Kam turned a corner to go into the main square and the newer section of the city when he noticed a group of seven people to one side of the square. Even in the empty stillness of what should have been the heart of the business district, he could hear nothing of what was being said.

He approached the group with the hopes of gaining some information about the lack of people in the streets when one of them, a woman, apparently caught his movement with the corner of her eye because she turned to face him. When Kam saw who it was his heart nearly stopped beating. Nycol's face was radiant in the morning sun, and her golden hair and equally golden eyes were even more striking, if that were possible.

She stared at him with a mixture of shock, longing and pain; the latter causing as much distress in Kam as the first time he saw it a year ago. He remembered it as clearly as if it had just happened. He told her he had to leave, and then seeing the pain and confusion in her face and feeling as though someone stuck a knife in his chest and twisted it.

At first, he didn't think he could utter a sound. He opened his mouth and moved his lips but only a whisper of air came out. But his heart! She had to be able to hear that. His ribs were being struck by his heart with every beat and with such strength he felt pain wrap around his torso like a giant serpent. He thought his whole body would start to vibrate with the beats until, like a house in a groundquake, he would finally collapse in a heap on the ground. His body would be completely shattered, but his heart would lay in the middle, still drumming his love for her.

He finally found the courage, or maybe it was just the necessity, to start to talk.

Your hair is even more golden now than the first day we met. Red said. *And your eyes sparkle with a radiance causing the sun to hide its face in shame.*

Golden HAIR? Gold replied. *Have you been drinking Lingonberry juice?*

"I haven't been drinking Lingonberry juice," Kam stated flatly. "And I didn't expect to see you here."

"I didn't say you had been drinking," a confused Nicole replied, glancing around at those who were with her as if to acquire confirmation of just such a fact. It was then she noticed he had a sword strung across his back. "Is that a new sword? Where's your old one, your father's sword?"

Sword? What sword? I don't have any weapons of man. Red's confusion was matched by Gold's. At that, he heard Blue bellow out a loud laugh, a deep, rolling sound only very large dragons make.

He's gone wormcrazy. And to think you were once banded to him.

I was your friend once, Red thought sourly. *And now you're trying to take my female. If you had any courage, you would have challenged me for her instead of trying to steal her when I wasn't there.*

"None of them are trying to steal me, Kam. And I didn't leave you, you left me, remember? And if I choose to be with someone else it's my decision, not yours."

Nycol's confusion was evident in her voice, and she glanced around again as if seeking verbal support from someone in her group. But Kam's confrontational outburst and calls for a challenge had all of them, especially the men, avoiding any eye contact with either of them. Kam himself felt angry and confused, feeling as though his best friend had just spoken out against him. But he didn't recognize any of the people here with Nycol.

With a roar, Red launched himself at Blue. He intended to fight him here and now. Blue answered his challenge and crouched down, preparing to take flight and fight when Gold abruptly placed herself between them and roared a call for silence as only a female can when trying to stop two males from doing something rash.

You both need to stop this right now. Red, you banished yourself and now you need to atone for that. No one can do that but you. Gold looked expectantly at Red, hoping for an answer that would allow him to avoid any more shame.

"Know this," Kam said "I...I think about you and I only left because... because..." He couldn't finish it. As he struggled to control his raging thoughts, he knew she would not only be ashamed for his father, but also for him. And her sympathy was something he would never be able to accept. He couldn't go through life knowing every time he looked into those beautiful eyes all he would see was sorrow and pity for him. That would drive him mad.

Anger pounded yet again in his head, anger he was sure came from Red, or at least he thought he was sure. He thrust the poem he had written and held all those months for her into her hands, turned, and strode briskly away. He knew she would never understand. Women could never understand what a man felt; they just weren't able to.

As Red strode away, he had to contain himself to make sure he didn't turn around and fly back at blue, tearing that smug look of his face at the same time he tore that ugly head from off of his neck. Or to gaze one last time at his banded Gold.

No, banded once a long ago; but not now. He knew if he saw that long neck, powerful body and fiery eyes one more time he would never be able to leave her again. It would be too difficult. And he knew that would cause her pain; something he didn't want to do ever again.

CHAPTER 25

Nycol watched as Kam stormed away, exasperation filling her soul. But that wasn't all. A confusing potpourri of other strong emotions had her mind spinning like a top. She had never told Kam how she truly felt about him; she could never bring herself to say it.

She knew there was something inside Kam, something dark buried deep inside. It was a place of intense sadness for him. He had never told her about it but she guessed it had to do with his father. She had never wanted to have Kam choose between her and the secret he harbored.

She always felt one day he would either tell her what it was or else put it behind him once and for all. She could see it tore him apart; yet she also saw it drove him to be the best at whatever he was doing. This was especially true of his first great love-his blade. Besides, everyone knew a woman couldn't tell a man that she cared for him before he told her. That put a fear in men causing them to trip over themselves trying to get away.

She looked down at the paper he had pushed into her hands. Like Kam it had two sides to it; on the one hand it was folded neatly into a perfect square while on the other it was heavily wrinkled. It gave her the impression he had been practicing with his sword while it was in his pocket.

As she carefully unfolded it, she noticed the smooth yet sturdy feel of the paper. It took her a moment to realize it was the expensive cloth-like stationary you could only find in the really big cities; not the cheap, rough paper most people used. She began to read the words silently to herself.

Doth light from yonder window spill
Upon this hallowed ground,
Causing the moon in shame to hide its face,

To light only itself, for none others to see?
Or doth the sacredness of this ground
Cheat fellow travelers from crossing
For fear of marring its golden beauty?
It guides and lures from lofty heights,
Beckoning and calling,
Begging for man to traverse chasms and dangers,
All for but a glimpse of its radiant glow.
Wise men doth avoid the call of that siren's song,
Sung in shades of gold and bronze
Rather than timeless tunes played on lute and lyre.
A witche's call, a wizard's ward, the beauty of Light's blessing
Giving all a peek into eternity's glory.
Could such light slay a thousand men with chariots
Or a thousand dragons
With scales dipped in reds and yellows and blues,
And end misery and famine?
Nay even causing the Dark One himself to shudder
At the very thought of its extinction?
Torches extinguishing in the agony of its splendor;
Flowers most fair,
Faces twisted and turned to watch the ground in humility.
Fauna cute and furry, large and violent,
Escape from leaving even shadows on gloried ground.
Touched by nothing save radiance from yonder window;
Radiance from love, true and strong.
Radiance from my one and only, the fairest of the fair.
My maiden, my princess, my queen.

She was entranced by the poem, by the language and the flow of
words. As always, whenever Kam gave her something romantic it started
her heart singing. It was an odd way to describe the feeling, she knew.
Yet that was exactly what happened each and every time.

She read it again, slower this time, to allow the full meaning of the
poem to distill upon her mind like the early morning dew upon the

grass back home. Her eyes started to water before she suddenly realized how quiet it was. She glanced up and noticed everyone was staring at her. She quickly wiped her eyes and, using a stronger voice than she felt, said, "What's the matter?"

"'What's the matter?' Your beau just challenged us all to a fight for your hand. That's the problem." Replied John, an overly thin man, boy really, of about eighteen years, who Nycol had known a few months now.

John was willing to talk tough about everything from the king's madness and insatiable greed to fighting for what he believed in. Nycole could agree with him on many of the topics he spoke on. But he honestly was just too scared to do anything but talk.

Fittingly John often wore clothes with faded colors, and today was no exception. His pale red shirt which was about two sizes too big for him and a pair of oddly striped blue pants gave him a comical appearance. When he spoke, his Adam's apple bobbed repeatedly, though from just speaking or because he was swallowing in nervousness she couldn't tell.

"He's not my beau!" she replied hastily, this time in nearly as strong a voice as she felt. "He's just…just a friend, a good friend. Well, maybe not a really good friend, just someone I know. Someone I know very well. No, someone I used to know very well. Not that I don't know him anymore. I still know him, of course. I just don't know him as well as I used to." As she glanced around at the other six who were with her, they just stared at her blankly, as if she had been speaking elfin or some other foreign language. Only Krystyna, one of Nycol's best friends and Kam's sister, was smiling. She had known Nycol her whole life and Nycol was sure Krys understood what she was talking about. She always did.

"She hasn't seen him in a long time and they still have an unresolved relationship." Krys said, still smiling.

What? How could Krys say that about her? Nycol thought, exasperation again filling her. "'Unresolved relationship?' Our relationship is not…"

"Let's get back to the subject at hand, please. We need to stay serious. If we are going to start then let's call it what it is-a revolution." Jerem interjected.

Jerem was wearing the purple and gold of royalty. He was both fairer and shorter than Nycol but carried an air of command wherever he went, giving him a sense of being much larger in size.

"I know what the king is like." Jerem continued. "I may not have been his favorite cousin, but I've been around him long enough to know how he'll react to someone disagreeing with him. And we aren't just talking about a simple difference of opinion here; we're talking about overthrowing him."

"And putting you in charge!" snapped Annabelle.

Annabelle currently preferred to be called Belle for short, but everyone knew her by her nickname-Sparrowhawk. Like the Sparrowhawk which was well known for attacking and fighting almost anything, including much larger birds of prey, she seemed to relish looking for an excuse to become angry or fight with someone.

She was a small, thin woman with a face which looked like it had the skin pulled too tight over her skull. She had a sharp beak of a nose and a large mouth which some would consider attractive if it wasn't constantly compressed into a frown.

Her eyes stood out more than any other physical feature aside from her size. They were large and luminous, a crisp blue-gray as if a storm were rolling in across the ocean. They could flash like lightening when pushed to anger though, which was often.

"I thought we had all agreed, I was the best one for the throne!" Jerem retorted, irritation clearly in his voice.

"For once I agree with you; *you* thought everyone agreed you should be the next ruler." Sparrowhawk replied.

Nycol sighed. Sparrowhawk had a sharp tongue and a sharper wit. Anyone who got on her wrong side was belittled unmercifully to a point where any physical blow would have been preferred.

The other girls feared her and not just for her ability to belittle and embarrass them in front of others. Her quotes were often repeated long after they were said, allowing the embarrassment to fester like an open wound.

But they also feared her nearly as much for her magical ability, which was considerable. There was more than one girl at the school wanting to get even with her but fearing any repercussions she might do. Her magic was more powerful than almost anyone at the school, including most of the professors. Unfortunately, she knew this too.

"At this point we can all agree that the king's greed is slowly strangling the life out of the kingdom. My family is already giving up half of all their crops and most of their money in taxes!" said Suki.

Suki's light brown skin and dark, almond-shaped eyes were complemented by the simple clothes she had on. She had practically grown up as Nycol's sister and she was levelheaded and took great pride in it. She also took great pride in being something of a peace-maker between all of the friends from Idyllwild.

Just then there was a loud thump off to one side. Startled, they all turned at the sound just as a huge, older boy threw a heavy bag of seed into a cart. The perpetrator of their surprise was well known to the girls; he was the school handyman and did odd jobs for room and board.

No one knew his real name so he became known as Moose, as much for his size as for his strength. He was shy and soft-spoken to the point of being mute Some said he was such a simpleton that he was given the work out of sympathy. However, no one could deny his strength. But everyone liked him for his generosity and eagerness to help; nearly everyone anyway.

As the girls watched, he glanced over and gave them a smile of embarrassment. All of the girls knew who the smile was intended for; it was Sparrowhawk. No one understood why he liked her; she was as mean to him as she was to everyone else. But somehow, in his simple, honest way, he seemed to see in her what no one else could.

Sparrowhawk gave a giggle and said, "Cowbell is all strength and no brains. Someone should teach him how to talk. Maybe let him know where the waterhouse is so he doesn't smell like horse all of the time." Then raising her voice, she said, "Isn't that right, Cowbell."

Moose looked up and then proceeded to look around before finally looking back at the girls and said, "There's no cowbell around here, Miss Annabelle."

Sparrowhawk chortled over what happened while the others just stared at her, speechless. "Only you can find a way to be mean to someone as nice as Moose." Krys said, frowning to try and look as menacing as possible so as to eliminate any possibility of a verbal reprisal.

It worked, partially. Sparrowhawk gave a loud hrumph and glared at Krys with such fire in her eyes Krys felt it got 20 degrees hotter.

"Anyway," Suki finally interrupted, "we do all agree we need to do something about the king, and about the *prison*." With her emphasis on the word prison everyone understood she was talking about the School for the Gifted.

Everyone was told the school was set up for the purpose of helping those with magical abilities to understand what they could do and give them a place to learn safely. But everyone who went there knew it was a place designed to hold them so the king wouldn't have to worry about being overthrown by magic users.

"We have enough students at the school supporting us to get rid of it and the king for good." said Matthew, an extremely tall man who felt strongly about having the king removed. He was also the most likely to support violence to subvert the king.

Oddly enough, the only magic he seemed capable of was the benign ability to entice plants to grow a little more quickly than they otherwise might. Nycol always found it interesting that Matthew always seemed to wear various shades of green but never any other color.

At that moment Moose came over and mumbled, "Everything's loaded up. We need to start heading back or Professor Harjdenove will have my backside."

At the professor's name all of them broke out laughing, leaving Moose with a confused look on his face as if everyone understood a joke which had just been said except for him. Which was, in fact, the case.

"Everyone's pet name for Professor Harjdenove is Professor Hard Nose." said Krys.

This again brought titters of laughter from the group, while Moose looked on with even more confusion, if that were possible.

"Never mind Moose," Krys called out sympathetically, "it's not important. Anyway, maybe we should be getting back to the school."

Everyone agreed and Nycol, Krys, Suki, Matthew and Moose all climbed into the wagon.

"Remember to keep your heads low and keep practicing your magic!" Jerem stated firmly. "Especially you Sparrow… I mean Annabelle." He hastily corrected.

Sparrowhawk seemed either not to have noticed Jerem's slip or choose to ignore it, and so he continued. "You have the strongest ability and we will need you on our side." He finished.

The last part brought a smile to her lips, although none of the other girls were happy about that. They all knew she was the most powerful, but no one wanted her to get any cockier.

They rode back in silence, more so because they didn't know what more they could say rather than because they didn't trust Moose. There was never any question as to where Moose's allegiance lay. Besides all they had to do was ask Belle to have Moose promise not to say a word, and he wouldn't.

When they arrived back at school the large clock in the tower in the middle of the campus was just ringing that it was 10:00. The girls jumped out of the cart and started running for their classes.

Matthew, the only one not with a morning class as all of the boys and men were required to do research every morning in the library, simply strolled back to continue his studies. He was also the only one in their group with permission to go to town with Moose and help him get seed.

The girls were making their way down the long, byzantine hallway when a voice suddenly rang out, "Girls, why are you late for your second morning classes?"

It was Professor Windam, one of the strictest professors at the school. He was extremely tall, easily head and shoulders over almost all of the students and professors. Although he was not what anyone would consider muscular, he was still a far cry from being considered thin. With him was Professor Gingham, one of the most beautiful women any of the girls had ever seen. She used her looks and a false sense of kindness to get what she wanted from the male students.

The girls all looked at each other imploringly, begging someone to step up with a reason as to why they were late. But before anyone could answer, Professor Windam continued, "You all need to get to your classes immediately and inform your professors that Ms. Gingham and I are requiring each of you to write whatever lesson you are given today five times in longhand."

The girls all groaned in unison. Professor Windam continued as if he hadn't noticed. "Annabelle, would you accompany Professor Gingham and me to the stables please. We would like to have a word with you in private."

The other girls, for once feeling sorry for Sparrowhawk, gave her looks of encouragement as they walked away. No one could be happy for someone having to face Professor Windam. He seemed to relish doling out punishment the way most girls enjoyed sharing sugar treats with their friends. Some even joked that he was an assistant for the Dark One, although no one would ever say that to his face.

As they walked towards the stables, Sparrowhawk saw Moose walking around towards the rear carrying the heavy sacks of seed. With one sack over each shoulder, it looked as though he were carrying light bags of laundry. She knew she teased him more than she should, but that's what made it so enjoyable.

The Professors didn't seem to notice Moose, so caught up in their own private conversation as they were. Annabelle couldn't hear a word they were saying, but they seemed to be enjoying themselves immensely.

Not for the first time Belle wondered if they had a relationship. She bet they did. But even if they didn't, that would be a fun piece of gossip to start. She giggled, then hastily covered her mouth with her hand so as to stifle any sound which they might hear.

As they approached the stables, Belle noticed the doors were wide open. *That's unusual* she thought to herself. *Those doors are always shut tight.*

In the middle of the stable was a large, round, metal trough for the horses to drink from. It was low, even by her standards, and full of fresh, clean water.

Cowbell must have just cleaned and refilled it. Belle reasoned, although she had to admit every time she saw it, it looked just as clean as it did right now.

She looked around to see if there was anyone else in the stables. She didn't see anyone until she happened to glance up and notice Moose in the hayloft watching them curiously. Not sure how he managed to get up there so quickly, she continued to stare at him until she caught his eye. He smiled at her with that lost little boy look. *How could any girl ever like Cowbell* Belle thought to herself, *he's just such a…*

Abruptly she sensed strong magic emanating all around her. One of her gifts, one which she had never told anyone about, was her ability to sense magic being used. She couldn't for the life of her figure out how that would in any way benefit her.

"Look deep into the water," Professor Windam said, "you'll be surprised at what you find there."

Belle was surprised at the request but she did as she was told. She leaned over as far as she could to make sure she wouldn't miss anything. The water, although not very deep, was dark in spite of the bright sunlight streaming in from all of the open-air windows most barns had. The still, glassy surface allowed her to see her own face clearly and she noticed not for the first time her large, beautiful eyes looking back at her. She also saw Professor Windam's hand hovering by her head.

With a painful start she felt the professor grab a handful of her hair and shove her face underwater. She was so surprised that for a few seconds all she could think of was how indignant she should be. But after the initial shock she realized he wasn't about to let her up. Yet even fully immersed she could hear that witch of a professor Gingham cackling.

Belle struggled to get air but couldn't lift her head even an inch. She put her hands up on the rim of the trough and tried to push herself up, but didn't have the strength to overcome the professor. She had the sickening feeling he was holding her down effortlessly and no amount of struggling would help her.

Belle squirmed sideways and tried to kick at him with her feet. She felt her legs connect against his, but it felt like she was kicking a tree trunk. And that laughter-she thought it would drive her crazy.

She desperately wanted to open her mouth and take in great gulps of air. But she knew if she did what her body screamed for her to do, that would be the end. She stopped struggling and gripped the edge of the trough even tighter. She concentrated on not opening her mouth. Her full concentration was on holding her breath and to stay alive; even if her life lasted just a few seconds more.

Belle's mind seemed to race from one thought to another quickly, briefly, as if to escape death by losing herself in a memory. She thought of many things. The last thing she remembered was Krys telling her how mean she had been to Cowbell. It was obvious he liked her. But she couldn't figure out... she couldn't... She stated to get dizzy and knew she only had a few more seconds of life. She realized she had treated him with such contempt and disdain. With such...

She was pulled back violently from out of the water and up into the air by her hair, which Professor Windham was still gripping. This caused her to land on her back with a loud thump. In ordinary circumstances she would have had the wind knocked out of her. But since she had no air left in her lungs it just jolted her into breathing again, allowing her to take in large gulps of air.

She looked up and there was Moose standing there, looking down at her with a concerned expression. She was confused; dazed also, but mostly confused. Where was Professor Windham?

Belle belatedly realized she had heard a piece of wood crash down and she looked over in the direction where the sound had come from. There was a hole in the side of the barn large enough for even Moose to walk through. She was sure she hadn't seen that hole there before.

Then it hit here, Moose must have thrown the Professor through the wall. But that was impossible-that wall was a good fifteen feet away. She looked back at Moose's worried face and remembered just how strong he really was. Still, to be able to throw a grown man fifteen feet through a well-built wooden wall... She had no idea how far the professor went, but she was grateful for Moose's appearance by her side.

She heard a gasp and looked in the other direction at Professor Gingham. Her eyes were large and round as she stared at Moose, her mouth wide open, gaping. She had the surprised appearance of a caught fish trying to catch its breath in an element which wasn't its own.

The professor regained her composure quickly however and her hands started to move. Belle could feel her start to cast some kind of spell, but she couldn't tell what. The wisps of magic which were cast passed her as they reached out towards Moose.

Belle wanted to warn Moose, to tell him to do something, anything, to keep him safe from the spell. But all she could do was wheeze heavily. She felt the magic emanating from the professor surround and encase Moose. She couldn't see the magic but rather felt it as it wrapped itself around Moose, binding his arms and legs together.

Moose's expression changed from that of concern for Belle to one of determination as he faced the professor. He tried to take a step towards her and found he couldn't. His face turned into a snarl and grew beet red as he strained to move towards the professor. Belle could feel the bands around his body tighten as the magic labored to secure him.

Moose slowly reached out with his arms and Belle felt the magic stretch and strain even more. She could sense the tension on the magic like a rubber hoop stretched to its limit. And like a rubber hoop stretched too far it gave way. With a surprised stumble forward he moved quickly towards the professor.

Professor Gingham, realizing her magic had dissipated, turned and ran. But she wasn't giving up just yet. As she ran Belle could sense her trying to cast another spell, something more deadly. As the professor ran, arrows appeared behind her hanging in the air. The arrows were wrapped in an ethereal green flame and hung in the air for a brief second before shooting towards Moose.

Moose, with surprising agility, quickly turned to the side and dove to the ground. The arrows streaked by where he had just been standing and flew into bales of hay used to feed the animals. The hay caught on fire and flared a spectacular variety of green hues, casting an eerie glow on the walls of the barn.

Belle could only watch in horror and point as the mystical fire started to grow and spread quickly. Moose, without wasting any time, grabbed a rectangular trough near him which was filled with water. Belle watched in disbelief as he lifted the trough over his head and dumped the water on the fire, effectively putting it out.

Belle was combing her hair, her hands still shaking from her brush with death. Her eyes were red and swollen from crying. The only benefit in having Cowbell nearby when it happened was that he provided her a shoulder to cry on. Well, that and the fact he saved her life.

She heard numerous footfalls running down the hall. It sounded like a stampede, which meant they heralded the arrival of her classmates coming to ask her about what happened. Obviously, Cowbell said something to them. With a start she realized she thought of them as her friends, but she had to wonder if they considered her their friend as well.

The girls burst into her room. All of them were breathless and looked as if they had just run across the school yard as fast as they could, which was probably what they had done. They all started talking at once, giving Belle the unique sensation of enjoying the attention and getting a headache at the same time.

"Stop, please, all of you," She said. "My head is still spinning."

The girls closed their mouths in unison, as if on cue from a master conductor who had orchestrated them to harmonize their questions at just the right pitch to cause an echo inside of Belle's head. As they all silently stared at her, Belle made her way to her bed and sat down on the edge of the straw-filled mattress. She abruptly realized the mattress was just as uncomfortable being sat on as lying down on.

"I saw Professor Gingham cast a spell without vocalizing," Belle began. She knew it was an odd place to start talking about nearly being murdered by two of the school's professors, but at the moment it seemed to be the most important information she had.

The other girls looked at each other, then back at Belle. "That's not possible. You have to vocalize incantations or they don't work. You have to." They harmonized again.

"You just had an experience few people will ever have. You were nearly killed. And that's not all; people you knew were the ones trying to do it. Maybe you just imagined it." Suki said.

Belle sighed. She had a hard time believing it too. It was something which was drilled into each student day in and day out. Everyone knew you had to vocalize magic or it wouldn't work. If she hadn't seen it herself, she wouldn't have believed it either.

"I know what I saw." Belle said defiantly.

The other girls quickly fell silent. They knew when Sparrowhawk got this way to just stop talking.

"Maybe the professors are Dark Ones!" Krys said.

The eyed each other disbelievingly; but in their hearts they were all wondering the same thing.

"If you're right…," Nycol started slowly, "then we desperately need to get the word out to the other students."

"You mean the other prisoners!" Exclaimed Belle. "And I, for one, am going to work on doing magic without vocalizing from now on."

All the girls looked at her. They all knew if anyone had the ability to accomplish that it would be her.

"But we need to do this quietly. If it's possible then we need to let others know too. And we can't trust the professors. Even if only some of them are Dark Ones, then we need to tread carefully." Nycol said.

The other girls nodded solemnly. They knew the seriousness of the pact they were making.

Suki said, "Even if there are some professors who are Dark Ones, I seriously doubt all of them are. Especially Summer, uh, I mean Professor Atrum."

"It's okay to call her Summer, Suki," Krys said. "She said that herself."

"But we should be careful how we refer to her outside of class. It's possible other professors, Dark Ones or not, might not be so understanding. We don't want to get the only nice professor here in trouble," Suki responded. "In fact, maybe we should warn her."

The girls all nodded their agreement.

"Well, I'm starving." Belle pronounced. "Let's go eat."

CHAPTER 26

" Look, I need to come with you. I don't know why, I just…do."
Kam said.

Wyk was becoming more impatient by the minute. He had no time
for this boy who seemed to come out of nowhere not far outside the city
to ask to come on their search with them. He was at the end of his wits
as it was with the people he was forced to bring with him to look for an
item of myth which he was sure didn't even exist. Now someone else
was trying to join the ranks of his group. It was looking more and more
as though they would just be going out on a camping trip.

"Please." Kam said desperately, trying to find the right words to
help change Wyk's mind. "I have to go with you." At least that's what
Nix had told him.

Wyk eyed Kam skeptically. He didn't know why this boy wanted to
go along so badly, but did it really matter? The king had already added
more people to go with them; including students from the School for
the Gifted no less.

Wyk, who was more than a little irritated, put his hand on his
sword. He didn't mean to actually draw on the boy, but he was hoping
to scare him off. What happened next was something that Wyk hoped
he'd never have to experience again.

While Kam took a half step back and put his hand on his own
sword, looking all the while as if he might actually try to defend himself,
there suddenly appeared a great, gaping jaw full of teeth. The white,
decidedly pointy teeth, were large, some even as long as his sword. The
mouth was so close he could have reached out and touched it, but the
hot, meaty breath kept that thought from coming to fruition.

Wyk froze. He had never seen a dragon's mouth before; he hadn't
even seen a dragon before. He didn't even know dragons actually
existed. He could see nothing else besides a large, open chasm filled

with rows of needle-sharp death next to him. But what was there could have been nothing else.

The dead silence which had erupted behind him where his companions were served to highlight that what he was seeing was not just in his imagination. Wyk swallowed hard, hoping the noise was not heard by the boy and his apparent pet. Or maybe it was his bodyguard?

"Um, sorry about him; he just wants to go home." Kam said, interrupting Wyk's thoughts and allowing his heart to start beating again.

Wyk slowly took his hand off his sword and raised both hands in front of him to show he had no intention of attacking Kam or the mouth of teeth.

Not that I have any weapon which could hurt that thing. Wyk thought to himself.

Wyk looked around and realized there was no place from where the dragon could have come from; no hills or ditches, not even a large tree. Since this was the main thoroughfare approaching the city most rocks and shrubs larger than a person's head had been cleared away so no enemies would have cover if they were to attack. That meant the dragon had to have flown in.

Wyk turned to gauge what the others were thinking, and he almost wished he hadn't. He noticed that the horses were skittish and quietly neighing nervously while everyone in the group had their jaws wide open and catching flies. Only two people weren't showing surprise or fear-Jesse, whom Wyk had never ever seen surprised or afraid, and astonishingly the king's guest, Sakura.

Wyk always felt he was a good judge of character. He thought that was exactly what made him a good leader. But he couldn't figure Sakura out. She said she had been attacked in the castle, which if true would explain her being in a state of shock. He had met women before who had survived violent attacks, and the one thing they all seemed to have in common afterwards was a sense of despair about them.

Sakura seemed to show the same effects of an attack in her demeanor, especially with her lack of emotion at the appearance of a dragon. Her clothing, however, said otherwise. Her well-fitted top and pants clearly showed her physical beauty to the world. Interestingly she was wearing the snug, one-sleeved shirt typical of swordsmen. The sleeveless shoulder was would be her sword arm, kept free of clothing to allow ease of swordplay. In recent times the wealthy had taken to wearing the same style of clothing, creating a senseless fashion for those who couldn't sword fight at all. Yet she had the figure of one who kept herself in shape. And she had a sword at her side.

"Excuse me." Kam said.

Wyk was instantly brought out of his reverie and gave himself a sharp mental kick. What was he doing? He was behaving badly and representing himself and his men poorly. He turned slowly, keeping his face blank, so as to seem unfazed by having a huge, man-eating dragon appear abruptly next to him.

"You two may come with us." He said to Kam.

The boy smiled and seemed to relax, as did his dragon, which finally closed its mouth, yet eerily still seemed to be smiling. Wyk had no idea if a dragon was truly even capable of smiling, but he imagined one which had a buffet the likes of this group walking with it might find reason to.

"We'll watch the rear." Kam said.

The boy then turned to the dragon and seemed to talk with it, with their conversation becoming increasingly animated. To Wyk it appeared they were having a soundless argument with the dragon's displeasure showing clearly in its eyes. Then they both abruptly headed towards the rear of the group, with the dragon hungrily eyeing the horses it passed. Or was it watching the riders? Wyk couldn't understand how anyone could argue with a dragon; or at least win an argument with one and live to tell about it.

"We're going to keep up a, uh, good pace. Don't fall behind" Wyk said, although since both Kam and the dragon turned to face him, he wasn't sure which he was talking to.

Wyk turned and yelled, "Forward!" although his mouth seemed to have suddenly become dry and he wasn't sure if those in the back heard him.

The group continued its trek and Wyk mentally tallied the bizarre group. There was a handful of the King's Guard led by himself along with a couple of girls from the School for the Gifted. He wasn't sure what they were doing here. Maybe the king thought they could use their magic to heat up their dinner.

Then there was the handyman, who was also from the school. He was the size of a barn and as strong as a horox by the looks of him. Wyk wondered if he could handle a sword. Even if he couldn't he might be able to hurl boulders at any enemies which might show up.

There was Sakura, the woman of the upper class who had been attacked. She was beautiful and carried a sword but would probably end up being useless. Then there was the boy and his dragon. What a group. At least robbers and highwaymen would think twice before attacking them, although that was more likely due to the fact that a dragon was traveling with them. Otherwise, they would seem to be an escort for the Lady Sakura.

"How far are we traveling?"

Wyk was again brought out of his reverie by the boy. Wyk did notice however that the boy rode very much like a soldier. Or at least one who had seen his fair share of fighting. Wyk made a mental note to challenge him to a friendly exercise of swords the next time they stopped.

"It should take a couple of months," Wyk responded.

Abruptly a short, barking laugh erupted from the boy's mouth. Wyk eyed him warily. He didn't need anyone to go soft in the head on this trip-especially since they had such a long way to go. The boy Kam seemed to sense the attention his offhanded guffaw aroused and turned his full attention on Wyk.

"I'm sorry, but sometimes his sense of humor about people is humorous in a very, uh… grim way."

Wyk had no idea what the boy was talking about and again had a sudden image of the boy losing his mind and the dragon…well, there was nowhere nice to go with that thought.

"Red and I are, um, connected…" Kam began.

Wyk looked at him, puzzled.

"The dragon; the dragon's name is Red."

Wyk glanced over at the dragon. *Well, that makes sense.* He thought. *The dragon was after all red.* Yet he had the odd feeling that Red wasn't called that just for his color, and the feeling that the group was a walking seven-course dinner for the dragon came to him again.

"Don't worry, dragons don't eat people. They can't stand the taste."

That was supposed to make him feel better? Wyk had eaten his fair share of nasty-tasting food, but he still ate it. Sometimes you didn't have a choice.

"We have a long way to go. Just get comfortable in your saddle."

A long way to go indeed.

CHAPTER 27

"What IS that thing?" Krys asked.

Krys must have ridden up while Kam had been talking with Wyk. He looked over at her and not for the first time noticed how much she had grown. She looked like a young woman and very much like their mother.

She had taken their surprising reunion well, although Kam was surprised to see her. He still didn't fully understand why she and her friend were on this trip. Krys said that the king had been told by someone to include magic users. Kam always thought the king hated people who could do magic.

Now he noticed her eyes wide with fear and...*envy*? Growing up, Krys had always showed a deep love for animals, even to the point of sometimes thinking she knew what they were thinking. She ate very little meat despite having grown up on a farm and having more meat than the average family would have been able to purchase. He was surprised she couldn't figure out now what kind of animal was with him.

"It's a..."

"DRAGON!" Krys finished for him.

Kam stared at her. Her fear vanished and was now completely replaced by excitement. Here was something new for her to bond with, a new animal to experience empathy for. Kam smiled to himself. His sister was in for a rude awakening if she thought she would enjoy being near a dragon, or at least this dragon.

Krys looked over her shoulder and watched as the dragon walked a shuffling, awkward-looking gait so as not to outpace the slow-moving group of people. She had no doubt the dragon could, even while being forced to stay flightless as he was now, easily keep up with horses going at a full gallop.

Krys suddenly turned to Kam and with a strained voice said, "He's sad and in pain."

Kam looked at her, surprise etched clearly in his face. Quickly he composed himself and as nonchalantly as possible asked, "How do you know?"

"I can feel that he's lonely. He's also been hurt by his family and someone he loved before. It's almost as though he feels he's been betrayed."

Kam swallowed hard. Krys had never been that descriptive about the condition of any animal before. Certainly not going into the feelings a pig might have about being eaten or about a horse having a person on its back. Perhaps it was the sheer size of Red which made it easier to understand or sense. But she was talking about it as if it were a person with feelings of betrayal and abandonment-something she had never done before.

"He also has a…a…uh!" she finally finished in exasperation. A shudder took hold and shook her whole body.

Kam swallowed again. *How is she doing this?* He thought. *It's as if she's looking right into the heart of Red. She's sensing what I've sensed before; a darkness that's rooted in his very soul.*

For a while they rode on in silence, but Kam knew his sister well enough to recognize the determined expression she now wore on her face. She was puzzling over what she sensed in the dragon, trying to understand it.

He knew she would never figure out what the dragon was feeling simply because she was incapable of comprehending the darkness. She was a naïve girl who always looked for answers in which everyone came out on top. She always had trouble comprehending the darker aspects of human nature. When she did come across it she always felt that love and forgiveness would make everything turn out. But this time…

"He has a deep, dark pain in his soul…" she began, interrupting Kam's thoughts. "And he senses you are helping him to overcome it. But he's not sure if he's happy about that or not."

Kam stared at her, speechless. He didn't know how to respond. She rode away and let the matter lie, at least for now. He knew however that at some point she would bring it up again.

"I appreciate you bringing me along." Sakura said. She watched as the Head of the King's Guard glanced over at her. He didn't seem surprised anymore at her having been allowed on this trip. However, he still seemed to be a little put out at having a woman along. Or maybe it was having a woman whom he felt couldn't defend herself.

She glanced back at the girls in their group. Everyone knew they were from The School, which meant they could do magic. She didn't know what kind of magic they were capable of, but any magic could be helpful in a difficult situation.

She turned back to look at Wyk again. He had a strong, handsome face; yet she could also see compassion in his eyes. If they were just two average people in the city, she could see them being together.

She shook her head violently. What was she thinking? She had a job to do. However, showing him what she *was* capable of might just give her a little more space and keep him from being around her too closely. She made a quick decision to show him a little of what she could do, something she rarely did. It was after all best to keep others at a disadvantage by keeping your skills a secret.

Again, she glanced over at him and again she noticed his handsome face. She briefly considered what he would think if he knew her true motives. *What am I thinking?* She thought. *Why do I care what he thinks on my being here? I have a job to do and I must do it.*

Suddenly he said, "The king asked me to bring you and I am. There is nothing you need to thank me for."

Well, that was abrupt. I guess he is like every other soldier-good for fighting but not for anything else. Maybe I will show him a thing or two about swordplay…and let him know what a real blademaster is capable of.

With that she slowed her horse just enough to fall back in behind him.

What about the dragon? She mused. *I didn't know there were any dragons outside of Dragonmount and Dark Alley. Where did it come from?*

She knew she wouldn't be getting any answers soon so she settled in for a long trip.

Jesse couldn't remember the last time he saw a woman as beautiful as Sakura. Her face was exquisite-looking, more like a work of art than that of a real person. Her blonde hair was up in a ponytail, something he had always found attractive. And the curves of her body were only barely contained beneath her pants and shirt.

He was used to getting women and took it for granted that any free woman was his for the taking…but this woman was different. She had paid absolutely no attention to him since they started their journey. He sighed. Soldiers didn't go on journeys, especially men of the King's Guard. They protected the royal family and sometimes their guests; that was all. They didn't do favors for the king, that's what servants were for.

He could tell Sakura had her heart set on someone else; that much anyone with two eyes could see. It would be interesting to see if the one she was noticing noticed her as well…

He sighed again. Maybe he would have a chance to win her over. He certainly had the time on this trip to show her he was the man she should be with, at least for a short time. Although there was something odd about her that he couldn't put his finger on just yet.

She was tired and hungry and she sensed everyone else was too. Or maybe she just thought she sensed in others what she was feeling. She glanced over at Cowbell who always seemed to know when she was looking at him. Sure enough, he turned his head and gave her a big country-boy smile.

She sighed. *Just because I owe him my life doesn't mean I have to like him.*

She turned away quickly, infuriated at herself for allowing her face to grow hot with embarrassment. She was the most powerful student at The School. In fact, she wasn't just the most powerful student, but she was more powerful than most of the professors as well. She should have been able to handle herself when she was attacked. But she didn't and it upset her to the point of…

Well, it upset her a lot. She hadn't been able to stop them from attacking her. She had been helpless and needed Cowbell's help. That's what really bothered her. But who could expect a girl in training to be able to handle herself like a soldier? It was the fact that it was Cowbell, that smelly, loose-minded man who was incredibly strong and cute, which bothered her.

She tried to calm herself, to still her thoughts. She used the meditation drills she learned from Mrs. Beesley. Sometimes Annabelle felt the only professor there who cared about her was Mrs. Beesley.

Surely she's not one of the Dark Ones.

"Hey Belle," Krys said, breaking through her thoughts with a snicker. "It looks like Moose still likes you."

Quickly Annabelle looked over at Cowbell and realized the joke Krys made on her behalf. To make matters worse Moose picked that moment to again look over at her and smile. Annabelle felt as if steam was coming out of her ears. She was so mad she wanted to scream.

Maybe she could use the dragon Kam brought with them for target practice later. She wondered if she had the magic to defeat a dragon. Now *THAT* was an interesting thought…

"…it was called a war hammer and it could shoot lightening and it was the most incredible weapon. It was powerful and Thor was a great warrior and he could…"

Wyk glanced over at Moose riding next to him and tried not to look bored. Moose was a good kid, well man really, but he seemed to have the mentality of a child. He seemed to be fixated on his horse's name. Wyk had to admit it was an unusual name. But now he was rambling on about a hammer? Well, it kept him happy and, with the exception of having to listen to him babble, he wasn't any trouble.

Besides this kid was STRONG. He had never seen anyone do the amount of work and lift the kind of weight Moose did. He did the work of five grown men and didn't seem to mind at all.

Wyk wondered how much weight he himself could lift. He knew he was strong, although not as strong as Moose, he was sure. Just then he had a bizarre vision came to him of Moose carrying his horse instead of the other way around.

While Moose was talking about hammers and unknown legendary warriors, Wyk thought about Red. He hated having a dragon with them, especially behind them where he couldn't be easily seen. What if he decided he was too hungry to wait around for his next meal and decided to gnaw on a person or four? Would they have the means of stopping him? Would Kam be able to control him? Wyk didn't think so.

The sound of arguing voices suddenly reached his ears. Behind him Krys and Belle seemed to be in a heated debate over their clothing. With a sigh and a quick "excuse me" he turned his mount Titan and rode back to see if there was anything he could do to stop their racket.

He knew it would be a mistake to get involved in an argument between two women as they would both suddenly turn on him as if he were the one who had started it, but at least it would get them to stop.

Moose hated riding. Most horses seemed too small for him and tired quickly. He also hated forcing another creature to do something it didn't seem to want to do on its own. But this horse that they got from the king's stables was far bigger than any one he had ever seen before. It was a good head and a half taller than any other horse in the group with the exception of Wyk's.

Wyk told him it was a special horse, a horse bred and trained for battle, the same as his. The only difference was that it had been put to pasture. Moose knew what that meant; it meant the horse was allowed to have fun with other horses. But the king's stable master told him this horse was never happy playing with other horses; that it was happiest in battle like any good warrior. And like a good warrior it wanted to die on the battlefield. Moose wasn't sure why anyone or anything would want to die on a battlefield-there was so much noise and blood and pain. He also knew sometimes you had to fight even if you didn't really want to.

The horse moved well under his weight, walking easily with its head held high, as if it was proud to be carrying Moose on its back. That part made him happy. Sometimes he wondered if he made anyone happy to be around him. Except for Annabelle; she seemed to like him.

She had even given him her own special nickname-Cowbell. No one else called him by her nickname and that was okay with him. It was her special name for him. She had always liked him and he had always known there was a special bond between them.

He patted his horse on its neck. The stable master told him his name was Thor. He wasn't sure what the name meant, but it sounded strong. The stable master told him the name was a very old and famous warrior's name; a warrior who fought with a magical hammer instead of a sword or spear.

He said the hammer could shoot lightening and no one else could use it. That sounded like the weapon for him. He didn't like swords because he was always cutting himself on them, especially when he sharpened them. He would have to ask his new friend Wyk if he could find him a hammer like the one in the story.

His stomach made a loud rumbling noise.

I'm starving and some of these horses look appetizing.

Kam swiveled around in his saddle to glare at Red. Of course, no one thought to bring along a few horses to munch on while on this little trip. And having to WALK; it was embarrassing. His stomach growled again and Kam gave him another stern look from the top of a potential meal. Red snorted. *People,* He thought angrily. *You can't live with them and you can't eat them.*

Red's stomach growled again and Kam gave him another withering look. Red snorted, louder this time so Kam would hear. If only dragons could stomach the taste of people; there were many here he thought the world could do without.

Although they had only been on this trip for a few hours, Red thought that the only human who had any decency was the big one-the one they called Moose. He had a quiet intelligence and strength about him. He also didn't seem to be afraid of him like the others were.

Moose seemed to accept him as an intelligent creature, even occasionally turning to look at him and wave. Although Red found that unusual, he sensed an almost Dragon-like greatness in Moose. There was a nobility and strength he didn't see in the others. Moose showed him a compassion and respect that everyone would be good to learn. Maybe he could find a way to acknowledge it.

Red found he could also sense a little of Moose's thoughts. It wasn't like the connection he had with Kam-that was different. It was more like how the sun would occasionally peak through a thick layer of clouds on a stormy day. Flashes of what Moose thought and felt seeped through into Red's head and gave him the feeling of soaring through an open sky with no cares in the world.

Red noticed Moose talking with the one who seemed to be the leader of the group. He was going over a specific type of weapon, but one he had never heard of before. He did, however, sense a different kind of strength in two of the women in the group. They were both very powerful in magic, but in different ways. Red wasn't sure how to describe it. Maybe if he was around women more often…

With that last thought Red started to choke and almost coughed out fire. Everyone turned at the sound with fear plainly written in their faces. Only two-Moose who was showing obvious concern for Red and Kam who looked at him with anger-didn't seem afraid. This was going to be a long trip.

CHAPTER 28

The next day they traveled along in peace. On the afternoon of the third day, Wyk started to marvel at the lack of complaining, especially among the girls and Kam. Usually on trips of this type he would have expected those without training to start grumbling about sleeping on the ground or the lack of baths. But the girls and the boy seemed to be holding up quite well.

Even Sakura, a woman with at the least the bearing of royalty if not the blood, seemed to be doing remarkably well. Apparently, she was tougher than she looked.

While they ate lunch, Wyk decided to give those who hadn't traveled outside of the kingdom before some information to help them on their journey.

"We will be traveling through some harsh lands and we may encounter things some of you may not have seen before."

Wyk glanced around at the group. Sakura had a bored expression, as though there was nothing he could say which would be new to her. The girls looked at each other skeptically while the boy kept eating with his head down. Moose sat up and actually looked excited. Wyk decided to spice up the conversation and see what would happen. "There are creatures such as Halfers and Darkbloods and, although I don't expect to encounter any, you need to understand what they are like just in case. Generally, they are fierce fighters, and in a group they can be dangerous. But individually they will be too afraid to come near us."

Krys raised her hand, which for some reason irked Wyk.

"Yes Krys?"

"What do they look like?"

Wyk paused, wondering how much he should say. Finally, he said, "Halfers are a combination of animal and man. They can be fierce fighters and utilize their animal traits to fight. Darkbloods may or may not have a shape like a person, but they tend to have natural boney armor. It will look as if their bones were on the outside of their body instead on inside.

"Both types of creatures have natural weapons like claws, but they can also have man-made weapons such as swords. If we happen to run into any of them, you non-fighters will need to get behind the Guardsmen as fast as you can. Understood?"

The girls nodded enthusiastically, Sakura still looked bored, the boy still had his head down, and Moose looked disappointed. This wasn't going to be a very enjoyable trip.

Perhaps, Wyk thought, *I should be grateful for us traveling in silence.*

After lunch everyone took a few minutes to relax a bit before starting out again. Wyk went over to Kam, who continued to exhibit the unnerving behavior of talking to his dragon without actually speaking.

"How about crossing blades with me?" he asked.

Kam looked at him, surprised. Wyk got the distinct feeling he had interrupted an important conversation. Hopefully it was not one where Kam had to plead with his partner not to consume them. But Wyk needed to know where this boy stood when and if there came time to defend the women.

Wyk could tell Kam wasn't sure why he was asking, but with a shrug Kam walked a short distance from the group and drew his sword. Wyk noticed the dragon came around and appeared to want to watch.

Wyk attacked first, moving easily and pausing after only a few blows. The boy parried him easily and again looked at him with that puzzled frown he seemed to wear a lot. It was almost as if someone was talking to him in a way only he could hear and understand.

Wyk attacked harder, pushing the boy, forcing him to parry quickly or risk getting cut on his arm or chest. Wyk had no intention of seriously hurting him of course, he just wanted to test his mettle. But the more he pushed and the faster he attacked the quicker the boy became. It got to the point all Wyk could see of his vicious attacks was a blur where Kam's sword was parrying him.

Wyk was starting to sweat and his breathing was beginning to become a little heavy. This boy wasn't just better than he thought; he was a lot better. In fact, Wyk was starting to wonder if Jesse would be able to take him. He knew he could eventually beat the boy, but still he was showing great skill with the blade.

"Hold." Wyk said, and stood straight up with his blade pointing skyward, the universal sign swordfighters everywhere used to signal they wanted to stop. Kam stood still, perspiration showing on his face and breathing hard through his mouth. Maybe this boy wasn't in great shape after all, but Wyk was still impressed by his skill.

Wyk turned to see the group had gathered around to watch. All of them were wearing faces of shock and surprise, although none more so than Jesse. As Wyk looked at them all he couldn't help but notice the dragon watching as well. Disturbingly, the dragon displayed what Wyk would swear was a smile of hope on its face.

"What's everyone looking at? We were just practicing for a few minutes. That's all."

"'A few minutes?' You've been at it now for over half an hour." Jesse said.

"Then…let's go. I mean get ready to move." Wyk said.

As he walked back to his horse, he passed Jesse who seemed to be snickering at him. Wyk glared at his back but knew he would have the last laugh over his friend. He would keep Jesse so busy that there would be no time for him to spend with any of the women on this trip. That gave him some sense of revenge.

As Kam was walking back to his horse, Krys came up, looking stern. "Why is the dragon upset?"

Kam eyed her warily. He knew his sister well enough to know she brought things up only when she was making a point, and the creator help the person who didn't understand the point she was trying to make.

"What makes you think he's upset?"

"I can sense it, along with everything else. It's almost as if I can sense his thoughts. You know from when I was young and could tell what animals were sometimes feeling? Well, it's deeper with the dragon, easier somehow. I can also tell he's very intelligent too. And he's not happy."

Kam stopped strapping his sword to his saddle and tried to focus on Red. He suddenly realized he had somehow grown used to the bond.

Maybe it was because of other people being around and distracting him. Whatever the reason, he had been paying less notice to him.

He now focused on Red and as he did the connection seemed to swirl around in his head. He again felt the icy-hot, greasy blackness which seemed to coat every thought and feeling Red had. He again felt the familiar desire to fall on his knees and throw up. But one thought did come through…and odd thought, but still a clear one.

Kam turned to Red and asked, *You want a hammer? A LARGE hammer?*

Yes.

Kam sighed. He didn't think he would ever understand the dragon. Why would he want a hammer in the first place? Kam sighed again and rode his horse over to the small supply wagon they had with them. He rummaged around for a few minutes, patiently searching. He finally found a cross pein hammer used for general wagon wheel repair and maintenance.

The hammer was large, larger than Kam would have expected, and looked well used. It was blackened by years of being used around forges and having soot and dirt ground into it. Surprisingly the leather grip that wound around the handle and formed the strap looked almost new, as if it had just been replaced.

Kam reached for the hammer and nearly dropped it. It was a large hammer but the weight didn't seem to fit. It had to be at least 20 pounds! Kam hefted it; it was like trying to lift a large rock with one hand.

Well Red should be able to lift this with no problem. Maybe he wants to knock out some meat stuck between his teeth.

Or maybe I should hit you over the head with it. Came Red's retort.

Kam jumped at the dragon's voice in his head. He reminded himself that while being with people distracted him from the bond, Red had no such distraction.

As Kam eased his horse back towards the back of the group, everyone gave him a friendly nod or greeting. He got the feeling some of them were being friendly just to get on his good side so he would keep Red from having them as an appetizer. However, most of the non-guardsmen he generally liked; the only exception was the beautiful one who held herself like a queen. She ignored him as she did everyone else.

As he slowed his horse down to pull next to Red his sister passed him. She shot him a look that could wither flowers. Now what was she mad about? Kam sighed. There was just no pleasing some people.

Take the girl that was with Krys, the one that wanted to be called Belle. She went around as if her undergarments were three sizes too small. She had a sour look on her face all of the time, which was too bad. She had pretty eyes and when she smiled it really caused her face to become almost pretty.

By the time Red caught up to him they were nearly to edge of the Eastern plains surrounding the city. You couldn't see the city anymore but the plains allowed for grazing for the royal herds as well as keeping any approaching armies from being hidden from the patrols as they approached the city.

Up ahead was the start of the Great Forest where the king and many of his subjects were allowed to hunt. Of course, to hunt in the forest meant you had to pay for the opportunity to be picked for that chance. If you were picked you then had to pay again to actually hunt, and then you paid based on the weight of the animal you caught. Kam began to think a dragon's life might be easier.

It isn't.

Kam jumped again and gave Red a sour look of his own. *You shouldn't be listening in on my thoughts. It isn't right. And where have you been?*

Red just snorted.

When Kam was about ten feet away Red turned his head and, without any warning, shot out his tongue. This caused Kam to jump. Red's tongue was long and sinuous, reaching nearly to him. The last four feet of it was split into two "fingers", snake-like, which caused Kam to shudder.

Kam knew what Red wanted so he hefted the hammer and placed it on one if the fingers, preparing to laugh heartily when the dragon's tongue hit the ground. However, Red merely rolled his tongue in on itself, taking the hammer with it as effortlessly as if Kam had just given him a flower.

You have a strong tongue. was all Kam managed to sputter while wiping off some of the dragon's spittle which had gotten on his hand. He was still surprised the saliva didn't cause his hand to catch on fire or burn it like acid; it just seemed to be saliva like any other animals'. He did however remember its ability to heal.

Abruptly Kam sensed some apprehension in Red and realized the dragon was wondering if he would be able to fit in and around the trees.

Don't worry; the road through the forest is very wide for a long distance.

I'm tired of walking. My wing is strong and completely healed; I need to be able to fly.

Don't be a baby. Kam thought back. *You'll be okay.*

With that last part Red gave him a look as harsh as any his sister would have given him. He sighed again and just spurred his horse on.

As they approached the forest, Red had to agree the road was very broad entering in, broad enough even for him. And the tops of the trees left plenty of room for him as well. Walking through the forest, at least this part of it anyway, was no problem.

But he hung back, waiting for the others to get out of eyesight for him to perform his own special magic-Dragonmagic. With the hammer still being held in his curled-up tongue he exhaled Dragonfire, but with a subtle difference. He didn't create flame but rather only smoke which filled his mouth and drifted out of his nostrils. The only way someone other than a dragon would know it was a form of magic, as opposed to regular smoke, would be its color.

The green tendrils which escaped through his nostrils wrapped around his head like an ethereal wreath crowning him lord of the forest. Eventually the smoke dissipated and Red extended his tongue and laid the hammer gently on the ground with far more care than anyone watching would have thought possible.

The hammer now looked new. Where it had once been dark and sooty now it was shiny, as if it had just been forged and polished. The sun gleaming off of its surface showed the metal now had a hint of green in its surface. Where the leather grip and strap had been now appeared to be dragon's skin. Yet its color remained a deep brown but now had overtones dark red in it. Red smiled at that; it was after all a piece of himself he was giving to Moose.

Now for the most difficult part-drawing on long-dormant magic shared with him by his banded Gold. He knew man could never understand the simplicity or the depth of Dragonlove, nor could they understand the sharing of Dragonmagic between two Dragons who agree to share their long lives together.

Each Dragon gives a bit of their magic to the other. It's not enough magic for the other Dragon to use, especially when it's a magic utterly foreign to its nature. But the magic still exists in more than enough quantity to be able to utilize. This was especially true for doing what Red had planned.

He touched the hammer gently with one claw. Then a bright light appeared from a small discharge of golden lightening starting just where the claw entered into Red's flesh. To anyone who might have seen this, it would have reminded them of the first bolt of lightning, reaching down from aa dark, overcast sky, to herald the beginning of a storm. The lightening arced around the claw and struck the hammer. When the arc died the hammer glowed softly, a deep golden yellow which gently faded.

Red didn't know what to expect as lightening was Gold's Dragonmagic, not his. He wasn't even completely sure how it would affect the hammer, especially with two completely different Dragonmagics being mixed together.

Red stared at the hammer for a long moment. He could sense both magics in it, but something else as well. The two types of magic seemed to be combining in a way he hadn't foreseen. They were affecting each other, becoming one new type magic, and far more powerful than he had anticipated. Well, he was still confident his idea would work, or at least he hoped it would. He picked up the hammer with his tongue again and started into the forest.

Red's mind was surprisingly occupied with a variety of thoughts, each struggling to come to the forefront and be noticed. When he had been alone, his thoughts focused on his anger and the mistakes of others. He had existed on a few memories, most of which were unpleasant. That was before he started traveling with the man.

But now a cornucopia of thoughts swirled in his head-most of which had nothing to do with him. Now his mind seemed open to the myriad potential in life, both for him and others he had met.

There were the girls who had magic within them; strong magic struggling to be free. Then there was the emotional symbiotic leeching of Kam. There was the well-deserved reverence of the large man called Moose. But, in the end, it was seeing the lightening magically infused into the hammer which brought back the strongest images-those of his Dragonlove.

She was a Gold Dragon, a Lightening Dragon, one of the rarest of all dragons. And she had been beautiful. No, she was still beautiful-she just wasn't in his life anymore. He hadn't realized when he lost her that her magic would stay within him and that he would still be able to use it. Red shook his head trying to clear his thoughts.

Abruptly he had to clumsily step to one side to keep from crushing Kam and his horse. The wagon in front of them had caught on a low hanging branch and come to a sudden stop. Kam looked up with an expression which gave Red all the information he needed. And he could have done without the yelling in his head and some words which he didn't understand.

But a new idea sprang into his head. Would the evil Dragonstaff which Kam carried to control him allow for a truly accidental death, even if it was caused by Red? Red mentally filed that thought away with the hope of causing some minor "accidents" later to see what would happen.

He noticed some movement out of the side of his eye and turned his head. It was the one who was smart enough to worship him, the one who the gift was for. He now seemed to be making sure Red was doing all right. Red knew he should probably be taking the man's attention as rude; after all who would ever think a dragon would need comfort or help from a person. But from this man Red found the attention exhilarating. If all humans looked up to dragons the way this one did the world would be a better place.

Red slowly extended his tongue with the hammer in it towards Moose. Moose looked up at him, the joy in his eyes for receiving a gift from such a glorious creature was obvious. And inevitable; the gift was, after all from a Dragon.

The man reached out and, with ecstasy on his face and his hands shaking, gently picked up the hammer. He looked it over and expressed his gratitude the only way he knew how-by profusely thanking Red with a barrage of sounds. Red knew it was all that this human could do, and so he relished in the adulation. The human rode slowly away, back towards the front of the group. Red was sure he would be showing the magnificent gift to all of the others.

Kam glanced over as Moose slowly rode past him, oblivious to everything around him. His attention seemed to be focused on something he was carrying, something very bright. With a start he realized it was a hammer, and judging by its size, the same one he had taken to Red. Only this one looked as if it had just been forged, although it had a faint chartreuse gleam to it.

"Do you mind, that is, would it be okay if I could see that?" Kam asked slowly.

"Sure, the dragon gave this to me."

It was also obvious Moose was excited to have received the gift. But why? It was a hammer, an old hammer which had been polished to look like new. As Moose started to hand it over an arc of what looked to be lightening seemed to jump from the hammer and struck Kam's hand. Kam quickly jerked his hand back while Moose, eyes wider than Kam thought would have been possible, quietly said, "Thor's hammer."

Kam looked at him then back down at his hand. Where the lightening had struck his hand and riding glove there was now a large burnt spot with a hole in the center of it. Kam took off his glove and inspected his hand. The point of contact left a red, tender spot which didn't seem bad, but it did hurt. Moose was still staring at him with those wide eyes when he said, "Where do you suppose he found Thor's hammer?"

"Who said he found Thor's hammer? And who is Thor?"

"I got this hammer from your dragon. He just gave it to me. Thor was a great warrior who lived a long time ago and he used this hammer to fight with. It's magical."

At that point Kam excused himself from Moose and edged his horse over a bit and thought angrily *What are you doing?* It was only at this point Kam realized he heard what he now knew to be Red's laughter inside his head and that it started when the lightning struck his hand.

You did that on purpose!

I didn't know that would happen. I was just giving my friend a gift.

It took a moment for the full impact of Red's words to sink in. 'I was just giving my friend a gift.'

Kam paused, he didn't care who Red gave gifts to, did he? He never expected to get anything other than the dragon's help while they were together. And if they survived whatever situation they eventually found themselves in, he had no qualms that Red would kill him as soon as he released the bond. But giving gifts to people? That didn't even sound like the same dragon.

He worships me. Came the explanation in his head.

Kam glanced back at Red and saw what he swore was fierce pride glowing in the dragon's eyes. He sighed. It WAS going to be a long trip.

CHAPTER 29

They had been traveling about a fortnight and still had many days to go and Kam was getting worried. The darkness which Kam noticed so distinctly in Red when they first met, which at times even seemed to have a life of its own, had now stopped exerting itself. It was as if the sun had suddenly risen on a new day after years of having forsaken the sky.

Kam could still feel the long, dark tendrils of what he had originally thought to be simply rage and bitterness, still inside of Red. Whatever was in Red was still there, but somehow it was different. It was as if it was slumbering, allowing its form to exist but without the emotional impact of its being truly awake.

What he sensed now was a new-found energy for life which had slowly taken over Red since this quest began. He also noticed that most of the people in their group had started to warm up to Red. He knew Red wouldn't eat anyone, but the fact that many of the group routinely went and talked with him seemed to please him.

Moose and Krys provided a seemingly endless supply of devotion to the dragon. And Krys's friend, the one who didn't seem to get enough to eat, had even been with the dragon on occasion. Then there were the King's Guards, many of whom had taken to routinely spending some of their free time with Red, including Wyk. Kam had to admit Red had been on his best behavior with the exception of a few minor accidents.

Sakura was the only one who seemed to avoid Red, almost as if she considered herself too delectable a tidbit for him to pass up. Kam chuckled to himself, a mirthless, dark sound which surprised even him when it escaped from his lips. He knew the revulsion Red felt when he even briefly considered eating some of the people, and he only considered that due to the lack of large animals for him to devour.

Unfortunately, the darkness which had been so prevalent in Red now seemed to be having the opposite effect in Kam. Within him it was like a festering wound, with its poison slowly creeping deeper and deeper into his body and causing ever more healthy flesh to turn sour and start to rot. He found himself becoming more and more distant and aggressive towards others, even including his sister, the one person he would never dare hurt.

He also felt the darkness affecting him in other ways-he wasn't sleeping well, he rarely felt hungry and lost his desire to eat, and he started having aches throughout his body and especially in his head. He even considered asking one of the women to see if they could do anything with their magic, but every time he approached them an argument seemed to break out. He found it best to just ride along in silence.

There were many occasions where he tried to communicate with Red, but he couldn't tell if the darkness he felt was more in Red or himself. He knew he would have to do something soon, only he wasn't sure what.

"Alright, break for lunch. And let's make it quick."Wyk yelled.

Kam didn't realize how far back he had let himself drift, riding a good thirty feet behind the others and forcing Red, who was making up the rear, to slow even more. As Kam approached the group, all of whom had already dismounted. Red again asked to be allowed to stretch his wings and fly. He had been asking that everyday but it was only in the past week that Wyk had agreed, as long as Red flew high and fast so as to not be clearly seen. It was a condition which Red didn't argue with.

Kam approached Wyk and, as if reading his mind, Wyk just nodded.

In an instant Red was up, glorying in his ability to soar over the heads of his traveling companions. Red had taken to looking for food from the air and then swooping down to get it, something which Kam was sure Wyk wouldn't agree to. But ever since he had told Red about the particular colloquialism that it's easier to ask for forgiveness than for permission, Red had taken it up almost as a mantra in his dealings with them. Kam figured it was to assuage his own conscious to the fact that he was listening to and even having to ask permission of Wyk.

"What are you thinking of?"

With a start Kam realized Krys was talking to him. He hadn't even noticed her coming over so intently had he been watching Red. He knew that the only time he truly enjoyed being bonded to Red was when he was flying. Not looking for food and certainly not worrying about all of the "insignificant" people around him; just when he was flying. The feeling of being free came through the bond as strongly as the darkness used to. Kam knew Red was hungry, but the feeling of freedom, probably due in no small respect to the fact Red was grounded for long periods of time, allowed the feeling to be magnified.

"I'm just…watching Red fly." Kam replied.

Krys looked up and watched the sky. Surprisingly she seemed to know where to look despite the fact Red wasn't anywhere to be seen.

"You're connected to him to, aren't you?" Kam asked.

Krys looked over at him and smiled. "I can sense where he is in the sky, but I'm not sure how. It's as if my connection to him is stronger than it is to other animals. I'm not sure if it's magic or something else but my connection to him is much more, uh, intense."

"It might be due to me." Kam started. "Don't forget about my magical connection to him. It's possible the magic may also be allowing you to sense him too."

Krys looked at him skeptically, a look Kam knew well. It seemed whenever Kam thought he had figured out something difficult or complex, Krys would disagree with him. But that wouldn't be so bad if she wasn't right most of the time.

"You think that because you're using a magical artifact that I can, what, siphon the magic out of the air and use it too?"

Kam had to admit it did sound farfetched.

"You know I've always had this gift, this ability. You know I could always tell what animals were sensing and feeling. But something else I've noticed…my ability hasn't increased with other animals on this trip. It has stayed the same. But either way I think you shouldn't be controlling him with magic; you should let him be here because he wants to be."

"But that's just it-he doesn't want to be with us." Kam said, trying to explain. "We need him to help us with what's coming. He's a dragon Krys, one of the most powerful and intelligent creatures in existence and we need him. Not just for us but for everyone."

Kam suddenly noticed a presence near him, as if someone had just walked up behind him. He turned and there was Red, having landed without a sound behind him and focused intently on every word between Kam and his sister. Strangely he felt a new feeling coming through their bond; a sensation of...what?

Kam couldn't say but he did notice an even greater lightening of the oppressiveness which was inside of Red. It was as if a hundred torches had been lit and the combined heat and light threw back the darkness and mist. It was a refreshingly invigorating feeling. A feeling which Kam wished would last.

"What are you two talking about?"

Belle's abrupt arrival startled Kam. He turned and noticed her eying Red hesitantly, as if she expected him to grab her with his claws and use her for a tooth pick. Apparently Red picked up on his thoughts because he caught an evil sense of agreement and humor coming through their bond.

"Well, what are you talking about?" Belle asked again.

Kam noticed Krys roll her eyes like she did when he said something which she didn't like. He wondered if Belle noticed it too. He couldn't imagine how she couldn't have. Then again with Belle staring up at Red maybe she did.

"It's okay." Kam said. "He won't hurt you. He doesn't like to eat people anyway."

She gave him such a look of shock that he wondered if in her apprehension that she misheard him, took it to be the opposite. Krys noticed her trepidation as well and a look came into her eyes that Kam knew only too well. With quick steps she walked over to Red, who calmly put his snout down for her to rub, almost as if he were a large horse with a trainer he trusted implicitly and was about to receive an apple for good behavior.

"Come over here Belle." Krys said.

Although Belle had communicated with Red before, she had never been closer than twenty feet from what Kam had seen. Now Belle looked over at the dragon uncertainly, as if even approaching him would cause Red to roar and breathe fire on everyone. She took a few hesitant steps towards him and started trembling like a leaf in a high wind. Kam was sure she would dirty her undergarments.

"It's okay. He won't hurt you." Krys continued.

Belle took a few more tentative steps until she was barely within touching distance. As she stretched out her hand Kam could see it was shaking so much that he couldn't understand how she didn't break a bone in her arm. As she lightly touched the end of the dragon's nose she slowly began to smile.

"It...it's not so bad." She squeaked weakly.

Abruptly Red snorted and with a small cry Belle fainted and fell straight to the ground. Kam rushed over while both Krys and Red started to laugh. Laugh! He couldn't help but notice Red's roaring laugh sounded eerily similar to Krys's.

"That's not funny!" Kam said in as stern a voice as he could under the circumstances. With a start he realized he was trying to hold back laughter as well. Moose, who always seemed to be near Belle, came over quickly and asked, "What's wrong? What happened?"

Kam noticed Red's frivolity suddenly turned to shame when Moose came over. *Why is he feeling shame?* Kam wondered. *He hates people.* But there was no response from Red if he heard Kam's musings.

"She fainted when she, uh, tried to um, pet...touch Red." Krys stammered. And she just...fainted. I think she's just afraid of him still."

Kam eyed Moose to see how he was taking the news. He was just glad it was Krys who explained what happened. He knew the whole truth and wouldn't have been able to keep it from him. Krys on the other hand had a way of telling someone the truth without telling them the whole truth and still feel good. This was true even if the partial truth she told gave someone the completely wrong idea, as in this case.

Moose gently lifted Belle off of the ground and carried her over to a shade tree. Some of the others saw him and went over to help. Moose called for some water and Kam noticed one of the guards run towards the wagon where the water barrels were kept. He then let out a sigh and turned back towards Krys and Red.

Krys seemed as if she would break out into laughter again at any moment. Her face was red and she was biting her lip to stifle any sound which might escape. But Red still had a feeling of shame emanating from him, although you couldn't tell from just looking at him.

What Kam really found interesting was that the shame Red was emanating completely pushed aside the vile darkness which he carried around. Kam would have thought that Red's shame and that darkness within him would have made great traveling companions. But it appeared the opposite to be true. That meant something important he knew, but he couldn't figure out what.

Kam heard some loud talking from where Moose had taken Belle and he looked over. Belle was sitting up and looking over at Red with eyes as large as plates. She looked okay, but Kam wasn't. It was a dirty trick that Krys and Red played on Belle and she had every right to be angry with them. Only, she didn't look angry. It was then Kam realized she didn't understand a joke had been played on her. She thought something innocent had happened and had a look as if she had done something wrong.

At that moment Red stepped into Kam's view and Kam looked up startled. Red took another step carefully towards Belle, being careful that he didn't step on anything in the area like horses and people. His steps were so careful and quiet that Kam thought he must have gone deaf.

Someone in the group congregated around Belle saw Red coming over and said something because they all seemed to look up at Red in unison. Everyone that is except for Belle whose eyes had been following Red the whole time. As Red approached the group he stopped about ten feet from them and slowly lowered his head to just a few feet above the ground. Most of those near Belle took a step back, while the guards looked at each other uncertainly, as if debating whether or not to draw their swords.

Red eventually dropped his head all the way down to the ground and laid it to rest there. Kam thought his action looked much like a dog's when it had been reprimanded and was showing remorse at what it had done. He also noticed that Red's tail was between his legs, and a recent memory tried to blossom in his mind but he pushed it away for the moment.

Moose then said something to Belle which Kam couldn't hear and helped Belle slowly to her feet. Moose then guided her over to Red himself, only this time she wasn't shaking nearly so much. She again held out her hand and gently stroked Red on the snout. Moose, smiling broadly, again said something which Kam couldn't hear; although he couldn't tell if he was addressing Belle, Red, or everyone in general.

Abruptly, and with great power, another feeling came through the bond. This one overshadowed both the shame and darkness Red had been feeling. It was one of calm satisfaction and contentment. *Satisfaction and contentment?* This was the first time Kam had ever sensed those emotions from Red.

As Kam started to walk over with Krys beside him, he saw everyone in the group around Belle move forward and start to stroke Red. Red was plainly enjoying the attention, which confused Kam no end. But he kept silent.

"Alright, let's get our things packed away and get going. We're burning daylight here." Wyk proclaimed loudly.

Everyone started to move away from Red except for Belle and Moose. Both of them wore broad smiles. Belle looked up into Red's eyes and said 'Thank you' in such a sincere way that Kam knew Krys must be feeling guilty over what she had done. As he cast a look sideways at her he could see she was very red in the face, her color almost matching Red's.

After Belle and Moose walked away Kam turned to face both Krys and Red. Red lifted his head off the ground by about a foot and turned it so he was facing Kam while Krys just looked at the ground and said, "It looks as if everything worked out for the best."

Kam was speechless, but he did know he wanted to try something. He took a few steps towards Red and reached out his hand to touch him. Red didn't move or make any sound as Kam ran his hand along

Red's face. Again, that feeling of calm serenity filled Kam's mind. This time however Kam noticed a happy satisfaction rising up in him as well.

He quickly tried to quell it, stifling it so Red wouldn't sense it; but it was too late. He could feel Red's emotional reaction to it, which was an amalgam of different feelings thrown together. He could sense Red's feeling of superiority, as if Kam should be happy that a dragon allowed him to touch it. He again felt the feeling of contentment, only stronger. And he felt other emotions depicting everything from relief to excitement, but very little of the darkness. It was as if the darkness was swallowed up for the moment in the other emotions. A brief thought of a snake swallowing a mouse came to mind and he quickly dismissed it.

Thoroughly confused Kam went back to his horse to mount up. Behind him he heard Krys talking softly to Red and wondered what she was saying. Whatever it was it helped to make the darkness dwindle even more.

Chapter 30

They had been traveling for two days due north since the incident with Belle and Red. Wyk was pleased how most of the group had managed to bond over the course of the trip so far. Even Red had integrated himself into their hearts. One person still concerned him though-Kam. He had gotten agitated and broody over the past several days.

Wyk glanced back at the 'traveling circus' as Jesse called them. He was amazed he could now look upon the group without feeling they were simply a large menagerie. Except for the dragon of course; that was just not something you saw every day. As usual his eyes gravitated towards Sakura. She rarely said anything but could still draw a man's attention away from even a large red dragon.

His thoughts drifted towards the previous evening when he had gone away from the camp late one night to relieve himself and had caught Sakura in a small open area practicing her bladework. She looked good; quick and agile with good form. He knew she probably had extensive training with swords as well as other things a lady prepping to be a queen would have. She definitely looked good on a horse.

Her horsemanship looks good. Wyk corrected himself mentally, although there was no one around to misconstrue his initial comment or know why he would chastise himself mentally.

He shook his head, which was all he seemed to be able to do around her. He also noticed she seemed ambidextrous, not a common quality among royalty or anyone else for that matter. Wyk's experience with rulers was that they seemed to do just enough of something so as to be considered fit to rule. However, striving to become physically able to wield a sword skillfully with either hand usually meant much more work than the monarchs were willing to invest in a single activity.

He continued to watch her practice. Her fluid motions and quick movements started him wondering just how good she really was. He had just begun to consider asking her to spar with him when, just as he shifted his weight, a small stick snapped underfoot.

She quickly turned towards the sound, facing him with sword extended and covered in a fine sheen of sweat. He noticed by the rise and fall of her chest that she wasn't breathing hard at all; a good sign for someone doing as strenuous a workout as she had.

"You, uh, look good. I mean your *bladework* looks good." He hastily added.

She continued to look at him, sword extended in front of her. For a moment Wyk thought he could see in her face contemplation as to whether or not she should attack him. Her face finally softened slightly and she lowered her sword.

It was then he noticed her blade in the silvery moonlight. Long, narrow, and slightly curved, he recognized its graceful beauty as coming from the Eastern Islands. He guessed some emissary had traveled a great distance to offer it up to her father as a token of friendship so that her kingdom might consider an alliance of friendship and trade between the two.

"Maybe we can spar together sometime. I would love to see some of your moves." He said, suddenly realizing how idiotic he sounded.

"You should not sneak up on people like that." She said huskily.

He felt heat creep up his neck and into his cheeks and hoped the moonlight filtering through the treetops behind her didn't provide enough illumination for her to notice. He swallowed, suddenly realizing how dry his mouth had become.

"Well, I, uh, am sorry about startling you. You should get back to the camp though. Although this area is still part of the kingdom there will be bandits this far out from the city."

She gave him a curt nod letting him know the conversation was at an end. He turned and strode back to the camp, completely forgetting the reason he had gone out that way in the first place.

Early the next morning Kam found Krys talking with Red.

"Why do you keep talking to him?" Kam asked his sister. "You know he can't understand what you're saying."

"Yes, but he understands my feelings towards him. Besides I'm just more comfortable talking to him out loud. I've found the more I talk with him the more…" She paused glancing at Red, whose snout she appeared to be fondling, and then with her voice lowered, "…the more I sense the darkness receding."

Kam glanced up at Red as well and noticed the dragon seemed to be enjoying the physical contact with his sister. His large eyes were closed and Kam would have believed him to be asleep if it weren't for the bond they had. He knew Red was awake, but Red seemed to be content just laying there, oozing a sense of satisfaction that *some* people knew how to treat dragons. Kam wasn't sure what that meant and he didn't think he wanted to know.

But she was right again. When she was near Red, giving him friendship and, dare he say it, *love,* the darkness seemed to slip away, drawing back into some small, hidden crevice deep in the dragon's mind. Kam had to wonder if the darkness was slowly leaving Red's soul or if it was just waiting for the right moment to burst forth again. Kam sighed; he *hated* it when Krys was right. Not only did it irk him no end but she usually made sure he didn't forget it anytime soon.

Well, live and learn. Kam slowly approached Red and extended his hand to stroke Red's snout as well when he suddenly felt a strange but subtle shift in his bond. He looked up at Red and noticed his eye was wide open and staring down at him. He wasn't sure what feelings were coming through their connection, but he now realized how unnerving it was to be that close to Red and have an eye as large as a shield staring down at you.

Kam slowly withdrew his hand, but only now noticed how human-like Red's eyes were. They had black pupils, only slightly elongated now, and they were surrounded by a ring of deep, dark reddish brown. Kam wondered if all dragons had the same eye color. There was something else; Red's eyes had large flecks of gold in them swimming in the ring of red. He didn't remember noticing that before and wondered if that had any special meaning.

It does, but it is not something I wish to tell you. Came the reply to Kam's thought.

Kam shook his head. Sometimes dragons could definitely be as mysterious and incomprehensible as any woman. He wondered if dragons somehow came from women. *That would make sense.* Kam thought. *That's why my sister and Red get along so well.*

As Kam walked away Jesse came up to him.

"Kam," Jesse called. "Do you have a minute?"

Kam stopped and looked at Jesse. He always felt Jesse was probably the second strongest man in their group, behind Moose. The man wasn't tall but was built like a wall. He always felt a little safer when Jesse was nearby; although with a dragon in your group the size of a man became a moot point.

"I saw you cross blades with Wyk the other day and I have never seen any man go that long with him. How would you like to practice sometime?"

Kam just looked at him in surprise. It seemed all the guards ever thought about was practicing their techniques. Well, he couldn't fault them for that. You would want a guard to be good at using weapons; that was their job after all.

Maybe he should practice with me came Red's opinion into Kam's head. Kam had to stifle a laugh. That would be something to see. He wouldn't put it past Jesse to find some way to win. He seemed like a very determined guy.

"We could do that." Kam managed to say.

"Could I practice too?"

Without their knowing it Moose had come up and he had his hammer in his hand. In fact, he always seemed to have his hammer in his hand. It was still shiny, sparkling in the early morning sun. But Kam noticed it seemed to have a golden gleam to it; a gleam that strangely reminded him of the gold flakes in Red's eyes.

Jesse just laughed and said, "We could practice now, if you like. It shouldn't take long."

Kam opened his mouth to warn Jesse, but before he could Jesse continued. "You country boys always think you can take a Guardsman down so easily. Well, it's time for you to learn."

Kam closed his mouth and smiled. *This should be good.*

Jesse and Moose went into the center of the clearing the group had stopped in to camp the night before. Jesse, wearing a large, battered breastplate, offered a similarly beat up one to Moose. Moose however just shook his head and smiled.

Holding the large wooden broadsword he used for practice, Jesse swung it around a few times to warm up. Moose just stood there patiently holding his hammer. Everyone gathered around to watch, including Wyk, who had a distinctly annoyed look on his face. Kam also felt Red coming over and stretching his long neck to watch.

Why are you watching them practice? Kam asked.

I want to see what will happen.

What do you mean?

Kam's question was met only with silence and it was at that point Jesse said, "Be on guard." to Moose.

They slowly circled each other. Moose, his face split by a large grin of excitement and Jesse, eyes set with determination. Kam could tell that no practice was taken lightly by Jesse; the man was deadly serious when it came to fighting.

Jesse swung hard, harder than Kam would have liked to see in practice. However, Moose moved nimbly to one side; so quickly for a man of his girth that everyone there gasped. Jesse, whose wooden practice sword swung harmlessly through the air, followed suit. Obviously, there was more to Moose than met the eye.

Kam spared a quick glance over at Krys and Belle and was surprised to find a large smile on the latter woman's face.

Odd, Kam thought, *she almost never smiles.*

Jesse swung again and Moose stepped to one side but this time he also swung his hammer upwards, catching the sword in the crook of the hammer. Jesse, a surprised look in his eyes at Moose's ability, withdrew a step.

Moose, now with a decidedly mischievous smile playing on his face, took his own swing at Jesse. But not knowing the basics of crossing blades, signaled his swing long before he started it, allowing Jesse to step back away from the swing. But as the swing came down swishing through the air, a bolt of greenish-gold lightning shot out of the hammer and struck Jesse full in the chest, sending him flying backwards.

Wyk, the first one to get to Jesse, asked, "Are you okay?"

Jesse sat up slowly, the old, dented breastplate he was wearing scored in the center with a blackened mark from where the lightening had struck it. Then looking around in confusion asked, "Wha…What just happened?"

Moose, who had also gone quickly to Jesse's side with concern written plainly on his face, said, "I'm sorry Jesse. I still don't know how to control the lightening very well. I just need more practice."

Kam felt a combination of surprise and amusement filter into his head courtesy of Red. *You think this is funny?* Kam asked. *Jesse could have been killed.*

He turned to look up at Red's face, but Red had no response except for the continual sense of surprise and amusement. Kam began to understand; Red didn't know exactly what he had done to the hammer, except that he had put magic into it. Magic which even he didn't seem to fully understand.

Kam walked over to Red, anger raging inside of him. He purposefully walked close to Red's front legs so the dragon would have to swing his head back around and face his own body and put him into an uncomfortable position. At least Kam hoped it was uncomfortable.

What did you do? Kam asked.

I used some of her magic. Red said.

Who are you talking about? Kam asked quietly.

There was a pause in Red's thoughts, but Kam could sense Red debating with himself about how much he should tell Kam. Finally Red continued.

When two Dragons agree to become one, to become banded, we share a little bit of ourselves, our Dragonmagic, with each other. It is not magic we can readily access or use. It is simply a small part of what we can do which we share. I used a little of both my ability and…

Red paused here for a moment and Kam sensed an overpowering sense of sadness before he continued…*Gold's ability to create the hammer. I didn't realize how the Dragonmagics would interact with each other. The result was far more powerful than I imagined.*

The lightening magic is from your mate?

No, not mate. She was promised to me. But yes, she was a Gold Dragon. Very rare among Dragons and her Dragonmagic was lightening. But there's something else, the magic in the hammer is growing. I do not know how strong the magic will become.

Suddenly a large amount of information came thundering into Kam's mind like a sudden winter storm over his home when he was a boy. He now understood so much more of what it meant to be a dragon. He understood about Red's companion, what he would call a promised one. He also understood how each dragon was differentiated not just by color, but by what ability each color could do.

He also realized that dragons had second names based on how a dragon behaved when it was young. Names like Boisterous, Humorous, Quick, and others gave a dragon another, more familiar name among his family and close friends.

He also saw Gold, Red's Gold, the one who was to be with him until they died. He saw her through Red's eyes and she was a beautiful shade of gold, like the color of the setting sun over the desert. A lustrous, fiery shade of gold like bronze heated to pliability in a blacksmith's shop.

Kam's breath caught for a moment at the wondrous beauty of her. He had always thought of Red's color as being magnificent, like the brilliant blood-red sunsets at his home, but hers was truly breathtaking.

But it wasn't just her coloring; her personality was just as stunning and it belonged to Red. No, not belonged to. It was a *part* of Red. Kam realized when dragon's share their ability, they also share a part of themselves, a part of who they are, with each other. They are truly mates for life as they will always have a connection which transcends simply being together. They carry a piece of their loved one around forever.

It was at that moment that Kam finally, and fully, understood the nature of the raging darkness within Red. That it had to exist. Mixed in with the rage and regret over having been excommunicated from his home and all of dragon society, Red was forced to leave his banded and a little part of himself.

The void left by all of that had to be filled-and it was filled with the only emotion strong enough to do it. Rage, mixed with a dark all-encompassing bitterness was all there was, all there could be. It was literally as if a part of Red had died and something needed to fill that gap or Red would have gone crazy.

Kam sagged with exhaustion, as if he had been working the fields in the summer sun all day. It took him a few seconds to even remember where he was. He realized that his connection with Red had so overpowered him that it was as if they became one. The flow of emotion coming from Red had pushed out with a force Kam could only compare to when the darkness had invaded his mind.

He looked over at Red. Red's head was hanging low and his body was slumped. Kam could feel that Red was emotionally drained from bringing up old, painful memories. He was also having a hard time sensing any of Red's feelings or thoughts now. It was as if Red's heart and mind were so drained by what had happened, he had nothing left for the moment.

He could now fully understand Red's emotions based on what happened, but he didn't believe Rage was the only emotion strong enough, vast enough to fill the chasm in Red's heart. But how could he make Red understand that?

CHAPTER 31

They finally reached the edge of woods which bordered the kingdom. They had been traveling half a fortnight through the woods just to get to this point and Belle noticed the difference. The road on this side of the border, which belonged to the kingdom was broad and the trees cleared back quite far so no robbers could lie in wait.

The road on the other side abruptly changed to a much narrower dirt path with trees bordering close on both sides. It was as if an invisible wall stood between the two areas and one side was forced to be as different from the other as much as possible. It reminded her of a children's story where a child passed between two worlds by going through a mirror. One side of the mirror showed her world while the other showed a nightmarish fantasy world.

It seemed to Belle like they were headed for a path from which there would be no turning back, a path which would close in behind them, preventing any retreat back to their kingdom. It was also noticeably darker, and she could easily imagine the group heading down the dark throat of a huge beast; one so large it dwarfed even Red into insignificance. The thought sent shudders through her petite body.

The group paused at the start of this new road with some of the men gathering together to discuss their plans.

Leave it to men to make a huge problem where none exist. Belle thought, feeling only mildly hypocritical due to her feelings of only a few seconds ago. The only one not at least partially involved in their quiet but earnest conversation was Moose. He had dismounted and was watering his horse at a small stream nearby.

He stood next to his horse for a minute before he looked over at Belle with that goofy but endearing smile of his. Why was he doing that? She knew he liked her, anyone with half a brain could see that. But she also knew what others thought of her. She was Sparrowhawk, everyone knew that.

What they didn't know was that she secretly loved her nickname, although she would never admit that to anyone. It gave her a feeling of power and that she could do anything given the chance. Especially if it involved the use of magic.

She glanced over at Moose again. He was still looking up at her, smiling his smile while turning red in the face. She would never tell anyone this either but she thought he was cute. That is, in a rural I'm-not-so-smart-but-I'm-as-strong-as-a-horox kind of way.

Her thoughts drifted and she imagined him lifting her effortlessly up in his arms and carrying her to a barn. He would then lay her down gently in a mountain of soft hay. As he leans over her, he whispers to her how much he loves her right before he gives her a kiss.

"Miss Belle, would you like me to water your horse as well?"

Moose had come right up to her but she had been so lost in thought she hadn't noticed. As she felt her face getting hot, she turned away quickly so he wouldn't notice.

"I, uh, I would appreciate that." She stammered quickly.

Moose took the reins and led her horse away. She looked over and saw Krys staring at her with a large smile on her face. Belle gave her as evil a look as she could muster under the circumstances and stormed away. She walked fast, brushing past people as she focused on looking straight ahead.

Those who saw her coming stepped aside to avoid being run over and, once they caught a glimpse of her expression, looked quickly away. She was so caught up in her emotions she finally stopped away from the group near a large tree to cry. She wasn't sure why she was crying but she knew she didn't want anyone to see her.

As her body sagged against the tree a million thoughts flowed through her head. Why did she get flustered when Moose came by? Why did Krys always seem to be around her when something embarrassing happened to her? Why was she forced to come on this trip? Why did she have to stay in that prison of a school? Why were people trying to kill her? And why couldn't she just be left alone?

With her emotions flaring she felt her magic welling up inside her. In the back of her mind, she knew heightened emotions could help strengthen magic, make her more powerful. Though her sobs wracked her body her magic filled her and wrapped itself around her like a blanket. As her pent-up emotional pain was released so was her magic. She let it fill her and expand around her to a point she had never felt before.

Suddenly she felt the tree trunk move slightly beneath her and she jumped back. Quickly wiping away her tears she tried to get her eyes to focus on the tree. Her mind kept telling her something was wrong but she couldn't put her finger on it. Uncomprehendingly she stared at it until it hit her-it was a red tree.

A red tree? She thought to herself. *Where do they have red trees?* Then it finally hit her and she looked up to see Red looking down at her, staring at her as if he would use her as a straw to drink water. With that image firmly in her mind she suddenly realized the dragon was laughing at her, although all she could hear was a roaring sound as if she were standing right next to a waterfall.

She sensed the dragon was saying something to her, telling her dragons didn't like to eat people. She shook her head, trying to clear it and wake from this dream she had obviously fallen into. The dragon also seemed to be telling her she could understand him because of the strength of her magic.

She looked up at Red again and this time noticed how human-looking his eyes were. They were a deep red, the shade of which she thought went very well with the crimson red of his scales. The pupil wasn't as elongated as she would have thought.

Red then lowered his head and brought it closer to her. She gave a tiny squeak but held her ground. The dragon's eyes weren't but a horse's length away and she was transfixed by them. She noticed now they had remarkable gold flecks floating within the red. They were beautiful in fact. She thought the dragon was thanking her for that comment and she even caught a note of surprise and pleasure in his thoughts.

She couldn't take anymore. With all of the events and emotional currents swirling around inside her, the realization that she could communicate with the dragon as well was just too much. She turned and strode back to the main group of people, who were standing around oblivious as to what had just taken place. She went over to another tree, after making sure it was just a tree, and slid to the ground trying to sort out all of her feelings.

She wasn't there more than a few seconds when she noticed Krys slowly walking towards her. Belle took a deep breath and held it while Krys came right up to her, sat down and slowly put her arm around her shoulders. Belle looked her straight in the eyes before leaning her head on her shoulder. She wasn't sure what to say so they sat there in silence for a little bit.

"I'm sorry." Krys said.

Belle lifted her head and looked her in the eyes again. She was surprised to see compassion there; a look of concern for her well-being. She was taken aback. Why did Krys feel sorry for her? Why did she even care how she felt? Suddenly a stab of darkness struck her, penetrating like a dagger thrust into her heart.

"Why are you sorry?" She demanded, and was instantly rewarded with feelings of guilt and shame coursing through her body. Krys was just being a friend, a commodity she had precious little of. However, if Krys noticed her tone she just ignored it.

"For a while now, we've made fun of you and Moose. But it wasn't nice. It wasn't nice to either of you. Moose is a good man: diligent, honest, sincere, kind and strong-really strong. But he didn't deserve our rudeness."

"What about me?" Belle asked hesitantly, wondering if she really wanted to hear the answer.

Krys didn't respond right away and Belle caught a swirling of emotions in Krys's face. Krys was plainly hurt by some of the things she had said in the past but she could also see something else; something akin to embarrassment.

"I'm not saying we should have teased you," Krys began slowly, "but you don't always make it easy to be around you."

Instantly another shot of darkness struck Belle in the heart and her first inclination was to strike out with venom. But she held her tongue, trying to focus on not giving in to her old habits. She turned her head slightly and glanced over at Moose who appeared to be animatedly talking with the horses, showing them his new hammer-thing.

She brought her eyes back to Krys's and taking a deep breath said, "I probably deserved it."

It was a confession which took a surprising amount of courage and energy for her to admit, yet it seemed as if a great toll had been lifted off of her. Not to mention that the darkness she had so recently felt seemed to have receded as well.

Abruptly Krys gave her a strong hug, squeezing the wind out of her. For a second she wondered if even Moose could have held her that tightly. That brief thought of Moose caused her to blush slightly and she could feel the heat rising up her neck. As Krys pulled away she noticed her coloring and immediately apologized.

"No, no. It's not you. I just, I'm not used to being hugged. That's all." Belle said, which was half truthful at least.

Krys said, "There's something else I need to apologize for."

Belle quickly backed away a little, holding up her hands as if in defense of a blow about to be struck. "No, it's okay. I understand sometimes I can be as mean as a mulee. You don't need to apologize anymore."

"But," Krys began. "We have been mean to you. And we have a, um, well kind of a, uh, not-so-nice nickname…" Krys let her voice trail off, not knowing what or how to say what she felt needed to be said.

"I know." Belle replied. "You call me Sparrowhawk. It's a name I actually like."

Krys just looked at her, mouth open in astonishment. Of course, Belle would like the name! She sighed and asked, "Do you want us to stop calling you that?"

Belle just smiled. "I would be happy if the only one who called me Belle was Moose." She finished, not understanding the large smile that formed on Krys's face.

"Okay then, Sparrowhawk it is."

Suddenly a question arose in Belle's mind, but she wasn't sure how to ask it. Something must have shown on her face though because Krys then asked, "What? What's the matter?"

"I seem to be able to, uh, sense what the dragon is feeling. How can I do that?"

Krys paused, not sure what to say. Finally, she said, "I can sense things with animals, at least with most animals. But with Red it's different. I seem to be able to actually communicate with him a little. His magic is very strong and I think that's what allows me to do it. Can you communicate with all animals?"

"No, no, just Red. And it's not really communicating. I can sense his feelings a little. That's all."

"I think it's his magic that allows you to do that. Or maybe your magic is strong enough. I really don't know."

"Girls, let's get going." Wyk interrupted, coming over unexpectedly. "We have a lot of ground to cover before nightfall."

Both of them ran back to their horses with questions about Red going through their minds.

Sakura sighed. The tedious nature of the trip was beginning to wear on her. She practiced as much as she could, which helped relieve the tension, but exercise could only help so much. She was curious about Moose's new weapon-the hammer which shot out lightning.

If the rumors were to be believed he had gotten it as a gift from the dragon. She wondered how he had accomplished that. A weapon of that power would be a benefit for her to have. She briefly considered stealing it, but with its size and weight it would be difficult to hide. Maybe when their journey was done…

Sakura glanced at Wyk, again admiring the chiseled cut of his face and the strong lines of his body. She had met many handsome men before, most of them far more beautiful than Wyk. But for some reason she just couldn't get him out of her mind.

She set her jaw as dark thoughts started to intrude into her consciousness yet again. The gray skinned man was looming over her, smiling his devilish smile. Images of him haunted her both night and day. She knew they would meet again; knew it as if she planned it. And she was terrified.

She looked up into the sun to clear her mind. Maybe if she became friends with the boy's dragon. She was sure he could stop the gray man-he was a dragon after all. But what if he couldn't?

That thought sent shivers running through her body. She shook off the feeling. She would need to stay alert, not live in nightmares. If and when she met the gray man again she would kill him, or at least try to. At this point that was all she could do.

CHAPTER 32

After a few days of traveling along the dirt path Kam began to feel claustrophobic. The thick forest here pressed in upon them darkly, with branches grabbing at them like skeletal arms. He knew part of the feeling emanated from Red, who he was unhappy about getting small branches stuck between his scales. He was also sure the rest of the group was feeling the oppressive nature as well as they now traveled in complete silence.

They came to a fork in the road which had one path heading in what appeared to be a northeasterly directing and the other going west. The westerly path was even narrower, not much more than a hiking trail for people traveling in single file. It was overgrown and showed no indication of having been used recently by anything other than small game.

Unfortunately, Wyk chose the trail headed west and Kam's feeling of being closed in only grew worse. The oppressive nature of the forest was amplified by the noise Red made as he struggled through the narrow pathway, snapping trees and branches and sounding like a herd of large animals stampeding through. Kam was surprised by Red's willingness to go down this path, but even more surprised at his lack of complaining.

After about half a day's traveling, they eventually came upon an area where the forest abruptly thinned out and no plant life of any kind seemed to be able to grow. The only exception being small, dark, twisted and leafless bushes with long, jagged thorns. It was as if the trees and grasses had agreed upon a line in the ground beyond which they wouldn't trespass. This created an open area of dark earth with many small, rolling hills.

Kam had passed this area once before, many years ago. He knew travelers passing through this part often went far out of their way to avoid traversing this area. The bizarre plants which grew here had thorns which were razor sharp and could even cut through leather. He couldn't understand why there was a great, dark bald spot in the middle of the forest.

"It's called 'The Dark Lord's Province.'"

Kam had caught up to Jesse without realizing it. The narrow trail had suddenly widened and became part of the desolate zone. As Kam glanced over at him, he continued. "They say it's where the Dark One and some of his conspirators stayed when they counseled in the war against the Light. The Light found out and came down to do battle with him. The Light cast the Dark One out and imprisoned some of his minions in the hills you see, but the battle so scarred the land that nothing has been able to grow here since."

Kam again looked around the barren area. It was roughly circular and it couldn't have been more than about six miles in diameter, yet it stood out by virtue of its low-laying hills and, more importantly, for its lack of vegetation or variance in color. Kam glanced back to see how Red was faring. As the dragon was exiting the trees into the open area Kam was surprised to see his sister riding along next to him, seemingly in deep conversation. He was also surprised to find he currently had no feelings coming through their bond.

"We need to stay on the trail. We must not leave it. They say those who venture off the trail are lost forever." said Wyk.

He hadn't noticed Wyk falling back but he had to admit this place, with its complete absence of life, was in its own way very distracting. Wyk then slowed his horse down even more, presumably to tell the others behind him.

Kam wondered how it would be possible to get lost in a place which was only a few miles across and barren enough to see the other side. Then it hit him-a strong sense of urgency emanating from Red.

Looking ahead he saw it. A ripple in the air, much like a rock thrown into a pond, distorting everything around it. And like a rock thrown into a pond, it was only the beginning of a series of waves expanding outward from that point.

Red's warning seemed to become even more urgent, if that was possible, and that was amplified by the terrified whinnying of the horses. Kam felt his horse shake with terror to the point it didn't seem able to move its legs.

Kam had no recollection of an incident like this happening before. Then again, if memory served, the last time he came through this area he had been laying on his back in a wagon with two arrows in his body.

As the ripples passed over them Kam had a headache attack his mind with the force of a dragon falling on top of him. For a second he even wondered if that was exactly what happened. His vision blurred before going completely dark and the bond through which Red had just tried to warn him suddenly went dead.

Kam sat perfectly still on his horse, hoping his mount could weather whatever was happening without throwing him or falling down. He strained his ears to see if he could find out anything about what was happening. Unfortunately, it was as if all of the sound had been sucked out of the area.

Abruptly Kam's vision cleared and the pain subsided to a degree that he felt he could stay on his horse while riding. His mount was still shaking, but to a far less degree than it had been. He was glad he had been offered a well-trained warhorse instead of just another strong animal to ride on.

Kam frowned and rubbed his temples. He looked over at Red who seemed to be having the same issue he was. Surprisingly Krys seemed to be unaffected but she was staring at the dragon with concern.

Kam felt something tickling his upper lip. He brushed at it and his hand came away with blood on it. But at this point he was in too much pain to care about a simple nose bleed. Then from a great distance he heard Wyk yell for everyone to ride quickly. He spurred his horse on, trying to focus on where he was going and ignore the pain.

He caught sight of a small dust devil. It appeared out of nowhere and moved quickly out of sight behind one of the small hills. Suddenly the pain stopped. There was a lingering aftereffect however, like an echo of the pain, which continued to bounce around inside his head and kept him from thinking clearly.

Kam looked around and saw that most of the group had managed to stay on their horses. He was even able to hear Red's thoughts again through the bond and was happy to hear Red say he was okay. But when he looked over at him, he saw Red slowly moving his head back and forth, as if he was looking for someone. Krys was still by his side, trying to talk to him, but Red seemed oblivious to what was going on around him.

With his head slowly clearing Kam followed a smaller, less used trail around the hill he had seen the dust devil go behind. What he saw surprised him so much he nearly fell off his horse. It was Nix from the magic shop. No one else seemed to have noticed that Kam had wandered off, which didn't surprise him given what had just happened.

Nix greeted Kam soberly. He seemed at a loss as to what to say. Kam took the opportunity to ask, "Where is your horse? How did you get here ahead of us without us seeing you?"

Before Nix could answer then the soft sound of footfalls in the dirt let Kam know someone else had come up behind them.

"Who are you?"

Kam instantly recognized the voice behind the question-it was Krys. He hadn't realized she had come over as well. The expression on Nix's face remained unchanged; Krys's appearance didn't seem to have surprised him at all.

Then just as abruptly as Krys had appeared, a long, oddly shaped shadow sheltered all three of them from the sun. Red swung his head around Kam and his sister so he was nearly nose-to-nose with Nix. He bared his teeth, the way a dog bares its teeth in warning right before an attack.

"Well friend, it's been a long time since I've seen any of your kind." Nix said.

Red continued to stare coldly at Nix and Kam was afraid Nix would become dragon chow. There was a sudden influx of emotion, so much so that Kam couldn't understand what Red was feeling. Then, reminiscent of when he had initially used the Dragonstaff, a flood of anger came pouring through. Only this anger was pure rage; there was no darkness lacing Red's emotions this time.

Nix looked unconcerned despite the dragon being nearly on top of him. Calmly he said, "Don't worry noble one, I am here to help."

"This is Nix, a friend of mine. He's okay, he's here to help." Kam said quickly, hoping to defuse whatever animosity Red felt towards Nix.

Kam usually couldn't tell what Red was thinking by looking at his face. He had always just assumed a dragon's face didn't have the dexterity to be as expressive as a human face. Yet now, looking at Red, he saw him staring at Nix with a dire look of enmity. Whatever had gone on before, whatever history there was between these two, he was clearly ready to attack.

Krys laid a gentle hand on Red's neck. It was a soft, gentle touch, the kind only a woman can give when she's stopping a man from doing something foolish. It was so soft that Kam was sure Red wouldn't be able to even feel it. But the dragon turned his head slightly and looked at Krys through one bright eye before turning his head away from Nix. Kam felt a strong diminishing of the rage he had felt just a few seconds before.

"I need to give you a warning," Nix said, turning to face Kam. "You need to get out of the waste as soon as possible. Do not camp or stay in the waste longer than you need to. It is imperative you leave this area as quickly as you can."

Kam nodded, then looked over at Krys and saw that she was still focused on Red, her hand still laid gently on his neck. He had to admit she was a compassionate person, especially when it came to animals. *And dragons* Kam added quickly to himself. More and more he viewed Red less as an animal and more as…well as something more than just an animal.

Nix took a few steps and stopped directly in front of Krys. She faced him, surprise written clearly on her face. Her hand still rested lightly on Red's neck, almost as if she were feeling for his pulse. Red turned his head back towards the shopkeeper and bared his teeth again.

Not only did the rage return as strong as before, but this time Red opened his mouth slightly, as if to warn Nix he could swallow him in one bite. For his part Nix seemed remarkably unconcerned about having a dragon threaten him.

Nix moved his lips as though he was talking with Krys, but no sound came out. Kam wondered what he had to say to Krys that he didn't want him to hear. Nix stood there for a few seconds, continuing his silent conversation with her. During that time Kam saw Red noticeably relax and he had to wonder what Red could hear that he couldn't.

When he was done Nix just turned and walked around to the opposite side of the hill. It was at that moment Wyk came over.

"We're losing daylight and we need to get across this barren piece of land and into the forest by nightfall." He said. "Let's go."

Krys and Red turned back from the way they had come to rejoin the group. Kam however went around the far side of the hill to talk with Nix a little more. He found though that when he circled the small hill there was no trace of Nix. Puzzled, wondering how Nix could disappear like that, he went back to the group.

She saw the dust devil go around the hill and right after Kam following it. Of course, right behind him were his sister and the dragon. She knew something was up but she wasn't sure what. In any case, that wasn't her mission.

She looked around at their little group and wondered if she would be the only one to survive their journey. The odds were that everyone would die, but she did give herself the best odds of surviving. Well, her and the dragon anyway.

She glanced over at Wyk helping the group after the whatever-it-was had given them headaches. He was a strong leader, one capable of leading men to do great things. She wondered if he would ever consider joining her group. But she didn't think so; he was far too honorable for that.

Sakura sighed. She knew this area well enough to know they needed to get out of it as quickly as possible. She was torn between spurring her mount on and leaving the rest behind or helping them to regroup and leave together. For now, she would help. But in the future she wouldn't hesitate to put her own concerns over that of the group.

After Nix visited with them, Kam found himself wondering what exactly Nix said to his sister. He tried to find the right moment to ask her, but after their experience in the Dark Lord's Province the group stayed together in a much tighter formation. Kam couldn't hold that against anyone; the experience they had was a bit unnerving. Even Red stayed much closer. Kam could feel the wind from Red's footfalls directly behind him while his head extended above and ahead of him.

As they continued through the wasteland Kam noticed something strange. Although he could easily see the other side of the barren area to where the trees were, probably not more than a few miles, they seemed to be making precious little headway. It was as if they were looking at the far side through an instrument which made it look closer than it actually was.

Kam also couldn't help but realize that there were no animal remains to be seen-none. Anywhere else they would have stumbled upon animal remains as the course of life took its toll, but here there was nothing. Not a single skeleton lying bleached in the sun or an animal scurrying away at the sound of their group. There was even the lack of insects buzzing around their ears.

The eeriness of this area being completely devoid of any life at all, past and present, bothered him. It felt like an ambush about to happen; until suddenly that's what it became.

CHAPTER 33

Belle's mount stumbled and stepped partially onto one of the many hills in the area. The hill was very soft and her horse sank into it up to its knees. It backed out easily but the whole hill started to tremble and dirt slid down the sides in huge quantities.

Out of the ground below the hill burst a creature Wyk had never laid eyes on before. It was massive; at least as big as the dragon, and it was ugly. It had a head faintly resembling that of a bull yet with four horns instead of only two. Two of the horns pointed skyward, but two pointed forward, curving around its head just below its front eyes.

Its mouth had mandibles and long, tentacle-like protrusions which waved madly around as if having a mind of their own, giving it the look of a crazed sea creature. It was obvious that if those tentacles grabbed one of them, they would be eaten instantly.

It raised itself more fully from under the hill where it apparently had been waiting. Its powerful legs looked to be some sort of mixture of animal and insect; although the fact that there were eight of them gave it less of a mammalian appearance and more of that of an arachnid.

Its body was long and was covered in some sort of natural body armor similar to insects, but very different from dragon scales. When it finally pulled itself all the way out of the ground Wyk felt his eyes widen at the three scorpion-like appendages sticking out of the rear of its body with mean looking barbs attached to them.

Its dark sandy color would have made it perfectly camouflaged in the desert-like barrenness of the place. The realization that it had been hiding its massive body under a hill caused Wyk's mind to go into tactical mode as he briefly scanned the numerous other small hills that dotted this Light-forsaken place.

The creature's sudden appearance threw the group into pandemonium. Wyk's battle-hardened mind watched everything as if it were unfolding in slow motion. He took only a few seconds to take stock of what each person was doing. His soldiers, taken aback by the swiftness of the attack, had been startled but for an instant. Within seconds his men had their swords drawn and tried to place themselves between the creature and the civilians.

Belle, who had been the closest to the creature when it attacked, had fallen to the ground when her horse had reared up at the creature's appearance. She appeared stunned and unable to move. Moose, who as usual had not been far from her side, moved with amazing speed and reached the creature before anyone else, swinging his hammer.

The creature lashed out with one of its tentacles, snagging Belle's wayward horse. Her mount in its fear had inadvertently run closer to the creature in its haste to get away. The horse struggled in the grasp of the tentacle but couldn't escape. The creature pulled the poor animal to its mouth and there was a loud, stomach-turning crunch as the horse was literally bitten in half.

While the creature was preoccupied with what was left of the horse, one of its tails which seemed to have a mind of its own, swung towards Belle who was still on the ground. But Moose was there quickly, standing over Belle and swinging his hammer. Lightening shot out of it, striking the tail midway between its base and tip. This caused the tail to fold in half and flop loosely at the creature's side.

The creature uttered a coarse, grotesque human–like scream as it turned to face Moose who stood resolutely over Belle. The Guardsmen, who had started attacking the creature on its side, found that their swords bounced harmlessly off the creature's natural armor. The Guardsmen's attack was so ineffectual that the creature ignored them completely.

Kam then charged forward and took a strong swing at the creature. Wyk was amazed to see his sword penetrate the armor, causing the creature to emit another horrendous, high-pitched shriek of pain. When Kam saw what his sword could do, he then swung sideways cutting one of the legs about half-way through. A great blob of thick, green blood belched out and drenched Kam. As the monster pivoted to face him, one of the tentacles swung violently at him and threw him back about fifteen feet.

Moose, who saw what Kam had done, moved in past another of the tails striking at him and swung his hammer at the base of it. There was a loud snap and the tail fell over like a felled tree. The creature then turned again, this time to face Moose with its full attention.

One of its tentacles shot out and wrapped itself around Moose's legs. Moose fell hard and lost his hammer when he was pulled violently towards the creature's mouth. Wyk moved quickly to help but one of the creature's legs was brought down right in front of him, nearly crushing him.

As if fighting one creature with nearly impenetrable armor wasn't enough, another creature emerged from a small nearby hill to join the fray. This new adversary was similar to the first with the exception of having claws in the front similar to a crab and only one tail.

Suddenly there was a loss of light, as if the sun had turned its face to avoid watching the ensuing massacre. Wyk knew it was a cloudless sky and looked up, expecting the worst. However, it was Red who had come to join the fight. Wyk wondered how well the dragon would fare against these creatures, but he didn't have long to wait to find out.

The initial creature had the misfortune of being the one Red attacked first. Red landed directly on top of the creature. He used one of his claws to grasp the creature's one remaining functional tail and another claw he used to pin the creature's head down. This caused it to release Moose and wrap its tentacles around Red's leg. The creature's legs buckled as Red's full weight was brought to bear.

Red bent over and, with an even louder crunch than when they had lost the horse, bit the creature in half. Wyk had heard and seen many horrific things since he became a member of the King's Guard, but for some reason this time the sound turned his stomach and he felt the need to throw up.

Red lifted his head and spat out large chunks of the creature. Green blood covered his mouth and green rivulets ran repulsively down his neck. The bright, perversely festive colors of the vivid shade of green nestled against the brilliant crimson of Red's scales brought a particularly macabre vision of the Day of Light Giving to Wyk's mind. It gave the traditionally festive holiday colors a truly surreal look.

Wyk didn't expect the Dragon to show emotion; it was after all a dragon. But he was sure he could see a look of revulsion in Red's eyes and he vomited the remains of the creature out of his mouth.

The other creature retreated a few steps after it saw its companion fall so quickly. It eyed Red warily, seemingly waiting for a chance to strike. Its barbed tail wickedly hovered over its head, ready to deal out death.

Red shot out fire at the creature, which surprised Wyk but not as much as the color of the flames-they were green. But not the vibrant green of the creature's blood, rather a mystical emerald green which carried the promise of strength. Wyk didn't think he had ever seen green fire before.

The creature seemed to fear the fire. So much so that it moved quickly to one side and crouched low, allowing the flames to pass by high and wide. It then took a few steps swiftly forward and struck at Red's chest with its tail. Wyk was impressed with the dexterity of the creature and even feared for Red. But the dragon wasn't about to be shown up.

Red used his long neck to bring his head down to the level of the creature's tail and strike from the side. He clamped his jaws on the tail in mid-strike, before it ever got near his chest. He then again shot bright green flame from his mouth, engulfing the tail.

An even louder screech than before came from the creature as the tail disintegrated where Red's fire came in contact with it. The tip of the tail fell to the ground, having the appearance of molten metal where Red's fire had dissolved it. Then faster than Wyk would have thought possible the creature turned and burrowed back into the earth where it came from.

There was a collective sigh of relief when the creature left, and Wyk took that moment to yell out, "Mount up. Let's get out of here."

It was at that moment he noticed Sakura standing many feet from him near the opposite side of the creature's lair. She was standing there covered in green and red slime. He ran over to her when he recognized what the red slime was.

"Are you all right? Where did you get hurt?" He asked, looking over her body for the injury.

"I'm alright." She said slowly. She had a long slash down her sword arm, and her blood had mingled with the green goo of the creature on her sword, giving it a truly ghastly appearance. Wyk belatedly realized she must have gone around behind the creature to the other side to fight it, but he couldn't figure out was how her sword managed to penetrate the creature's armor.

"How did your sword…?" He began, wondering if her sword was magical.

"It's a very sharp sword, made in a very special way." She said cryptically, then she turned and walked away.

Wyk just shook his head. This woman had gone around to the back side of the creature alone to fight it. She had obviously injured it. She would never cease to amaze him. He tried to ignore the strange sense of pride he felt welling up inside of him and instead went to inspect the melted tail Red had taken off.

He noticed a dark orb just above the barbed end of the tail which had the appearance of being filled with some sort of fluid. It was also a sandy color, which explained why he hadn't noticed it before. As Wyk watched, a lid partially closed over it and then stopped before it could close all the way. His heart froze for a moment as he realized the significance of what he just saw.

The orb was an eye, one of two he now noticed, above the barb on the tail. He figured that was how the creature's tail seemed to work and attack simultaneously and independent of whatever else the creature was doing. Wyk turned and returned to the group, wondering what sort of evil under the Light created this kind of creature. And what other dark incarnations existed in this place.

The group mounted quickly. Moose helped Belle onto one of the pack horses and was rewarded with a pretty smile, causing him to turn a deep shade of red. He then went back to his horse then rode over to Red to thank him.

Kam also walked over to Red and said something which caused the dragon to nod its head in agreement. Wyk held no reservations about their having the ability to defeat the creatures without the aid of Red. He also made a mental note to approach Red later to offer thanks when they stopped again.

With that last thought Wyk become conscious of the fact he was using both Red's name and referring to him as a 'him' instead of an 'it'. He glanced over at Red and saw Red looking over at him, causing Wyk to wonder if he could read his thoughts.

As they began their trek again it was with a renewed sense of urgency, a feeling that they needed to leave this desolate area as quickly as possible. Yet again the land seemed destined to play some dark joke on them, seeming to stretch the area while they crossed. It took them until well after nightfall to finally reach the line of trees on the far side, even with the group pushing the horses to their limit.

They went into the forest some distance before setting up camp to be as far away from the waste as possible before going to sleep. Wyk could see the exhaustion in both the riders and their mounts but was impressed by the spirit of the group, This was especially true of those without any military training.

They finally decided to set up camp when they came to a small, open area and were able to get water from a nearby stream. After the horses were watered and brushed Wyk looked around and took a quick head count. They were one short, and he knew just who it was.

"Has anyone seen Sakura?" Wyk asked.

Everyone responded in the negative. Except for Belle who said, "Maybe she's at the watering hole. I was hoping to go down there myself after I ate, but now I am just too tired."

Wyk's eyes narrowed. "Where is it?"

"Just follow the stream back from the way we came," Belle said. "It's not far."

"I'll go and get her. Everyone else just finish your supper." Wyk said.

Wyk strode quickly away, hoping to find Sakura so he could get back and eat while his food was still warm. He strode down the narrow path which paralleled the river for about fifty yards. The river then widened into a small pond, which was really little more than a shallow indentation, a pock mark really, where the water collected before moving on. Wyk eyed the river as it continued past the pond and its course deviated drastically, heading in a direction away from the wasteland.

Even the water avoids that place. Wyk thought.

Wyk heard some sounds coming from behind a large tree to one side of him. With his hand on the hilt of his sword he rounded the tree and found Sakura. She was damp from a bath and had just finished putting her clothes back on.

Her clothes, already well fitted, now clung dangerously to her curves with the dampness of her body. Her blonde hair, darker now due to the wetness, was pulled back into a ponytail behind her. She looked at him with those large, luminescent blue eyes and gave him a quizzical look. Quickly he focused his eyes on hers so as to avoid any looks to areas which might get him in trouble.

"You took a bath?" He asked, not quite sure why she would take one here as opposed to a spot in the stream closer to where they had set up camp.

"I felt…dirty." Was her response and she abruptly walked around him and back to the camp.

Wyk pondered what she said. He was not be one of the City Guard who would normally be the ones to question people in regards to crimes. He always felt though that he had a knack for knowing when people weren't being completely honest. And Sakura was definitely hiding something; that much he knew.

Wyk returned to camp to find that everyone had finished their meal. He went over and got his food, now just barely above the ambient air temperature, and started to eat. As he ate his mind was swirling as he puzzled over everything going on.

He looked over at the girls from the school. He had yet to see them perform any magic tricks. He needed to know what they could do and how it would benefit the group. He knew the capabilities of his men, their strengths and weaknesses. He now knew what Red was capable of. He even knew that both Kam and Sakura knew their way around in a battle. He could even appreciate Moose's courage. But the girls? They were an enigma.

It was obvious Moose liked Belle, and the feeling seemed to be reciprocated. Maybe Moose could give him some information on them.

Even now, with everyone settling down for sleep, the silence was broken by the chattering of the two girls. Wyk caught snatches of their conversation and it centered on nothing. They talked about everything that could conceivably be talked about which had no meaning.

Just give me a battlefield and opposing armies and I understand the world. Wyk thought. Life under those conditions tended to be much simpler.

Sakura woke an hour before sunrise, yet she got quickly out of her sleeping roll and started stretching. Her training from childhood had been intensive and complete, allowing her the luxury of needing only a few hours sleep each night. She also knew that staying in bed after she had woken up was an invitation for sluggishness throughout the day. After her stretching exercises, which only took a short time, she threw on some clothes and crept out of her tent.

She paused by her tent opening to wait for the sounds of the forest to differentiate from the sounds of the guards so she could focus on where she wanted to go. It took her a full twenty minutes to finally place the soldiers on watch. She knew that these men were very well trained so she crept slowly and silently between them and out into the forest.

She had to go about half a mile to find a suitable area with enough open space to do her exercises. The exercises were also something she had been taught since she was a child. In fact, everything she knew about life she had been taught since she was very young.

She knew other people allowed their children to have fun when they were young and then gave them progressively more responsibility as they grew older. But her parents were different. Their livelihoods, their very survival, focused on them being the best at what they did. This was the way of her people. They were different; they were a hard people, a people feared by others. Yet no one knew who they were.

As she continued her exercises, doing them very slowly so as to control her muscles and focus on her balance, she allowed her thoughts to wander. This was a gift her people did not have; that of being able to partition their mind so they could focus on one aspect while doing something else entirely. She could train, spar, anything while at the same time allow other thoughts of problems, of a job she was on, even of her childhood to take some of her attention.

When she had told her father of this ability, he had told her to stop. He said that one day this 'infection' of her mind by other thoughts would be her downfall. He said she needed to stay focused completely on what she was doing at that moment in order to succeed. She finally stopped telling him about it as she realized he could never understand this ability.

She continued her slow ballet of movement, knees bent, and arms in various positions of striking and blocking. As she did so her mind again returned to the one thought that haunted her her whole life; her looks. Her people were a people of color, she was not. They had tan skin, dark, almond-shaped eyes, black hair. The women had slim, athletic bodies. She had light skin, large, blue eyes, blonde hair and a figure with curves.

Her father never had an answer for why she was different-he just always said she was special. All of the boys thought so too. She continually got looks of desire and smiles of hope whenever she was around them. She was different and that's why they wanted her.

All she wanted were strong friendships with her people and she couldn't have that. She soon realized she would never, could never, have a relationship with any of them. What they desired was something she didn't want to give.

And the girls! They all wanted to kill her for stealing their dreams of being with the man they liked. But they knew as long as she was around they couldn't trust their own mate to be true to them. No, she knew she could never have a special relationship with any of her people; she accepted that and let it make her stronger.

She did her 'Dance of Death' as her father liked to call it, and went into some quick fighting forms to work up a sweat and get her heart pumping. This was her favorite part. Although she did her slow workout nearly every day it was the fast, fighting forms which she loved. Her ability to fight hand-to-hand had gotten her out of more than one situation where she didn't have her sword handy.

After about thirty minutes of kicks, punches and jumps she stopped. She felt good. Her muscles were loose and her skin was warm and tingling with the emergence of sweat. It was a wonderful feeling she never tired of. She glanced around making sure there was no one near, although she already knew that as she always kept part of her mind focused on what was going on around her.

She slowly took her top off. This helped her to cool down and her skin to dry off faster. Her body glistened with the sheen of perspiration and in the light of the full moon her curves were highlighted-the round fullness of her breasts, her slim, taught stomach and the strong, lean curves of her arms.

She tilted her head so as to see her shoulder tattoo. Hers was a thick tangle of slim branches, leaves and beautiful red and white blossoms which extended from around her left shoulder down to nearly her elbow. It was what set her people apart and everyone got one specifically for them.

Most girls got their tattoo on their sixteenth birthday and it was up to them to choose what they wanted. A lot of the girls she knew got small animals like birds or fish representing a smoothness of movement and an ease of fighting. Not her. She had always been inspired by the Sakura flower.

When used in moderation it could be a drug to get someone untrained to tell the truth. In larger concentrations and combined with a few other herbs it could knock someone out or kill them quickly; or slowly if that was what was needed. She even liked its nickname-poppy. But perhaps the greatest reason she liked it was that for some reason it reminded her of her mother, yet she wasn't sure why.

Her mother died when she was young, and she had been the closest thing to a friend she ever had in her life. She knew her mother had loved her unconditionally and that had always inspired her to work towards being the best she could. Yet she couldn't understand why the Sakura reminded her of her mother. She never understood it but she did accept it. Her mother never knew of her choice, of course, as she was already dead by that time. But Sakura knew, and that was enough.

By this time her skin had completely dried off and her body had cooled back down to its normal temperature. She had pulled her top back down over her head and turned to go back to camp when she saw him. Her breath caught in her throat and she thought her heart would stop beating.

She had never been afraid of any person before, man or woman, but she was afraid of him. She had never gotten his name, but the memory of the attempted rape in the room with the mural she would never forget. She knew that moment would haunt her for the rest of her life.

"Don't get dressed on my account." He sneered.

She looked at him, watching him as she had never watched anyone before. She thought she could hear her heart pounding, hitting her ribs with every beat. Hitting them so hard she thought they would actually crack under the force.

Her breaths came in little gasps. The very act of breathing was an exertion requiring a great amount of strength. It was as if a tremendous weight was resting on her chest. No one ever had ever made her feel this way.

She understood his attack had a little to do with it, but there was something more. She just didn't understand what it was. It was as if his mere presence cultivated feelings of despair and hopelessness.

"I have another job for you. Well two; but obviously the time isn't right for us to be together yet. I want to go slow and enjoy that moment when we get to it." And with that he gave a smile as evil as any she had ever seen. His teeth shone black in the moonlight like obsidian stones, each polished and smooth like river rocks and contrasting with the cadaver gray of his skin.

She felt a drop of sweat course down the back of her neck. She risked a sidelong glance at her sword, which she had hung on a broken branch of a nearby tree. She knew she wouldn't get to it in time; she didn't know how she knew but she did. She also had a feeling that despite this creature not appearing to have any weapon on him her sword would be of little use.

Thoughts of their previous meeting swirled in her head and she fought desperately to take control of her emotions. She focused on breathing slowly, controlling her air flow and forcing herself to calm down. She began doing some simple mental exercises to offset the influence he seemed able to exert over her.

"I will come by to see you on occasion to get information on what you find on your search. It is of the utmost importance you relay exact information to me each time I visit. Do you understand?"

She paused in her mental routines and thought about what he was saying. For what reason would a being as powerful and emotionally influential as he was need her to give him information? He could just as easily pick anyone in the group and get the same answers, couldn't he? What was different about her? She needed more information.

"Why me? There are many others here. Why can't you ask one of them?" She asked.

As she waited for his response she tried to put on a courageous face, one which might cause him to think twice about attacking her again.

"The others? They are not like you. Aside from the heat you seem to be able to stir in my heart; well in the area of my body where my heart should be anyway. They are too sociable. They are with each other all of the time. Solitude is a lost art which you seem to have perfected my dear. And then there's that vile creature and the girls with their magic…" he stopped suddenly, as if realizing only now that he might have acknowledged something he shouldn't have, and his face grew gravely dark.

He took a step towards her and her heart seemed to stop beating completely. Her body grew deathly cold; but whether due to his proximity to her or her own fear and loathing she wasn't sure. Just then a light thump came from a short distance away. And then another, louder.

The creature looked beyond her, trying to see whatever was making the noise. He gave her one more look of pure evil and spun so fast Sakura would swear he became a dust devil. Then that quick he seemed to melt into the ground.

As she instinctively turned to see what had caused the creature to leave, a large head loomed from behind the trees. She was startled until she realized it was the boy's dragon. It looked around her, then right at her as if to ask, "Are you all right?" She gaped at it, wondering if the dragon could sense her feelings and thoughts. It seemed to give her a reassuring look before lifting its head back around the trees and thumping away.

She gathered her things and went back to the group, pondering on all she had heard. He had said 'that creature'. He couldn't have meant the horses as there were many of them and the only other creature that she knew of was the dragon. Maybe dragons and the creature, whatever it was, were enemies. It also sounded like he was going to mention magic. Maybe it's a creature of magic. If that was the case then maybe other magic, good magic, was an anathema to it.

Well, she decided. *It's time for me to make some friends.*

CHAPTER 34

They had been traveling for three weeks and had finally exited the forest. For a group as diverse and having as many non-trained people as this one, Jesse thought they were doing pretty well. They even had a *dragon* of all things.

The food appeared to have become completely rotten, including the dried and pickled items. He had heard some of the others blame the Dark Lord's Province. He wasn't sure they were wrong.

They were forced to hunt nearly every day as they traveled. Unfortunately, there was only small game in the area. Jesse kept his eyes peeled for anything larger than a jackrabbit but to no avail. All he could do was hope for a quick change in scenery where larger game might be found.

Jesse sighed and tried to put his mind onto other things. He glanced over at Sakura.

Now she's nice to look at. He thought. *Unfortunately, she treats me as if she were married, although lately she has become...* Jesse paused in his own thoughts, trying to come up with just the right word... *friendlier in the past little bit. But not friendly enough to warrant a little moonlight handholding.*

Jesse sighed again. At least she was treating him like a human being. She still seemed to ignore Wyk altogether, but then she fawned over that blasted dragon more than everyone else put together! That just wasn't right-choosing a dragon over a handsome man like himself. It just wasn't right.

At least that girl Krys has been nice to me. She is a bit young though. With those thoughts Jesse glanced back at Krys, who was now riding a little behind as the trail narrowed considerably through the rocky terrain. She threw him a smile when she noticed him looking and he turned quickly. It wasn't good to let women know you were too interested. If they found that out before you had them hooked, they might just spit the hook out and swim to someone else's bait.

No. Jesse shook his head, more for himself than anything else. She's too young. She's barely of age. She won't know what it means to romance someone or to enjoy their company. She would be very serious and say things like "you can't go on a quest for the king" and "but I love you" and "what do you see in her" and "I'll join the Guard so I can be with you" and other silly things like that. That's why he liked women a little more mature, a little more down-to-earth. Still, she was very pretty...

He glanced down at his hand which had started aching again. He flexed it hoping for some relief. Not even Krys could take the pain away with her magic, although the Light knows she tried. Maybe the dragon could help with that.

It was that stupid hammer! He had to try it himself, but all he got was stabbing pain like the lightening was going up under his skin. He could only hold on to it for a few seconds but the shock it sent through his body was too much. Both Belle and Krys said they felt its magic growing, which Jesse didn't understand at all. How could its magic grow? Magic wasn't a living thing and neither was the hammer. There had to be something else going on.

Jesse sighed for the third time. He wasn't looking forward to reaching their destination. Wyk said there would be water and he hated water. He knew they would have to get on a boat or find some other way across it.

He liked being on land. If man was supposed travel on the water the Light would have, well, would have given him gills or boats for feet or a fish's tail. Obviously, man wasn't meant to go anywhere near the water. It just wasn't natural.

Wyk put up his hand and everyone stopped. Jesse glanced around, hand on the hilt of his sword looking for trouble. He couldn't see any danger and it was far too early in the day to stop for lunch. A noise reached his ears, a noise which grew. It soon became a cacophony of sounds.

It started to sound like one of those traveling bands, those menageries with animals and people who did tricks and clowns and the like. He never understood what people saw in those things, although he did like the big cats. Like the lions and tigroxes.

Tigrox, now there was an animal. Looking vaguely like a broad horse but with teeth, claws, horns and very powerful legs it was the fastest non-flying creature Jesse knew of. He had heard once of a whole group of men sent to hunt one which had taken up near a town and started to slaughter the people and animals. It was said fifty men went out to kill it but only ten made it back.

The ones in menageries didn't seem so vicious; but he knew the temperament of caged animals could be deceiving. They knew they couldn't get out and they were being fed so they were content to wait for their moment of escape and retribution. Jesse could understand that.

Another, softer sound came to Jesse's ears; a faint growling coming from behind him. He knew what it was-the dragon was hearing the other sounds as well and was getting ready for a fight. He was always amazed how a creature built for flying and as large as Red was able to walk as lightly as he did. He was also surprised at how Red had become the de facto protector of the group, making sure everyone was safe whenever he felt something out of the ordinary was going on.

When he had first seen the dragon, he was overwhelmed. After all, how could anyone protect people from *that*? Yet as time wore on more and more of them warmed up to him, even that mouse of a girl Belle who seemed utterly terrified of everything. And Red seemed to bask in their friendship.

Some had said there were those in the group who very nearly worshipped him! But Red just drank it up. Even Jesse now expected the dragon to help in tough situations. The only one who seemed surprised by any of it was the boy Kam and he's the one who supposedly knew the dragon best.

By now the sounds had become much louder and Wyk deployed the soldiers to the front to protect the group from whatever was heading their way. Red had moved up towards the front as well, standing off the road in a large, rocky field bordering the road. Those that could do magic were ordered to stay together and watch the rear. Kam and Moose were in the middle as bodyguards for the women.

A large group of mounted men stopped about half a mile in front of them. The noises emanated from them. Wyk pulled out his long glass and studied the mounted figures for a moment.

"It is the guard from the kingdom of Alagastor, the bordering kingdom…" Wyk said then paused for a moment. When he continued his voice took on a slightly higher pitch as if he were asking himself a question. "…and our allies."

Kam looked over at the mounted group ahead of them. They looked more like a small army than a simple border patrol. After a brief pause Wyk slowly put down the long glass and seemed deep in thought.

They want to fight us. Came Red's thoughts.

As Kam looked, he noticed some of the mounted men looked odd. They were low to the ground for being on a horse and the movements also seemed odd for a horse.

That is because they are on lizaerds. Red said, sounding excited.

Kam understood instantly what Red meant. The thought of the large lizaerds being ridden by men seemed out of place for this kingdom. Apparently Wyk agreed.

"Instead of horses many of them are riding large lizards. This could prove to be a problem." Wyk announced.

"Those are lizaerds and they live mostly around Dragonmount," Kam said. "But why is a simple border patrol near a kingdom, and its ally, present such a show of force?"

"That's a good question." Jesse said.

Kam pulled out his own long glass, one which he got from his father, and looked at the opposing group himself. There were some men on horseback but most of the 20 or so men there appeared to be on the large lizards Red recognized.

The horse-mounted men easily had their horses stable and under control while the men on the lizaerds were having problems controlling them. The lizaerds were skittish and looked as though they wanted to head in the opposite direction. Kam wondered why, if they were so difficult to control, they would be used as mounts in the first place.

They sense me. Red said. *They know I'm here and they are afraid I will eat them, as they should be.*

"Wyk, are we going to have to fight?" Kam asked.

Wyk looked thoughtful for a moment before responding, "No. I'll go on ahead alone and will parley with their captain. We should be able to settle this quickly."

Wyk rode slowly ahead and Kam saw three of the other group's men ride out to meet him. He saw them clearly, even being able to see the weapons they carried. He couldn't understand how he could see those men as clearly as he did without using his long glass, which he now held at his side. He finally understood he wasn't seeing the men with his own eyes, but rather he saw them as Red saw them.

Red, what's going on? How come I can see what you're seeing?

I don't know. But I can see what you see as well.

The three men met with Wyk in the middle between the two groups. Kam saw the other men point first towards their group and then towards Red. Kam could feel the intensely familiar dark rage which Red harbored swell and threaten to engulf him again. This time however Kam noticed a sense of pride and devotion mixed in. This puzzled him until he remembered how everyone in the group had been fawning over Red.

As he turned to glance at the dragon, he saw the scales along the back of Red's neck appear to protrude up slightly, almost like a dog raising its hackles. Red bared his teeth as well, again reminding Kam of an angry dog. His scales had become a slightly deeper shade of red and appeared luminescent, as if they were giving off their own light. But when Kam looked at the ground around Red there was no reflection of light there.

Abruptly Wyk returned to their group, taking Kam's attention away from Red.

"They don't want us going past," Wyk said. "They are afraid we're an advance group preparing to launch an invasion. And they want to know how we got a dragon to help us."

"How long would it take us to go around their kingdom?" Kam asked.

"Too long, and we don't have time to waste." Wyk said somberly.

"So they're just going to sit there and watch us until we leave?" asked Krys, who had ridden up from her rear position.

"No. they'll probably give us ten minutes to decide what to do before they attack us." interjected Sakura, surprising Wyk. He was starting to come under the impression that none of the women were ever going to listen to what he said, especially when it involved keeping them safe and allowing the men to protect them.

"Actually, it was five minutes." Wyk put in dryly.

"So, what are we going to do about it?" This time it was Belle's turn to surprise Wyk. Well, at least they were staying together.

"Why don't we just send in the dragon?" Jesse asked. "They can't hurt him and the women will be safe."

All of the women gave Jesse a vicious look, forcing Kam to stifle a laugh. Red, for his part, moved forward a step like a huge, red, guard dog sensing trouble and ready to be unleashed. It was as if he understood what Jesse had just said.

"No one was even supposed to know we had a dragon." Wyk said sourly.

"Does this mean we have to kill everybody?" It was Belle again and she almost sounded excited at the prospect.

Again, to Wyk's surprise, which seemed to be happening a lot lately, Moose remained completely silent. Yet if there was anyone who should have felt some excitement at the likelihood of a fight it should have been him. Wyk glanced over at him and noticed a somber, almost melancholy look on his face at the prospect.

But before Wyk could respond to Belle, there was a loud cry and the other soldiers came at them. The lizaerds ran as fast the horses, only with an awkward looking gait caused by their bodies moving side-to-side with each step. Even more amazing was the fact that the horses didn't trip over the long, whip-like tails sweeping back-and-forth. Their answer left Wyk no choice.

"Prepare to engage and defend!" he yelled. "Women and non-Guardsmen move to the rear!"

Unfortunately for the Alagastor troops none of Wyk's group listened. The first one out was Moose. He held his hammer forward, like a lance, and as he rode his hammer shot out a large bolt of lightning. The bolt was far larger than any Wyk had yet seen.

The bolt headed towards one of the men leading the charge when it suddenly splintered and, like chain lightening from the sky, branched out and struck many men at once, throwing them off of whatever mount they were riding. All the men went down with large scorch marks on their chest plates and leaving the metal looking as if it had been partially dissolved.

Red also advanced but seemed to avoid going directly between the two groups. Instead, he stayed to the side and quickly knocked off three of the men riding lizaerds. Then, just as quickly he ate the lizaerds, leaving the men on the ground stunned for a moment until they got up and ran frantically in the opposite direction.

Kam drew his sword tentatively. This was not a battle he was wanted to fight. He knew the men they were confronting were just following orders; but why were they trying to keep men from a kingdom friendly to theirs outside of their borders? He hoped no blood would be spilt in this skirmish.

But before he had a chance to join Wyk and his men he felt the hairs on the back of his neck start to rise as a chill swept through his body, sending shudders down to his toes. Over to his right both his sister and Belle sat on their horses with their hands outstretched, their mouths moving. He couldn't hear what they were saying, but their faces were masks of concentration.

A strong gust of wind swirled around his sister's hands, as if a hurricane was being born. It grew in size and strength until it fled her hands, blowing a path along the ground straight towards the fighting.

The mini cyclone went between Wyk and one of his men he thought was Glenne and went directly into the three men charging at them. The wind lifted the first soldier and his lizaerd high into the air. The rider held on tightly to his mount but the lizaerd was twisted so violently that he ended up spinning around in the tempest, looking so much like a whirling top.

The lizaerd's tail struck one of the mounted men behind it knocking him off. The twisting wind picked up the second lizaerd as well. With both of the lizaerds twisting violently in the air Red caught both of them in his mouth and bit each nearly in half. Kam sensed a deep satisfaction emanating from Red with this intake of food.

The magic coming from Belle was of an entirely different nature however. Waves of what Kam thought to be magic shot out from her hand, distorting the air around it like heat off of a cobbled road. Kam tried to follow the distortion with his eyes but it moved too fast. All he could see was the outcome-three of the Alagastorian soldiers and their lizaerds were cut cleanly in half.

The three men's frozen faces held inert expressions of confusion and surprise while the lizaerds' bodies were still writhing on the ground. As he spared a glance back at Belle, he saw an expression of shock and horror. Kam knew from personal experience she would never forget the day she took someone else's life.

One soldier on a horse somehow got past the confusion and headed straight towards Belle. Quickly Kam rode forward and cut him off. The soldier swung his sword and Kam parried. The two exchanged swings with neither gaining the advantage as their horses skipped around each other. Kam risked a fleeting glance at Belle and saw she was too immobilized by what she had done to contribute more.

As the other soldier's mount danced nimbly around Kam, he was forced to turn to block another swing. Belatedly Kam saw that the soldier had maneuvered past him and was now between him and Belle. Knowing he only had one chance before Belle would be killed Kam swung his sword with all he had.

The soldier raised his sword to parry it, but Kam's sword cut it cleanly in two. The soldier looked at his broken sword for a second before wheeling his horse around and riding off as fast as he could.

Kam looked around and saw there were no more soldiers attacking. He could see that most of them had been killed or had their mounts slaughtered. He took a quick head check and found none of the Guards who came with them were killed. Some of them were injured, seriously. He breathed a sigh of relief when he saw that his sister and Belle were uninjured.

He also saw the bits and pieces of lizaerds on the ground and knew Red had gorged himself. The only ones left which hadn't been torn to pieces were the two which Belle had cut in half.

Red was nuzzling the still faintly writhing bodies of those lizaerds, yet Kam knew he refused to eat them. All he could sense through the bond was that Red having an unsettling sense of…smell? No, it was something more, something innate.

Kam cleared his mind and finally understood. Red could sense that magic had been used on the lizaerds. It was Belle's magic which unsettled him and was why he refused to eat them.

He wasn't expecting the girls, especially his sister, to use their magic so viciously and effectively. He also wasn't prepared for Red's help and his successfully taking out so many of the mounts without Kam seeing him kill a single man. It was too much of a coincidence to think a dragon out in the middle of a battle could kill mounts but not the riders.

I'm very full.

Kam, startled, looked over at Red and found the dragon looking at him and feeling very bloated.

How many lizaerds did you eat? Kam asked, thinking that dragons seemed a lot like children at times.

I don't know, but many.

Kam sighed. He knew from his bond with Red that dragons could eat a great deal of food and then not eat again for days. He didn't understand how they did it but at least Red could still walk. That was the important thing.

You killed many mounts but kept from killing the men. Why?

I did not need to. The men were of no danger to me. Their weapons couldn't have hurt me.

Kam looked hard at Red's speckled eyes but saw no sign of emotion. Yet through the bond he knew Red was keeping something from him. Something important but he couldn't figure it out. He wondered how Red could hold something back from him through the bond.

Wyk chose that moment to walk up beside Kam, leaving his musings unfinished.

"I wanted to thank your dragon, for the help he gave us in the fight. His support was invaluable in turning the tide in our favor."

Kam turned to look at Red and relay what Wyk had said when Red abruptly opened his mouth wide and gave a ferocious belch. The force of it caught both Kam and Wyk off guard and blew them to the ground. But it was the stench which hit them hardest, causing them both to gasp for air.

Choking, and with tears streaming down his face, Kam looked up at Red and he could swear the dragon was smiling at him.

CHAPTER 35

Krys was in shock. She had never seen so much carnage before. It was true most of what was on the ground was probably bits and pieces of the slaughtered mounts the other soldiers were riding. Mainly those ugly lizard things she saw Red wolf down with astonishing speed and vigor. She had also caught the dragon eating a horse or two.

Still, there were many of the other soldiers who were lying dead on the ground. Some had arrows in them which left surprisingly little blood; but others had stab wounds and even parts of their bodies cut off and they were in pools of their own gore. Yet instead of feeling sick she felt sorry for them.

Then there was the magic. She didn't even know she had it in her. She had simply wanted a little gust to blow dust into the eyes of the other soldiers, but the magic welled up inside of her like never before. Instead of a stiff breeze a large dust devil came out of her. She had trouble believing it even as it happened.

She looked over and saw that both Moose and Belle had dismounted and were talking softly. Her head was buried in his shoulder and her body was racked with sobs. Key had seen what Belle had done and it unnerved her a little. She didn't think Belle knew what she was capable of either.

She looked around to see where her brother was. She saw him walking over to something which lay on the ground by where Belle had been during the fighting. It was the blade end of a sword, but there was no hilt to it. Why her brother would pick that up she had no idea.

Maybe he wants it as a trophy. She thought. *Men do the strangest things.*

Moose held Belle gently. He had never seen her this upset before. Between sobs she managed to choke out what she had done. He was amazed; proud of her but amazed. He could see the remains of her magic-she had cut men in half as if they were paper. But he knew she was a gentle person at heart and was bothered by the violence which had erupted out of her.

She fought because she felt she needed to help and he understood that. She was brave but she didn't have the heart of a warrior like him and the other Guardsmen. She was little more than a girl, a kind, loving, and exceptionally beautiful girl.

She sobbed quietly into his shoulder and he held her. Her soft, girlish body was shaking like a leaf in a strong wind. He wanted to help her. To do something, to push away the dread she felt at what she had done, but he knew there was nothing he could do. She had to come to terms with what she did on her own.

Eventually her crying subsided and pulled back just enough to look up at him. Her tear-streaked face nearly broke his heart, but he knew she had overcome the worst of it. He wasn't sure how he knew, but he did. She pulled out of his arms slowly, as if she never wanted to leave his embrace. That part made him happy, but he didn't envy what she had to do next.

She walked slowly over to where the bodies of those she had killed lay on the ground. There was an oppressive silence, like a heavy winter blanket, which seemed to cover the entire area and even stifle his breathing.

He looked around and saw nearly everyone in their group was watching her as well. They all stood still, like statues frozen in a moment of time, to watch what she would do.

They saw what she did, Moose thought. *They understand what she's feeling.*

Belle stood over one of the men she had killed. She went deathly pale and for a moment Moose was sure she would be sick. But then she stood a little taller, a little straighter and Moose knew she turned a corner. She accepted what she did. That she did what she had to do to help her friends and protect herself. At that moment Moose loved her more than he ever thought he could.

Wyk was always saddened at the loss of life which battle brought. He never reveled in fighting and killing; he just knew it sometimes had to be done. His men performed admirably, as had Moose and Kam. And even the girls he admitted grudgingly. He now knew what his group was capable of, and for the first time he felt as though they actually had a chance to accomplish what they set out to do.

He watched as Sakura wandered among the dead soldiers. *It looks like she's looking for something.* He thought.

He had seen her in action-moving among the soldiers like a ghost. Their swords seemed to miss her, pass right through her. But her sword found its mark every time. There was one who Wyk thought was the leader of the group, who fought very well. It actually took her about one minute to finish him off. Her bladework was easily that of a blademaster.

When the fighting was over, he caught her wiping the blade of her sword off on the body of one of their dead. He hadn't realized how much blood had been on her blade until she cleaned it off. Then it shone like a thousand stars as the sun reflected off of it. Her sword's long, gracefully curved blade reminded him of the sensuousness of her body.

He then realized she had looked up and caught him staring at her, and for a moment the surprise in her eyes turned to embarrassment. He thought he saw a smile tug at the corners of her mouth, just starting to pull her those beautifully full lips up into an expression of delight at being looked at by him. Then, as quickly as it had come, it left her face and she turned and walked back to her horse.

Wyk shook his head and turned away. He needed to keep his head in this journey or he might just get everyone killed. He heard the soft clomping of a horse as it approached and looked up to see Kam riding slowly over to him. He held a short sword in his hand.

"Wyk, can I speak with you a moment?" Kam asked.

Wyk nodded. Kam dismounted and handed Wyk the sword. Wyk reached for it and saw that it wasn't a short sword at all, but rather a blade which had broken off of the hilt. Wyk inspected it closely. It appeared to be made of pig iron; a terrible metal for weapons. It was cheap and could break over time.

"Where did you get this?" Wyk asked.

"One of their soldiers had this sword on him. When we fought my sword broke his. Doesn't it seem substandard for soldiers to have?" Kam asked, leaving out the part about his sword having cut through it.

Wyk looked at the broken end. The edge was smooth and straight and looked like it had been cut rather than broken, like a hot knife slicing through butter. He knew that when metal broke it tended to shatter and have a ragged edge. He had seen it happen before. And with metal of this type the shattered area should be even more jagged. He made a mental note to ask Kam about that later.

"You're right. Have you told anyone else about this?"

"No."

"Don't. There is something going on here which I don't completely understand. I recognized a couple of the men we fought-they're lowlife's who spend all day in taverns and will slice your throat for a few coins. They are definitely not the kind to become soldiers for the crown. I suspected most of the others were mercenaries, and this weapon confirms that. I can't believe soldiers of Alagastor would settle for cheap weapons."

Kam was puzzled. Why would someone want to stop them? It was obvious by the sheer number of the Alagastorian soldiers that someone wanted to overwhelm them and end this fight quickly. If Red hadn't been there, their plan might have succeeded.

"I believe these men were sent here to stop us, but for what reason I don't know, Wyk said. "This is the farthest corner of Alagastor and it is rarely patrolled. Certainly not be a group as large as the one we encountered today. We have to assume anyone of us might be the reason we were attacked, especially after seeing how powerful Belle and Krys are. You must not mention this to anyone. Do you understand?"

Kam nodded, irritated Wyk would think so little of him as to feel the need to tell him not to talk to anyone else about their suspicions.

"Also, did you recognize what those creatures were some of the men were riding on?" Wyk asked.

"Those were lizaerds and they have a distinct advantage over a horse."

"Lizaerds?"

"They're mainly around Dragonmount. Dragons eat them for food."

Wyk glanced over at Red and saw Sakura standing by him and she appeared to be *petting* him.

"We need to get moving. I don't want another surprise like this one." Wyk said.

Kam had to agree. Neither mentioned what they were both thinking-that there could be someone in their group who might have been behind this.

Krys walked over to Belle and Moose. Belle had gone back over to Moose and was resting her head lightly on his shoulder. Moose had his arms around her and was holding her in a surprisingly tender way for a man as large as he was. His hammer hung at his side on his belt by the stout leather cord he had wrapped around it.

Krys could imagine what Belle was feeling. She had never used magic as a weapon before. She knew she had had to be strong and pull her own weight and she accepted that. She wouldn't force anyone else to defend her when she could do it herself. But that didn't make it any easier. She decided to walk over and offer her support.

As she approached them she overheard Belle saying, "I…I've never killed anyone before. I knew I had too; at least I felt I had to help. You and the others were putting your lives in danger for us and I felt I needed to do something too. It's just that, I didn't know I had it in me."

At the same moment both Moose and Belle seemed to sense her presence and turned to look at her. Krys wasn't sure what to say. She felt tongue tied but she managed to blurt out, "I understand. It was the first time I've done anything like that myself. But," Krys sighed, "we needed to. We needed to do something."

Belle's eyes were still damp, but Krys imagined being in the strong arms of someone who loved her helped. Belle slowly nodded her head, almost s if she heard Krys's thoughts. Krys smiled and laid a hand on Belle's shoulder.

Another large belch erupted from Red. Everyone turned quickly at the sound before realizing there was no danger present. Krys and Belle turned and looked at each other, the tension having been reduced for the moment. They both started to giggle while Moose, uncomprehendingly, still stood with a confused look on his face.

Krys was surprised to see Belle smile at her. It wasn't the normal, gentle smile of camaraderie; but it was a bit more relaxed than her usual dour expression. But when she turned to look at Moose, her face lit up.

As Belle and Moose gave doe-eyes to each other Krys took the time to back away surreptitiously. She found it hard to imagine two people more disparate than those two, and she had to wonder how they would get along. Would love blossom and unite them or were they just so different that any attempt at a relationship was doomed to failure? She imagined any relationship could succeed if people decided to put all of their heart, mind and strength behind it. How could it fail then? But she realized it would take both parties to participate for it to succeed.

Krys sighed. Life could be so difficult at times. She was so intent on getting her friends out of the school and able to use their magic openly. With all of that on her plate she wondered if she would ever be able to get into a relationship herself.

She did think one of the soldiers in their group was kind of cute. She thought his name was Glenne. But she could never have a relationship with him. She was sure his life as a Guardsman would be too busy to allow him to have woman be a part of it.

She wandered around looking for her brother and found him with Red. However, before she could say anything to him Wyk called out for them to get going. Krys hurried over to her horse and climbed on. As she waited for the group to get moving, Glenne rode past and gave her a quick glance and a nod of his head. Without even knowing why she felt her face flush with heat. She tried to flash him a smile but he had already ridden past and was looking away.

She gave a deep sigh of irritation at herself. She was behaving like a silly farm maid! She rode over to where Belle was and reigned in her horse in next to hers. She knew Moose would now be somewhere up near the front of the column talking with whichever Guardsmen would lend him his ear. She turned around and saw Sakura riding by herself as she always did, no closer than fifteen feet to anyone else.

"Maybe we should go and talk with Sakura." Krys said to Belle.

Belle glanced back in Sakura's direction. "She's always by herself. I don't think she likes anybody." She said.

"But, shouldn't we make her feel wanted. You know, being the only girls here and all."

Belle eyed her curiously. "You want to be someone's friend who doesn't want you around?"

Krys looked at Belle uncomprehendingly. Could Belle really not see the irony in what she just said? Krys decided to let it pass.

The group started forward, passing through the bloodied ground which only a short time before had been an active field of battle. Krys kept her eyes focused straight ahead. She was afraid she would break down in tears at the sight of the dead bodies, some lying torn apart on the ground. She did spare a sidelong glance at Belle and noticed she appeared to be sitting straight up on her horse trying to do the same thing.

They rode in silence for a while. Krys sensed everyone seemed to have the recent attack weighing on them to the point of evading any opportunity for talk. She understood how they felt; the images of the dead bodies were still fresh in her mind.

Then she started to catch impressions from Red again. Only this time they were different. The sensations she got had a distinctive human quality about them. With a start she suddenly understood she was vicariously sensing her brother's feelings through his bond with Red.

The realization sent chills through her body. For some reason being able to have a connection with Red was vastly different, and more acceptable, than knowing what her brother was feeling. Perhaps it was due to her lifelong ability to communicate with animals. Or maybe it was just the fact that he was her brother. Either way she tried to shut all of the sensations emanating from Red out of her mind.

She glanced up ahead at Glenne and thought what it would be like to have his broad shoulders to cry on, his strong arms around her giving her strength and protection. And with his deep, blue eyes to gaze into. At least she thought they were blue. She shook her head, trying to keep her thinking on track. She had been thinking about his face coming close to hers, his lips, slightly parted, were...

"Talking to yourself again?" Kam asked.

Krys looked up, startled out of her ruminations. He had ridden up next to her without a sound, yet again interrupting one of her delicious thoughts. How did he always manage to do that?

"No, I, uh, I was just thinking, wondering what we would do now."

Kam's eyes scanned ahead of her, taking in their little group.

"Who were you thinking about *this* time? I'll bet it was Jerome, wasn't it?" Kam said. "He's a nice guy, good with the sword too. But I think you'd have competition with his horse. I think he loves that animal more than anything else."

Krys turned away, hiding her face so her brother wouldn't see how red it got. She hated when he assumed she was thinking about men. It's not like she did it all of the time. Besides, a girl had to know what her options were. Although Jerome *was* nice looking, and those eyes of his. She was pretty sure they were blue.

She glanced over at Kam and found him staring at her.

"What?" she asked.

Kam looked down, his brow furrowing in concentration.

"Can you do me a favor?" he asked.

"What is it?"

"Can you try and sense why Red has a, um, living darkness in him? Something bad happened to him and I want to help." Kam said.

The question was not what Krystyna had expected. At times she had sensed something in Red, like a disease, eating away at him but she wasn't sure what it was. Or what she could do about it. However, her ability might prove useful in helping him and that was important to her. With a small sigh and a brief nod, she eased her horse back, letting herself ride a little slower so as to allow Red to catch up to her.

The large dragon came up next to her and she was surprised to realize just how light on his feet he was. For a flying animal he had taken to walking very easily. As she looked up at Red, she was startled to see him watching her. She turned away quickly, hoping he hadn't seen too much of her thoughts.

Interestingly she sensed a humorous feeling emanating from him, almost as if he enjoyed sensing her views on dragons. Yet beneath his enjoyment ran the darkness, like a fast-flowing river of black molten rock. She knew if she got caught in it, she could easily get carried away into its inky depths, causing her to be lost.

She looked up again, trying to fathom Red's emotions, his inner turmoil. She wanted him to know her concerns about what she felt. This time it was Red's turn to turn away and Krys could have sworn his beautiful red scales turned a shade deeper. She wondered if that were even possible.

She looked up at him again and he doggedly looked straight ahead, oblivious to her. But she could sense his emotions in turmoil, rampaging like a vast storm inside of him. She slowly guided her horse closer to him and gently laid a hand on his side.

She could sense that he felt her touch, even thought of it as being warm and soft. Abruptly he stopped and she pulled her horse up next to him, marveling at the horse being able to be this close to a dragon and not be skittish.

Again, Red turned to look at her and she kept her hand on his side, marveling at both the dragon's response to her touch and the warmth she felt emanating from him. That was something she hadn't noticed before. She then abruptly realized that his scales were probably hollow, closer to pot-hard on the outside but protecting a soft spot and blood vessels inside. It was a discovery which, for some reason, sent chills of excitement racing through her although she couldn't say why.

She reached out with her mind, letting Red know of her purpose in communicating with him. She felt herself in the dragon's mind, approaching the black, tar-like river of flowing emotion. She could swear she could feel it radiate heat as she tentatively approached it with her mind. Somehow she knew if she were to enter it she would become unbelievably cold.

She could sense Red's thoughts on it-he viewed it as a companion. It was almost as if it were a living entity, with the two of them enjoying a type of symbiotic relationship. She took her mind away from the river and into another part of Red's mind, trying to find the head of the river. Red stood perfectly still, almost as if he was afraid if he moved their connection would be broken.

She was traveling through his memories. She could sense Red there, apart from the memories but with her too. It was if he wanted to both guide her and watch her experience what he experienced, to understand how he became this way.

Suddenly she was there. She didn't know how or why, but she was at the root cause of Red's anger. And it wasn't just his feelings she was sensing. It was as if she could see his memories with her own eyes, as if she had been there and were reliving her memories of the incidents which had so twisted Red's life.

It was a single memory, a very old and cherished memory. Why did he cherish this memory? She didn't know, but still she watched the memory play out in her mind. She saw his parents, knew of their love for him, saw a fight with the leader of the dragons and saw the dragons turn away from Red. They were disgusted with him and they put their tails between their legs.

All of them except a beautiful golden dragon, the color of the sun shining off of a highly polished bronze plate. She was magnificent. She knew all of the male dragons were envious of Red for being the one she wanted to be with. Her tail was not down, but up. And that gave Red more happiness than Krys had ever felt before in her own life and a joy unmatched by any other incident in Red's. Yet the moment brought sadness too. Red left, and she chose not to go with him.

Krys realized she was breathing hard, her breathing matching that of Red's. She felt exhilaration for having had the opportunity to share in Red's life, to experience what he experienced. And, strangely enough, she felt as though Red not only understood her feelings, but agreed with them. Their souls had touched and both were the better for it.

Krys put her hand down and started to walk towards Kam but felt her world slipping away. As she started to fall, she vaguely saw Kam gallop towards her, arms outstretched to catch her. Then blackness enveloped her.

CHAPTER 36

He was getting desperate. Their puppet-ruler in that mud hole of a kingdom thought he could turn against him. Give a small man a little power and he feels he can rule the world. He would have to deal with him one of these days; perhaps even sooner rather than later. But he couldn't kill him, not yet. He needed him too much to eliminate him now.

He started to pace restlessly as his thoughts spun around in his head just as impatiently. He could use his favorite obedience inducer. Pain tended to be a great motivator for mortals. Some pain might just be the antidote to the king's reckless arrogance. He would need to be taught a lesson and one he would never forget.

His thoughts strayed briefly. He could sense her magic; sense its strength and power. He felt a kinship to this girl. Her magic was how magic should be. It was dominating and destructive, full of passion and heat. Her magic was strong and he could sense the way she decimated his guards. No small feat considering he gave the guards their magic himself.

Of course, all his guards combined couldn't stop him. He would never forget what his master had taught him so many years ago-to provide your servants the means of your destruction was to provide others with your downfall. It was a wise saying and a reminder that even he couldn't defeat his master.

He looked down at his own massive body, powerfully muscled and a beautiful deep, dark green. Although in this room with its limited lighting his skin took on a deathly charcoal look to it, as if his body had been consumed in a funeral pyre. Keeping its outward shape but burnt through to the bones.

Through the crack under the door, he saw an extremely bright light. A powerful, almost overpowering shade of green which made him shield his eyes. The light gave his floor, made up of a combination of dark slate-gray granite and lava rock, an oddly twisted checkerboard look.

The smooth, reflective granite with its flecks of minerals reflected the light and had the appearance of a million green stars in dark sky. The slightly unfinished rough lava rock seemed to absorb any light which got close to it, causing the "sky" to look as if it were full of holes.

He loved this floor; it made him think of the uneven nature of life. Yet even the highly polished granite with its reflective specks of minerals couldn't brighten the room much. He knew he was the cause of that-his magic seemed to absorb whatever mystical energy came close to him.

He was like a giant leech living off of the energy of everything else which existed. That was what his master called him, Leech. He hated the name but he didn't have any choice in the matter.

He could sense how she didn't weaken when she used her magic, as most did. Instead, she gained strength in its use. For anyone else she would be a formidable, virtually unassailable, opponent. But for him she would be merely a waste of life.

He stood still, waiting for her. He could, through being able to sense her magic, almost see her through the door. Her magic was a brilliant, angry green. It was blindingly bright but alive, and as intensely green as the most beautiful, verdant valley. Ironically it was just the opposite of extremely dark green of his body, which color looked more like the last moments of life of a dying mountaintop.

He knew what she was thinking, that she could burn her way through anyone and anything until she got to him. She'd never had an obstacle which didn't fall before her flame. But then again, she's never met him.

His anger briefly flared as he again thought about that pig of a king who presumed he could send her here to do his dirty work. Thoughts of his having to deal with that mortal briefly interrupted his excitement, but he quelled it quickly. He would have time to deal with that issue later.

As he looked at the door again, he witnesses something he realized he would probably never see again. The thick, heavy wooden door got hot, green with heat in fact. And the wood actually melted. Melted! It is a wondrous sight and something which even he, with all of his years and experience, had never before seen.

Then she was there. Her magic was strong and beautiful, and its color reminded him of lush fields of grassflowers with their brilliant green blossoms. As she entered, he smiled slowly, expectantly. He knew this would be an enjoyable confrontation with her green fire and the passion and heat it generated.

He felt a slight trickle of wetness begin to creep down the side of his chin, leaving a slimy, moist trail behind it and he quickly brushed the irritation away with the back of his hand. He wanted no distractions for the coming event and the pleasure it would bring him.

She moved quickly, lightly. It was as if her whole being existed simply as flame, with no corporal body attached. But he stood still, his excitement so great he felt his own heat rise up. His body shivered with anticipation and he didn't bother to pretend he needed to defend himself.

In a second she was on him. She leaped up and wrapped her legs around his waist and her arms around his neck and put out as much of her magic as she could, as though someone were stoking a simple fire to create more warmth on a cold winter's night.

After a few seconds she tilted her head back and looked him straight in the eyes, confusion written plainly on her flickering face. She was confused, but not impotent. She pushed her magic to its apex with all of her strength and ability.

He knew if not for his own power he would be cinders by now; no, less than cinders. His body would have nothing left to show for its existence except a black smudge on the floor. Her power was enticing and addicting; an aphrodisiac for others who also craved power. And as he stood there basking in the feeling of being around someone with as much power as any mortal he had ever come across, she realized her error.

She released him and started to back away, moving to exit the place as quickly as she could. But as fast as she was, moving as quickly and smoothly as real fire, he was faster. He reached out to her and with one hand grabbed her head, his hand so large it completely engulfed her face, covering her nose and mouth. She struggled against him, awkwardly trying to push away with her arms as she twisted and turned in his grasp.

She started to make a noise, a high-pitched squeal like a pig does when you slit its throat, but without the blood. His other hand twitched by his side as though aching to join in the fray, but it was not needed. Between his fingers he sees that her eyes are wide, wider than he'd ever have thought possible, and with a beautiful green sparkle to them.

As her flame began to die down, she struggled with what strength she had left. Her hands grasped his wrist and they are almost white hot as she focused all of her magic into them. Her body however lost its ethereal quality and became solid again.

With most of her body corporal, the few flames which still flickered on her gave the appearance of her body being consumed by fire rather than being constructed of it. Her flames slowly dwindled, becoming limited to just her hair and hands, as well as the ironically celebratory sparkling green embers which were reflected in her eyes.

At this point he felt it well up inside of him-the rapture. His body started to tingle and his head began to pound. He felt his own breathing became a deep pant which he was told sounded like the death gasps of a dying horse.

Tears started to trickle down the sides of her face, appearing as little drops of emerald fire cutting glowing green pathways down her cheeks. The flames on her hands finally went completely out. This left only her hair with a much paler, faintly flickering green; an embarrassingly weak imitation of how she started out. Her struggles had almost stopped, but still she sobbed silently for…for what? Was it for her life or her inability to stop him?

He almost released her, the desire to give her wondrous magic another chance at life filling his chest. But he knew her life was forfeit when she killed his guards and attacked him. He also knew that when he was this close to the rapture, he didn't have the strength to stop. It was coming and he had to let it come. Ironically it was the one thing he knew which was too strong for him to control. It was and always would be joyously more powerful than him.

The faintly flickering flames which were her hair slowly extinguished from the lack of air. He finally felt the same rush of ecstasy, that feeling of pure joy, which came only from the closest of lovers. Finally, as the sparkling green diamonds within her eyes went out and her movements stopped completely, he let out a roar of pure pleasure. His body shook in frenzied delight.

He took a moment to catch his breath, savoring the exceptionally strong response he had towards this woman's death. He wondered if it were possible to use His power, the Dark Lord's own energy, to resurrect her. Not that he desired to assuage any guilt he might have felt in his conscience; in fact he was fairly certain he didn't even have a conscience. No, this was for purely selfish reasons. He wanted to see if he had the power to bring her back and then he wanted to have that same rush with her death again.

As he looked down at her body he felt his magic, the dark magic of Him who he chose to follow all those years ago, course through his body. He focused on what he wanted and tried to will her back to life. Nothing happened. He gritted his teeth in impatience.

Now that he set his mind into having her come back it was all he could think of. He tried again only this time he tried pushing his magic into her body, to put life back into it. At first nothing happened. Then with a spasm of heaving coughs which caused her body to convulse she sat up.

He was ecstatic. He wondered if the Dark Lord knew he had enough power to do what he just did. He wasn't sure but he wouldn't say anything until the Dark One himself questioned him about it.

Once she caught her breath and was breathing quietly, she looked around in a confused manner. He again placed his hand over her face, covering her mouth and nose. She looked up at him, recognition instantly flooding her eyes. She again struggled against him. She kicked and pulled but didn't use any magic, which he found odd. She again struggled until her body slumped and the same pure rush of pleasure flooded his body, although to a much lesser degree than before.

As he looked over her body once more, he wondered if her inability to use her magic was a result of dark magic bringing her back to life.

As if bringing someone back with the use of his magic resulted in an imperfect resurrection. Maybe a dark resurrection, unlike the famous resurrection of Light, didn't allow people to return completely whole. Or maybe it caused some damage to their minds. Either way it didn't matter to him; he would still able to enjoy his toys over and over.

There was a clicking noise in the shadows to his right. He knew no new guards had arrived since the woman killed the others, not that it mattered. He had guards befitting his station, not because he needed their protection. And if she had gotten past his guards and into his room, he would have had to kill them anyway. He couldn't allow them to see his cravings and addictions. That would show weakness and he couldn't afford to do that. But he knew the sound wasn't from any of his guards.

"Come here little one," he said gently, almost lovingly, in sharp contrast to the acts he just performed. "I will bring this one back again and you may have her then, but you mustn't kill her. I want her to stay alive. Do you understand?"

The happy clicking sounds he heard were enough. He would bring her back again and let his pet play with her for a while until he wanted that feeling again. He chuckled to himself.

He knew eventually he would need to send his new toy to the kingdom. They were always in need of his puppets over there. This time he would trade for some of those young ones in the school they had. It was perfect.

Unfortunately, now he needed to take the time to talk with his partners. He hated the elementals. They felt themselves to be the most powerful beings and required subservience from all who were around them. But they would show him respect. Or rather fear, which for him was even better.

He wasn't completely sure how many of them there were; only that he knew of seven of them. Well, six he could use. There was that traitorous one he wanted to kill himself but the Dark Lord forbade it. He was going to do something himself about that one. Now THAT would be fun.

He magically called to them and knew they would come soon enough. He had new plans for them, all of them. They needed to be ready to do what was asked.

He briefly thought again about how many of those vile things the Dark Lord kept back. He knew the Dark Lord was holding the others in reserve until the last, great battle; the one where his master would become supreme ruler of this planet. Then he would spread his dominion outwards to other planets. He chuckled again, his master was nothing if not ambitious.

Life was good.

Krys awoke to find both Glenne and Jerome hovering over her, looking down with some concern. As she looked up at them, she realized she had been wrong about both of them. Glenne's eyes were a beautiful shade of green while Jerome's were a stunning maroon. She decided then that she could put up with having either color in her life.

"How are you feeling sis?" Kam asked softly. Krys lifted her chin to look up at Kam.

"I'm okay," she said. "I feel fine. It's just that the bond I have with Red overwhelmed me a bit. That's all."

As she sat up, she noticed Red also hovering nearby, his long neck curled nearly into an "O" over the top of the group so he could be close without blocking anyone from checking on her. Krys started to giggle as she imagined it as a giant halo sent down from the Light itself.

Focusing on Red she felt embarrassment coming from him and understood he had some concern about having caused her harm. She smiled at him and said, "I'm okay you big lizard. I just wasn't expecting it."

That quickly she felt irritation flow through to her but also a sense of relief. She smiled at Red again and the dragon moved away.

As she got up, Jerome helping on one side and Glenne on the other, each with one of her arms, she would swear she could hear Kam snort behind her.

I wish my brother understood how to treat women. Krys thought to herself. *These two are true gentlemen.*

As she got her bearings, she saw Wyk staring at her, and he didn't look happy.

"She's fine, let's go!" he shouted. We've wasted too much time here."

And with that they once again set out on the quest no one really believed in.

As they rode Kam slowly pulled up next to Krys so they could talk. Belle, who knew something was up, pulled up on the other side of Krys.

"Well?" Kam asked. "What did you see?"

Krys paused, looking over at Belle, wondering how much she should say. Kam didn't think her presence here was important enough to defer getting the information he wanted so maybe she shouldn't either. It was just that she now felt an even stronger connection to Red than before. A connection she couldn't fully explain yet something she couldn't deny either. It was as if Red became her best friend and soul mate in a matter of seconds. So, she did what any girl in her place would do, she sighed.

Kam groaned inwardly; or at least so he thought. But judging by the looks both Belle and his sister gave him some of that groan must have escaped his lips.

Girls, he thought to himself. *Why did they always have to make things more difficult than they were? All I want is understand my dragon better.*

With that he paused. He didn't understand why he referred to Red as *his* dragon. He searched his feelings and realized he didn't think of Red as a possession, like a pet, but more as a friend. A friend with whom he had a relationship with and others didn't. He also realized he was jealous of others having a part of that relationship in their lives as well.

He didn't understand why. Maybe he was trying to protect others from having the burden of a relationship with a creature which was, in many ways, as intelligent as a man and yet as complicated as a woman. Without Red's dark rage however, Kam could see them truly connecting, having a special means of communicating and allowing them a deeply personal method of understanding each other. It was a bond which Kam found to be stronger than any other he experienced.

"He has had problems with other dragons." Krys began, speaking so softly that Kam had to reign his horse over and lean towards her in order to hear.

Before she continued, he felt a horse brush against his leg and realized Belle was also getting closer in order to hear, which was why Krys was whispering in the first place. He held up his hand to Krys and turned to look at Belle, giving her his best questioning look so she would know not to hover. She seemed to understand as she gave a loud sniff and turned her horse around to fall back in with the group somewhere well behind him and his sister.

"He was, um, what's the word when a group kicks someone out and tells them they can never come back?" Krys continued as though nothing had happened.

"Ostracized," Kam said.

"That's right. He was ostracized. They kicked him out because he defeated their king or ruler or whatever they call the head dragon. Well, it wasn't just because of that. They fought on the ground, like two tigroxes. Dragons can't do that. When they fight each other, it has to be in the air."

Kam paused, and in the back of his mind he sensed Red listening in, like a large bird watching what was going on and waiting to pounce on its hapless prey when the time was right. Kam was surprised not to sense any animosity at either himself or his sister despite the ever-present layer of raging blackness which seeped through every aspect of Red's thoughts and emotions. He was sure Krys had to have sensed it as well.

"Thanks, Krys, I owe you one."

"Yes, you do," Krys said more to herself than to Kam.

Kam pondered what she said. There was nothing new in the information she gave him, nothing he didn't already know. But coming from someone else allowed him to confirm what Red had told him before. The only question now was what they could do to help him.

As Kam eased his horse back to try and be next to Red, Belle passed him, giving him a look which could boil water and cut meat. Kam shivered inwardly. He could fight other men, kill horrendous creatures, battle Dark Ones and bond with a dragon, but he didn't dare face an angry woman. And the fact Belle knew magic only compounded matters. He would never be comfortable knowing a woman had that much power. It just wasn't right.

He finally fell back enough so that Red caught up with him; or rather Red's head caught up with him. He knew he didn't have to be physically next to Red to sense him. Their bond could span…well, how far they could separate before he wouldn't be able to sense him, he didn't know. But he did know from experience that even when Red was flying so high he couldn't be seen he could still sense him.

Kam tried to explain why he wanted to know what Krys felt with her connection to Red. He also wanted him to understand why she felt the need to explain it to him.

He looked up and saw Red looking down with a strong sense of bemusement. Apparently, dragons didn't care about why someone did something, only that they did it. Kam realized with some surprise that was how he felt. He wondered if that made dragons similar to humans or humans similar to dragons.

Chapter 37

They were almost out of the kingdom of Alagastor, with its famous rugged mountains surrounding it on three sides. Wyk wondered how popular their king was in Alagastor. He had heard stories about King Roane and they weren't flattering. It seemed that both their kingdom of Austine and the kingdom of Alagastor were now being led by men who appeared to have dark ties and darker ambitions.

As they headed north over one of the tall mountain ranges protecting this kingdom Wyk wondered if he should be concerned for the dragon. He had no idea what temperatures dragons felt comfortable in or could even physically tolerate. As the temperature started dropping, he glanced back and saw Red continue to plod along, looking more and more comfortable walking. He didn't know why but for some reason that irked him.

He had seen Red fly before. There was a sense of elegance about it, a gracefulness as he flew, which made it seem as though his ability to fly was more than just a necessity. It was as though it was one of enjoyment as well.

As terrifying as dragons were, both for their size and ferocity, the latter of which he had now seen firsthand, he had to admit having a dragon along gave him a sense of comfort. It was as though he and this group were in fact being protected by this magnificent animal, but an animal with the intelligence of a man.

Suddenly, as if coming out of a trance, Wyk realized he was staring at Red and that Red was staring back. He had no idea how long the dragon had been looking at him but felt it must have been a while. Yet Red seemed to be showing no signs of animosity towards him. That was contrary to when he first met him and felt as though the dragon would chew him up and spit him out with no hesitation whatsoever.

He turned around and wondered about that. Were dragons, like people, capable of growing to like someone as they got to know them? Were they able to even have likes and dislikes, live out their lives making friends and raising families, living beyond the capacity to just survive and procreate? Or were they more like the lizards they seemed to come from?

His instincts told him they were more than their apparent smaller cousins. All of the information he had gotten from Kam and Krys seemed to confirm that. He wished he could communicate with Red, to find out what the dragon was thinking and why he was the way he was.

"I hope you're not thinking that hard about me."

Wyk turned to his left, surprised that Sakura had been able to ride up next to him without his noticing. Leave it to a woman to interrupt a man having important thoughts though.

"Not at all. A man of my standing would never sully even the ethereal image of one as beautiful as you."

She eyed him suspiciously, as if his words had some special, hidden meaning designed to make her appear foolish without her knowledge. Just like a woman, to take a compliment and twist it around to something bad!

Her features softened somewhat and she said, "I would like to cross blades with you sometime. You are one of the best bladesman I have ever seen."

His eyes narrowed and it was his turn to look at her as though her words held a darker secret. But her face looked back with all innocence and he felt a true sincerity in her voice. Not knowing exactly how to respond he simply nodded his head.

He had to admit that she was one of the best bladesman he had ever seen as well. Or would it be bladeswoman? Well, it didn't matter; she was one of the best and could probably give him a run for his money.

Her strength, though, was her unassuming demeanor and beauty. She would make a great intelligence gatherer. As much as Wyk hated to admit it, most men became idiots around a pretty face, showing less intelligence than a flea in order to gain the attention of a pretty girl.

And with Sakura's beauty and athleticism, men would go far beyond acting like schoolboys. Some might even kill for her.

That last thought brought Wyk's train of thought to an abrupt halt. What if Sakura wasn't all she seemed to be? What if she was there to cause confusion or to gain knowledge for someone else?

Wyk glanced over at her again and she seemed to sense his renewed interest in her and glanced back at him. He looked quickly away, feeling even more like an idiot for her having noticed his looking at her again. But he had to admit her beauty was beyond any woman he had ever seen. He also had a hard time believing she could harbor any darkness in a heart hidden in that wonderfully curved bosom of hers.

He's looking at me again.

Sakura had to wonder if Wyk was suspecting something. She had never known any man to see past her façade. In her experience men either stared at her face or stared at her bosom, which was a shame. She felt her legs were her best asset. Not that it mattered; men could be so predictable and childish at times. Well, all the time in fact.

But Wyk was different. His roughly-cut face, looking at times like a sculpture which hadn't been finished yet and still needed some smoothing away, drew her attention. No, he wasn't a beautiful man. More like a ruggedly handsome, somewhat austere looking one. But that suited her just fine. Those pretty men in their fine silks did nothing for her.

She always appreciated those men who could take care of themselves-hunt, fish and just got their hands dirty. Yet also knew how to be civilized and treat a woman. And have a modicum of intelligence to their name. Although Wyk had more than his fair share of smarts, she could see that. And that's what worried her. Of anyone here, he was the only one she felt could figure her out, who could decipher her true intentions.

She would just have to continue on as she had been and hope her part in this would remain undiscovered long enough for her to accomplish what was required. Yet she found herself in the unenviable position of feeling both guilty whenever Wyk was around and hoping he would figure out what she was doing here and stop her.

She sighed softly; she couldn't let that happen.

Sakura had another worry-the dragon. She also didn't want to underestimate Red. Although she couldn't figure out what was going through his head, apparently Kam and Krys could. And from their talk that dragon was at least as smart as a man and maybe even as smart as a woman.

After a brief stop for lunch Sakura found herself following Wyk in among the trees. She had no idea where he was going or what he was going to do, but after her earlier thoughts about him she seemed to be unable to stop following him. She did so quietly though and he didn't seem to notice. She was amazed trees could grow here in an area which looked to be more rock than dirt.

Wyk was drawn over to a large tree where he stopped as if inspecting it for a flaw. After a moment she heard what sounded like a small waterfall flowing and understanding finally dawned on her.

She turned to go and found herself face to face with *him*. It was the same evil, vile creature who currently employed her and who had nearly raped her only a few weeks before. He was smiling that half-smile of his, condescending and tortured, as if just the act of trying to smile caused him pain. Yet unknown to her was that he had to smile; for the evil he was about to inflict was what made him happy, what drove his life.

She turned and ran, up around some scraggly trees and onto a barren, rocky spot. She hoped it would slow him down but somehow doubted it would. Knowing she shouldn't she turned her head to see where he was and saw nothing. She turned her head back around and was rewarded with a quick glimpse of him standing in front of her before she ran full into him. It was like running into a full sack of milled flour, a very large and heavy sack of flour.

She went down gasping, her breath knocked out of her. As he stood over her, his dark eyes caressing her body and causing her to feel sick, a loud voice said, "Get away from her."

She looked over and saw Wyk, sans pants and with sword drawn, coming to her rescue. The gray man looked over at him and for a moment it looked as if his painful smile edged up slightly. He raised an empty hand and a strange spear with a long, curved blade grew out of it.

Without missing a beat Wyk charged forward. The gray man swung his spear high, going for the head. Wyk ducked, but felt the wind as the blade narrowly missed him. He was sure he saw his hairs, now newly trimmed from the top of his head, pepper the ground.

He stepped back and the gray man thrust at him. But he was too far away for the spear to even touch him. Then, suddenly the spear grew, as if a living tendril of the gray man, coming straight for his stomach. Wyk twisted, using his quick reflexes to try and avoid the point, but he wasn't fast enough. Although not a killing blow, the blade sliced through his side in the fleshy part of his abdomen just above his hip.

Pain shot through him to his very core. He had been stabbed before, many times to his dismay. But this was different, the pain was different. It was like a cold ice storm radiating out from the wound, raging through his body and penetrating all of his muscles and nerves. He didn't understand what was going on, but he knew he had to do something quickly before the pain and loss of blood effectively ended this confrontation.

Wyk started to get up but the gray man swung the butt end of his spear at his head. Wyk lifted his sword to parry it, but the gray man strength was such that his spear pushed through Wyk's block and hit him in the head, knocking him unconscious.

The gray man turned to face Sakura who then decided it was best to leave and hopefully draw him away from Wyk. She took off running as fast as she could, not daring to risk looking behind this time even thought she heard no sounds of pursuit. She ran towards a large tree, the largest of the scraggly trees in the area, and quickly ducked behind it. She stood there, breathing heavily, and waited with a pounding heart and drawn sword.

After a few seconds she still couldn't hear any sound of pursuit and she peeked around the edge of the tree. There was no one there. She turned back around and leaned against the tree with her eyes shut.

A sudden sense of someone watching her caused her to open her eyes and look straight into the face of the gray man. Before she could react, he grabbed her around the throat and threw her fifteen feet onto to a hard, rocky area. She landed with a resounding thump and lost both her sword and breath.

As she lay there trying to get up the emotional strength to face him again, she felt a slowly creeping coldness along the backs of her legs and arms. Numbness spread throughout her body, freezing her muscles. It was as if someone had glued her to the ground with ice and completely incapacitated her.

The coldness moved up her legs and wrapped around her knees so she couldn't bend her legs. The same thing happened at her elbows. A cold chill went up her spine and she shivered; but the cold refused to go away.

Whatever this stone was, it was alive; growing and extending itself up across her body. A band of the rock went around her head and over her mouth, covering it so she couldn't make a sound.

The rock slipped under her clothes and formed a band around her torso. It felt like she was wearing a girdle of granite. The coldness of the rock again sent chills through her body but now she was so encased in stone she was unable to even move enough to shiver. The pressure increased on her chest and she had difficulty breathing.

From her knees the coldness slowly moved up her thighs, but only along the inside of them. And as the stone moved up towards that precious place where the apex of her legs came together, she knew. She knew what was about to happen and for the first time in her life she started to cry. She had been helpless when they had met before, her and this minion of the dark. But then she had been able to keep fighting, to keep pushing herself to do what it took to keep this thing off of her.

He seemed to sense what she was thinking and started to laugh maniacally.

Her mind raced frantically, trying to think of a way to escape. She didn't want to accept the realization of what was about to happen and that this time there was no hope. The cold reached the top of her thigh, and for a moment it stopped; or rather it hesitated. Then it slowly entered her and there was nothing she could do. As the cold started to penetrate her body tears started flowing freely down her face, and her only thought at that moment was that she wanted to die.

CHAPTER 38

Wyk sat up in a daze. He wasn't sure what had happened but would bet it had something to do with magic. Then it came back to him and he looked around for Sakura. He didn't see her anywhere.

He got up and half-ran half-stumbled his way back to the others. He was hoping she had somehow made her way back to the group. He found them where he had left them, packing up everything to move on. He made his way to Jesse and asked about Sakura.

"No, I haven't seen her." He replied. "We all saw her go with you into the wooded area." Jesse glanced down and continued, "where are your pants?"

"Quick, get everyone together. We need to go out and search for her. And there could be a Dark One with her."

Jesse gathered up everyone and they went out searching for Sakura. Wyk grabbed a spare pair of pants and went out looking for Sakura while trying to pull them up. What would he do if that creature had gotten to her? What if she was dead? It didn't matter if the creature was the Dark Lord himself, he knew he would be his fault for not protecting Sakura.

He first went to the area where he had fought the gray man and he tried to find footprints which might lead him to her. Any clue which could tell him something about which way he should go to find her. As he struggled with emotions he didn't know he had, there was a sound of someone running on the hard, rocky soil and he turned, sword half drawn. However, it was only Glenne.

"Wyk sir, they've found her. She's back with the others. And she um, needed some help"

Wyk took off at a full sprint, not caring about the low branches which whipped against his face or the rocks he slammed his foot on. All he knew was he needed to get back and see that she was okay.

When he reached their camp he looked around. Everyone seemed to have formed a rough circle. When they saw him they suddenly looked away and turned and found other things to do. *What was going on here? Why was everyone acting so strangely?*

He made his way towards what would have been the epicenter of everyone's attention and saw Krys and Belle standing next to someone. He walked up, trepidation in his heart over what he might see. When they saw him, they too turned away and allowed him to see Sakura.

She was sitting on a large rock, a blanket wrapped around her and her head bowed. His heart broke at the very sight of her. He knew something was wrong only he wasn't sure what. No one was tending to wounds or setting broken bones. It didn't make any sense. Then she seemed to sense his presence and looked up.

When he looked in her eyes he saw something he knew, something which he had seen many, many times before. It was death. Not the literal death of the body but spiritual and emotional death. It was the kind of death which left a body just as lifeless. When someone lost that which was most precious to them, they acquired that look. It was the death of the soul. And with that death came a real longing for the physical death to follow, an end to the suffering and pain.

He wasn't sure what to say or do to help. He guessed she wouldn't talk to him. Why should she? To her he was just a soldier, a man who fought for his king. He looked around for the girls but they seemed to have moved off, as if allowing him the chance to be with her. He wasn't sure why they would do that. He tried to think about who might be her friend and came to the realization that no one in their group was close to her. At least not that he had seen.

He looked at her face, at one time so full of beauty and life. Now it looked like a hollow image of her, a statue made of clay showing just the external appearance but with nothing inside. A tear slowly slid down her check and all of that proud confidence she once wore confidently, now completely evaporated.

Then it finally hit him. He understood what had happened. He didn't even know how he understood; it was as if she communicated to him without talking, but he knew. The realization brought to him a coldness which seemed to permeate his body despite the warmth from the sun hitting him. It was as if he went through a doorway from one season to another-leaving the heat of summer and going into the dead of winter. He knew, and with that knowledge something else came, something which he had never experienced before in his life.

As he stood there, tears started sliding down his face. Tears of sadness yes, but also tears of commitment and of rage. Tears which committed him to searching out the animal which had so hurt this woman. He knew he would not stop until he found out who did this. Then the justice of his wrath would be taken out in full force through the painful infliction of his judgment.

As he stood there more tears formed and fell, sliding slowly down his cheeks until they reached the bottom of his jaw. From there they fell onto the ground, mixing with the dampness already there from her tears.

Their painstakingly slow pace, now kept slower by the extra vigilance and the shock of the attack, put everyone in a sour mood. Wyk desperately wanted to meet the gray man again and salvage something of Sakura's honor by placing his blade through the vile thing's heart. Unfortunately, there was no sign of any living thing in the area.

They were over halfway up the side of the mountain. The trail up so far had been relatively easy. It was still far too early for snow to fall at this level but the coolness of air left a refreshing tingle on everyone's skin.

The climb wasn't difficult, but Belle knew there was a lot of emotion going through everyone. She knew what had happened to Sakura, understood immediately after looking into her eyes. She just wished she could do more for her.

She had seen the anger in so many of the men's eyes, including her Moose. Seeing it even frightened her. She knew Moose would never hurt her; he would rather lay down his life that hurt a hair on her head. She knew that. But seeing his expression still frightened her. She was used to seeing that boyish face beam with happiness whenever he was around her. He had changed. Not a lot, but he had. He had grown up on this journey.

Krys and she had agreed that one of them should always be by Sakura's side to provide support. It was the kind of support only a woman could offer another woman in these situations. It was an understanding, an acceptance, that it could just as easily have happened to any one of them. Men could be animals and sometimes women just had to accept that.

She had been surprised at one thing though. Well, two things actually. The first was Wyk's reaction. She knew Wyk and Sakura weren't close, but by the way he reacted you would have thought they were lovers. Belle felt that his support, more than anyone else's, did more to help give Sakura strength.

Then there was Red. The dragon had approached Sakura while everyone was finishing their packing to leave the area. Krys had offered to pack up Sakura's things for her and she was able to sit there for a few more minutes alone. Red came over and laid his massive head on her shoulder. His jaw only lightly caressed her but it was still an extremely touching moment. The funny thing was Sakura hadn't seemed the least bit surprised by Red's actions.

Belle risked a peek over at Sakura. She rode head down staring at the mane on her horse. Belle wondered what thoughts were going through her head. Revenge, most likely. Belle could understand that. But who attacked her? Their group had wandered around for an hour trying to find the culprit but found nothing. And Sakura remained very tight-lipped about who it had been.

They rode for a while with nothing but the soft clops and heavy breathing of the horses to break the echoing silence. Belle found the mountain air as invigorating as the beautiful landscape. Rugged outcroppings, green plateaus and trees growing on the edges of cliffs kept her eyes wandering from here to there. The lightly dusted snow which capped the highest peaks bore warning of a stiff winter to come and sent shivers down her spine.

They reached a plateau which looked to be the last one before they crested the summit. It was broad and fairly level so Belle wasn't surprised when Wyk called for them to stay the night. Darkness had already started to settle in and it was extremely difficult to see the trail.

They sat down for a quiet dinner. Nearby Belle found some wild snapapple trees and their bland meal was brightened slightly by the bitter-sour taste of the fruit. It also seemed to compliment their mood Belle thought morosely.

A stiff breeze suddenly tossed her hair into her face, but it ended as quickly as it started. Belle smiled to herself; she recognized it as the sign Red had taken flight. Belle wondered if he was hungry. She hadn't seen him eat since the fight at the border.

The memory of the fight came back to her with the force of Moose's hammer. She again saw the men she had killed in her mind and it tore her heart. She wondered if she would ever get over what she had done. She needed to learn to control her magic better.

"If you need to go behind the bushes I can stay with Sakura."

Belle turned, startled by Krys's sudden appearance. She had been so caught up in her own problems she forgot about Sakura!

"Okay, thanks. I'll be back in a minute." Belle murmured.

She was exhausted and grateful when they all finally laid down that night. She had barely closed her eyes when darkness settled in around her.

They finally reached the north western boundary, or the summit of the mountain, of the kingdom of Alagastor. They view from the top of the mountain was spectacular, showing the entire main valley. They needed to traverse that valley as well as a honeycomb of smaller valleys interconnecting with it.

Wyk eyed the rugged descent warily. He had been told this was the smoothest way to get to the artifact, but the mountain disagreed with him. There didn't seem to be any "smooth" way down. He focused on the green valley below and thoughts of the kingdom of Austine came to him. He could remember the beautiful fields of grice, which dotted the landscape all around the city, and orchards of apple and sugarplum trees.

"Can you see our destination from here?" Sakura asked.

Wyk turned and looked her in the eyes. The pain was still there, he could see it clearly. She had the haunted look of a lost soul. He hoped she was doing better. He knew he wasn't, not about her anyway.

"We're headed to Minotaur Flats. That's the series of buttes over there. Inside one of them is a chamber where we'll find what we came to get." He said.

Sakura looked to where Wyk was pointing. The flats looked to be a number of shallow valleys interconnecting around a number of small mountains which all had their top half sheared off. The small valleys between the buttes helped them form a checkerboard pattern. It looked like it would be easy to get lost in those ravines.

Wyk knew the trip would take a decidedly dangerous turn here traveling down into the valleys, some of which were not much wider than the width of a horse. Besides falling rocks and the distinct possibility of getting lost, roving bands of criminals were said to hide out here. It was also rumored to house the Guild of Assassins, although Wyk was sure that rumor was more speculation than anything else.

"The legend has it that one of those buttes has a large cavern inside and you could find a cache of treasure in it. But it isn't the treasure we're after; it's an object of incredible magical power. Some say it's an ancient artifact which has the ability to call on supernatural powers from the creator himself." Wyk said. Although he didn't believe in such nonsense the king did, and that was what mattered.

Sakura gave no indication as to whether or not she believed the rumors. Her stoic face tried but failed to hide the pain in her eyes and Wyk's heart broke a little more.

This far into the relatively isolated and mountainous northwest region of Alagastor, Wyk felt it would be okay if he allowed Red to exercise his wings. Red took off with jubilation. Wyk felt if the dragon was kept well exercised then he might just stay happy. After all, no one wanted a cranky dragon. As Red soared far over their heads Kam got information on how far ahead the flats were.

"He says that at the rate we are traveling it will take us another four days to reach the flats." Kam said.

Wyk shook his head. This quest of the king's was taking far too long. It was almost as if the king wanted them to stay away from the kingdom. Wyk turned to Kam and asked, "Could Red fly us over to the flats? He could probably do it in half a day."

Kam's expression was a combination of surprise, shock and what looked like dismay. Wyk didn't understand what the problem was. Red was a big, strong dragon and should easily be able to carry at least two riders and their mounts at a time.

Kam moved his horse over to a large, flat area and waited. About a minute later Red landed next to him. Kam looked up to face Red, although Wyk was sure he didn't need to actually see the dragon in order to communicate with him. But before Kam could say anything Red interrupted his thoughts.

This is not the right way. We need to travel in the other direction.

"Wyk, I think Red found what were looking for. He said we need to travel northwest."

Wyk frowned and looked in the direction Kam meant. He could see in the distance where the flats ended and a plain of dusty green color washed up against it. Within that area there rose up another butte. It was smaller than those which made up the flats but stood out due to the flatlands around it, and the unsettling way it seemed to move in the wind.

There is something of great power in that direction. But I cannot fully sense it; its power is being partially blocked. It is difficult to say exactly where it is.

Then how can you sense it at all?

I'm not sure. I can only say that there is magic blocking the location of whatever it is.

"He senses something magical, something which has a lot of power. But he isn't exactly sure where it is." Kam said to Wyk.

Wyk frowned, then recited the lines the king had him memorize.

A mountain with no summit
But a summit it will have
Not of rock but of leaf
To make a wondrous salve

It sits alone in a sea
Though many are near

A watery grave to besiege you
And green waves you can't hear

Deep below the ground
In the darkest cavern you must cope
Lay dangers waiting to strike
And the power to raise all hope

Wyk studied the forlorn butte with apprehension. In some ways that butte fit the directions detailing where they had to go. But he wanted to be sure, and safe.

"Kam, ask Red to fly over to the butte over there. See if he can sense the power more clearly. And ask him what's on the ground. It looks like it's moving."

Kam nodded and relayed the information to Red. As Wyk watched Red took off and sped directly towards the butte. It looked as though he was almost there when he suddenly stopped short and started to plummet to the ground. Red caught himself and slowly flew back towards them. Wyk frowned. He couldn't figure out why the dragon stopped so abruptly.

He turned to ask Kam what had happened and only then noticed he had fallen to the ground in agony, his face deathly pale.

"Kam what is it? What's the matter?"

Kam regained his composure and color in just a few seconds. He sat up slowly, rubbing his head.

"He can't get any closer; at least not without us being there with him."

"What? Why not?"

"I'm not sure. But we have to be closer before Red can get any nearer to it."

You did not tell them the truth.

No, I didn't. He doesn't need to know about the Dragonstaff.

I have flown farther away from you before. Why did it stop me this time?

I don't know. Kam said.

Kam watched as Red slowly circled around in the air above them. He hadn't yet relayed the request Wyk asked him to. He wondered how Red would react.

I will tell you, said Red. *I am not happy about it.*

Kam mentally kicked himself for thinking about what Wyk had asked him. He should have known that Red would pick up on it.

How about if you take me halfway? Kam suggested. *That way you can finish with everyone else then come and get me last.*

Kam could almost hear Red turning the suggestion over and over in his mind. He could sense the darkness, conspicuous by its silence, and felt what could only be called vibrations. It was the darkness trembling; but for what reason Kam didn't know. Was it excitement thinking it could influence Red to drop who he was carrying and have them plummet to their death? Or maybe it was rage at the thought of helping them get to their destination?

Kam wasn't sure which it was but he wasn't looking forward to finding out. He knew he would be safe-the magic of the Dragonstaff would see to that. But as to the others…

CHAPTER 39

Krys was terrified. She had waited until everyone else had gone, but now it was her turn. She looked over at Belle and Sakura. Sakura didn't seem to mind doing it, but then it was hard to tell how she felt about anything anymore. Belle, who looked like she would fall off of her horse at any moment because she was trembling so hard, looked as scared as Krys felt.

It wasn't that she didn't trust Red. She knew the dragon would try not to drop them. But being in the air! It wasn't right. Then there was the issue of the horses. Most of the poor animals had just gotten used to being around Red when they were now asked to be flown down the side of a mountain in his claws! She didn't blame the horses one bit for being scared.

As Krys had her horse move closer to Red's waiting claw, she replayed Glenne's trip in her mind. His horse had struggled hard to free itself from Red's grasp. It was terrified. Even at a distance Krys could feel its fear thinking it would be eaten. It struggled so hard that it slipped out of Red's grasp. Glenne's screams echoed the horse's as the plunged straight down. Fortunately, Red was able to swoop down and catch them before they became a permanent mark on the ground below.

She edged nearer to the waiting claw. Her horse started to dance nervously, letting her know how unreasonable she was being in having it move closer towards its death. She tried to comfort it, both physically and mentally, but it was no use. She felt her horse's fear inside of her and it magnified her own.

She should have taken Wyk up on his offer to blindfold her horse as well. But the other horses still seemed to know what was going on. Besides, with her connection to animals she didn't think it would do a bit of good.

Slowly Red's claw closed around them. She pushed out with her mind as hard as she could and tried to stifle the horse's movements. It helped a little. She could sense the surprise in her animal's inability to move around. But it pushed back hard! Krys had never felt an animal fight so hard mentally as her horse did right now.

Before she knew it, they were airborne. There had been no warning from Red, which she found a bit rude. But then again, she was halfway to Kam before she even looked down.

The mountainside flew by them so fast it was a blur of whites, browns and greens. She caught a bit of satisfaction from Red about his own superior intelligence. He figured out to have his claws below the horses' hooves so as to trick them into thinking they were still on the ground. She decided not to mention the fact that he should be able to think of things like that. He wasn't just smarter than a horse, he was as smart as any person she knew.

Fortunately, the ride was brief. The horses calmed down quickly once their blindfolds were taken off and Red moved back a short distance. Sakura appeared unfazed by the whole experience. With the exception of her windblown hair, you wouldn't have been able to have guessed she had just been on a ride with a dragon.

They were taken to the edge of a swamp. Tall green and tan grasses grew out of the stagnant water and gave the appearance of green waves as the wind blew across them. Out a short distance stood the lone butte, rising out of the water like a monolithic alter to whatever creatures ruled this putrid area. But even more amazing was the gigantic tree growing out of the top of the butte. If Krys didn't know better she would swear the butte was the trunk of the tree. But no tree was that large!

Krys looked around and saw that Red had just brought Kam over. But there was something strange going on; Kam was shaking his head slowly, as in some deep disagreement with Red. However, she knew that it wasn't a conversation Red was having. Rather she could feel in her mind that Red was experiencing pain, and that it had gotten worse the closer he got to the swampy area.

She wanted to do something, to help him. But she wasn't sure what she could do. She decided for the moment to let Kam and Red try to figure out what was happening while she went to be by Sakura.

As she approached Sakura, her friend gave her a lifeless expression. Krys shivered inside. She wished she could do something to help her but wasn't sure there was anything she could do. She knew that sometimes just being with a friend helped during trying circumstances. So, she had her horse stand right next to hers. She didn't say anything; she knew she didn't have to.

Red, what's going on? Where did this headache come from?

Red just looked at him with pained eyes.

Red?

It is the magic of that place. There is magic there doing this. It is made to keep dragons away.

Kam paused at that; magic to keep just dragons away? He had never heard of such a thing.

It's very old magic, from the Dragonwars.

Kam paused again. Magic from the dragon wars? That happened millennia ago! And the magic used at that time was still working? He wondered if his sister or Belle could somehow turn off the magic so they would stop having this blasted headache.

Red grounded and Kam started to head directly to his sister when Wyk cut him off.

"This is the place," Wyk said. "The king described what to look for and this is it."

Wyk paused for a moment to take in the butte. Or rather, the bottom half of the butte. The top half was a giant tree. They tall swamp grass blowing in the wind appeared to be waves of water when they looked at it from the mountain top.

"The king said he said he didn't know how deep the swamp was but warned us to keep from trying to swim across. He said there are traps in the water and we might set them off. But he mentioned that there should be a walkway going across somewhere nearby."

"How does the king know so much about this place?" Kam asked. "Red said there's magic here dating back to the Dragon Wars. What are we looking for anyway?"

"What do you mean magic? How do you know there is magic?" Wyk asked.

"Red can feel it coming from the butte. It's some kind of anti-dragon magic." Was all Kam could say with his head pounding like there was a thunderstorm raging inside of it.

"We'll set up camp here. I want all Guardsmen to form two groups and head out in opposite directions around that tree. There's supposed to be a walkway and we need to find it." Wyk said.

One group of guards came back after only a few minutes. Kam glanced up but shaded his face so the glare wouldn't exacerbate the pain behind his eyes. Glenne looked wet and had some of the reeds sticking out of his pants at odd angles. If he wasn't in such pain Kam would have laughed.

Me too. Red agreed.

Glenne said his horse got spooked by a noise and ran towards the water. By the time he regained control the horse was twenty yards out from the shore. From that position he could look straight down into the water and see he was on a strip of ground about two feet underwater which looked to extend all the way to the tree.

After sending one of the guards to get the other group, they headed out to where Glenne's horse ran into the water. From the edge of the swamp you couldn't tell that there was any difference at that particular spot. But Wyk walked in where the hoof prints led and as soon as he was five feet out, he announced he could see the path.

The group had a small lunch of dried rabbit and prepared to go to the butte-tree. They formed a single file and started across. Kam asked Red if he could fly but Red said the pounding in his head is too much for him to do anything but walk. As they ventured out into the water Kam kept his eyes on the submerged path which he guessed was about ten feet wide. Definitely wide enough for a wagon, or a dragon.

Every so often he saw large footprints on the path beneath the surface. He also noticed that these were three-toed footprints as opposed to Red's own five-toed feet. Outside the edges of the path the water became deep and Kam couldn't see the bottom.

Kam's headache had grown worse in the short distance they traveled out towards the butte-tree. He stared at the sight, unsure of what he saw. The lower part of the butte was definitely stone, but it looked as though about half way up it turned into a tree. The broken, jagged edges of the dark gray rock became a lighter brown-gray where the rough bark started.

Kam turned to see if Red had noticed the unusual butte-tree as well. Red however was sniffing the water. Kam tried to focus on what Red was doing, although the pain made it difficult. He did get the impression Red was trying to determine what creature had left the three-toed footprints. But sniffing the water?

Kam saw that the others had also noticed Red sniffing the water and now looked at Kam strangely, obviously expecting an explanation from him.

Why are they looking at me? Kam thought. *Just because Red and I are bonded doesn't mean I always understand what he's doing.*

This place is not good for Dragons. Red said, and Kam had to agree. His headache was so bad now he felt he would get sick. Kam wondered how Red could even stand up with the pain he was in.

Abruptly and in unison Belle and Krys turned around in their saddles and said something. Kam couldn't make out what it was, but it didn't sound like any language he knew. When they finished, the headache in Kam's head decreased by about half. Not as much as he would have wanted but a lot considering he wasn't expecting it. The throbbing pain still made communicating with Red difficult though.

They finally crossed the swamp and were able to spread out a little on the narrow strip of rocky beach which surrounded the butte. Everyone turned to Wyk to see what he wanted to do next when the shrill sound of a horn cut through the air. The reverberations permeated even Kam's throbbing headache and seemed to add another layer of tortuous discomfort to his already anguished mind.

Men appeared, coming out of an extremely narrow canyon which seemed to have been sliced by a very sharp, thin knife. As the men approached Kam saw they were wearing armor which looked to be stone. But as they got closer, he could see that they weren't wearing armor at all but were in fact made of stone.

"Gargoyles." Wyk and Jesse yelled in unison while two of the guards notched and let fly two arrows. The arrows shattered harmlessly as the struck the gargoyles. The gargoyles moved faster than Kam would have thought possible. Yet he also thought he could outrun them given the right motivation, such as them charging at him.

"Kam, you, Red and the women go around the bend and find the way in. Bring us back the artifact. The rest of us will stay here and hold the gargoyles back. Go!"

Kam paused, knowing the difficult time the others would have fighting creatures of stone. "Maybe Red should stay here with you and…"

"No. You will need him with what you're going to go through." Wyk interrupted. "We can take care of these things. Go."

They started around the butte, leaving behind the guard to protect their rear. Kam hated leaving people behind but he knew Wyk was right. Then Kam sensed something from Red and he turned to watch what the dragon was planning.

Red turned and breathed out a huge plume of green flame directly at the gargoyles. Kam couldn't believe Red was able to use his magic with the pain in his head, and doubted he could do it again. The pain was magnified tenfold after Red used his magic and it nearly drove Kam to the ground.

Fortunately, when the flames died down all Kam saw were piles of molten rock sizzling on the beach. But before Kam could celebrate two more of the gargoyles came directly out of the side of the butte, from solid rock.

It was then Kam noticed that Belle had stayed behind and was throwing what looked to be arrows with her hand. Her arrows flew straight and true and penetrated into the gargoyles' rocky exterior and seemed to cause them a great amount of pain. Moose ran forward and smashed his hammer into the chest of one of the creatures. There was a bright light and the gargoyle blew apart, sending shards of rock everywhere.

They rounded the bend and Kam lost sight of the fight. He turned his attention back to where they were headed. Large snake-like tendrils, some as thick as his torso, cascaded down from the massive branches above him. Some of them had buried themselves into the beach and formed new, smaller trunks to support the massive weight of the branches far above them.

Kam glanced over the side of the beach to peer into the unknown depths of the water. He noticed he still couldn't gauge how dip the water was. He had assumed the water would be fairly shallow, but seeing a large, silvery-gray mass which he guessed to be at least fifty yards long swim by just beneath the surface caused him to reassess his assumption.

As they continued moving around the butte Kam stretched his neck and looked up at the tree. He could see the branches overhanging past the edge of the butte and he started to understand just how large the tree really was. The tree was larger than many of the large hills near his hometown.

He began to wonder if there were snakes or some other animals living in the tree ready to pounce on unwary travelers below. The thought made Kam shudder and he hoped the sight of Red would be enough to scare them off.

Then, almost as if in answer to Kam's thoughts, strange, guttural sounds punctuated by loud screeches and animalistic screams penetrated the air. It was as if an alarm were being raised by the denizens of the tree as a warning to the other inhabitants. He wondered briefly if snakes made noises like the ones he was hearing.

The ground hurts.

Kam tried to focus on Red, pushing through the pain caused by whatever magic existed here. In doing so he felt…more pain. But this pain was different. It radiated from Red's feet and up into his legs. Walking was becoming tortuous for Red. Kam wondered how he would fare if he didn't have the luxury of riding a horse. He was afraid he would soon find out.

Krys stopped at what appeared to be a crevice, although it was extremely narrow. It was obvious the horses would need to stay on the beach. Kam and Krys had just dismounted when Kam heard another horse behind him and he nearly jumped. To his surprise he saw that one of the guards had followed them.

He recognized the guard as one whom always seemed to have his helmet on, even during the hottest time of the day. His name was Alyx and he was also the thinnest guard with them. Surprisingly, Alyx took this moment to take off his helmet. When he did his delicate features came clearly into focus, causing Kam to gasp in amazement.

"You're, you're a woman!" Kam gasped.

Interestingly enough Krys didn't seem fazed by this revelation.

"Alyx, where do we go now?" Krys asked the onetime male guard.

Alyx went close to the crevice to inspect it. She turned away, disappointment written clearly on her face.

"This isn't it. We need to keep moving until we find an entrance into the interior of this place and then make our way down into an underground chamber. We will find the artifact there."

They continued around the butte, moving slowly as Alyx surveyed every nook and cranny they came across. It was a surprise when they came across a huge opening large enough for even Red to enter. The sides of the opening were bordered by two massive trunks which extended down from the tree above them.

They decided to leave the horses tied up outside and they lit a torch and entered. Kam held the torch while his sister created a ball of light which seemed to follow her every movement like a love sick boy.

Show off. Kam thought.

A trickle of amusement found its way into Kam's head through all the pain. Kam gave Red a glare but said nothing.

Not far into the tunnel the path split. The way to the right was larger and less cluttered. The path on the left, although wide enough for Red if he tucked his wings in, had large rocks strewn across the floor as if the ceiling had partially caved in.

Alyx glanced over at Red, then looking at Kam said, "I'll go with Krys to the left. You and your..." she paused here as if debating with herself what she should say, then continued, "...friend can go that way." She finished, pointing to the right, which Kam thought was very considerate of her.

Kam and Red turned and went down the tunnel. The darkness was oppressive, seeming more like thick smoke than just blackness due to a lack of light. Kam's torch seemed pitiful, with the darkness overpowering its meager radiance more and more with each step. It got so bad that there were times Kam wondered if his torch was even still lit.

It was with relief Kam noticed the walls of the tunnel start to glow with a faint luminosity which contributed a great deal towards the battle between the light of the torch and the surrounding darkness. Upon closer inspection Kam saw that was a peculiar type of moss growing on the wall which glowed lightly. It shone with a pale green light which, despite its meager radiance, nevertheless made Kam feel safer.

Kam hoped that, in spite of the pain Red was feeling, he would be able to guide them towards whatever magic they were looking for. They had walked for about an hour when Red seemed to become even more agitated, although Kam wasn't sure how that could happen. The pain in his head had gradually increased until it was about as bad as it had been before the girls did their magic on them.

The tunnel abruptly widened into a huge chamber. Kam looked up and the ceiling was lost in the darkness. The glow coming from the walls picked up noticeably in the chamber, but Kam's range of vision was still only about thirty feet. As Kam looked around a guttural growl pierced the air and echoed hollowly around them. Kam crouched, sword drawn, trying to pinpoint the exact location of the sound. It was at that moment the creatures choose to appear.

There were two of them, with bodies not in proportion to their extremities. Their heads were too large and their arms, which had wicked looking claws on the ends, were too small. They walked upright on massively muscled legs and were nearly as tall as Red. But it was their jaws, and the wicked-looking six-inch long teeth inside of them, which caught Kam's attention. One bite to the throat could easily take out Red. Kam knew through the bond that Red was incapable of fighting very well at this time.

The first creature advanced followed closely behind by the second. Kam saw that the second one was slightly smaller, and assumed it was the female and mate of the first. They approached cautiously; their gaze fixed solely on Red. Thick drool escaped their mouths and dripped menacingly slow to the ground, leaving behind puddles of the thick goo.

The two creatures stopped about twenty feet away and faced Red. The smaller one, slightly behind the larger, started to move around to Red's side. Red pivoted around the larger creature so as to put it again between him and the smaller one.

Kam's head still throbbed from the headache Red was feeling, but through the fog of pain he knew that Red understood the tactics the creatures were employing. The larger one would viscously attack him from the front and keep him occupied while the smaller one would then use the opportunity to swing around and attack a soft spot on the side or rear. Although Kam didn't know if the long, sharp teeth of the creatures could penetrate dragon scales, the massive, powerful jaws and heavy bodies could surely break bones, causing a slow and painful death.

Red kept his wings tightly folded against his body so as to keep them from being damaged in the fight. But the creatures kept their tactics up-the larger one moved close and would feint with its claws then snap at him with its powerful jaws. The smaller one would try and go around to attack from the side. Red continued to dodge the attacks while he side-stepped as best he could to keep the larger creature between him and the smaller one.

Kam knew Red couldn't keep this up. The pain in his head made it difficult for Red to stay focused on the fight and to keep moving. It was only a matter of time before the patience of the creatures would prove to be the deciding factor.

With a start Kam realized Red had an idea, and it was a dangerous one. Kam cried out but Red's plan had already been put into motion. As the larger creature came forward and snapped its jaws, instead of dodging completely Red turned his head and neck away and lifted up his front leg so the powerful jaws came down on his foreleg. Kam heard himself scream as his arm caught fire from the pain he was experiencing through his connection with Red.

Red went down in great pain, but he wasn't as incapacitated as the smaller creature thought. With the larger one still biting down Red's front leg the second creature, moving remarkably quick for its size, coming around and going for his exposed underbelly. At the last moment Red swung his long neck around so he could reach in and close his jaws on the smaller creature's throat. The creature opened its mouth to scream in pain, but no sound came out.

Blood gushed out around Red's jaws. He brought brought his hind legs around, one on the side of the smaller creature's throat and the other on the back of its head just below its skull, and clawed viscously. The creature went motionless for a second and then fell down, lying still. Kam realized that the leg to the back of the head had probably broken the creature's neck.

The other creature, noticing its partner was down, let go and stepped back, surveying what had happened. It let out a loud roar which deafened Kam and echoed though the chamber. Kam didn't know if these creatures were intelligent or not but he thought he saw a new sense of rage glowing in its eyes.

At that moment Red swung his tail against the legs of the larger creature to trip it. But the creature was too large and heavy. It didn't fall down and regained its balance with surprising agility.

Wrap your tail around its legs, Kam thought, *and then pull.*

Surprisingly Red heard Kam through all of the pain. This time instead of just trying to hit the legs he wrapped his tail all the way around them, like a rope, and pulled. The creature went down with a heavy thud and grunt of pain.

Red lunged at his fallen foe, but as he jumped the creature lifted its hind legs in defense. Red landed on the thing's powerful hind legs. It then kicked violently, throwing Red backwards onto his back. Both of them got quickly to their feet and warily eyed each other. Kam tried to communicate with Red through the pain in his head and arm as well as through Red's battle lust.

Red, Kam thought, *it mainly uses its legs and jaw to fight. That's its weakness.*

Red, understanding Kam's thoughts, awkwardly stood up on his hind legs and rushed forward to attack the creature head on. Red then used his uninjured front leg to push the creature's head back and away. The creature then grabbed Red with its underdeveloped front legs.

Now able to use the creature as leverage, Red lifted up one of his hind legs and, stretching it out in front of him, clawed the creature's belly. With its guts spilling out on the ground, the creature went down for the last time.

CHAPTER 40

Kam rushed over to Red's side. He had concern etched clearly on his face.

Are you okay? He asked worriedly, although the burning in his arm let him know the answer, at least in part.

Red got up slowly and hobbled over to the wall of the cavern, leaving a trail of blood from the bite on his front leg. He sniffed the glowing moss which seemed to be everywhere and started to lick it. The moss somehow looked familiar to Kam, yet he couldn't remember why.

Why are you eating the moss? Kam asked.

This plant will help with the pain. It looks different here but I know the scent.

As Red talked Kam realized that the burning in his arm was so intense it momentarily surpassed the headache he had. But after a few minutes, as the pain in his arm started to subside, the throbbing in his head manifested itself again. He wondered why the moss didn't help with their shared headache too. It was at that moment Krys and Alyx choose to burst into the chamber from behind them, breathing hard.

"We came as soon as we could," Krys said breathlessly. "We heard a lot of noise and…" at that moment she noticed the creatures lying in their gore. She quickly turned as she caught the scent of the aftermath of the fight and threw up noisily.

Alyx eyed Red with a critical eye, noticing the injury. "How are you Red? Can you walk?"

Kam let out a hard sigh. People were still talking to Red as if he was a person capable of responding to their direct inquiries. Even if Red chose to answer, either he or Krys had act as a go-between in order to provide his response. People just didn't seem to get it.

"Good." Alyx said, apparently talking only to herself. "Well then keep eating. My guess is we will need your help again later."

Kam frowned then talked with Red through the haze that was their shared headache. *Can you communicate with her?* He asked.

The magic surrounding this island and causing me pain also seems to allow talking with others who I wouldn't normally be able to. Red said as he continued to lick the sides of the cavern.

Kam frowned again. He certainly wasn't one who understood magic, but the scenario Red painted seemed a bit farfetched. An idea came to him but he decided to let it rest for now. There were far more pressing matters going on at the moment, not the least of which was making sure Red didn't die from blood loss.

I shouldn't die from loss of blood. A Dragon's scales work by covering and closing a wound. The blood allows the scales to stick to the wounded area, keeping more blood from coming out. I think your idea about the one called Alyx may be correct, she…

Red stopped abruptly as another roar cut through the air. It didn't sound close by to Kam but in the tunnels he couldn't be sure. He did know he wasn't in the mood to hang around and see what made it.

"What do we need to look for now?" Kam asked Alyx.

"It will be some kind of entrance allowing us to descend." Alyx replied.

"Descend? We're surrounded by swamp. If we go lower, won't we end up in water?" Krys asked, feeling well enough to finally be able to talk.

"I don't know." Alyx replied. "We'll just have to wait and see. But from the information Wyk gave me we need to go down deeper. And I think maybe we should stay together this time. This seems like the main path anyway."

They started walking again. Krys created a string of ethereal, floating balls of light to prevent a surprise visit from another subterranean inhabitant.

Wyk took a moment to catch his breath. He wondered again if getting off of their horses had been a good idea. The horses were well trained and wouldn't stray far, but staying on their mounts might have given them an advantage, however slight.

He watched as Moose smashed another gargoyle in the chest. Only this time not only did he cave in the creature's chest, causing it to shatter into a thousand pieces, but lightening shot out the back of it and struck another one. That one didn't explode but the lightening seemed to disable the magic which held it together. This caused the seemingly solid piece of man-shaped rock to fall apart into various smaller rocks.

The other men were having a rougher time of it than Moose. Their swords, made with some of the best steel, could barely even scratch the surface of the gargoyles. Fortunately, Belle, who had disobeyed him to stay back and help, was keeping the monsters at bay.

Her magic arrows, thrown from her hands with surprising accuracy, inflicted a great deal of pain. When enough arrows hit a gargoyle, it also fell to pieces. Unfortunately, whenever one of the creatures was destroyed, another seemed to take its place almost immediately by simply walking out of the side of the butte.

Only Sakura's sword was able to penetrate the tough, rocky hide of the gargoyles. Wyk marveled at her innate intelligence and ability with the sword. She caught on to the fact that killing the gargoyles simply made more of them and she changed her tactics. She merely cut off their arms and legs, which left them rolling around on the ground making horrible noises.

Her plan worked for a time, until the number of gargoyles coming out of the side of the butte started to increase. Wyk then knew he had to figure out another plan or face being overwhelmed by sheer numbers. He formulated a plan which he hoped would work, but without any other options they had no choice. He just hoped that these gargoyles truly had rocks in their heads.

"Everyone, get back to the path, and hurry!" Wyk yelled.

Everyone slowly moved towards the mouth of the path, going into the water up to their knees.

"Hold here!" Wyk shouted. "Form a crescent around the end of the path."

The gargoyles instinctively moved to surround them and attack from the sides as well as the front. But when they entered the water their weight in the soft silt slowed them down considerably. Then as they took a few more steps, they disappeared altogether, dropping into the depths of the swamp.

Suddenly a huge silvery body raised itself on one side of the path and long, spidery arms extended out of the water and wrapped themselves around the gargoyles. The arms squeezed the gargoyles until their rock bodies were crushed to powder. Other arms, which had claws on the ends much like a lion's, swiped at the stone figures and tore them to shards.

Another silver body emerged on the opposite side of the group and also started to attack the gargoyles. But the silver bodies didn't stop with the Gargoyles in the water; they started to go after even those which were on the beach. The only ones the water creatures didn't touch were Wyk's group, all of whom were on the path.

One of the gargoyles fared a little better than its friends as it walked straight out to them. It apparently made the lucky choice of staying completely on the path. Before anyone could do anything, Jesse gave it a tremendous roundhouse kick to the head.

If the gargoyle had been made out of anything but stone Jesse's kick would have sent it flying. As it was it simply lost its balance and stepped partially over the side, but it was enough. Two slender silver arms came out of the water to greet it and promptly tore it in two.

Wyk heard Belle gasp as the two halves of the gargoyle's body were sent flying. One of the pieces came precariously close to taking out some of his men. But their quick wits and quicker reflexes saved them as they ducked and had the piece fly just inches over their heads.

Wyk watched the side of the butte as more of the gargoyles kept coming out. The question was which would give out first-the water monsters or the magic churning out the gargoyles?

"Krys, bring the light closer. I want to see something." Kam said.

Krys brought a few of her glowing globs of light over to where Kam was standing. He had been inspecting one section of the wall closely. After a few more seconds of eyeing the wall intently he ran his hand over the surface.

"Look at this." He said excitedly. "The wall is now made of wood, like bark. We're headed in the right direction."

Alyx looked at him doubtfully but Kam continued through her visual skepticism.

"The tree is growing out of the middle of the rock. This is important. There must be a way down through the tree."

Krys, who had moved on ahead, said, "Here it is. I found it."

Alyx and Kam went up to where Krys was looking into a hole. It was a hollow shaft within the tree filled with impenetrable blackness. Hanging down from somewhere above were thick, rope-like extensions of the tree like the ones they had seen outside.

"It looks like we're going down." Krys said.

"I don't know…" Kam began but before he could finish Krys grabbed some of the vine-like growths and started climbing down with three of her globes of light in tow. Kam had forgotten how strong and agile his sister was. It was almost as if her empathetic ability to communicate with animals also gave her some of the athletic characteristics of certain species.

Krys quickly climbed down with the ease and grace of a cat. Alyx went next, also moving with surprising agility. Red had stuck his head in the shaft and Kam thought he was seeing if he could fit. But he was sniffing the air instead.

Kam sensed both puzzlement and recognition from Red concerning the odor he just inhaled, but couldn't make out the specifics. For some reason he felt this wouldn't be the right time to ask Red about it and let it go. He did however mentally file it, with about a half dozen other question he had but couldn't seem to find the right time to ask.

Will you be able to fit down the hole? Kam asked. *It seems a little too narrow for you.*

Red abruptly stepped in front of Kam and started to squeeze down the hole. Although the hole was large, Kam still had misgivings about Red being able to fit. But amazingly the dragon wedged his head in and worked his way down, making loud scraping sounds in the process as his scales ran along the wooden sides of the shaft.

Red's tail finally went down and out of sight. Kam sighed and grabbed onto one of the tendrils and lowered himself. It was pitch dark inside and he belatedly wondered why he didn't ask Krys if she had put some of her shiny things in the passage. He did see a faint light coming from an opening which he assumed was the bottom of the chute after about 60 seconds of repelling.

He dropped down the last couple of feet in to land in front of a doorway of sorts which led into another chamber. Again, he was amazed that Red managed to fit through. He tried to determine if it was difficult for Red to maneuver through the shaft but all he got was the continuous pain from the headache and leg.

They hadn't walked far when their path ended abruptly at a wall. The wall was another part of the tree, covered with bark and solid to the touch.

"It looks like we made a mistake. Let's go back up and see if we can't find the entrance." Alyx said.

"No. This is it, I know it." Krys said.

Red gently pushed them aside and put his nose right up to the wall. He sniffed loudly then paused. Abruptly he opened his mouth wide and bit deeply into the wall, leaving behind a massive gouge. It looked eerily like the side of a giant apple which had a giant bite taken out of it.

At the deepest point of the bite there was a small hole, much like a worm hole one would find in an apple after taking a bite, and left Kam with a sickly feeling in his gut.

The hole was large enough for a person to wiggle through but nowhere near large enough to allow Red into its depths. Red then placed his foot into the newly created gouge and hooked two of his claws into the small hole and pulled.

A massive chunk of the wall came away, leaving behind a smooth, semi-circular opening. It had the appearance of a doorway from which the door had been pulled off of its hinges.

The three of them looked at each other and then at Red who stood there with a surprisingly sheepish look on his face.

"I don't know what we would have done without you," Alyx said. "You have been such a great help so far. You've even saved our lives on more than one occasion."

It's nice to be seen as something more than just a pet dragged along on the end of a magical rope. Red thought.

Alyx and Krys gave a chuckle. Kam, for his part, didn't see the humor in it. All he could imagine was walking down a broad road in the middle of town with him holding a rope leading to Red's neck and people running away screaming.

The doorway was now large enough for Red to squeeze through. As soon as they went through the doorway the first thing Kam noticed was a dramatic lessoning of the pain both in his arm and especially his head, of which he was very grateful for. Before that moment he had serious doubts of even being able to lift his sword.

This passageway was smooth and descended slowly. Kam couldn't tell if it was wood or stone. Behind him he heard Red spitting out the wood which was in his mouth. Before he could laugh, the sensation of having just eaten a tree hit him strongly. With the headache diminished he could sense things easily from Red again. That left him with the unfortunate sensation of feeling as though he had just eaten a handful of toothpicks.

They walked down the passageway with Kam fervently trying to wipe his tongue off with his tunic. In his head he sensed Red laughing. Apparently, a dragon's mouth was used to having rough, splintery things in it like wood and bone.

From the light cast from Krys's magical orbs Kam saw that the passageway had small stalactites hanging down. But upon closer inspection he could see they were actually bushes, growing upside-down from the ceiling of the tunnel. But these plants had leaves which were opaque and nearly colorless.

He heard Alyx utter a single, quiet oath in surprise and Red's single-word thought came through as *wrong*. The eerie, unearthly quality created from the plants made all of them feel as though they were in a surreal nightmare.

Krys's conclusion that the lifeless looking plants above them were some of the tree's roots which really irritated him. He wasn't sure if it was her constant know-it-all attitude or the fact she was almost always right which bothered him the most.

They continued forward, the only sound around them was the sharp clicking as Red's claws struck the hard floor with each step. They continued on this way for some time until the tunnel grew wider, as if anticipating a large cavern approaching.

"We've traveled back under the swamp and are headed towards the Flats." Alyx said, although how she knew that Kam had no idea. He figured they had walked a good two and a half miles when the tunnel opened into a huge underground chamber. Suddenly, a powerful stench, which somehow seemed to stay within only the cavern, caused them to cover their noses in revulsion.

Red was aware of the smell to such an extent it nearly drowned out the remaining pain in his head and leg. He also heard a scurrying sound much like a lizaerd running across rocks. The sound intensified and came from above them but when Red looked up all he could see was pitch darkness. He did however feel heat emanating from the darkness.

The ground beneath his feet grew softer somehow, spongy like the sand around Dragonmount. He tried to see if Kam had noticed it as well but Kam said he couldn't because of the overpowering smell.

Krys lifted her hand and the balls of light ascended until just below a dark, writhing mass which comprised the top of the cavern. For a second Red's heart stopped. It looked like the same caliginous blackness which lived inside of him, twisting and gnawing at him on the inside. But this was the first time he had ever seen it outside of his body.

Kam, Krys and Alyx all made various sounds of surprise and disgust, but he could felt most strongly Kam's revulsion at the undulating ceiling. Through Kam, Red could sense a commonality of understanding at what they were looking at. Kam too felt the mass somehow represented the boiling cold darkness which threatened to drive him Dragonwylde.

Suddenly a piece of the mass broke apart and fell towards Kam and his friends. It appeared as if the seething darkness was stretching out one long, dark tentacle to ensnare them. The piece moved quickly, maneuvering through the air with a will of its own.

As it descended Red instinctively swung his tail to swat it, but it deftly avoided it and continued reaching down. Kam drew his sword but it evaded his attempt to slash it as well. It finally attached itself to the back of Krys's arm. Krys screamed in agony while Alyx pulled it free.

Red could see the creature was large-its wingspan was much wider than the height of Kam. The body was similar to the large bats of Dragonmount, yet that was where the similarity ended. Despite the fact its face was covered in Krys's blood, Red could distinctly make out its very human features.

The creature squirmed in Alyx's grasp, nearly lifting her of off her feet with the frantic beating of its wings. Finding it impossible to escape it opened its mouth and a horrendous sound escaped. To Red's ears it was part human scream, part piercing screech, and it sent shivers down Red's back and caused his head to ring with sharp pain again.

Kam quickly swung his sword downward, cleaving it in half. Red could sense through the bond with Kam and the newly acquired bonds with the others that they felt revulsion like nothing they had ever felt before. He sensed it was due to the human, albeit distorted, looking face.

Suddenly there were more of the flying creatures swirling around them. Kam and the others were fighting them off as best they could, but despite the flailing of their weapons they were getting scratched and bitten at every turn. Many of the flying things tried to attack Red as well, but his scales prevented them from injuring him.

Krys yelled something and the other two covered their faces. Red understood what she planned and closed his eyes just as a bright light pierced through his eyelids, making him see stars. The cacophony which followed deafened him for a few minutes.

When Red opened his eyes, he saw that the flying people-bat things had retreated back up towards the ceiling in their attempt to retreat from the unexpected and unnatural light. But they weren't staying away for long. They started to glide down again, moving lower and lower to their dinner.

Red vaguely sensed that the light Krys created had weakened her, and that she wouldn't be able to keep creating it for long. Red decided to take things into his own claws and let out a rush of red-hot fire above them. He aimed above the three to try and kill those starting to get close to them and hopefully keep the rest of them from flying down and attacking.

The burned and burning carcasses he toasted started raining down on them. He noticed with some satisfaction that not a few hit Kam, causing him to utter oaths at Red. The noise in the cavern quickly grew in volume to a point of having Red's vision blur and feeling he was about to black out.

Get under me, quickly! Red said to all of them.

As they crouched under him Red lowered his body and wrapped his tail around himself to try and keep them completely encircled. Then he put out as much fire as he could, both around him and then aimed at the ceiling. He did this for what seemed an eternity, finally stopping to catch his breath. Unfortunately, what he inhaled was less air than acrid stench and ash.

But the downpour of dead bodies gave Red immense satisfaction. His body kept the others from being hit, but he couldn't help but notice just how many bodies were piling up. They were up to his shoulders and still falling, yet he knew there were many, many more of them. He started to think he had barely scratched the surface of the layer upon layer of these creatures, somehow living crowded upon each other hanging from the ceiling.

The bodies were nearly over his wings and he was worried even he would get trapped down here, drowned in a sea of bodies. He decided he needed to take a chance, and so he grabbed each of his companions in a claw and he leapt straight up.

It was difficult to flap his wings while creatures were still falling down around him. And as he dove into the sea of life which still swarmed above him, he felt himself brushing by large chunks of rock which were hanging down from the ceiling. One of the pillars of rock hit him hard in his chest, but still he continued upward.

Through the writhing mass of bodies which had now slowed his momentum considerably he saw a faint light. Pale, but definitely there. He tried to aim for it, to go towards it, but the writhing mass partially diverted him. He tried to claw his way through the living, pulsating blackness; but it was soft and malleable and didn't give him any traction.

He continued to beat his wings but he felt as though he were swimming rather than flying as his wings pushed against bodies instead of air. His forward momentum stopped completely and he felt as if he were adrift as the moving bodies buffeted him back and forth. They carried him to a different destination other than where he wanted to go, away from the light.

He brushed up against another of the rock pillars and he wrapped his legs around it. He knew what he had to do, but also knew if he had to explain it Kam and the girls wouldn't agree. Before they could understand what he was thinking, he worked each of his claws up to his mouth and popped each of them in.

It was definitely a disconcerting feeling. When he put something in his mouth it would eventually stop moving. Since he wasn't trying to eat them their movements continued, distracting him. He finally wrapped his tongue around them to keep them still.

Now that he had his claws free, he used them to dig into the rock and climb up. He slowly put one leg in front of the other, climbing through the blackness-the blackness which was poised to overwhelm him at any moment. His own personal darkness enveloped his mind as the darkness around him seemed to penetrate his body and into his soul. It felt like the physical and emotional darkness enveloping him were one and the same. Losing to either meant losing to both.

There was a whisper in Red's head; a soft, sweet, seductive whisper. It chose now to talk to him again. The disturbing darkness which had been patiently waiting for so long now spoke again. Red frantically tried to sense Kam, but the magic which connected them ceased to exist. The only other being in Red's head now was the living madness.

Red continued to climb. The pressure against his physical body from the creatures was quickly tiring him. He felt as if he had four Dragons hanging on to him trying to keep him from ascending to the light. Then there was the pressure in his mind, the beautiful promises of the dark temptress residing in his soul.

His forward movement paused and his dark companion, the one who seethed in the hot darkness he kept secure in his mind, laughed. It wasn't a loud, boisterous laugh or a laugh of frivolity or enjoyment or camaraderie. It wasn't even the freely given laugh done out of love. It was a selfish laugh, done solely out of spite.

He knew then what the darkness wanted-it wanted him to fail. It wanted him to give into the temptation to give up, to rest and let himself and the others with him drown in the eternal darkness that swirled both within and around him. It wanted the end of all things and it wanted Red dead.

He thought about Gold and his love for her. Then about Blue and the rejection he felt from him. He remembered the fight, *the* fight, and the rage which he used to harbor before the darkness took over filled him.

He roared. Not his fiercest cry as the darkness muffled the sound and seemed to absorb it. But the effort inspired him. With a rush he burst into a crazy tangle of roots and bushes, which for a second pulled at him like a giant net, before he burst blindly through into blindingly bright light. He closed his eyes and gasped for air feeling as though he had been holding his breath for an eternity.

His eyes acclimated quickly and he realized the light wasn't bright at all but was simply vast amounts of the glowing moss within another cavern. He felt revitalized in a way he hadn't felt for a very long time. He looked back at the hole he had made and found the plants had already grown over where he had exited and that no flying man-faces had followed him. With a cough he unceremoniously dumped his passengers in a slimy heap on the hard floor.

CHAPTER 41

The light which had been suddenly thrust upon Kam, Krys and Alyx glowed eerily. For a moment all of them thought the glow was coming from within Red. In Kam's case he thought the dragon had swallowed them and he was seeing spirits in the next life. But his eyes gradually adjusted form the total blackness within Red's mouth and he saw they were in a chamber, smaller than the last, but without any of the flying minions of the Dark Lord.

He knew he was covered in Red's spit, but still he felt as if he had been thoroughly cleaned. Under closer inspection he saw that he was covered in blood too. He knew it wasn't his blood so he quickly checked the women.

It is my blood.

Kam looked at Red uncomprehendingly. He had many questions running through his head.

What did you do? He asked.

Red told them about what had happened and why they ended up in his mouth.

I bet you were tempted to eat me. Kam said.

Red just looked at him, bemusement coming through the bond strongly.

"Red just saved our lives." Krys said, eyeing Red to make sure he caught what she was saying. "The only thing I don't understand is why you roared. My ears are still ringing."

It was for…inspiration.

"That's okay. But how's your tongue? Is there anything we can do for it?" Alyx asked.

I am fine. It's a small cut from Kam's sword. He was holding it when I placed all of you in my mouth.

Both women gave Kam dirty looks as if he had done something terrible.

Great, Kam thought. *Now everybody hates me for hurting their friend.*

Kam decided the best way to get out of this was to be busy, so he started to look around this new chamber. But a nagging thought tried to break into his consciousness, begging to be noticed. He shuffled it to the back of his mind to focus on his first thought-that neither he nor Red had any pain in their heads anymore.

How are you doing? He asked.

I am good. Red replied while gazing down at him with soulful eyes.

We owe you our lives. Kam stated simply, as more of a comment than any soul-searching commentary or inspired gratitude.

I was worried for the females. They were in pain. Red said.

Kam frowned at him, unsure of how to take Red's last comment or how to respond. He felt he should feel insulted but for some reason he sensed it wasn't said that way. Yet with dragons it seemed you never knew.

The nagging thought came again, fairly yelling to get Kam's attention. Kam allowed it to come forward and when it did, he gasped.

Red, I don't sense darkness in you anymore. None!

Red said nothing, but the women caught the emotion in Kam's connection and looked at Red as well.

"He's right." Krys said.

"Right about what?" Alyx asked.

"She must not have had a connection strong enough to feel it." Kam said.

"Feel what?"

"Never mind, I'll tell you about it later." Krys said.

Alyx looked a little miffed at not being told something which she gathered was important. But more importantly Kam knew they had to continue on with their task, and being in a chamber with no exit was important.

"Did you notice that there is no…"

"…exit." The women finished for him.

There was a moment of silence as they all looked at each other, the only sound being the soft dripping of water. They headed over to the sound, up against one of the walls, and found a small pool of water being fed by a slow but steady stream of drips coming from a tiny crack near the ceiling.

"It's water which has collected here. It's not a lot but we can get cleaned up." Kam said.

As they cleaned off the slime and blood from Red's mouth Krys wondered how far they had traveled through the tunnel. It didn't seem very far at the time but now she wasn't so sure. As she looked around the cavern for a second time, she still couldn't find any possible exit with the exception of going down the way they came in.

Red sensed what she was thinking as he walked over to one side and pointed with his snout at one part of the wall.

There is an opening here. Magic is hiding it but I think I can break through with Dragonfire.

With that he shot out a thin stream of green flame, hitting the rock wall in a very precise manner. There was a blindingly bright light with wonderful shades of green in it that they were all able to see before they turned quickly and covered their eyes. When they were able to see again, they could make out a hole in the rock in the shape of a very large doorway. It led into what appeared to be a hallway.

Krys looked at Kam, who had a determined look on his face, and then at Alyx who just shrugged. Then acquiring her own determined look, she started towards the doorway.

Krys stopped hesitantly in front of the opening however and slowly raised her hand. She half expected to feel something of substance rather than the nothingness it passed through. She heard Red give a loud snort behind them. It sounded chillingly like one of Kam's chortles when he saw someone, usually her, do something he deemed foolish. Alyx strode passed her without slowing, followed closely by Kam. Krys glanced at Red then went in as well.

They had entered another long hallway, stretching out as far as they could see. This hallway however was lined with dimly lit torches providing just enough late dusk-like light so as to allow them to walk slowly down without the fear of tripping over a dead animal or stray body.

"How are these torches lit?" Alyx asked. "Are they always lit? Are they magical?"

"They may just ignite when someone passes through the doorway." Kam stated casually, as if anyone should have been able to figure that out.

Krys moved hesitantly up to Kam, wondering if she should provide more light with her magic. She decided not to as the bright luminosity would carry far down the hall and allow anyone waiting there to see them coming from a distance. As no one made a comment about it she assumed they had reached the same conclusion she had.

They made their way slowly down the corridor. Krys ran through her mind the different magical defenses she could use against possible assailants. She wondered if she was limited to whatever magic already existed within her, such as being able to release wind, or if she could learn to do some sort of magical arrows like Belle. She was wary of doing the wind magic again as she felt she couldn't control it well enough.

Maybe my magic is limited only by what I can conceive of. She thought.

There are no limitations as to what your magic is capable of. Even the strength of your power can increase if you work at it. Like Dragons you have areas of strength and ability.

The voice in her head brought a knowledge and surety that what it said was accurate. She knew it was Red; yet she had never heard him quite so clearly before. She wondered why and Red continued. *It is because the magic in here is strong and is affecting you.*

As they continued down the corridor faint sounds came to them. Sounds of people eating and talking came softly to them. They were the sounds you might hear in a tavern Krys realized. She wondered if they were finally going to be going above ground or if this huge, underground labyrinth continued on forever. She was hoping the former as she was starting to feel a little claustrophobic. It was a feeling she was not used to.

They had not gone more than a hundred feet when two doors abruptly materialized in front of them. The doors were of a dark wood and seemed to absorb light. They were extremely large and could easily accommodate two Reds entering side-by-side. It was obvious to all of them the sounds they heard were coming from behind the giant-sized doors.

"The real question is," Alyx began, "that if it is nearly impossible to get into the room in front of us based on those hideous gargoyles we had to fight, then does that mean…"

"…there is another entrance." Kam finished for her.

"Another concern is whether the doors are made this large to house something which is so huge it requires doors of this size." Alyx continued.

While the three of them stood there staring at the doors it was Red who, after a loud, derisive snort, took a step forward and pushed against the massive doors with his head. The doors slowly opened soundlessly, which surprised them all. Inside they were greeted by an unusually bizarre scene. People, and a couple of human-like creatures they didn't recognize, were sitting around in a huge roomful of tables eating, drinking, and talking.

As they slowly entered the room it everyone turned to look at them. When they finally focused on Red, who at this point only had his head inside, they stopped what they were doing and an oppressive silence filled the large room.

Once inside the room unusual scents assailed their noses. Krys thought she caught the sour, pungent odor of rotten meat; although she wondered if it was meat or the normal smell of some of the creatures she saw here. Or possibly just some of the patrons who hadn't bathed in a month or two.

The walls appeared to be a combination of rock and wood and had the distinctive appearance of having been hewn right out of the natural rock and trunk of the butte-tree. Whoever made it only did enough to create the room and didn't bother to smooth out the rough edges, given the whole room an appearance of being unfinished.

They continued to walk slowly into the room with Krys taking great comfort in the sound of Red's claws clicking on the stone/wood floor and the sensation of him in the back of her mind. She saw some things which looked more animal than human. And there was one creature which had the head of an insect, five arms, and was the size of three men put together.

Krys then noticed something she would soon wish she hadn't. On a raised dais in the middle of the room on a supercilious chair which appeared to be made of intricately wrought gold sat a woman. Darkness covered her head like a veil, but her body was surrounded by a soft, pale light. It was barely covered and what she saw of it was flawless.

Krys felt herself start to blush, in part for the amount of skin showing but also for noticing the woman's perfect curves. She looked straight ahead and couldn't help but follow the curves of the body upwards, taking in every line and roundness, gaping at the sheer beauty and perfection of the legs and torso as the person sat comfortably in her throne.

She heard Kam gasp behind her and knew his typical immature manliness was in full swing. The only problem was she agreed with him this time. The body showed such magnificence in its flawlessness that even she was awed. Until she started thinking that the beauty of the woman's body was magically enhanced.

As her gaze finally reached the head of the individual she gasped again. She had thought the head to be shrouded in darkness, as if the lighting had been set up just to amplify the wondrous body the head sat on. Or maybe it was just the perfection of her curves blinding her to everything else. But in fact, she could clearly see the woman's face, if indeed it was a woman.

She heard Kam let out a strangled gasp and had to smile. Served him right for being a man! The woman's face, if that's what you would call it, was as hideous as the body was beautiful. The closest comparison Krys could make was that it was a cross between a woman, a dog, and a horse, with some extraneous features thrown in.

The head, which seemed too large for the body, had a large snout coming out with a distinctively horse-like mouth and oversized teeth. The snout curved up to large, dark eyes which looked glazed over as if the woman was dead. Her…its dark brown hair stood out on top at bizarre angle as if most of it had been pulled out in handfuls by the roots, leaving only twisted tufts. But the ears were definitely dog-like. She wondered if the horse-woman had a mane but couldn't see down her/its back.

Krys was torn between admiring the female's unblemished body and her revulsion at its perfectly repulsive face. She finally understood that magic had to be involved somehow and she wasn't about to let herself be a victim of anyone's magic.

She strode forward to the dais, to the "queen" of the place, watching those dead eyes following her. She heard chairs scrape on the stone floor but couldn't take her eyes off the thing in the gilded chair. She thought she heard Kam say something behind her but continued forward.

She had to reach the queen and let her know she would do anything for her. She had to tell the queen that her love was unconditional and she would lay down her life for her.

In the back of her mind, she knew it was wrong. That what she was feeling was unnatural and caused by magic. But she still went forward to pay homage to this wonderful, glorious creature. She knew it! She knew magic was involved. But even so, she couldn't get her mind to think of anything but worshiping the horse-woman.

She tried to take another step towards the goddess when her feet suddenly froze as if ice had formed around them and the floor, keeping her attached to the spot she was in. She struggled to continue forward, to lift her legs so she might approach and worship Her Greatness, The One-Whose-Beauty-Surpasses-All-Those-Around-Her. It was if she were in a dream; she could see what she was doing but at the same time couldn't change anything.

She could hear the grunts of those behind her and knew Kam and Alyx were having the same problem. She tried to sense what Red was feeling but sensed only a feeling of euphoria even stronger than hers.

"You must worship me."

The horse-woman's words were understandable, but with an odd accent. Krys didn't picture it sounding that way; but then she had no idea how a horse should sound or what kind of accent it would have if it could speak.

"You must worship me."

The words came again and Krys felt she was losing herself in them. It was as if she were falling into a deep hole, and the deeper she fell the more likely she was not to come out alive.

"You must worship me."

This time she felt as if she were leaving her body. Whatever it was that made her who she was slowly drained out of her. Her thoughts and character were being replaced as the horse-woman kept speaking those words. The more she said them the more of Krys faded away, only to be replaced with someone who did truly worship the creature. Soon there would be nothing left of herself. She would be only a husk, a shell, whose only objective in life would be to serve this vile thing.

"Drop to your knees."

This time even though it wasn't the horse-woman speaking but her brother. The words impacted her with just about the same force as those spoken by the glorious being on the throne. Falling down onto her knees was something which would be easy. It would show reverence to the queen even though what was left of "her" mind and "her" will said not to. She had to allow herself to worship this being and the best way was to bow down and kiss the ground upon which it sat.

She fell down to her knees and wept with the joy of being in the presence of the beautiful goddess in front of her. This was not what she wanted to do. What was left of her mind fought it but in the end the creature controlled her too much. As she prostrated herself before its unspoiled glory, she knew with its next words she would cease being Krys, sister of Kam, friend of…friend of… she couldn't even remember the names of her friends anymore.

As she waited for the last time for the Holiest-Of-Devine-Ones to speak to her as Krys, she felt a breath of air by her ear and a soft whistling. She knew She-Who-Sat-Upon-The-Heavenly-Throne-Of-Love was going to speak directly to her and her alone…

A loud cry shattered her reverie of worship and subservience. She looked up at the creature to see Kam's sword protruding out of its perfect chest. Deep crimson blood quickly spread across its beautiful white garment. It shivered once then slumped over, its gore quickly spreading on the floor beneath it.

As Krys stood up she looked around and saw the entire tavern of people seemingly staring out into space as if in a trance. She watched as some of them were already shaking their heads and trying to stand up. It seemed without the creature's hold over them the magic wore off quickly.

Kam walked over to the now Inglorious-Queen-Who-Lay-Dead-At-The-Foot-Of-Her-Golden-Throne. A couple of large, not-so-bright men brushed past Kam and tried to lift the throne to take it with them. When they found it to be too heavy to filch, they each grabbed a side and pulled. The throne started to give; then suddenly both arms came off in the hands of the men while the former monarch's body fell to the floor with a loud thump.

The men looked at their pieces, then at the bulk of the throne which still rested on the dais. They looked at each other and apparently came to an unspoken agreement that the bulk of the throne would still be too heavy to lift and they left with their spoils.

Krys went up to Kam but before she could ask how he managed to overcome her magic an exceptionally large man walked over to what was left of the throne. He was at least as big as both of the previous men who had gone up there but with the head of what looked to be an insect. After admiring what was left of the golden throne, he picked it up with ease and ran off.

The smell Krys noticed when they had entered the room was much stronger around the deceased monarch, and the odor assailed her nostrils with such force as to cause tears to come to her eyes. With the ornate chair now gone she saw that there had been a large carcass hidden behind it. It appeared to be that of a dead horse, which brought a strong sense irony to the situation.

The animal's carcass had fresh bites taken out of it which appeared to fit the queen's mouth. As Krys stood there transfixed by repulsion, and with nausea hitting her hard in the stomach like a punch, Red's head came into view. He Quickly scooped up the remains in one large mouthful. Krys couldn't hold back any more and with one loud grunt threw up what little she had in her stomach. Yet through it all a feeling of well-being came strongly from Red.

Krys glanced over at Kam and found him wiping his sword on the dead queen's white clothing, seemingly unconcerned that Red had just eaten rotten meat.

That's so typical Krys thought. *Only a man can ignore disgusting things like she had just witnessed, but when a pretty girl walks by they give her their full attention.*

Krys watched as Kam then walked over to a long counter on one side of the room. Alyx was already there and she grabbed an uneaten loaf of bread laying there and tore it in half, giving Kam one of the halves. As they ate Krys looked away, again appalled by what she was seeing. How they could eat at a time like this was beyond her.

Her eyes drifted away from them and somehow found their way back to the body lying nearly at her feet. As she looked at the bizarre face of the creature she noticed the eyes, which still had the same glazed look to them. On the creatures neck she saw a gold chin. Hanging on the chain was a bright object which she remembered noticing hanging from the creature's neck.

She grabbed it and looked hard at it. It was a medallion, perfectly round and brightly polished. On the medallion was a strikingly etched picture of a man and a woman chained together and looking imploringly at each other. Krys felt a strange sensation of tingling on her fingertips as she held it, a feeling which she hadn't ever felt before. And for some reason it gave her the sensation of magic.

She quickly dumped the item into her pocket and walked over to the other two, avoiding the other people in the room as they started to walk around looking for an exit. Krys consciously avoided looking at Red as he gave a loud, and extremely smelly, belch. She felt a feeling of his being contented emanate from him.

When she got to her brother and Alyx, she noticed they had found some cheese on one of the tables and had started to wolf it down as well. Kam shoved the rest of his food into his mouth before handing a small plate of bread and cheese over to her. As she reached for it, she suddenly noticed a ravaging hunger in her belly and was grateful for the food.

She started to take a bite of the cheese and glanced over at Red. He was picking his teeth with the tip of his tail, flicking out rather large chunks of putrid meat onto the floor. She turned away in disgust and saw Kam picking at his teeth with a sliver of wood, having small chunks of bread and cheese flick onto the counter. Her appetite immediately vanished and she wrapped her food in the cheesecloth it was on and stuffed it into her large side pocket.

"That was pretty good, huh?" Kam asked, walking up to his sister. "I don't think I've ever thrown anything that well before in my life." Krys was a bit disgusted at Kam's overindulgence in his killing of the creature; although she was grateful his arm had been true.

"Listen you ivory tower philosopher, you're still just a boy. When you've experienced the kind of fighting I've seen then you can gloat over your accomplishments."

Alex's strong words brought a surprised look from Krys and a hurt one from Kam. He was still young but Krys knew Kam's heart was in the right place, and he did just save them after all.

"When need to get moving," Alyx said, "We need to find the orb."

Krys and Kam look at each other.

"What orb?" Kam asked.

"It's a magical orb somewhere in here. It's the task the king sent us on in the first place. The king wants us to bring it back to him."

As Alyx led them past the body of the horse-woman lying on the ground Krys noticed for the first time a large hole in the ground behind the dais. She didn't notice it before as the cadaver of the horse had been on top of it. There were stairs leading down into what Krys imagined was a pit filled with loathsome creatures. But before she could comment on her thoughts Alyx led the way down.

Chapter 42

The magic of this area must have a mind of its own and realized there was no way to win against the large, silver creatures in the water. Wyk reasoned to himself. *That's why it finally stopped creating the gargoyles. Either that or the magic creating the gargoyles ran out.*

Even so, their group was not without its injured. Everyone except Belle looked to have fallen off of a cliff, hitting every rock on the way down. Wyk could see that among the injuries were some broken bones, including his arm.

The intensity of Moose's attacks and the damage his hammer did with shattering the gargoyles was nothing short of amazing. But the sea creatures seemed to glory in ripping apart the gargoyles, causing pieces of them to go flying in all directions like shrapnel.

Moose was now quietly talking with Belle, who had made a good accounting of herself as well with her arrows. Right now however, she had a forlorn look in her eyes. Wyk had seen it before; men who wanted to do the right thing by fighting their enemy but not always knowing how to justify the pain and killing that accompanied it. Wyk knew not everyone could kill, even given the right circumstances. But he always felt that sometimes people had no other option.

He approached Belle and Moose. When they saw him, they stopped talking and looked at him expectantly.

"You did well today, Miss Belle. You saved our lives. You did a good job too, Moose." Wyk said, glancing over at him. "Miss Belle, would you be able to heal the men? Do you have the, ah, magical ability to do that?"

Belle glanced at Moose before answering, although for what reason Wyk couldn't fathom.

"I can try, but I've never healed any serious injuries before; and certainly not broken bones. I think I probably could. Healing that much will exhaust both myself and the person being healed."

Wyk thought about that for a moment. "Then we need to get somewhere safe before you do that. Someplace where we can't be found, yet is easily defensible."

He looked around but saw no sign of the horses. Nor was there any sign of their blood or carcasses. Just shattered pieces of rock.

"Anyone know where the horses are?"

The men looked around sheepishly, each glancing at the others.

"Maybe the dragon ate them." Jerome offered.

"Red wouldn't have eaten them!" Moose said defensively.

"I don't think Red ate them either." Wyk said. "In any case, we need to get to higher ground, maybe a cave."

They looked around for a few seconds before Jerome pointed partway up the butte.

The cave was close and not too high, but with their injuries it would still have been a difficult climb. It was Moose and Jesse who came to the rescue. They assisted those who couldn't climb well and carried those who were more seriously injured. Wyk decided he was curious about which of them would win an arm-wrestling match.

Fortunately for them there were no more attacks and they were able to get to the cave without further incident. It took them the better part of an hour for all of them to get up there.

Once inside, Wyk had Belle heal everyone. Sakura gave Wyk a melancholy look while her cuts and scrapes slowly closed up and disappeared under Belle's hands. He only wished Belle could heal her emotional pain as easily as she healed her body. Sakura's usual radiant beauty was muted, like sunlight being filtered through a heavily overcast sky. He wished desperately he could find the demon that hurt her. He wouldn't let it get away next time.

Everyone ate a light dinner and lay down to sleep with Moose and Jesse taking the first watch. Wyk was willing to give Alyx and the others until morning to find the orb before sending everyone out looking for them. He had faith that anyone under him was capable enough to get the job done. Plus, they had Red with them and that couldn't hurt.

Alyx frowned. She couldn't understand where they were. She looked around at the steep sides of the windowless circular prison they were now in. It looked like rough rock all the way around. There was no ceiling and she could see the dark sky brilliantly lit with multitudes of sparkling diamonds shimmering in the clear air.

She grunted in frustration and turned to look at the others. They just stood there watching her, even that stupid dragon, expecting her to make the decision as to where to go next. Well, it was her decision to go through the entrance behind the dais. But who could have expected it to lead here? On top of that, the doorway disappeared behind them, becoming part of the rock so they couldn't go back the way they came.

She looked up again and wondered if Red would be willing to fly up to the ridge and see where they were. She hated asking him to do menial tasks like that but he was the only one capable of…

With a loud sound of flapping wings and a gust of air across her face, Alyx realized he had done just that. In a moment he was resting on the ridge, his form outlined against the stars like some celestial being of great beauty and strength watching over his universal domain. For a moment Alyx's heart skipped a beat and her breath caught in her throat. He really was a magnificent creature.

"He doesn't know where we are." Kam said. "He doesn't recognize the area."

Alyx bit her lip in exasperation. Where had she led them? What kind of place was this?

"It looks a lot like a caldera," Kam said, responding to her unspoken question.

Alyx just stared uncomprehendingly at him.

"A what?" She asked.

"A caldera. It's an old volcano."

Alyx frowned, taking in what Kam just said. She didn't know of any volcanoes in the area, or in any area for that matter. She had never even seen one before; at least not until now.

She looked around the inside of the caldera again. The only thing at all besides blank rock walls was an unusual lizard-like skeleton up against the side.

"Everyone, walk around the inside of the caldera and try to find anything unusual. We got in here so there must be a way to the orb." Alyx said.

Krys created a series of her glowing blobs of light which circled the inside of the small, dead volcano.

At least I hope it's dead. Kam thought.

It is Dead. Red said.

Kam looked up at Red's silhouette framed against the black sky with bright stars outlining it. He looked like a statue carved from dark marble and set in a majestic pose for all who entered to admire. He thought about the Dragon Wars and wondered what would cause man to fight against such wonderful animals.

He knew what Red would say to that so he carefully changed his thinking to the more mundane idea of finding a way to the orb. This place, this caldera, had to be a link to another path. Otherwise, there would be more than just one lizaerd skeleton in it.

It is not a lizaerd.

Kam looked again at the remains. Although difficult to see even with Krys's magical stars encircling the inside of the caldera, it still had the appearance of one of the giant lizards Kam had seen.

Are you sure? Kam asked.

Yes. It has neither the scent nor the form of a lizaerd.

Kam was taken aback. A skeleton which looked to have absolutely no flesh remaining on its carcass could still have a scent? As for its form, it looked like a lizaerd to Kam, but then he knew he should probably trust Red's expertise on this one.

What is it? Kam asked.

I don't know. I haven't seen anything like it before.

Kam gave a small sigh. This was ridicules. They could miss so much in the dim light of his sister's magic and the play of shadows along the wall could easily hide a clue which could help them. On top of everything else he knew they all were exhausted.

"Alyx, I think we should get some sleep. In the morning we'll be refreshed and in the sunlight we would be able to see more clearly.

Alyx mulled over Kam's suggestion. The caldera wasn't very large and in the sunlight they probably could discover a way out quickly.

"Okay. Have Red get back inside. He can be easily seen up there."

As if on cue Red swooped down and laid with his back against the wall in the general vicinity of where they had entered, effectively keeping anyone else from coming in the same way.

Krys and Alyx went straight over and curled up in the curl of Red's tail. Kam looked at Red cautiously before slowly making his way over to lie down next to his sister and waited for Red to protest. Red peered at him with golden red eyes before laying his head on his front legs. Kam could sense Red was asleep in a matter of seconds. With a deep sigh he rolled over on his side and fell into a blissful blackness.

Wyk awoke with a start. The sun had just topped the cave entrance and breached his eyelids. He sat up with a start, realizing the sun had already started its laborious climb across the fresh, crisp blue sky. He got his bearings and realized he slept well past his usual routine waking hour. Something he had not done since…well, since ever. As far back as he could remember he always awoke at about the same time every morning.

A thought of his parents came into his mind-of them getting up and seeing him having been awake for some time and saying how he should find something to do since he got up so early. That led him to his first job, milking the neighbor's cows every morning. Wyk shook his head to clear his wandering thoughts, trying to disperse them like stray cats with a clod of dirt thrown at them.

He figured the healing must have been more taxing than he had first thought. He got up and noticed everyone else was still asleep; everyone that was except for Moose. The more he learned about Moose the more his admiration for him grew. He would make a fine soldier one day if that was what he wanted to do.

"Morning Mister Wyk."

"I told you Moose, just Wyk is fine. You're not in the Guards. Not yet anyway." With that last comment Wyk saw a smile pop onto Moose' face, and knew his speculation was dead on.

"Is anyone else awake?"

"No Mist… uh Wyk."

Wyk smiled. He always had problems with his men at the beginning, when they first joined him. Although a stickler for protocol most of the time, he felt being on a first name basis with his men allowed himself to be accessible to them and to keep himself grounded. The best leaders throughout history kept themselves from being put on a pedestal. That could lead a man into thinking he knew everything there was to know and eventually become immune to listening to others. That was not good.

Wyk sighed. He realized, based on everything they had been through, that the others needed sleep. Apparently, the very act of healing was traumatic enough on the body that it behaved as if it was still injured and needed time to recuperate. He would have to ask Belle if there were any other way for a someone to be healed. It wouldn't help to be on a battlefield healing your injured men and having them go right to sleep.

He looked out over the landscape in the early morning light. In the bright light of the newly reborn day, he saw that the cave had a less severe incline up to it than appeared the previous night. That would make this cave easily accessible, which meant if there were any living things around, they would probably use this particular cave as shelter.

"Moose, has anyone gone to the back of the cave to see if there was anything living here?"

"No." Moose said sheepishly, as if he were the one who was responsible for that very thing.

Suddenly a movement caught his eye. At the base of the butte, he saw Sakura practicing her forms. As usual, her movements were crisp and precise, but that didn't lesson the danger to her.

"She must be crazy to be down there alone!" Wyk exclaimed, without realizing he said what he had been thinking out loud. He looked back and saw that his outburst attracted not only Moose's attention, but also woke up nearly everyone else.

With Moose and Jesse, who had woken up quickly at Wyk's outburst, searching the back of the cave for any potential dangers, Wyk went quickly outside to talk with Sakura. *It's almost as if she wants to get herself killed,* he thought.

He half-ran, half-slid down the side of the butte. He must have made a lot of noise because she turned towards him before he was even half way down. He ran up to her, furious at her lack of concern for her own well-being. He stopped directly in front of her, ready to give her a piece of his mind. Then he focused on her eyes; those beautiful, sad eyes of hers. Looking at her then he realized even a slow-witted man like himself should see she was troubled and lost.

His anger unraveled and all he could feel was pity. And regret. Regret that he couldn't stop one demon from hurting the one woman he ever had feelings for. He vowed he would take revenge out on that thing. One day, but for know she needed a different kind of help from him.

He stepped forward and gently put his arms around her. She was startled, that much was abundantly obvious, even to him. He moved close to her and looked her straight into her eyes. He could see they were haunted by a devastating memory. He then and there committed to himself would do his best to protect her from that memory.

She kept her eyes on him, looking so deep into his own eyes that he thought she was looking through him. Then with a small sob, the kind a frightened little girl might make, she fell forward into his embrace. He heard her sword hit the ground as she released it, but the sound seemed tinny, distant. All he knew now was she needed him and he wanted to be here for her.

As they walked deeper into the cave, Jesse couldn't help but notice that Moose's hammer started to glow with an undulation of green-gold light. It made the torch he brought seem useless. It also made it appear lightening was flowing over and around them as they walked along, giving the whole area a dreamlike effect.

He watched the shadows play along the walls as the hammer cast its cheery radiance. The shadows it created were eerie; sometimes there and sometimes not. The rippling of light made the shadows seem as if they had a life of their own. The shadows danced around them as if they were their bodyguards celebrating their arrival and gleefully searching for some dark evil to fight and protect their masters from.

"How does your hammer do that?" Jesse asked, still spellbound by the images.

"I'm not sure," was Moose's reply. "I think something, like right now I wanted light, and the hammer provided it for me. Isn't it great?"

Jesse grunted in response, realizing he was more than a little jealous of the hammer. Everyone had magic! Belle and Krys could do magic, Wyk had the Dragon Armor and even that boy Kam said he had some kind of magical sword.

He briefly wondered what would happen if Wyk's armor went up against the hammer. The armor was old magic, and powerful. But the hammer was dragon magic, another old and powerful type of enchantment.

Without realizing it Jesse had slowed slightly while lost in his thoughts of a magical battle and Moose ended up being a little ahead of him. Just as Moose stopped and said "end of the trail" Jesse felt himself bump into a large boulder, darker than their guardian shadows. With a grunt Jesse reached out and ran hand his hand across it. This boulder had stiff, bristly hair growing out of it. In a heartbeat he knew what it was.

"Moose, we have to get out of here, now!" Jesse whispered fiercely.

Like a well-trained guardsman Moose wheeled around and started to retrace their steps quickly, without hesitation and without asking why. They reversed their course and headed back at a much quicker pace than the set out with. But Jesse felt an icy cold hand grip his stomach when a muffled grunting sound followed them. He quickly pulled out his sword and whispered to Moose, "Make sure everyone's awake and ready to leave. We won't have much time."

Moose grunted in response, giving Jesse the impression he knew exactly what was happening and, more importantly, what would soon happen. Jesse found himself wishing the dragon was still with them.

With that maw, and that appetite, the animal following them should be nothing more than a snack for Red.

As they approached the front of the cave, more light spilled around them, illuminating the darkness despite the early morning hour. Jesse turned and started to walk backwards, sword held out in front of him, with the hope that just the view of something shiny and sharp might slow the animal down or at least give it cause for hesitation.

At that moment Jesse heard a multitude of sounds behind him-Moose calling to Jerome to help while rousing those who still slept, the voices of some of the guardsmen who had apparently already woken up and the girls trying to ask what was happening. The continued grunting of the animal, which now seemed to be only a few feet in front of Jesse, was accompanied by a short yet sharp growl. Although his own shadow falling across the creature made it difficult to make out, Jesse was fairly certain he knew that it was a saber-toothed cave bear coming after him.

As he got closer to the cave entrance, enough light streamed into the cave to provide Jesse with a much clearer view of what was following him. He now had a clear look at the face of the bear, which was as high as his own head even though it was still on all fours. The two, long, dagger-like fangs were still retracted, which Jesse had heard was a good sign. But the growling certainly wasn't.

The worst part of it though were the eyes-they glowed a deep crimson. the color caused Jesse to think that the bear could see his blood pumping through his body and wanted a sip to quench its thirst. It was a thought which didn't sit well with him.

Jesse slowed his backtracking to allow the others time to exit the cave. He could hear sounds of people stumbling as they quickly retreated to the mouth of the cave. Everyone that is, except for Moose. He came back and stood next to Jesse.

With the two of them forming a barrier across the passageway Jesse hoped they would intimidate the bear enough to cause it to retreat back into the solitude of the rear of the cave. But to Jesse's surprise instead of readying his hammer to fight, as Jesse expected him to do, Moose tossed the bear a large chunk of dried beef.

The bear sniffed it, nudged it carefully with its nose and then took the large chunk into its mouth with one bite. Jesse looked at Moose gratefully and together they backed away from the bear and out of the cave quickly.

Jesse ran down the slope doing a mental head count to make sure everyone else had reached the bottom. What he wasn't expecting was to see was Wyk and Sakura pulling away from each other as if they had just been hugging. At the bottom of the slope Jesse looked back up towards the mouth of the cave but saw no sign of the bear.

"Let's go," he said urgently.

Wyk and the others moved blindly down the narrow beach. They had gone about partway around the butte when a large crack in the side of the mountain came into view. It was wide enough to allow them to go into the crevice easily, but the path lay couched in darkness, as if the shadow formed was at war with the sun and refused to give ground.

"We're going into the gorge." Wyk said, although calling the crack in the butte a gorge seemed overly generous to the rest of the group. This was especially true since they had to walk single file. They walked through the dimly lit passageway slowly, unsure of what lay ahead of them. The eerily lit corridor gave Wyk the ominous feeling that they were being watched.

They walked through the morning, with the surrounding high walls causing feelings of claustrophobia in the group. The temperature was decidedly cooler in the crevice, which at least kept them from sweating as much as they did when they were out in the open sun.

Wyk worried that the group might start to feel hopeless given the situation. But when he heard the soft laughter behind him as the joke of naming this narrow walkway 'butt crack' got passed around he relaxed somewhat.

Wyk let his mind wander and his thoughts led him to Sakura. He wondered how she was doing, but as she was directly behind him he thought it inappropriate to turn around in their narrow confines and look. As silence settled over the group his apprehension for them, and especially Sakura, again grew. He couldn't even hear her breathing despite the long hike and narrow confines.

It was well into the day when they finally found the end to valley butt crack. The quick transformation from dim, claustrophobic confines to a bright, open space was almost painful to the senses. Where they had been walking single file and were pressed close together, now they were in a large bowl-shaped area open to the azure sky.

It wasn't large, maybe fifty feet in diameter, but everything was different. The light, which had been muted in the narrow confines of the crevice, now was blindingly bright. The sun was directly overhead and lit up the area clearly.

The smell of sour sweat and the echoing of deep, even breathing were now gone. They had been replaced by a woodsy scent, as if they had somehow stumbled into a forest, with a distinctive silence. Wyk eyed the walls all the way up and saw the transformation of the rock into the trunk of the large tree which made up the top part of the butte. But directly overhead there was a gap, as if the tree accepted that sunlight needed to come all the way down to the bottom of the shaft.

Wyk was amazed at how the confines of their day's walk had been affecting him. He felt like a great pressure had been released, as if he had been holding his breath all morning long. He felt he was finally able to exhale and breathe again when he walked out of the restricting confines of the passageway.

There was only one entrance into the section they were in and that was the crevice they came through. And except for some writing on one part of the wall there were no other markings anywhere. Wyk walked over to the writing and studied it.

He didn't recognize the language, but that wasn't the only unusual aspect to it. The writing started at the ground and when straight up about eight feet where it curved and formed an arch before going back down and ending at the ground. It had the peculiar aspect of forming a doorway directly onto the rock wall.

Just then there were some loud grunting noises behind Wyk. He turned and saw the backs of everyone as the stared at the crevice they had just come through,

"I think something's coming through the butt crack." Moose said, although any sense of humor the group might have gotten out of that comment was lost in the tension of the moment.

Jerome came up to Wyk and asked, "What do we do? I think it's that animal that was in the cave with us."

Another loud grunt came from the crevice, as if it were the mouth of a large creature getting ready for some lunch.

Jerome, who was next to Wyk, tuned around to face the opening too quickly and tripped, causing him to fall backwards into the wall. Except that he didn't hit the wall. He fell between the words, passing through solid rock and before disappearing from sight. It took Wyk only a moment to grasp what had happened before he yelled, "Everyone through this doorway. Quickly."

Everyone went through the doorway of words, with Wyk being the last as he watched the crevice for anything to come out. By the time he went through the doorway he still hadn't seen whatever it was which was following them.

CHAPTER 43

Wyk felt nothing. He was surprised; with the power of the magic that transported them he would have expected dizziness or nausea or *something*. But there was nothing. One second he was in a small bowl-shaped area of rock, and the next he was in a bigger bowl-shaped area of rock.

He looked at his men to see if there was any adverse reaction to the magical corridor they just traveled through, but they all seemed to be fine. Out of the corner of his eye he saw that a large section of the rock in this area had a distinctive red coloring to it. A deep crimson color in fact. It drew his attention away from his group and he followed the splash of color until it came to a head-a dragon's head.

He gave a massive sigh of relief. He quickly spotted Alyx and the siblings and went over. Everyone gathered around them and bombarded them with questions, although his main concern was whether or not they were able to accomplish their objective.

The reunion improved everyone's spirits, and smiles went around quickly. The only person who seemed unaffected by it all was Sakura. Her expression, which had been one of sad determination, softened slightly when she met with the others. But no smile cracked her face until she noticed Wyk looking at her. Then and only then did she force a tired smile to her lips, one that Wyk imagined was for him and him alone.

Wyk scanned the area for a path to lead them out of wherever they were now. Unfortunately, he couldn't see anything. He frowned as he tried to understand how the others had entered when it came to him that Red must have flown them in. But after a brief meeting with them he understood. This place was rife with magic, something which made him extremely uncomfortable.

After explaining how he and the others came to this place a renewed sense of urgency and understanding flooded Wyk's mind. It was entirely possible there was another hidden doorway which led to the artifact. It seemed to Wyk that whoever had hidden it had gone to great lengths to keep it from being found. And maybe more importantly, kept people from leaving like an elaborate rat trap.

A loud cry erupted behind him and he turned quickly. What met his eyes was a sight he could have gone his whole life without seeing and been happy. A large bear had entered into the area behind them. Wyk drew his sword and barked out orders. He had assumed the animal following them would not know how to pass through the magical portal. But he was wrong.

All of his men quickly drew their weapons and faced the beast. It was huge, at least as big as a small wagon, and it looked hungry. Behind Wyk a menacing growl erupted and he nearly jumped out of his skin before realizing it was Red. He knew that as large as the bear was it would be no match for the dragon.

If the bear hadn't noticed Red before it did now. Long, curved tusks slowly pushed their way out of its upper snout and they curved menacingly down past its lower jaw. Wyk doubted those teeth, as sharp as they were, would be able to penetrate Red's scales.

"Wait!"

Without warning and before anyone could comprehend what she was doing, Krys ran up to the bear and started to talk to it. Wyk could hear her voice but couldn't make out what she was saying, but the bear's posture changed instantly.

It sat back on its haunches and its dagger-like fangs receded into its mouth. Its eyes, which had been mere slits, were now wide open. And as Krys scratched it behind its ears it looked like nothing more than a very, very large dog.

Wyk couldn't begin to comprehend what magic Krys used to calm the bear. But whatever magic it was, it was effective. Now she was scratching its belly! Not only that, but the bear seemed to be enjoying her attention.

He shook his head; this was a strange set of circumstances he was involved in. Things which belonged in stories for old men to talk about around a pint late at night and which were more artistic than accurate. They were the type of stories which were meant to be legend makers and to gain an audience's ear and to be taken with a grain of salt.

"What's that?" Jerome asked.

Up against the wall, near where Wyk and his group came through, was a large animal on the ground. It looked to have been killed recently. The bear calmly went over to the carcass and dragged it over to Moose where it unceremoniously dropped it at his feet. Before Wyk could stop him, Moose reached out and pet the bear. For its part the bear seemed content with the situation.

"I think it's repaying us." said Jesse.

Wyk looked at him then back at the dead animal.

"Well, it's time for lunch anyway," Wyk said, trying to take everything in stride, "let's get a fire going."

His men got a small fire started with what little wood they had on them. The bear, after it had deposited its gift and made sure they were going to eat it, turned and walked about thirty feet from them and sat down. On its way it threw a growl at Jerome, who nearly passed out. Wyk noticed it seemed comfortable with everyone in the group except for Jerome. Whenever it looked at him it growled, causing Jerome to cast it side-long glances and to stay on the far side of the group.

After they were finished eating Wyk got up and slowly circled the entire area, walking right next to the wall and gently tapping it with his scabbard. After one full circumference he couldn't find any magical hidden doorway to lead them out of the enclosure they were currently in.

Sakura slowly approached the area directly in front of the skeleton of the giant lizard and peered intently at the wall for a minute. Wyk walked over to her and looked at the bones. It had a definite lizaerd look to the body similar to the ones they saw when they fought the men in Algastor. But the skull was different; it had an eerily human look to it except that it was elongated. Looking at it gave Wyk the chills.

"It's a salamander."

Wyk looked at Sakura intently. "A what?" He asked.

"A salamander; it was a creature said to be part human and part lizard. They say it was the precursor to the dragons."

Wyk's brow furrowed. "What does that mean?"

Sakura gave him a small, sad smile before she said, "It means some people think dragons developed from them."

Wyk eyed the skull again. It was creepy how human-like it was.

He looked at Sakura again and saw she was gently rolling some sort of coin or medallion between her fingers as she stared at one point on the wall. Wyk tried to gauge where she was looking and bent in to get a closer look. He saw a narrow slit just above where the skeleton's skull lay. It appeared it was using whatever nose it once had to point to it.

As he stood there trying to figure out the puzzle, he again felt that familiar warmth he felt whenever he was close to Sakura. With a slight smile and a nod of his head he stepped aside and allowed her to inspect the slit up close. With another small smile of her own, one which never reached her eyes Wyk noticed, she took the coin and inserted it into the wall.

There was a soft sound Wyk couldn't place and then a dark opening appeared directly in front of Sakura. It was pitch black and showed no signs of a room or hallway behind it. Not even the overhead sun was able to penetrate its blackened depths. It had the look of a doorway being painted on the rock and having no depth to it.

A chill suddenly went through Wyk's body as a sensation of cold seemed to emanate from the blackness. He couldn't tell whether the coldness was real or imagined. Sakura turned and looked into Wyk's eyes.

"That is the way we must go." She said.

Wyk frowned. He wasn't sure how Sakura knew that was the way or where she got the coin or whatever it was, but she seemed to know a lot about what was going on. She turned and pulled the coin, which apparently hadn't completely entered the slit, from the wall but the doorway remained.

"How did you know about the slit in the wall and where did you get that coin?"

She peered at him as if debating what she should tell him. Finally, she said, "I knew the salamander skeleton was the key. The coin was something I've had my whole life."

She stopped and gave Wyk a look that said *please don't ask me any more questions.*

Wyk sighed. He would never be able to figure this woman out. Then he said, "I will go through first."

Sakura opened her mouth to say something but Wyk shook his head. It would do no good to have a women go ahead of him into a potentially dangerous area. What kind of man would he be if he allowed that?

Wyk faced the doorway and took a deep breath. He strode forward and waited for his foot to hit the ground on the other side of the darkness, although he half expected his foot to meet only air and to plummet to his death.

His foot made contact with the ground, but he was now in total darkness and unable to see, smell or hear anything. What he could sense, the only thing he could sense, was an extreme cold of a nature he had never experienced before. It chilled him to the bone and caused his whole body to ache.

He took a tentative second step and emerged into the subdued light of a bizarre landscape. The cold was gone, but what he saw was straight out of his worst nightmares. A soft groan escaped his lips.

As far as his eyes could see there was nothing but bones; human, animal, whatever. The bones were piled nearly to his shoulders in some areas and gave the grisly appearance of a dumping ground for the bodies of everything that had ever died since the world began.

He looked up, half expecting to see he was at the bottom of a huge grave with bones falling as rain from the sky. But all he saw was a strange purple canopy with two dim suns peering down at him like the eyes of the Dark Lord watching over the souls of the damned.

Suddenly a chill went through Wyk's body as a fearful thought crossed his mind.

"Wait! No one else come in!" He yelled frantically as he turned, but it was too late. Appearing in front of him coming out of a stone obelisk about ten feet tall was Sakura. She looked at him quizzically, hand reaching for her sword, trying to figure out what he was warning them about. As her eyes scanned the grisly dreamscape behind him, he saw in her eyes that she grasped the same conclusion he did.

She turned quickly and yelled, "Don't come in."

The response from Jesse sounded hollow and far away, as if he were answering back from down a long shaft. "Okay." he said.

Wyk and Sakura gave each other glances of understanding and the acceptance of possible death, something Wyk found rare in a woman. Of course, Sakura was no ordinary woman. She was probably the most capable person, man or woman, he had ever met.

Wyk said, "Don't move. You just came in and I can't see anything but solid rock behind you. But maybe it's possible to exit exactly the way we entered."

He bent down and picked up a bone near him and threw it at the obelisk. It went into the rock as though it wasn't there. A sharp cry of pain went up on the other side. Both Wyk and Sakura breathed a sigh of relief.

Maybe she doesn't know as much about what's going on here as I thought. Wyk thought to himself.

He turned back to the graveyard. He recognized some of the skeletons, including two which appeared to be similar to the bear which was following them. He saw many of what he thought were the salamanders Sakura mentioned. He also saw an enormous skeleton, larger than Red, which also had large legs as thick as tree trunks.

It took him a minute to see there appeared to be a raised pedestal one hundred yards away. It looked about the height of a man and beautifully colored a bright golden-white. There was a narrow path between the bones leading out to it.

"Wait here." Wyk said, and saw a flash of anger rise in Sakura's eyes. But he knew she would stay. Or at least he thought so.

Wyk started to head over to the pedestal. He hadn't gone more than ten feet however when he heard a sharp whistle behind him. He turned just as Sakura tossed something to him. He caught it easily and looked into his hand. It was her coin, the means of their entrance into this bizarre place. He looked up at her and she said, "Take it. You may need it."

He then turned and continued towards the pedestal. When he was nearly there, he heard a rustling under some nearby bones. He stopped and drew his sword, not knowing what to expect.

An exceptionally large squirlion scuttled up a massive rib bone from what appeared to be an exceptionally large dragon. Its short, smooth fur ended just past its second set of legs while its third set of legs and long, barbed tail were covered in a dark, metallic-looking exoskeleton. Its mouth, while not large, was full of razor-sharp teeth which flashed menacingly.

They eyed each other warily. Its body, while as long as his arm, was not what he focused on. It was the tail, curved up over its head and easily as long as its body, which drew his attention. Wyk knew they were fast and that a sting from its tail could prove to be fatal.

Wyk slowly released his grip on his sword and instead slowly reached for his knife. He would have only one shot to kill it. If he missed, he knew there would be no way to outmaneuver it in the tangled jungle of bones surrounding him.

With a quick flash a knife was sent flying into it. The dagger flew straight and true and caught the squirpion dead center. It writhed in pain, using its tail to continually sting the knife again and again, causing poison to cover the handle and ooze down its sides thickly. The only problem-it wasn't Wyk's knife.

Although she had forsaken his warning about following him, she was still a good twenty yards away. It was a nearly impossible distance for anyone to throw a knife with any accuracy. Yet she done it and surprised Wyk yet again.

With a sheepish look on her face, she turned and walked slowly back towards the obelisk they had entered in from. Wyk, for his part, found it hard to be angry at her considering she had just saved his life.

He turned back and looked at the impaled squirlion one last time. It twitched a few more times and then shuddered and stopped moving for good. He also noted the beautifully crafted throwing knife which was now coated with sticky, white death. Shaking his head he then turned and continued until he reached the pedestal.

It was indeed about his height and appeared perfectly formed with no flaws, marks or indentations. It had the look of being made out of a single large piece of white marble with gold veins running through it. He didn't recall ever seeing marble that exact color before.

There was a circular area around it, cleared of bones, which allowed him to circle it and try to figure out what he needed to do. He walked around it completely but saw no indication of what it was other than a simple piece of sculpted marble with a perfectly smooth finish.

It was on his third rotation that he finally noticed a small slit about halfway down the side facing away from the obelisk. The slit was narrow with one side straight and smooth and the other having little bumps protruding into the opening, much like a keyhole. He was about to put his sword tip into it to try and force whatever it was open when a sharp whistle cut through the otherwise heavy silence.

She was pointing at him and then at her hand. He looked at the coin and realized that while one side of the coin was smooth and without any inscription, the opposite side had a raised image on it. He put the coin by the slot and rotated it until the bumps matched the indentations in the hole and pushed it in.

When the coin was inserted, there was a faint click and the pedestal started to move. At first Wyk thought the pedestal was lowering into the ground but quickly realized it was separating into six equal sections with each section pulling away from the rest. When the sections pulled back far enough, he could see that there was a dark hole going down. The darkness of this hole, like the doorway of darkness he entered to reach this mass graveyard, was untouched by the ambient light.

When the pedestal pieces finally stopped moving Wyk took a deep breath and put his hand into the hole. He knew he was operating on a leap of faith, hoping someone didn't go through all this trouble just to put a squirlion, or some other nasty trap, into the pedestal as a grisly joke.

As his arm extended into the opening, he lost sight of his hand immediately. Sweat broke out on his forehead and started to make its way down his face. As he reached further into the hole, he could feel his heart pounding palpably and inanely wondered if anyone had ever had their heart burst in their chest from beating too hard.

Abruptly his hand came in contact with a large, smooth sphere which felt oddly warm to the touch. It was large enough where he couldn't get his hand around it enough to pull it up and was thus contemplating inserting his other arm when he felt it stick to his hand. It wasn't sticky, it just adhered to his hand and he was able to retrieve it easily.

When he pulled it out his first thought was that it was made of the same marble the pedestal was. It was a beautiful pure white with gold veins running through it. But these veins didn't seem to be running through it randomly as with the pedestal. Also the weight was much lighter than it should have been for a sphere that size made of marble.

As he turned to let Sakura know he had found the orb he gave a start; she was standing right next to him. He hadn't heard her at all. Wyk felt his face redden and thought, *how does this woman do that?*

"May I hold the orb?" Sakura asked.

He looked at the orb and wondered if it would know to stop sticking to his hand so he could give it to her. She reached for it and it went easily to her. She gazed at it reverently, as if it held the answers to all the secrets in the world. Without realizing it she even started to lightly caress it.

Wyk went over to the part of the pedestal which held the coin. He used his smallest knife that he kept with him wherever he went to pry the coin out. Just as it fell into his hand Sakura yelled out, "No!"

Each of the six pieces of the pedestal collapsed in on itself. They splintered into little pieces as though the gold veins running through them became a multitude of cracks marring their integrity. Cracks which started to enlarge and shatter the pedestal.

Right after the pedestal broke apart Wyk felt the ground under his feet start to shake. The movement grew so violent that he fell to his knees. It stopped shaking only a few seconds later, but which felt much longer to Wyk. He turned to look back at the way they had come but bones were now scattered everywhere, covering up the narrow trail they had used to get here.

He tried to find the obelisk but it must have fallen as it was nowhere to be seen. He looked over at Sakura who was staring at him with a very effective this-is-all-your-fault look, causing him to turn away in embarrassment.

Still looking away from her he asked, "Um, do you know which way to go?"

"I was facing away from the obelisk when you pulled the coin out, so it's straight back in that direction." she said, pointing directly behind her. "Can you see the tall rib standing straight up? The obelisk was right next to it. But we need to hurry; there is a time limit for returning once you remove the coin."

Wyk gave her a weak smile and started out ahead of her. He kept the one giant rib, which looked like it could have belonged to a huge dragon much larger than Red, in his sight as he pushed other bones out of the way to make a path for her. It was tough work as most of the bones were tangled up with each other, making it impossible to move one at a time.

"The magic won't last," Sakura said. "We need to walk on the bones to get there in time."

With that she nimbly hopped up and began to walk across the bones as if they were wide paths. Wyk watched her for a few seconds, envious of her agility. *There's just no end to what this woman can do,* he thought.

Sakura led the way back through what was now a tangle of bones strewn across the ground. She did so with a sense of surety, as though she still recognized the landscape and the bones were secure even as she put her weight on them. Wyk had more than a few problems with his weight often shifting the bones, causing him to fall and scrape his legs.

She frequently glanced back at Wyk, lines of worry creasing her face more and more. Wyk knew what she was thinking-that they would both be stuck here forever. He also knew what he had to do.

"Go on ahead," he said. "Even if I don't make it at least you'll be safe."

She gave him a look he didn't recognize, though if he had to guess he would say it was a combination of worry, anger and compassion.

She nimbly ran ahead, reaching the rib while Wyk was barely half way there. He saw her bend over and knew she was at the obelisk. He heard her saying something but couldn't make out what it was. Then she stood up, her hands empty.

"Go through!" He shouted. "Don't wait for me!"

But still she stood there, looking all the while like a beautiful goddess watching over the bones of the subjects in her care. At that moment Wyk knew he would never be able to be apart from her again.

"Hurry up! The doorway's closing!"

Wyk knew that Sakura wouldn't go through without him, and he didn't want to be the reason she got left behind in this light forsaken place. He took a deep breath and started leaping from bone to bone, looking for the largest ones to jump to. He covered the remaining distance in a matter of seconds and reached the obelisk in time to see a look of disbelief invade Sakura's face.

"Quickly, jump through." She said.

Wyk looked down at the obelisk. Its color was different; where before it had a brownish hue to it now it was turning gray. Without thinking he grabbed Sakura around the waist, to which she gave a small cry of surprise, and dropped her through. He waited a second then held his arms straight up and jumped.

Wyk landed flat on his back looking up at the now darkening sky. He frowned, how long had they been inside? He quickly sat up and saw Sakura standing next to Jesse, who was holding his stomach as if he had just gotten punched while Sakura looked a little embarrassed.

"How long have we been gone?" Wyk asked to no one in particular.

"About 5 hours." Jesse replied, still holding his gut. "If you hadn't gotten the orb to us when you did, we were going to go in looking for you."

Wyk stood up and dusted himself off. "We might as well make camp here." He said. "We can worry about getting out of here in the morning."

Dinner was leftovers from lunch, which of course had been the meat of an animal no one recognized except the bear. As they ate Wyk looked over his group. They seemed content now that they had the orb. Even the bear was curled up near them.

Two things bothered Wyk. The first of course was how Kam had joined their group back at the palace. He couldn't have known where they were going or what they were looking for. In fact, he behaved as if he didn't care, just so long as he was with them. That didn't sit right with Wyk.

The other was Red. Since they had returned Red had been watching Wyk with narrowed eyes. He didn't look happy and Wyk wondered what he had done to upset the dragon. It was something he needed to address later when he had time.

After dinner they decided to retire to bed early. Kam watched as Krys used her new-found friend as her bed, snuggling up to the big bear like it was a giant pillow. She offered the same amenity to her girlfriends, but none of them took her up on her offer.

Red however was another story. He flew around in circles overhead endlessly. When Kam asked him what was wrong, he couldn't explain it. Red did say that there was something close that was bothering him, something magical. Kam couldn't figure out what that was, but he knew enough to trust Red's instincts.

He glanced around their little group, observing how everyone stayed close to the ones they knew. Belle was sound asleep with Moose right next to her, ready to use his hammer on whomever or whatever came at her. The Guardsmen all stayed together-no surprise there. And Sakura, who was usually alone, was with Wyk tonight and they were talking quietly.

And of course he had Red.

Don't flatter yourself.

Kam smiled at Red's comment. He was starting to enjoy having Red in his head, especially lately with the darkness gone. There was still rage in Red; Kam could feel that much. But even his rage seemed to have dwindled of late. Kam felt that was in part due to the people Red was having contact with. Between his sister, Belle, Moose and some of the others, Red was starting to see the good side of people.

They're certainly better than you. They haven't tried to use magic to control me.

Kam paused at that. He had wondered lately if Red would still help them even if he wasn't controlled by the Dragonstaff. He had thought about it every so often but Red never commented on it.

Well, would you? Kam asked.

There was only silence. Kam sighed; he wished he could get the dragon to understand how important he was to the plan. It wasn't a great plan, but it was definitely doomed to fail without Red's help.

Kam laid back with his head on his arms. *Good night, Red,* he thought. There was no reply, only agitation that Kam could feel plainly. The last thing Kam saw before he fell asleep was Red slowly circling overhead.

She smiled; it was a relaxing and surprisingly humorous smile. The exception was her eyes which still held extreme sadness in their depths. Otherwise, it lit up her face and caused what Wyk had already thought to be a face of perfect beauty turn into a truly breath-taking and vibrant one. It took Wyk a moment to remember to breath and he was only able to do that by looking away for a moment.

"Truce?" Sakura asked, forcing Wyk to look up at her exquisiteness again. Her eyes were wide and of the deepest blue imaginable. He wondered if her eye color changed based on her moods. Now at least it looked like the deepest blue of the lake where he and his father used to go fishing on beautiful summer days, with the blue in the very center of the lake seemingly drawing him into its wondrous depths. But he couldn't help but notice they also held the foreshadowing of a summer storm as well.

Wyk smiled. It was a simple, pure smile of contentment that he got when a difficult task was accomplished. Then he simply nodded.

He wondered what magic women had over men that they could seemingly control them with a smile. Never before had Wyk ever been ensnared by a woman's look as he now was with Sakura's. He would be the first to admit he had met some beautiful women before. Yet her smile, imprisoning though it was, also had an element of liberation as well. Though his body and emotions were held captive by her, his spirit was set to soaring with exhilaration.

He shook his head and tried to clear his thoughts. This woman was obviously using some sort of magic on him to make him feel like a drunk, moon-struck youngling.

"What's the matter?" She asked concern in her voice.

He again looked up at her. "I'm just tired, that's all," he said. "Jesse's got first watch so I think I'll get some shut eye."

She smiled a small, soft smile which seemed to say get-some-rest-and-I'll-see-you-in-the-morning. He got up and went to his bedroll. He paused as he thought about Sakura and her complex-yet-enticing smiles and realized that all of them of late had been tinged with sadness, and maybe even a little despair. As he fell asleep, he again vowed that if he had the chance he would make the demon pay for what it did to her.

CHAPTER 44

Krys awoke the next morning feeling as though the earth was shaking beneath her. The sun wasn't up yet and it was still dark, with just enough light from the moon to make out people packing their things. As she sat up, she realized the bear was growling at Jerome who had come over. He froze at the sound, tentatively watching to see if the bear would attack him.

"Krys, we are having Red fly us out of the area. We are going to have breakfast on the other side of the cliff." Jerome said in a tentative voice.

"Thanks." She said. She then patted her new friend to try and calm her down. She couldn't understand why the bear seemed so nervous about having Jerome near her. She didn't react that way to anyone else.

The fly out over the rim was quick, although Krys could tell there was something bothering Red. His thoughts and emotions were such a jumble though that she couldn't make heads or tails out of them.

Once out of the caldera she looked around but didn't recognize where they were. In the air she did see a couple of watering holes; one by where they were set down and the other on the far side of the small volcano they had been in.

There was scrub brush around and soon they had a small fire burning. Her bear laid down again to snooze some more and she took the opportunity to join her. A few more minutes of sleep couldn't hurt.

This time she sensed rather than physically felt the bear's agitation. She looked up and saw Jerome standing about ten feet away and holding a plate of food. He had a wild look in his eyes as if he might drop the plate at any moment and run away. He put the plate on the ground and backed away slowly, walking backwards so he could keep his eyes on the bear.

Krys giggled in spite of herself. She could sense the bear was upset but she still couldn't understand why. She wondered if he had done something. In any case the bear seemed very protective of her, especially when Jerome was around.

She got up she reached for the plate and sniffed it. The meat still seemed edible but looked odd; it had a stringy look to it. The bear seemed to be looking at it hungrily, with drool slowly dripping out of its mouth. She tossed it over and she caught it in the air, swallowing it without even chewing. She was content to nibble on the dried fruit, which this morning had some wild nuts mixed in, and drink water.

She looked around the camp and saw Red a ways off by himself. She tried to reach out to see what he was feeling. All she could make out were wave after wave of strong emotions; confusion, anger and hope, all jumbled together.

She walked over to him with the bear in tow. She didn't know how the animals would react to each other but hoped her presence might prove to be a catalyst for them to be friendly with each other. She approached Red slowly, trying to get a read from either animal. She sensed no animosity from either Red or the bear towards each other. They seemed to be able to get along with ease. The effortless way with which they accepted each other, however, surprised her.

As she got close to Red she realized his emotions seemed to be focused on Wyk. She glanced over at him and wondered why Red was feeling the way he was. Wyk seemed to be the same; the only difference was the knapsack he started keeping with him all the time. Then it hit her-the knapsack had the orb in it!

"Wyk, come over here please," Krys called out. "Kam, can you come too please."

Both of the men looked at each other and then came dutifully over with Wyk having the knapsack in tow. Before either of them could say anything, she said, "Wyk, please take the orb out of the knapsack and show it to Red."

Both men again looked at each other. Then with a confused look in his eye Wyk took out the orb. Red brought his head low so he could look at it. Then he got agitated and started shifting his weight back and forth, making Wyk very nervous.

Krys could sense Red's emotions intensify, but she couldn't grasp what was going through his mind. But by the look in Kam's eyes, he did. Kam turned to Wyk and, completely ignoring Krys which upset her no end, said, "The orb is special to Red. I'm not sure why but I can tell it belonged to an ancient dragon many, many years ago."

With those words Kam looked again at Red and his expression changed. Krys knew Kam well enough to know she had only seen this expression one time before. It was when their mother told them that their father had died. Kam's face had taken on a different hue, turning almost completely ashen, and having a look of confusion and disbelief.

"What? What is it?" Krys asked.

"The orb is an eye, a dragon's eye. And it holds a lot of power"

Wyk stared at the orb in disbelief, as if a joke were being played on him. The orb, large as it was, was nowhere near as large as Red's eyes. It was like comparing a man's head to an apple.

"I don't understand." Wyk said. "Red's eyes are much larger than this is. Is it from a much smaller dragon?"

The jumble of thoughts which came from Red overwhelmed Krys. She was starting to get a headache. But it wasn't just from the confusing potpourri of thoughts that poured out of Red, it was the strong emotions attached to them as well.

"Red says that a dragon's eye is made up of two balls. The larger one is the one we see, and within that there is another ball which is what they actually see out of. It's like the pupil in our eye only it's solid." Kam explained.

They all looked at each other. Wyk looked like he was ready to drop the orb after Kam's explanation, and Krys wouldn't blame him. Who would want to hold onto a dragon's eye? But this still didn't explain why Red was acting the way he was.

Krys looked up at Red and the dragon was as still as a statue, staring at them with eerily gleaming eyes that Krys was sure had tears in them. *Why did this eye mean so much to Red?*

Wyk turned his full attention on Kam. "I don't know what's going on here but you need to talk with your dragon and get all the information you can," he said. "I want to know everything there is to know about this orb, or uh, this eye that we have."

Kam nodded and Wyk strode purposefully away. Krys felt unwanted as she didn't have quite the same connection her brother did to Red and felt useless standing there. She turned quickly to walk away and nearly tripped over the bear. She had forgotten about him being there. The bear was looking at her with concern in its eyes and she felt its concern for her through her bond with it.

She smiled and rubbed its head for a few moments before stepping around it to walk away. She heard it padding softly after her, making very little noise for a creature so large.

Wyk quietly watched the small fire burn down. It reminded him of a childhood long since dispersed into distant memories. Of times past which were mostly forgotten and the rest hidden in the mists of time.

The low morning sun created a bloody massacre among the distant clouds and made them appear as soldiers' bodies strewn across the sky. It made Wyk think of a great conflict among the gods which turned the heavens into a battlefield high above that of mortal man. Bizarrely, is also reminded him of the painting in the Pious Room where the figures seemed to move of their own accord.

He got up and started walking around the circumference of the caldera they had been in only an hour before. The massive tree on the top of the butte towered over them, now seemingly as big as a mountain. Wyk was now thinking it wasn't just a single tree, but many trees very close together which allowed a small volcano and streams of water to be in the middle. Or maybe the massive tree grew around everything; he just didn't know.

It seemed to be the center of magical conduits leading to and from places he didn't even know existed a day ago. Then there was the orb. Wyk knew it was what the king wanted, but why? And why did its presence bother Red so much?

Lost in thought, Wyk had walked about halfway around the caldera without even realizing it. He was about to turn back when a sudden, small movement caught his eye and he turned. Being in an area he didn't recognize he instinctively reached for his sword. His tension quickly relaxed and turned to one of pleasant surprise as he noticed Sakura bathing in a shallow watering hole.

Her back was to him but she was turned enough so as to allow him a view of her right side. His breath caught at the simple, curvaceous beauty of her profile. He felt his face flush hot with embarrassment as he realized he was staring at a woman who, for all intents and purposes, believed herself to be alone and able to bathe in privacy.

As he started to turn away from her view she turned also, allowing him to see her full back and left arm. As the image hit him, his blood turned to ice and he felt a hand grasp his heart in a steely, vice-like grip. Her left arm, which had been hidden from his view, now showed off its full splendor.

Splashes of green, red, yellow and orange were highlighted by smaller splotches of blue and black. Even at this distance the pattern of color on her arm showed just as much beauty, albeit in a different way, as her profile had just moments before. It was a beauty which also foretold a hidden secret, and a dangerous one at that.

Unknowingly Wyk moved slightly towards his left, shifting his weight and stepping on a small, dead plant which cracked like a whip in the stillness of the morning. Wyk moved as quickly as a trained military man could, spinning and going into a crouch behind a small tree he had been next to. His heart pounding, he sat dazedly, feeling like a man caught for murder and awaiting the lever to be pulled to drop him to his death at the end of a rope.

She's an assassin! He thought to himself. Her beautifully complex and colorful tattoo still fresh in his mind. *And a member of the Yakaza.*

As he slowly stilled his heart from the shock and betrayal he felt, he slowly moved away. He kept the tree between him and her and made sure she couldn't either see or hear him. He had no idea what he should do next when inspiration struck him as a thunderbolt.

He would let her play out her part as a thespian on stage, waiting to see where her actions would take her. Perhaps even to the chance of dealing a crippling blow against the Assassins' Guild itself, something which had not been done in generations. He walked slowly back to camp, a plan forming in his mind, allowing him to, temporarily at least, keep the emotions which were thundering inside of him, at bay.

While simultaneously clearing her eyes of the tears she had only a second before been shedding, she spun quickly and effortlessly in the cool water. She moved into a low crouch at the sharp sound she heard, ready for anything. The water was shallow but she went low enough for the water to cover her markings.

She felt naked and not just because she was. She felt that way whenever she didn't have her sword on her. She always thought she could walk down a busy thorough-fare in the middle of a large city without a stitch of clothing on, but if she had her sword in hand, she would not feel the least bit self-conscious.

In spite of herself, and causing heat to rise to her face when she realized it, she had instinctively reached for her sword. However, that same sword was even now on the bank of this serene pond many feet away. She didn't care if her instinct was to reach for a weapon, even if the sound which startled her was probably caused by some small animal wondering along the edge of the lake. She felt silly because her instincts should have reminded her that she had no weapon on her body.

She sighed and used a brief meditation technique to calm her nerves before leaving her solitary bath behind. Sakura was used to going for long periods of time without bathing. There were times an assassin just couldn't ask for a break and jump into the nearest lake or river to clean off. But she wondered if she was going soft.

She risked cleaning herself off far too close to camp, where someone might have wondered off and seen her tattoo. But she knew that wasn't what she feared. It was that thing, that creature sent by the Dark Lord. Her nightmarish meeting with it the last time still left her shaking after another night terror, and frequently left her sobbing quietly to herself in the middle of the night.

She left the water quickly, rushing over to a group of small, low branches which had grown close to the water and went inside the shelter. It was as if someone had made the branches grow here so as to create a little changing room of sorts. She dried herself off with a small piece of cloth which she always carried with her and slipped into her clothes, making sure tattoo was completely covered.

The dark pit in her stomach, which seemed to fill her soul as well, always got larger when she thought about the attack. There were times she just wanted to kill herself and get it over with. She used thoughts of revenge and of killing that thing as motivation for living, for moving on. She didn't know how to kill it, but she would find a way.

As she finished dressing, thoughts of Wyk crept into her mind and she felt her face break into a little smile. She didn't know what it was about him but he seemed to make the darkness disperse a little. It was like the sun breaking through the clouds after a heavy storm, brightening not just the landscape but everyone's mood as well.

She knew he wouldn't want her now though. Not after what happened. She had been used, soiled by a creature so hideous, so evil, that it had to have marked her. How could Wyk want to be with her after she had been with that thing?

She thought she felt the dark pit in her stomach grow and spread its vile corruption further through her body like a vine growing over and around anything in its path. She knew at some point it would leave her withered and broken inside. She knew she had to find a way to destroy the demon before she became incapable of doing anything.

She trudged back to the camp feeling desolate and dispirited. An overwhelming feeling to just curl up and cry nearly overpowered her, but she fought it and forced herself to continue. She entered the small camp they had set up to plan what to do next. She saw everyone except Wyk. As she glanced around, she saw him coming over and she gave him the best smile she could. His appearance always seemed to give her a reprieve from the dark seed of despair growing inside of her. He however, seemed not to have noticed her and kept walking towards the group.

He looks like how I feel, she thought to herself. She wondered what might have happened to cause him to feel the way she did. In any case it didn't matter; she had a job to do and needed to find out how to accomplish it. She wondered if the dragon could help her. Surely the dragon knew what the dark creature was and how to kill it.

She turned and started to walk away from the camp. She was telling herself she was looking for Red, but really she just needed to get away. She needed to find a place to…

As if reading her thoughts the dragon's head appeared in front of her, held just a few feet off of the ground. She had been so deep in thought she had almost walked into him. In fact, if he had had his mouth open, she wouldn't have been surprised if she had walked all the way down into his stomach before noticing where she was.

Red stared quietly at her, as if he could read her mind simply by looking at her. Everyone said he couldn't, but it was eerie the way he gave off that feeling. She knew dragons were intelligent maybe some of them were mind-readers too. Or maybe Red could see, or at least sense, the black, evil taint she had on her.

And then it hit. There was no fighting it this time. It came as a torrential flood, destroying everything in its path.

The tears and the huge, heaving sobs causing her to literally fall forward and land on the dragon's snout. Tracks of water flowed between his scales, forming small rivulets and miniature waterfalls. She clung to him for what seemed like hours, sobbing uncontrollably. Her body was wracked with an emotional pain she couldn't understand. She clung there, like a little girl clinging to her father's leg after a terrible fright, oblivious to everything except her own pain.

After a moment she started to slide down to the ground, her legs too weak to do anything but hang from her body like dead branches on a tree. But she never reached the ground. Instead, she felt something soft and damp catch her.

She didn't know what it was but it felt like a blanket brought in from the rain and strung up hammock-like to dry. She felt a warm, dry breeze gently rush over her and it became a calming salve for her butchered soul. There was a tranquil strength to it; a support for her soul to not just lean on, but to be fortified by.

For a moment she felt alive, more alive than she ever remembered having felt before. Yet her first thought was that of Wyk, as if it were his strong arms granting her empowerment. His love giving her asylum from the darkness which now followed her constantly.

She felt guilty for thinking about Wyk in a moment of tribulation where it was the dragon providing the moral support, not another person. She wondered if Red knew what he was doing or if it was just some ambient dragon magic according her this momentary reprieve from the filthiness she felt inside.

Her sobs subsided and she found the strength to stand on her own two feet again. Her rising allowed Red to pull his tongue back into his mouth. As she stood up facing Red, she looked deep into his eyes. She saw something there, an ageless intelligence and an emotional depth, which she knew not all people had.

Impulsively, and thus uncharacteristically, she reached out and gave Red's snout a hug. Her arms barely went around the end of his nose but that didn't matter. In that moment she gave all of her emotion, all of herself, in one expression of gratitude. Right now, when she needed it most, it was Red, not another person, who gave her the ability to go on another day. And for that she was grateful.

With tear tracks still glistening on her cheeks she gave him a big kiss. Surprisingly Red didn't seem either shocked or repulsed by everything which had just taken place. Rather, he exuded the same quiet strength, the same serene devotion to amending a situation and helping to improve it. The same characteristics one would find in a family member or loved one.

She turned to go, giving Red one last, parting look of gratitude, then moved away. She was grateful for his support, but knew in the end her moving past the attack, the rape by that thing, would end up being of her own volition. Unfortunately, she felt the only way she could move past this emotional turmoil was to kill that thing, something she wasn't sure was even possible. It seemed to be an insurmountable problem. The thing couldn't be killed by steel, and she imagined wood and stone wouldn't fare any better. So, what then? What was out there that could kill it?

In the end there was only one possible solution-magic. It had potent magic at its command. No, IT was potent magic. Created by the Dark Lord himself. Its very essence, its very existence, owed itself to powerful magic. That said, it would follow that only magic could defeat it, and powerful magic at that.

She felt a little better thinking about destroying the creature. Although in truth she would rather castrate and torture it before she killed it. Make it suffer the way she suffered; the way she was still suffering.

But the despair was still there. It was just below the surface, like a strong under current just beneath the waves which could easily pull you out to sea. That despair threatened to break out of her self-imposed constraints and drown her in darkness.

She did feel a little better, a little lighter in her soul, since Red was there for her. She wondered if he used some magic of his own to help her to cope with the situation she was going through. She wondered if a dragon's magic was strong enough to defeat the dark spawn. She knew dragons had magic, but would it be strong enough to destroy the creature?

She decided the best thing she could do was just to go at it one day at a time. She would keep busy and focus on her job and on her ultimate goal of destroying the creature. It seemed as if only time would tell if she could accomplish that.

Sakura turned back and gave Red another soft kiss on his now damp snout. She then turned and walked back to the others. She could only hope that Red could understand exactly how much he helped her.

CHAPTER 45

In the end it was Alyx who recognized where they were. After finding other portals on the butte, the picked one and went through. This magic portal had dropped them off in a caldera which was known to the small town she was from. It was considered a place of dark magic and everyone avoided the area. But as a child she often snuck out to the area to swim in the ponds.

She was able to lead them to the town which was only about ten miles away. It only took them about half a day of walking to reach it. Red however stayed back at the caldera so as not to frighten any of the townspeople.

They had the good fortune of finding a herdmaster of surprisingly docile bullbears and horsecrabs to ride, for a nominal fee of many crowns of gold of course. Most of them rode on horsecrabs, which moved fast but also caused squeamishness to their riders when the animals took to skittering sideways, which Kam noted was of great amusement to Red.

After half a day of hard riding they found a spot near a lake to camp for the evening. As everyone moved around to set up camp, Sakura watched as Wyk fed and watered the animals. He hadn't spoken much to her the past few days and she was beginning to wonder if she had unknowingly done something wrong.

She slowly walked over to him, unsure of what to say. All she knew was that she missed his company. He heard her approach and looked at her, but she could see in his eyes that he wasn't looking at her the same way. The sheer joy which used to be in his face when she was near always brought a smile to hers. But now that was gone, replaced by something else, something unsettling.

He looked at her now as if she had killed his sibling. There was animosity in his look, anger at…what? Dare she ask him? She knew if she didn't ask him things might never get back to how they used to be. And right now, she needed him to be there for her.

"Wyk, I need to ask you something."

"Sure." He said, but it was forced. He didn't want to talk with her, that much was obvious.

"Have I done something to upset you?"

He looked at her with pure malice in his eyes and she was afraid of what he might say. That maybe she had done something inadvertently to hurt him. She would be willing to apologize. She had to have him back as her friend, as her…

"No." He said.

She waited, but he didn't seem inclined to say anything more about it. What could it be? She thought back to their quest. She tried to remember the last time he had spoken to her and treated her with kindness and respect. It was after they had retrieved the sacred sphere. Could that have put some kind of curse on him? But he was okay until that one morning after she had finished bathing…

Her heart nearly stopped beating. A cold filled her body, almost as cold as when that vile dark thing abused her. Her mind remembered hearing a small branch snap while she was bathing. She had assumed it was a small animal, but what if it had been him? What if he had seen her markings?

That's not possible she thought. I looked and there was no one there. Besides, the laws in all of the lands dictate that anyone representing any of the kings may summarily kill anyone from the Assassin's Guild. Surely, he would have killed her if he knew what she was.

Still her blood felt like ice water in her veins. She didn't want to believe it, couldn't believe it. But there was no other answer for the change in his behavior towards her. No, she wouldn't jump to conclusions. She would ask Kam to ask the dragon about the orb. Everyone said the dragon knew what it was. If it was a curse maybe Red could use his magic to lift it.

She slowly turned and walked away, half expecting at any moment to hear him running after her, to hear him draw his sword. No, she wouldn't let her mind play tricks on her. It had to be the sacred sphere. She would get Red to lift the curse and Wyk would be Wyk again.

She spied Kam talking with his sister, Belle and Moose and headed straight to them.

"That's not right!" Krys said ardently. Belle and Moose both nodded their agreement emphatically.

Kam sighed. "Look, I'm not saying I disagree with you. I'm just saying that it could hold the key to us winning the war that's coming."

"I think Red should be able to return it to the dragons." Krys continued. "Every time one of you brings it out, I get a head full of so much emotion from him it hurts! It obviously means a lot to him and we should give it back."

Kam sighed again. He really did agree with his sister and her friends. It just wasn't that simple.

"Red gave me this hammer and it's saved our lives many times already. He has saved our lives and been a good friend to all of us. In all that time he hasn't ever asked for anything. I think the least we can do is give the eye back to him."

Kam hadn't heard Moose say that many words since…well since ever. But he still wasn't convinced it was something he or the rest of the dragons would want or even use. He waited for Red to chime in with some thought or other but his head remained quiet.

"Uh, am I interrupting something?"

They all turned to face Sakura. Her usually blue eyes were reflecting the colors of the setting sun, giving them a purple cast. Her face displayed a seriousness which helped to quiet them all down.

"What is it, Sakura?" Krys asked gently.

"The sacred sphe…I mean the orb. Could it have put a curse on somebody?"

The others looked at each other uncertainly. It wasn't a question they expected to hear.

"Kam was just going to talk with Red about it." Krys said helpfully.

Kam gave her a withering look. He had already told them Red wasn't interested in talking about the orb, but maybe if they all went to him together. They needed to know what the orb could do.

"Why don't we all go together? Maybe then he'll give us some answers."

Everyone was in agreement, although Kam noticed that Sakura didn't seem too happy about it. It was almost as if she was afraid she might get an answer she didn't want to hear.

After Kam called Red asking him to come, they all walked over to where he was. He had started playing with the saber-toothed bear. The bear was trying to catch Red's tail, but Red flicked his tail so quickly that the bear caught only air.

"Red, we want to talk to you about the orb we found."

Red turned to face them, the gold in his eyes sparkling in the setting sun. The bear seemed to sense a change in Red's mood and she came around and flopped down right in front of him

Kam wasn't sure where to begin. It was almost as if the orb was so special that Red didn't want to talk about it with them. But he couldn't see how an old dragon eye could be that special.

It is the eye of our greatest leader and was stolen from us after he was killed in the Dragon Wars. Man took the eye to find a way to defeat dragons, all dragons.

Kam was shocked. He still didn't understand why it would be important for man to have it or how they could harness its magic. But he reiterated what Red told him to the others, although Krys seemed to already know what Red said.

His magic was so great that it took many sorcerers and all three of the Dragon Armors to slay him.

Kam again repeated what Red had said. There was shocked silence for a moment until Sakura asked, "Does the orb contain magic?"

Yes, Red replied. *It has very powerful magic in it-Dragonmagic.*

Sakura was watching Kam intently, but when he repeated what Red had said she continued, "But can it curse someone. If someone carries it, can it curse them?"

Kam frowned but asked Red, although he suspected he already knew the answer.

No. Tell Goldenhair that it does not curse the person carrying it, and that I'm sorry.

Kam repeated what Red had said, but she too seemed to know the answer already. She turned away quickly and Kam thought he saw her start to cry.

I won't say any more about it. Red said, then flew off.

It was easy for her to move away from the group. The others were busy talking about Red and the sacred sphere. They didn't even notice that she slipped away. But now she had another problem-she was fairly certain Wyk had seen her while she was bathing. If she thought he knew what she was, then she was required by the guild to kill him.

She gave a small sob. They each had a reason to end each other's life. She didn't really think he would kill her. Men weren't strong like that. Most of them couldn't hurt a woman no matter what she'd done, especially honorable men. Now men in the guild-that was another story. They wouldn't hesitate to kill a woman if it suited their needs. But Wyk was different.

She walked around the camp slowly, trying to make sense of thoughts and feelings she had never felt before; which she had been trained not to think or feel. Focusing on her training helped to bring her back into equilibrium. A state of acceptance of who she was, what she did, and what she had to do. The Guild had taught her that- what they called the basic three. She knew what she had to do and knew she could do it.

She passed by Wyk who gave her a smile and wave. She couldn't help but notice that the smile was cold and never reached his eyes and the wave was half-hearted at best. No, there was definitely something wrong. But was she sure it was him that made the noise by the pond that night? Was she willing to kill him and risk bringing attention to the fact that someone in the group was an assassin? What about the other one in the group, the traitor? Did he have orders to kill Wyk? If he did then she wouldn't need to.

With a growing sense of dread she accepted that she might have to be the one to kill him. But she knew she would have to wait; at least until they returned to the palace. That way no one would suspect her. And if they did, she would just have to kill them too. Her mission was all important. She couldn't allow anyone to stand in her way.

They reached the southern border of the kingdom the next day. The tension in the group had grown noticeably to the point Belle felt as if some in the group might start fighting each other. There was Red and the eye of his great-great-great-whatever ancestor or something like that.

Then there was Sakura who had gone back to being a loner after she and Krys had tried so hard to befriend her. And there was Sakura's relationship with Wyk. Belle would have bet that those two would have gotten together but something happened on their journey, causing a deep chasm to form between them. One which she was sure others noticed as well.

At least there was Moose. He was strong, loving and always steadfast. She knew he would never leave her, although sometimes she wished he would leave his hammer somewhere and lose it. He was always handling it, practicing with it, and polishing it. It was enough to make a girl sick! And the way he talked about the King's Guard. You would think he actually had a chance to join.

Belle cared for Moose immensely; but she didn't really believe he could join the Guard. She just wished the others would stop putting foolish notions into his head. He was a good man and would someday make a good husband and farmer, but that's all he could ever be. Maybe she could get Moose to give his hammer to the king for some good farmland not far from the city. Now *that* was an idea.

Chapter 46

The past few nights the group had camped within the borders of the kingdom as they made their way back to the palace. This was especially heartwarming to Jesse who was glad to finally be home. It felt like they had been gone years instead of just a few months.

The quest had taken its toll on everyone. Even Red seemed a little put off by all that had happened. Although in Red's case, Jesse figured the fact they had an artifact which belonged to dragons was what made him unhappy.

If the orb really did belong to the dragons, then it would be something they would want back. But Red should know they would never use it against him or his kind. Not as long as they didn't attack them anyway.

Jesse sighed and let his mind wander. He had come to miss many things on their journey-good, fresh food and ale, his regimented schedule of practice and work, and of course the company of women. He missed a lot of things, but having a pretty woman in his arms to kiss was definitely near the top of the list.

He looked over at a field of wheat grass and saw a young woman. She had just stood up and was straightening her clothes while she watched them walk by. She was stunning, but had a concerned look on her face.

Jesse looked at her more closely and saw she had on the clothes of someone who had coin, yet she was here out in the fields. She definitely wasn't a farmer, so who was she?

After a minute of staring at them, the woman apparently figured it was best to just stay where she was and threw herself back down on the ground. Jesse lost sight of her and realized that's what the woman wanted. She was hiding, but from who?

He had no time to contemplate why the woman was there. As they rounded one of the last large hills before the palace came into view a scene appeared before him which took his breath away.

The plains around the city walls were filled with a bizarre army the likes of which he had never witnessed before. Jesse recognized some of the creatures there as being from the Dark Lord's Province-the large insect-like things which looked half-scorpion and half-evil. Only these had riders on them.

There were also groups of Halfers and Darkbloods wandering around looking as if they were about to fight each other. Then there were other things which looked to be made up of a conglomoration of different creatures thrown together, almost as if the creator was playing a joke on the world.

"Non-military people stay here," Wyk yelled to his group. "Everyone else follow me."

He said this knowing full well no one would stay behind. He knew all of them well enough, from the boy to the girls to Red, to appreciate the fact they would all help fight to defend the city. As he charged forward his chest swelled with pride knowing every last one of them would die if necessary fighting for the kingdom. All of them that is except for Sakura.

As they charged forward a shadow passed overhead, briefly blotting out the sun. They all knew who it was even before Red landed with his full weight on top of an especially hideous looking creature ridden by a Halfer. Both the Halfer and its mount were flattened into the dust.

Wyk knew from experience the scorpion-mounts hade tough hides, so he left those for Kam, Moose and Red as they were the only ones who could do any real damage to them. The others, including the girls, he led on swift attacks against the combatants which were on foot.

Attacking from the rear they caught many of the roaming groups of Halfers and Darkbloods by surprise, taking them out fairly quickly. It wasn't until later when some of the other creatures took notice that Wyk worried. However, even though they were heavily outnumbered, Krys's windstorm magic took out large groups of the enemy.

Then there were Belle's deadly green arrows, which eliminated those who Wyk thought were leaders. This left many of the surviving fighters without any direction and they roamed the battlefield like rudderless boats, allowing them to be killed easily. This benefited Wyk's little group immensely.

Some of the more intellectually inclined Darkbloods grouped together and tried flanking them and attacking from the rear. Wyk quickly sent Alyx and a few of his men to head them off and keep them away from the group. Unfortunately, he couldn't keep track of them as he had his own hands full.

Burrowing up from beneath them a huge animal which looked like a combination of a gopher, spider and tick. Wyk had never even heard of an animal like that before and its size took his breath away. He briefly wondered how a creature that large could live undetected by anyone.

Krys sent a powerful gust of wind, which quickly formed into a small tornado, at it. However, its weight proved to be too great for the wind to have any effect. The only thing which happened was that it started to slide a little until it used its eight massive legs to push its long, spiderlike claws deep into the ground.

Out of the corner of his eyes Wyk saw a large bulk run up to the monstrous creature and attack one of its spider-like claws. It was Krys's bear. But the creature flicked its claw and the bear went flying backwards about twenty feet.

Wyk drew a deep breath and wondered how they could stop something so huge. Fortunately, Red seemed to know what they were facing and landed hard on the creature's back. But even Red's bulk did nothing to stop the creature, which again used its massive legs to thwart an attack against it by absorbing the shock of Red's fall.

Three of its middle legs were brought up and it bent them at the middle joints. From the joint itself pincers appeared. These grabbed hold of Red's legs and bit down. Two of the pincers bit hard enough to pierce Red's scales and draw blood, although the amount of blood coming out was minimal.

Red growled in anger and bit down just behind the large, insect-like head. The creature's mandibles clicked loudly, and a wraith-like wail pierced the air, causing Wyk's eyes to water.

With a stomach-turning crunch Red pulled the head clean off. The body shuddered for a moment before collapsing on the ground. Red let out a ferocious roar before leaping strongly into the air and taking flight again.

Finally, the denizens of the dark army seemed to realize they were being attacked from behind and turned to face them. With a loud cry they rushed in, hoping to do with numbers what they had thus far not accomplished with skill. But in their haste to get at Wyk and the others they invariably ran into each other.

The history of bad blood between the Halfers and the Darkbloods soon had them at each others' throats. The battlefield quickly became a free-for-all of fighting. It was the worst, and most disoriented, battle Wyk had ever been a part of.

"Make your way towards the main gate!" Wyk shouted, hoping everyone heard him.

As a group they stayed in a tight formation, defending themselves and each other. Wyk tried to find a path which would lead them to safety within the city's walls. That proved challenging as the many confrontations which had already broken out within the opposing forces grew more numerous and inhumanly vicious.

Other men from the city were fighting as well. When they were near, Wyk yelled for them to join their group and make their way back towards the city. Unfortunately, for every two men that joined their group Wyk would see one fall. He also lost sight of the girls and Moose.

He did see Red wreaking havoc among all who were near him and assumed Kam was fighting by his side. Even without using his magical green fire, Red was still an unstoppable force. He shredded the giant insect creatures with his claws while decimating anything on foot which happened to be around him.

At one point, Wyk surveyed the battlefield, and on one of the distant hills he swore he saw an enormous green man watching. But he only saw him for a second before he again had to focus on protecting himself and his men.

The only other thought which came to him concerned Sakura. He had not seen her in a while and began to wonder how she was doing. He didn't expect her to be fighting-this was the group she was working for after all-but he had lost sight of her completely since their initial charge.

As his group, now about forty strong, got close to the main gate to the city, another massive creature suddenly appeared and blocked their way. It was vaguely arachnid but had a wickedly barbed tail extending from behind and hovering over its body.

It had three heads, although two of the heads were partially fused and formed one large deformed appendage, and multiple legs. Three barbed stingers on willowy arms extended from its mouth and dripped poison. Each of its legs had barbed stingers on extendable arms making it virtually impossible to attack.

Each time they advanced on it one of the barbed extensions on the legs would lash out at them. There were numerous times when the men were nearly killed. Wyk finally called over his men and explained the tactics they would need to use.

His men then attacked each of the legs in pairs-one man would get the stinger to slash at him while the other would then slice at one of the leg joints, cutting it off. When the creature was sufficiently hobbled his men were able to go around it and get into the city safely.

With the initial group inside and safe Wyk turned to find others he could help. At this point all he wanted to do was get the city's protectors to safety while the dark spawn attacked and killed each other.

Suddenly he saw the two girls and Moose running towards the city wall. He ran towards them hoping to meet them halfway and provide some support as they tried to reach safety. Suddenly a turtle-like animal with a multitude of flailing tentacles where its head should have been attacked them.

Before Wyk could help them, Moose swung his hammer and smashed it into the creature's shell. A large section of the shell cracked and fell off, exposing a soft, blue jelly-like body underneath. Belle was able to pincushion it with her magical green arrows and the creature soon stopped moving completely. Belle, Krys and Moose then ran to the main gate.

But Wyk saw many others, good men, get killed. He cried out his rage at the insanity of it and started to hew down whatever got in front of him. His bloodlust lashed out and the dark spawn at the receiving end of it had no chance.

A loud roar filled the air and a dragon with two heads, one on top of the other, landed with a crash. It roared out another challenge and looked around for something to fight. Its body, instead of having protective scales like Red's, had a rough, rocky outer skin, giving it a diseased look.

Some of the other creatures attacked it, seemingly driven to a fighting frenzy by its war cry. But nothing seemed able to penetrate its hard exterior. It roared its challenge again and waited.

Then an answering cry, one so loud it drew everyone's attention away from the screams and roars on the battlefield, came from above. Red, flying high in the sky, was roaring his acceptance to the other dragon's challenge. Instantly it took off and headed straight for Red.

They fought high above the others, who were shackled to the ground with chains of gravity. Their fight was one of graceful pirouettes and fast lunges. Their graceful aerial ballet took everyone's breath away

Red swooped in many times to slash at it but the other dragon's thick skin seemed impervious to all attacks. Even Red's normal fire did nothing to slow it down. It took all of the punishment Red could throw at it and kept coming.

Then the other dragon swooped towards Red and then stopped at the last minute while swinging its tail. This caused a hailstorm of rocks to dislodge and hurl at Red with incredible force.

Some of the rocks hit Red and made him roar out in pain. Kam also felt the rock-like projectiles as they struck Red, causing him intense pain in his body and shoulders. Kam knew, through the bond, that Red's wings were still okay.

Then Red flew straight at the other dragon with such speed it couldn't dodge him. Red used his legs to grasp the other dragon's limbs to protect his wings. Then he latched onto the base of the other dragon's throat with his jaws before engulfing it in bright green flames.

Most of the neck with the heads suddenly detached from the body and fell to the ground like a toppled tree. The body, released from Red's grip, also fell, taking out a large contingent of Halfers.

I thought dragons weren't allowed to use their magic on other dragons. Kam said.

That wasn't a dragon. Was Red's reply.

They fought on, helping and supporting each other with strength and emotional sustenance neither had individually. Between Red and the fact the Halfers and Darkbloods had turned on each other turned the tide of the battle. Whatever was left of the forces which had surrounded the city turned and fled. Leaderless and without the stomach for death there was no reason for them to stay and fight.

The plains were now red with the blood of dead and dying. Unearthly sounds filled the air as creatures screamed out their last in the throes of death. Kam noticed with some satisfaction that many of the larger creatures were also dead, thanks in no small part to Red.

Thank you, said Red, sounding very proud.

CHAPTER 47

Wyk turned at a sound behind him. Although he knew there was really nothing left standing, he also knew you couldn't lose your focus and make stupid mistakes at any point when you were on a field of battle.

It was Sakura. She was covered from head to toe in red and her sword dripped blood, although he knew her well enough to know it wasn't hers. She looked at him with a combination of feral menace and sublime anguish.

He wondered if she fought to make herself look good in his eyes. Maybe she was hoping for a reprieve for their friendship or maybe she was just hoping to finish her mission. Whatever it was Wyk didn't want to know, but he knew he didn't trust her anymore and never would.

They stood there and looked at each other. The two of them both understood and accepted that their relationship, whatever it had been, no longer existed.

They were caged animals which, given the opportunity and released, would go for each other's throat. Unlike those animals however, their cages were not physical but emotional and self-imposed in nature. And neither knew if or when those cages would be opened.

EPILOGUE

"Where is he?"

The first man, who had gray skin and black hair, eyes and teeth, asked his companion who was a mirror image of himself.

"He said he needed to go and punish the king," Replied his twin. "He said he would be back soon."

The first man looked over the plains encompassing the city of Austine. "Does he not care about the battle?"

"He said the battle was merely a warning to those that had power granted to them by the Master. They needed to understand that their power was a gift and that they needed to continue to prove they earned it."

"Then why is he going to punish the king?"

"He did something, tried to get an artifact he wasn't supposed to. But more importantly brother, if he finds out what you did to the assassin, he will be very angry."

Silex glanced over at his twin. He knew he meant well, but he couldn't help it. She was beautiful and he hadn't been with a woman in a long time. No, that was a poor excuse and he knew it. Excuses were not tolerated by either the Master or his green giant lackey.

Silex sighed. She was more than beautiful, more than desirable. She was far more enticing than any woman he had ever seen, and he had seen many, many women in his long life.

The assassin had a charisma which was as powerful as any magic in snaring and holding his heart. She had something special about her that he couldn't put his finger on, but whatever it was he wanted it. Besides, what did it matter whom he bedded?

Cephas regarded his brother with a mixture of understanding, love and concern.

"Just be careful; if he finds out he could hurt you…"

Silex snorted. It was a harsh sound like two rocks being rubbed together. The green giant didn't scare him. Besides, his brother would always watch his back, as he always watched his. And the assassin was beautiful. Maybe he would go and visit her again…

EPILOGUE 2

The huge green man had skin so dark it almost looked black. But there was no confusing his mood, which was darker than usual.

"What shall we do with her?"

The question was almost rhetorical in its ridiculousness. His new guard knew what was expected-she was to return to the kingdom. But before he could chastise his supposed protector, he looked at the girl closely.

Her face was downcast, staring at the floor as if it was a means to leave this life and transport her to a new, kinder universe. Her shoulders were slumped forward and her body held all the emotion of a soggy pickle. It was obvious she wanted to leave this life and leave it for good.

Her body, covered in cuts, scratches, and abrasions from being used as a plaything by his pet, gave the impression of her having been whipped numerous times. He knew she had neither the desire nor the strength to ignite herself as she once had when she had first arrived.

The green man snorted loudly. The sound echoed off of the walls and gained volume rather than losing it as noise often does in an enclosed space. The giant man knew what he had to do, he needed to make her forget all that had happened here.

Giving his guards a stern look, one they knew meant for them to leave quickly, he turned towards the girl. She apparently realized that the others who were with her had left and gave a small squeak while shaking her head with a terrified look in her eyes.

The giant smiled, a cold, calculated expression meant to reassure her but only added to her terror. With an angry grunt he grabbed her and focused his magic in a way he never had before. He focused on her thoughts and sought to soften them, allowing them to slowly sink deep into her subconscious like a stone sinking to the bottom of a pool of water.

Gradually her eyes softened and she passed out, although the latter caught the giant off guard. Her lack of consciousness would make it easier to transport her back to the kingdom.

He called to his transporter, a large, ungainly creature which looked to be half bird and half dragon. It hissed angrily at him for having to carry the girl instead of eating her. But the giant, in an almost a loving voice, told his friend that he would give it something good to eat when it got back.

After he placed the unconscious body of the girl on its back, the bird-dragon disappeared using its special gift of magic. He knew it would be able to make the round trip to and from the kingdom very quickly.

He sat back on his large chair and contemplated what he would do next. He knew what Silex had done to the assassin, but he also knew Silex didn't know he knew. He decided to give him a chance to come forward on his own before he took any action.

He really didn't care that Silex raped the assassin. He probably would have done the same thing after he saw what she looked like. But that was not his mission. Not only that but he might have permanently broken her spirit, and that the giant couldn't have. She was far too valuable in the overall scheme of things.

He sat back and listened to the sound of his pet clicking away happily as it ate its dinner. It was a sound which always soothed him. And which always made him happy.